WHY ON EARTH wasn't I dead?

Cass, Eloise, and Marco were floating lifelessly in front of me. Their oxygen, like mine, had run out. I swam toward them. This seemed impossible. *How could I be functioning and not Marco?*

I could feel the Loculus moving and I looked down.

In . . . out . . .

I was holding it tight to my chest. *That's* what was moving. I was . . .

No. Impossible. I couldn't be breathing underwater.

But my mouth was shut. My nostrils were sealed. What on earth had just happened to me?

In the Belly of the Beast

THE
LEGEND
OF THE
RIFT

PETER LERANGIS

HARPER
An Imprint of HarperCollinsPublishers

Seven Wonders Book 5: The Legend of the Rift
Text by Peter Lerangis, copyright © 2016 by HarperCollins Publishers
Illustrations copyright © 2016 by Torstein Norstrand
Map art by Mike Regan, copyright © 2016 by HarperCollins Publishers

Library of Congress Control Number: 2016932062
ISBN 978-0-06-207053-1

Design by Joe Merkel
16 17 18 19 20   CG/OPM   10 9 8 7 6 5 4 3 2 1
❖
First paperback edition, 2016

THIS BOOK IS DEDICATED TO
SEVEN WONDERS READERS AROUND THE WORLD.
YOU'RE ALL SELECTS TO ME.

SEVEN·WONDERS
of the Ancient World

BLACK·SEA

THE·TEMPLE·OF·ARTEMIS
AT·EPHESUS

ATHENS

THE·MAUSOLEUM
AT·HALICARNASSUS

THE·STATUE·OF·ZEUS
AT·OLYMPIA

THE·COLOSSUS
OF·RHODES

M E D I T E R R A N E A N · S E A

THE·LIGHTHOUSE·OF·ALEXANDRIA

THE·GREAT·PYRAMID·OF·GIZA

NILE

TIGRIS

EUPHRATES

THE · HANGING · GARDENS
OF · BABYLON

USALEM

PERSIAN · GULF

SEA

MILES

0   100   200   300   400   500

FIRST DAY OF THE END OF THE WORLD

YOU KNOW YOU'VE reached rock bottom when you're standing on a beach, looking to the horizon, and you don't notice you're ankle-deep in dead fish.

If I'd been there ten minutes earlier, the water would be up to my shoulders. Now I was at the top of a wet, sloping plain. It was littered with rocks, ropes, bottles, crabs, fish, a massive but motionless shark, and the rotted hull of an old shipwreck.

Our tropical island had shot upward like an express elevator. Ten minutes ago, King Uhla'ar of Atlantis had opened a rift in time, which according to legend would make the great continent rise again. But I wasn't really thinking about legends right then. Because when he jumped into that rift, he took Aly Black with him. One minute there, the next minute *boom*! Down and gone. Back into time. Back to Atlantis.

Losing Aly was like losing a part of myself.

So on the first day of the end of the world, I, Jack McKinley, felt like someone had reached down my throat and torn out my heart.

"Jack! Marco! Cass! Eloise!"

Mom.

I spun around at her voice. She was back on the sandy part of the beach, glancing over her shoulder. Behind us, a group of frightened Massa soldiers streamed out of the jungle. Marco Ramsay, Cass Williams, and his sister, Eloise, were standing at either side of me. And that was when I began to notice the fish. Because a really ugly one whipped my left ankle with its fin.

"They look nasty," Eloise said.

"They speak highly of you," Cass replied.

Eloise looked at him, completely baffled. "Who, the Massa?"

"No, the fish," Cass said. "Aren't you talking about the—"

"I'm talking about *those* guys!" Eloise said, pointing to the frantic soldiers. "Do you hear Sister Nancy—I mean, Jack's mom? She's warning us to stay out of their way."

From deep in the trees, I could hear the shrill screech

2

of a poison-spitting vizzeet—followed by the guttural cry of a soldier in great pain. The Massa headquarters was on the other side of the jungle, and their soldiers and scientists were running here to see what had happened.

They'd felt the rumble, but they had no idea about the rift. And about the monsters who had escaped.

"Aw, man, what a trap," said Marco. "Those critters? They're like, woo-hoo, Greek dinner, free delivery!"

Some of the Massa were laying their bloodied pals on the sand. Others were running in confusion and panic down the muddy, fish-strewn beach toward us. Some were barfing in the reeds, nauseated by the violent motion of the earth. Mom was trying to calm them all down, tell them what had happened in the caldera. She wore a Massa-brown robelike uniform like something from a fashion catalog in 1643. The soldiers respected her, but they didn't know she was (a) my mom and (b) a rebel spy. And Torquin, our beloved seven-foot bodyguard, was directly behind us, picking his nose, which he did when he was nervous.

"We watched Aly go, Jack," Cass said. "What are we going to do?"

It was hard to think. There was another huge problem none of us wanted to talk about—Uhla'ar had taken the Loculus of Strength with him. If we didn't find all seven of the magic Atlantean Loculi, our G7W gene would kill us on schedule by our fourteenth birthdays. So if even one

Loculus was missing, we were toast.

The fish were distracting me now, and I pulled us all back onto more solid ground. As we moved, the Massa bellowed to each other, mostly in Greek. They were pushing and jostling, positioning themselves to ogle the shipwreck. Fifty or so yards down the muddy slope the ship's remains rose out of the muck like a dinosaur skeleton. It canted to one side, its mast tilted and cracked. Seaweed hung from its crossbeams like long-forgotten laundry, and the wooden hull was lumped with barnacles. Weirdly, after more than a century underwater, the ship's name was still visible on the hull.

The *Enigma.*

"Dudes, call me crazy," Marco said, pushing a couple of the soldiers out of our way, "but you think the answer might be out there, in the ship?"

"You're crazy," Cass said.

Marco's size-thirteen feet made slurping sounds in the mud as he stepped toward the ship. "Okay, stay with me now . . . That ship belonged to what's his face, right? The guy who discovered the island in the eighteen hundreds. Marvin or Berman."

"Herman Wenders," Cass said.

"Right," Marco said. "So I'm thinking, we go out there and explore the ruins. Wenders was supposed to be a genius, right? What if he left behind important stuff—you know, maps, notebooks, secrets? I mean, this is the guy that discovered the rift, right? Maybe he knows how to get in and out of it without all the bad consequences."

"We'll be like pirates." Eloise began striding toward the ship with an exaggerated limp. *"Argggh!* Yo-ho-ho, avast and ahoy! Batten the britches! Poop the decks!"

From the look on Cass's face, he wished his long-lost sister were still lost.

Torquin's gloomy expression melted, and he snorted bubbles through his freshly picked bulbous nose. That would be a disturbing sight under normal conditions, but it was worse now. These days he looked like the Hulk dipped into an acid bath. His face was still black with burn marks from a car explosion in Greece, and his once-red hair was just a few blackened clumps. "Ha. She said poop. Funny girl."

"I say we go back to the rift and offer the king a trade," Cass murmured. "We take Aly, he takes Eloise."

Hearing that, Eloise picked up a dead eel and threw it at him. He giggled and ducked. Like typical sibs who'd been fighting all their lives. Which was strange because until recently Cass didn't even know he had a sister. With their parents in jail and their lives scattered among foster families, it was like they needed to make up for lost time.

"So I try to be serious," Marco said with exasperation, "and this is what I get."

"They're blowing off steam," I said. "Trying to be normal."

I couldn't blame them. If old Herman Wenders hadn't

come to this godforsaken island in the first place, maybe the Karai followers would never have organized the institute. And then no one would have discovered the Atlantean G7W gene that made a superpower out of your biggest talent, but killed you at fourteen. And I would be a normal thirteen-year-old kid in Indiana, worrying about math and sometimes being whomped by Barry Reese. True, I'd be about to drop dead, but at least I'd be blissfully ignorant about that. And I wouldn't have wasted all these past weeks looking for seven Loculi to cure us—which we now knew we would never find. And Aly would still be here.

But he had, and they did, and it was, and I'm not, and we did, and she isn't. So in four months I would be an ex-Jack, the G7W Kid with No Talent.

I wondered if I'd have a chance to say good-bye to my dad. Was he still in the airport in Greece, where we'd left him? Would I ever be able to contact him?

"Earth to Jack?" Cass said.

I looked around into the mass of confusion. "Okay, if we do nothing, we're dead," I said. "The Massa are up in a twist about the earthquake and the ship. That won't last forever. They're going to turn on us. Marco, visiting the ship is a cool idea. But I say we try to get Aly now."

"Us and what army?" Cass said, looking back toward the jungle.

Marco puffed out his chest. "Who needs an army when

6

you have Marco the Magnificent?"

"Did you see that . . . *thing* that was stuck in the rift?" Cass said. "It was huge. And . . . and . . . green. And magnificenter than you!"

"You mean the thing that I stabbed, thank you very much?" Marco said.

"Yeah, but what about all those disgusting creatures who escaped? Listen. Just listen!" Cass turned toward the jungle, which echoed with the hooting and cackling of panicked animals. "You see what's been happening to the Massa. There are vizzeets and griffins and vromaskis in there—hundreds of them!"

Marco nodded thoughtfully. "Well, yeah, even human physical perfection has its limits."

"That's the most modest thing I've ever heard you say," Cass said.

"So we'll use the Loculus of Invisibility and the Loculus of Flight. Just pass 'em by. They won't even know we're—" Marco cut himself off in midsentence. "Uh, one of you guys did take the backpack, didn't you?"

Cass shook his head. I shook my head. My heart was dropping like a freight elevator.

"Nope," Torquin added.

"And the shards of the Loculus of Healing?" Marco continued.

"Everything happened so fast—" I said.

Marco put his palm over his face. "Man. I thought I was supposed to be the dumb one! Guess I'll dust off three seats in the doofus corner."

"Five," Torquin said, counting on his sausage-sized fingers. "I mean, four."

A deep rumbling noise cut the conversation short. For a moment I saw two Casses. The ground shook, as if a silent subway train were passing underneath. I bent my knees instinctively. I could hear a distant *crawwwwwk*—the *Enigma* creaking as it shifted with the earth's movement.

Cass held on to Marco. I held on to Torquin. My body lurched left, right, up, down, as if the world itself had slipped on its axis. Every other noise—seagulls, the distant crashing of the surf—stopped.

Then, as quickly as the movement began, it ended.

In the silence, I could hear Brother Dimitrios's voice cry, *"Earthquake!"*

"Duh," Torquin said.

Cass groaned. "Ohhhh, I feel motion sick. The world is about to end and I am going to die in a pile of my own puke."

"Swallow three raw eggs," Torquin said. "Very good for nausea."

"This is just the beginning," Cass moaned. "It's like Aly said. If the rift opened, Atlantis would rise, and the continental plates would shift. Then, *wham*. Tidal waves, earthquakes. New York and LA go underwater. Massive fires sweep the land . . . dust clouds block the sun."

"Cass, we can't panic," I said.

"Don't be a denier, Jack!" Cass said. "This is *exactly* what happened in the time of the dinosaurs—and you know what became of them."

Marco wiped sweat from his brow. "I don't think we have a choice. Jack's right. Face down those critters! *Into the rift!*"

Whenever Marco moved, he moved fast. In a microsecond he was dragging a protesting Cass back up the beach toward the jungle. I followed behind.

A scream greeted us as we got to the tree line. It was loud and human, maybe twenty yards deep into the jungle. It rose to a horrific, pained bellow, then stopped abruptly. I squinted into the trees, dreading what I might see. But even in the brightness of the afternoon sun, the thick treetops cast shadows, making the jungle nearly pitch-dark.

"Wh-wh-who do you think that is?" Cass asked.

"*Was*, from the sound of it," Marco said.

"S-see what I mean?" Cass said, backing away. "Someone just died in there. We could be next. I am staying out here in the light. I'll take goons in robes over human-eating beasts any day."

An acrid stench of rotten flesh wafted out of the jungle, and Cass gagged.

"Whoa. Beans for lunch, Torquin?" Marco said, waving his arms.

"No. A Twinkie," Torquin replied.

I was focusing on a dark shadow in the jungle behind Cass. "Guys . . ." I squeaked. "Look."

Marco's eyes fixed on the black shape. His body tensed. "Cass," he said softly. "Do. Not. Move."

Cass spun around. With a sound that was halfway between an animal roar and the grinding of metal, a hose-beaked vromaski emerged from the jungle shadows. It launched its boar-like body toward Cass. It flexed its claws and its nose tube folded backward, revealing three sets of razor teeth.

CHAPTER TWO

DINNER FOR TWEETY

IN MOVIES AND books, it always seemed dumb to me when a character shouts "No-o-o-o!" to an attacking wild animal. As if the animal understands English. As if it'll stop in midattack and say, "Pardon me, you'd prefer not to be torn apart limb from limb? All right then, I'll go away, so sorry."

So what did I say when the vromaski was about to sink its teeth into Cass?

"No-o-o!"

Here's the weird thing. The beast seemed to freeze for a nanosecond in midair. Its eyes flickered toward me, but I felt no fear. Everything seemed to stop and I had this crazy feeling I could reach into its brain and make it change course.

Then I blinked, and Marco threw me to the ground out of harm's way.

I rolled away to the left, then scrambled to my feet. That crazy frozen moment had flown out of my head, and I looked around frantically. Where was Cass? I dreaded what I would see. I didn't expect that it would be Marco with his right hand wrapped around the vromaski's left tusk. The creature was spitting and squealing, its legs flailing in the air.

Marco's left hand pinched his own nose shut. "Whew, take a bath, Bruno," he said. Planting his feet firmly, Marco flung the vromaski away from Cass. In a spray of its own saliva, the beast rocketed over the tree canopy, disappearing into darkness. I waited for the thud it would make as it hit the ground. But that didn't happen.

Instead, the beast's growls became helpless squeals, high overhead. It was stuck in the branches.

"That was emosewa. . . ." squeaked Cass. "Thanks."

Torquin nodded. "What he said."

Grimacing, Marco wiped his hand on the trunk of a nearby tree. "Anybody have a Handi Wipe? Let's get on with this before Porky comes back for revenge."

Cass struggled to his feet. "So . . . wait. We're just going to move on, like this didn't happen? Just march into the woods like four walking snack bars?"

"Hey, I protected you once, didn't I?" Marco said,

putting his arm around Cass.

I had to admit, I admired Marco's bravery. But I was having doubts about his sanity.

"Stay with me, you two," he said. "Think about Aly."

I already was. In my mind I could still hear her screams, see her struggling. She was tough and fearless and smart. But against Uhla'ar she didn't stand a chance. Especially if he had the Loculus of Strength.

We couldn't just abandon Aly. If she was still alive, somewhere in the past, we had to get her.

I glanced toward Cass. He looked tiny and vulnerable under Marco's arm. "What about my sister?" he said.

Eloise. Out of the corner of my eye I saw her still striding toward the ship. "Going back will be a risk," I said. "They don't seem to be noticing her."

"She's nine," Marco added. "She was the best of all the trainees, and the Massa respected her. They'll take care of her. Hey, if we can rescue Aly, it'll be a piece of cake rescuing Eloise when we come back."

Cass nodded. He was too smart to protest the plan. He knew the stakes.

And so did I.

I took a deep breath. "Let's roll, guys."

As I stepped forward, I spotted a fluttering of wings from the cloudy sky, a streak of red. At the bloodthirsty *caaaw* of an Atlantean griffin, we had only one choice—duck for cover. The half eagle, half lion hurtled downward, spreading its haunches and flexing its eagle's wings.

You'd think we'd be used to this. We fought one in Greece. We flew on the back of another through the underworld. But even a thousand encounters wouldn't make this monster less frightening. Its body was thick and furred, its talons like swords. Sizing us up with yellow, red-rimmed eyes, it snapped open its beak, revealing a rigid forked tongue that could skewer me like souvlaki.

"AAAAAAAHHH!" screamed Cass. Or maybe it was me.

My arms sheltering my head, I counted to five and realized that if I were actually able to count to five, the griffin must have been skewering someone else.

I peeked out. I could see the griffin's tail disappearing into the branches of the trees high above us. The bird's shadow merged with the vromaski's. As the two beasts growled and spat, branches snapped and thick leaves rained around us.

"Run away!" Marco shouted. "That tree is coming down!"

We sprinted back toward the beach, but the tree didn't fall. Instead, the vromaski's fearsome growls thinned to a whimper, and then silence.

I heard an odd noise that could very well have been a griffin burp.

Marco let out a hoot of triumph. "Supper for Tweety. Free-range vromaski on a bed of tangy jungle leaves."

Torquin stood, wiping his forehead in relief. "Hope he leaves tip."

"Wait—you guys are joking? You think this is funny?" Cass looked at them both in disbelief. "We could have gotten killed. We *will* be killed. We haven't even stepped into the jungle yet! These monsters are crazed, hungry, and . . . kcisemit."

"I stink at Backwardish," Marco said.

"Timesick?" I offered.

"Exactly," Cass said. "Like carsick or seasick—which happens when you travel in three dimensions. Imagine what it feels like to travel through time."

Marco scratched his head. "Wait. Is that a real thing—timesick?"

"I don't know!" Cass said. "The point is, we can't jump into this. We have to do something radically different from what we usually do."

"Which is—?" Marco said.

"*Think*," Cass replied. "In plain Frontwardish. Not just rush, rush, rush, then fight, fight, fight. Maybe that works for you, Marco, but think about it. This place has gone nuts. We're dead if we stay; we're dead if we go."

"What do you suggest?" I asked.

"I don't know that either!" Cass began pacing, running

15

his hand through his tightly coiled hair. "I'm trying to channel Professor Bhegad. He always always told us to think against the grain, not just react to every little thing. So let's take a few minutes. Recalculate."

He was interrupted by distant high-pitched screams, back toward the beach. I squinted, but all I could see was a growing crowd of Massa at the edge of the fish-strewn plain. "Was that Eloise?" I asked.

Cass cringed. "She must have seen us. I'll bet she thinks this is so unfair. In two seconds she'll be running toward us, with Massa goons behind her. Just what we need."

My eyes narrowed. Someone *was* running toward us, but it wasn't Eloise. It was one of the Massa, wiry, thin, and athletic, with a hood pulled over his face.

As I tensed to run, the hood fell away. First, it wasn't a he. Second, it was a Karai in disguise, someone we knew very well. "Nirvana?" I said.

The Karai rebel pulled the hood back over her head. Her eyes, no longer rimmed with thick black mascara the way I remembered them at the KI, were softer. Urgent. She grabbed both Cass and me by the hand. "Listen closely. I've been gathering Massa weapons while they're distracted. The rebels are in the jungle and we'll help you. We know about your mom, Jack. We know exactly who she is, and she'll be working with us as much as she can. She has the backpack with the Loculi of Flight and Invisibility—and also the sack that contains the shards of the Loculus of Healing. Fritz tracked her down as she came through the jungle."

"The Massa haven't found out?" I asked, my heart pounding.

"No, and they won't, as long as I'm alive." Nirvana smiled. "All of it is in hiding. We'll figure a way to get them to you. Now go—go save Aly. Get her out of the rift. Get the Loculus of Strength back. We'll look after Eloise and the other Massa trainees. We have our ways. Whenever you need us, we'll be waiting. This will be our signal."

She inserted two fingers into her mouth and whistled an earsplitting version of the first few bars of "Happy Birthday."

"Oh, cifirret," Cass said. "The one tune none of wants to hear."

Nirvana cringed. "Sorry."

Then, with a nod, she headed for the trees. But she stopped in her tracks when the carcass of the half-eaten vromaski tumbled from the branches.

It hit the ground with a dull thump, sending a spurt of cold green vromaski blood onto my ankle. Both of its eyes were missing, its body was in shreds, and a torn piece of flesh clung to my ankle. As I jumped back in horror, I heard a loud *craaaaack* echoing from the beach like a cannon shot.

I spun around. The rotted mast of the *Enigma* was splitting up the middle. Either half alone could crush a person. And there was exactly one person standing near enough for that to happen.

Eloise.

"What is she doing?" Cass said, running toward the beach. "GET BACK!"

For some reason, Eloise wasn't moving. And even though the Massa were clumping around to watch, no one was pulling her out of danger's way.

As I raced after Cass, I saw Mom out of the corner of my eye. She cupped her hand over her mouth and shouted one word.

"Quicksand!"

CHAPTER THREE

COWBOY CASS

THE WOOD GROANED. Splinters spat into the air like sparks. The two halves of the mast split apart into a V shape, connected only by thin shards of wood that were snapping one by one.

With each step, my feet sank deeper into the mud. Far ahead of me, in the area just before the ship, four Massa soldiers were stuck in a huge patch of quicksand uncovered by the receding sea. They twisted as if doing some creepy tropical dance. The other soldiers had clumped behind them, too wary to move forward.

With another sickening *craaack*, the broken mast split apart, toppling downward—directly toward Eloise.

As I screamed her name, a blur of brown passed me to

the right. I knew it was Marco. No one else could possibly move like that. What happened next was so quick I could only piece it together a few moments later.

He stopped just before reaching the crowd of soldiers. Heaving his arm back, he hurled something toward the ship, hard. I wasn't sure what it was at first, maybe some kind of log. But when it finally hit the mast, I knew.

It was the remains of the vromaski, a hulking projectile of bone and gristle. On impact it sent off a spray of green blood, its head separating clean off and spinning into the muck. The weight of the animal seemed to knock the mast off its course—but not by much.

I flinched. My eyes darted away, and I heard the mast hit the ground with a soft, sickening whump. And Cass's voice, yelling for his sister.

The Massa were rushing toward the scene now. I forced myself to look, but their bodies blocked my view. I glimpsed Marco in the crowd and headed for him as fast as I could. Elbowing my way through the clutch of people, I saw part of the mast embedded in the mud but no signs of Eloise. Was she underneath? Weren't they going to lift it?

I fought my way past a phalanx of robed monks until I was finally standing next to Marco. He—and several other Massa—had stopped short. "Stay right there, Brother Jack!" Marco urged. "Don't move."

About twenty feet away, inches from the sinking mast,

Eloise was standing thigh-deep in quicksand. Alive.

She was peeling a piece of dead vromaski from her cheek. *"EWWW,"* she cried out. "What is this green glob? And why are you all just staring at me?"

Now I could see Cass, carefully high-stepping through the muck toward his sister. "Eloise, you have to try to reach toward me—"

"You did this on purpose, Casper!" she shouted. "You waited till my feet were stuck and then pelted me with this . . . disgusting *thing*."

"Cassius," he said, trying to reach across the expanse of quicksand.

"What?" she snapped.

"My name is Cassius, not Casper," he replied. "Now come on—reach out to me!"

She threw the hunk of flesh at him, but he ducked. Marco lunged forward, pulling Cass back by the shoulder. "Easy, Brother Cass. Or we're going to have two dead Williams in the quicksand."

"Williamses," Cass said.

"This is quicksand?" Eloise shrieked, jerking her body left and right.

She wasn't the only one. At least five Massa were stuck, too, squirming helplessly. "Don't fight it!" someone yelled.

"Lie down!" someone else yelled.

"Don't lie down!"

"Grab the mast!"

Everyone was shouting at once. Eloise froze. Tears began streaming down her face.

"We need a branch—something long!" Marco said. "Now!"

Everyone around us began scouring the beach. I could feel my feet sinking immediately, and I instinctively backed away. My heel clipped the top of a large rock, and I fell.

I landed butt first in the mud, and I could see a black, pointed object jutting upward. I hadn't tripped on a rock at all.

It was an anchor.

Where there was an anchor, there was a rope. I dug hard with my hands until I found the anchor's ring. *There.* A thick, barnacle-encrusted rope was tied to it securely. "Marco!" I shouted.

He was instantly at my side. "Sweet," he said, yanking the rope from my hand. The thing was stiff from the centuries of mud and seawater. But Marco was Marco, and he managed to pry it loose, holding the end upward. "What now?"

I was about to tell him to throw it to her, but I vaguely remembered something that Cass had once told me about his childhood. "Cass, can you throw a lasso?"

He looked at me funny. "Third place for ten-year-olds in the Laramie junior rodeo. How did you—?"

"Marco, give him the rope!" I said.

Marco quickly massaged the stiffness out of the rope and tossed it to Cass. His face all grim and focused, Cass began fashioning the end of the rope into a fancy loop. I glanced out toward Eloise. She had sunk at least a foot more, nearly up to her shoulders. "Stay still, Eloise!" I cried out.

"No-o-o-o!" she screamed.

She was squirming, jerking her body left and right. Panicking.

"Eloise, listen to me—quicksand behaves like a liquid!" I shouted. "If you stay still, you'll rise to the top and float."

Eloise cocked her head and looked at me curiously.

"You're doing it!" Marco called out. "Nice!"

"Do you feel the difference?" I asked.

Eloise's panicked expression dissolved. "Um . . . yeah!"

She wasn't going anywhere, but at least she wasn't sinking. Beside me, I could see Cass beginning to twirl the rope awkwardly over his head. I took a deep breath.

Marco looked doubtful. "You sure you don't want me to try?"

"Git along, little dogie—yee-hah!" Cass cried out.

My jaw dropped. Unathletic, geeky Cass reared back and tossed a perfect loop that dropped neatly over Eloise's head. He immediately pulled back and it cinched around her chest, just below the shoulders.

"What did you call me?" Eloise said.

"Just go with this, Eloise!" I called out. "Go limp!"

She did, and Cass began to pull. Slowly she leaned backward. Her torso emerged from the sand . . . her knees . . . A moment later she was flat on her back, floating toward us at the end of the rope.

"Way to go, Cowboy Cass!" Marco shouted.

I wasn't aware that my mom had approached me from farther up the beach, so her voice made me jump. "How did you know that Cass could do that?" she asked.

She was looking toward Eloise, not at me. For years Mom had kept her real identity secret from the Massa and she couldn't risk any suspicion. I did the same.

"When I was nine," I said softly, "a few years after you died . . . or after we thought you did . . . a family from Wyoming moved to Belleville. The kids were sad we didn't have rodeo, because they'd all competed in it. I always thought it would have been cool to grow up in Wyoming. Anyway, back at the KI when I first met Cass, over lunch one day he listed all the places he'd lived in all those foster homes."

Mom smiled. "And you remembered one of them was in Wyoming," she guessed.

"Yup, it was his longest stay. Two and a half years."

"So you figured he might know how to handle a rope, like those other kids."

I nodded.

"And the quicksand info?" she asked.

"I read it in a *Superman* comic," I explained.

"Good, Jack," she said. "Very good."

Her voice was warm and admiring. I had to turn away from her, or I'd start to cry. Or hug her. Or both. And then we'd be in deep Massa doo-doo. Okay, yeah, I'm thirteen, but imagine finding out your mom is alive after six years of thinking she's not. It does things to you.

"Thanks," I said.

Her voice dropped to an urgent whisper. "I have to go. Don't follow."

She began crossing behind me, as if just passing me randomly on the beach. In my peripheral vision, I could see Brother Dimitrios and some of his henchpeople heading for her. Dimitrios was gesturing toward a line of injured Massa lying in the sand. Mom took him by the shoulder, pointing him away from me.

Had he noticed me? I couldn't tell.

It took every ounce of my strength not to run after Mom. But she had told me not to follow, and the last thing I needed was Brother Dimitrios's attention right now.

From the opposite direction, a very soggy Eloise was storming angrily toward me. Just beyond her, Marco was doubled over with laughter. Cass was wiping a huge glob of mud from his face. The lasso lay on the ground next to him.

"Welcome back, Eloise!" I said. "Are you okay?"

"At least *you* were nice to me, Jack," she snapped, jerking a thumb back toward her brother. "He called me a doggie."

CHAPTER FOUR

TINKERS AND TRAILERS

"*DOGIE*, NOT *DOGGY*!" Cass cried out to his sister. "Dogie means *calf*."

"Oh, so I look like a *cow*?" Eloise stormed away, toward the Massa.

This was our chance. We could take her with us. I tried to pull her back, but she shook me off angrily.

"Eloise, we have to get out of here," I protested. "You don't want to go in that direction. You betrayed the Massa. They are not going to be nice to you."

"Pfff," Eloise said. "You saw them. They tried to save my life."

"But I *did* save your life," Cass pointed out.

"But I hate you!" she protested.

26

"Eloise, please." I looked out toward the ship, where the Massa were all frantically trying to pull each other out of the quicksand with the rope. "This place is chaos. They're distracted by the earthquake and the quicksand. Give them a few minutes, and they'll be on us. They're the enemy. So let's go before it's—"

"Um . . . too late?" Eloise murmured, her eyes flickering farther up the beach.

Mom and Brother Dimitrios were heading toward us across the wet sand, with two guards in tow. Mom was tucking a clipboard under her arm. Dimitrios looked stern and tight-lipped. "Well, that was an admirable deed of derring-do," he said, then turned to the guards. "Seize them!"

One of the guards grabbed Eloise, but she bit him on the wrist. As the other guard jumped in to help, Mom raced toward me. Her eyes were frantic as she grabbed my arm.

I didn't know what to do. She drew me close. I could feel her shoving something into my pocket. Then she rasped the word *go* into my ear and fell back as if I'd hit her. I fought the instinct to help her up, but she was staring at me with a fierce look that was unmistakable. *Leave fast.*

She had done that on purpose. To make it look like I'd pushed her. She didn't want the Massa to suspect that I'd escaped her clutches without a fight.

As I pushed Marco and Cass toward the jungle, Brother Dimitrios and the guards dragged a screaming Eloise away.

* * *

We ducked behind a bush near the tree line. As we peered over, I caught my breath.

"Now what?" Cass said.

"Why'd you make us run?" Marco said. "We had the chance to extract Eloise."

"Because Mom wanted it that way." I scanned the beach—or what used to be a beach. Mom was being helped to her feet by a couple of guards. Behind one of their backs, she was shooting us a thumbs-up gesture. "Now she's giving us an okay signal. We have to trust her. She's no Dimitrios. She knows what she's doing."

"Are you sure you're not just saying that because she's your mom?" Cass said.

I shook my head. "Here's what I know, Cass. One, she's the smartest person on this island. Two, she probably just saved our butts. And three, she'll take care of Eloise. I don't know her exact plan, but we have no choice. Unless we want to be captured."

Cass gave me a barely noticeable nod and stared glumly through the branches. Eloise was surrounded by Massa now, and Mom was fake limping toward her with a towel to wipe her face. Farther to the right, a team of Massa had fallen into line, one behind the other, holding on to the rope like a bunch of overgrown preschool kids. They looked like they were testing the mud for quicksand. Trying to

28

find a safe path toward the *Enigma*. An exploratory mission, maybe. Behind them, Brother Dimitrios was barking orders in an agitated voice. He had a cell phone or walkie-talkie to his ear.

He was also looking around, probably for us. Dimitrios was nasty and sadistic, and don't get me started about his breath. He'd been there at the fight in the jungle with the rebels, and he knew about Marco's defection back to the Karai side.

The only person I feared more on this island was his boss, the head of Massa. Her name was Aliyah, but everyone in the Massa called her Number One. I looked over my shoulder. We were maybe twenty feet from the jungle. Was she in there? Back at headquarters? Eaten by a vromaski?

Beside me, Marco was running his palm from his forehead to his chin and flinging away sweat. He was breathing heavily from the run.

"I think this is the first time I've ever seen Marco the Magnificent out of breath," I said.

Marco smiled. "Must be the shock of seeing Casso the Lasso in action. You were amazing."

"Too bad my sister didn't think so," Cass said.

Marco tried to hold back a laugh, but it spat out of him so explosively that he started to cough.

"What's in your pocket?" Cass asked.

"Huh?" I said.

"A piece of paper in your back pocket," Cass replied. "I didn't see that before."

Mom's note.

I reached around, pulled out the paper, and unfolded it:

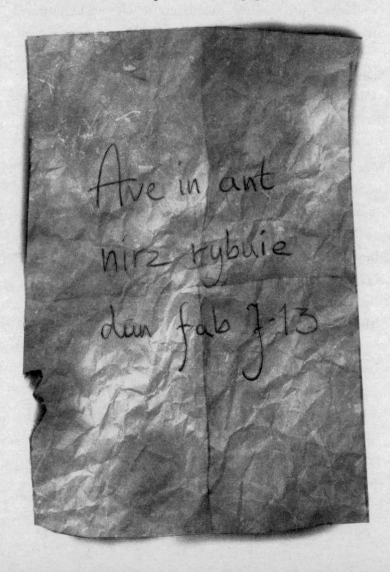

"A code," Cass said. "Cool."

"Um, can we deal with this later?" Marco said. "Maybe after we get to Mount Onyx?"

Cass shook his head. "What if she's warning us about a trap? Let's crack it now. All of us together, we can do it in no time."

Marco groaned. "I'm the Soldier. Soldiers don't do codes. Soldiers keep watch." He crouched, parting the branches of the bush with his fingers. But his eyes were slits. "Codes are solved by . . . Tinkers and Trailers."

Cass glanced up from the note. "Trailers? I think you inhaled quicksand, Marco."

"Whoa, what did I just say?" Marco murmured to himself, blinking hard. "Okay. Cass is the *Sailor* 'cause his brain is a GPS, Aly's the Tinker for the killer tech ability. And Tailor Jack . . ." He let out a massive yawn.

"Maybe I can sew your eyelids open," I said.

Marco ignored the comment. His sleepy eyes sprang wide. "Whoa, put that code away, boys. Here comes Obi-Wan Kenobi."

Cass and I huddled closer to the ground and looked through the bush. I shoved the note back into my pocket.

Stomping up the beach toward us was an SUV-sized Massa with a hooded robe that could have doubled for a tent. "Let's book," Marco cried. "That ain't Nirvana."

I tensed to go, until the guy let out a juicy, enthusiastic belch.

31

"The greeting call of Torquin," Cass murmured, his body relaxing.

"Heyyyy, if it isn't the no-hair giant formerly known as Red Beard!" Marco called out. "In Massa fall-fashion wardrobe."

"Disguise," Torquin grunted, patting the sides of his robes. "Smuggling stuff underneath."

"Vizzeet antidote and griffin vaporizers, I hope," Marco said. As he stood to greet Torquin, he slipped and fell to the dirt.

"Marco . . . ?" I said.

"Whoops," Marco replied. "My—"

The word *bad* caught in his throat. His eyes rolled up into his lids. A shudder began in his fingers then traveled up his body. Gagging uncontrollably, he began to convulse.

"Marco?" Cass cried out. "Is this some kind of joke? Because you're freaking me out."

"He's having a G7W episode!" I said.

"He said he was immune," Cass pointed out.

We watched in shock as Marco's body contorted and lurched like one of the fish on the beach.

Without wasting a moment, Torquin scooped up Marco in his soot-stained arms. "We go to Massa hospital. Now."

Chapter Five
All You Need Is Lohv

A SLINGSHOT ROCK cracked the skull of the first vizzeet. An arrow pierced the leg of the second. In mid-spring, a vromaski took a bullet to the head.

The Karai rebels were armed and all around us in the jungle. We saw only flashes of them as we stumbled through the brush, but they were picking off Atlantean predators left and right. Torquin nearly fell a couple of times. But he held Marco tight over his shoulder.

"Is he . . . alive?" Cass shouted, panting with the effort to follow at Torquin's pace.

"Marco tough," Torquin replied.

I pushed my way through brambles and over roots. Marco's skin was pale, his body limp. I tried to avert my eyes from at least three Massa corpses I saw lying in the brush on either side. Had the entire compound been abandoned for the beach?

"How do we know . . . that anyone . . . will be at the hospital . . . ?" I asked.

"Doctors . . . do not leave patients . . ." Torquin shot back. "Hypocritic oath."

"I think that's the wrong word," Cass said.

I could see a brightening in front of us, which meant we were heading out of the jungle darkness and into the Massa headquarters.

Near the end of the jungle path stood the man who was once the Karai head chef. Old Brutus's clothes hung loosely from his once beefy frame, and a thick rag was wrapped over his left eye. "What happened to you?" Cass asked.

"Vizzeet spit," he explained, barking a short laugh. "Didn't need that eye anyway. Coast should be clear. You're almost there. When this is all over, we'll make a fine meal out of these critters. Oh. Your mama told us to give you this."

He unhooked a backpack from his shoulders. As he swung it around, I could see the familiar bulbous shapes of the two Loculi. "You guys are amazing," I said. "Thank you."

"She said she would get the shards to you. . . ." Brutus continued, but his voice tailed off as he spotted Marco on Torquin's back. "Isn't that kid the traitor?"

"He's one of us again," I replied.

"Then good luck," Brutus said with a curt nod, and he disappeared back into the jungle.

In a few minutes we emerged into the compound that was once the Karai Institute. After the Massa attack, the lawns had become brown, overgrown, and cratered from bomb blasts. The stately brick buildings, which once looked like some Ivy League college teleported to the tropics, were battered and patched with plaster. When we were last here, most of the structures were surrounded by scaffolding. But the earthquake had turned those into mangled steel and piles of planks.

As we raced to the hospital I heard a burst of excited voices, like kids in a playground. Between two of the buildings, I spotted the Massa trainees—Eloise's friends—all grouped together near their training yard. One of them called out Marco's name before a couple of goons ushered them away and out of sight. I was glad they were safe.

Turning back to the hospital, I called out "Hello?"

With his free arm, Torquin pounded on a wall so hard I thought for sure he'd punch a hole in it.

The lobby was brightly lit and reeked of that superme-dicinal hospital smell. I couldn't see anyone at the front or elsewhere in the vast lobby. But above us, on a second floor balcony, a white-coated doctor emerged from a door. He looked startled by the noise, but when he laid eyes on Marco, he immediately said, "Bring him upstairs. The elevators are out."

A wide staircase led to the balcony and we raced upward.

"Call me Brother Asclepius," the doctor said, gesturing to an open door.

"This is Marco—" I began.

"I know Mr. Ramsay," the doctor said. "Please, lay him on the bed."

Torquin did as he was told. As Cass and I began to explain what had happened, Brother Asclepius gently cut us off. He had dark brown skin and probing eyes that seemed to grow with concern. "Yes, this is a G7W episode. Treatable, but a harbinger of the final deadly effect of the gene—"

"So you can fix him?" Cass said hopefully.

The doctor's calm gaze faltered. "I—I'm afraid the equipment for this procedure was in the east wing, which was destroyed."

I felt as if my entire body were dropping through the floor.

"Destroyed?" Cass said. "Why would anyone destroy medical equipment?"

"The Massa are canny, but often reckless," Brother Asclepius replied. "They did not properly identify this building as a hospital during the liberation."

"It wasn't a liberation!" Cass spluttered. "It was an attack. Professor Bhegad told us these episodes will kill us if they're not treated! Isn't there anything you can do?"

"Ohhhhhrrrrrrgh . . ." Marco groaned, clenching and unclenching his fists.

"A strong young man. Stubborn," Asclepius said. "I can sedate him. I can use every technique in my power to keep him alive, but I'm limited without access to the right resources. Maybe the Karai staff have knowledge of an emergency supply of medications somewhere. They were the ones who built this hospital. But without the right equipment, there's only so much I can do."

"Call for the rebels, Jack," Cass said. "With that super-loud whistle, like Nirvana did. With the fingers in the mouth."

"I don't know how," I said. "I thought you did."

Cass shook his head. We both looked at Brother Asclepius, who gave us a helpless shrug.

I glanced around for Torquin, but he'd slipped out of the room. I spotted him through the second-story window—outside, pacing back and forth at the edge of the jungle.

I threw open the window and shouted, "Torquin! We need the Karai!"

Torquin turned toward me. His eyes were glazed, his face sweaty, and for a moment I thought he might have had an episode, too. As he looked up, he said something in a choked, squeaky voice that sounded like complete nonsense.

"Was that English?" Cass yelled.

"Ohhh . . . yes . . . pardon me," Torquin said.

"*Pardon me?*" Cass said. "Did you just say—?"

"*The Karai, Torquin!*" I said. "Can you do the whistle?"

Torquin snapped to, gave me a stubby thumbs-up, turned toward the trees, and inserted two fingers into his mouth.

A pathetic little tune puffed out, mostly breath.

"Oh, great," Cass said. "He has so lost his mojo. They'll never hear that."

"Hey, he's lucky to be alive. Give him a chance. The rebels are listening for us. They'll hear him." I turned to Brother Asclepius. He was injecting Marco with something, hooking him up to IVs. From the beeping of the monitors attached to Marco, he seemed to have stabilized.

Cass and I both breathed a sigh of relief. For now.

"Okay, come on, Torquin . . ." Cass murmured, glancing toward the window.

From outside came a strong "Happy Birthday" whistle that echoed off the hospital wall. Outside, Torquin threw us a big grin.

Brother Asclepius turned from Marco and wiped some sweat from his brow. "Well, I was able to buy us a little time at least."

Cass smiled wanly. "Thank goodness for the Hypodermic oath."

"Hippocratic," Asclepius said gently. "After the ancient healer Hippocrates."

"I knew that sounded wrong," Cass said.

I took Cass by the arm, pulling him out of the room onto the long balcony that overlooked the lobby. There I sat on the carpet and pulled out Mom's note. "Can we do this while we wait? We may need it."

Cass plopped down next to me as I unfolded the sheet of paper:

I could sense Cass trying hard to concentrate. "Did she just make this up on the beach, with all that stuff going on around her?" he asked.

"We started to talk, but Dimitrios was noticing us," I said. "She must have written this when they were taking Eloise away."

Cass stared at the message. "She couldn't just write regular words?"

"What if someone intercepted it?" I pointed out. "Her cover would be blown. Mom is supersmart and superfast. But so are you, Code Guy. Any ideas?"

"Okay . . ." Cass said, narrowing his eyes at the paper. "I'm seeing a bunch of letters. . . ."

"I got that, too."

"Except for the very end. The thirteen. Those are digits."

I looked at him. "So?"

"So," Cass said, "that thirteen could be some sort of key to the rest of the message. Like, 'read every thirteenth letter.'"

"I'll get a pen." I ran back into the exam room and grabbed a pen from a counter. While there, I took a quick look at Marco's chest.

In, out. In, out.

Good.

I ran back out and quickly went to work, numbering the letters first and then circling every thirteenth:

AVE IN ANT NIRZ
1 2 3 4 5 6 7 8 9 10 11 12

RYBUIE DUN FAB J-13
13 14 15 16 17 18 19 20 21 22 23 24 25 26 27

40

"*R* one?" I said. "That can't be right."

"Duh, it's not," Cass said. "Okay. Okay. Maybe this is just a substitution code. Where each letter represents another one."

"Like the one you gave me at the Comestibule, when I first came to the island," I said.

"Ylesicerp," Cass replied, scribbling on the paper. "First you need to number the letters of the alphabet."

He angled the sheet toward me:

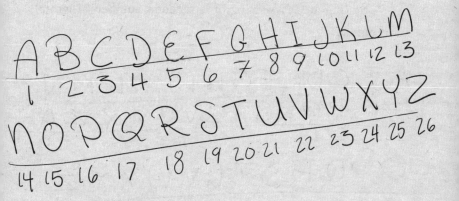

"Now, let's look at that code again," Jack said. "I'm thinking the 'thirteen' is our key. Like, replace every letter in the message with the one thirteen letters ahead of it."

I nodded. "So if you see *A*, you go thirteen letters to the right, and you replace it with *N*. Which is the fourteenth letter."

"Yup," Cass replied. "So if each *A* is an *N*, then each *B* is an *O*, each *C* is a *P*—"

"Then you get to *M*, which is *Z*," I said. "What happens after that?"

"You wrap around," Cass replied. "Go back to the beginning. So *N* becomes *A*, and *O* becomes *B*, and so on."

"Got it."

"Good. Next step, write the alphabet on top and the replacement letters underneath. Makes it easier."

Staring at Cass's string of letters and numbers, I wrote it out:

ABCDEFGHIJKLMN
NOPQRSTUVWXYZA

OPQRSTUVWXYZ
BCDEFGHIJKLM

"Ognib," Cass said. "Now solve that message."

I didn't want to get anything wrong. I quickly wrote out Mom's message and replaced each letter, using the key I'd just made:

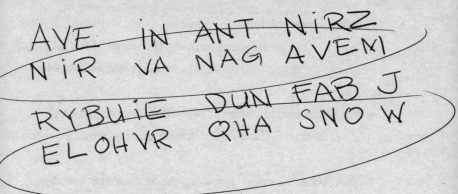

AVE IN ANT NIRZ
NIR VA NAG AVEM
RYBUIE DUN FAB J
ELOHVR QHA SNO W

"Aha!" Cass said, grabbing the paper from my hand. As he read it, his face fell. "Uhhh, guess not . . ."

As if in answer, Marco let out a low, unconscious groan from the table.

"Even in a coma, he lets us know we messed up," Cass said.

"Maybe the substitution works in the opposite direction," I said. "We went thirteen letters to the right. What if we go to the left?"

Cass shook his head. "The alphabet has twenty-six letters—twice thirteen—so it would be the same either way."

"Maybe we're not seeing something. . . ." I unfolded the paper and sounded out the letters softly: "Nir va nag avem elohvr . . ."

"Wait . . ." Cass said. "Read that again, but don't pause for the spaces."

"Nirvanagavemelohvr—" I began.

"Stop," Cass interrupted, pulling the paper closer so he could see. "You said *Nirvana*. There it is, plain as day! *Nirvana gave me . . .*"

My heartbeat quickened. "Nirvana . . . gave me love?"

"*L, o, h, v* . . ." Cass said. "Your mom has trouble with spelling?"

"No, Cass," I said. "Look at the rest of the message. Everything after 'Nirvana gave me' is gibberish—*lohvrqha snow*. No matter how you put spaces in it, it makes no sense."

"The second half of the message could be in a different code. . . ."

I stared intently at the letters. "*L, O, H, V, R, Q, H, A*—maybe the letters stand for something . . . like an acronym."

"For what?" Cass said.

"*L, O, H,*" I replied. "That could be Loculus of Healing."

Cass nearly hit the ceiling. "Nirvana gave me the Loculus of Healing!"

"*V, R, Q* . . ." I said.

"Followed by *H, A, S, N, O, W*—that's two real words, not anagrams," Cass said. *"Has now!"*

"Yes!" My fingers trembled. "So it says, 'Nirvana gave me the Loculus of Healing. *VRQ* has now.' What's a *VRQ*?"

Cass began pacing. "Very Rough Question. Virtual Reality Quiz."

"Victory Round Quaffle," I said. "Virginia Royal Queen . . ."

"*VRQ* . . . it has to be a name, right? Vinnie. Victoria. Virgil."

"That's it!" I said.

"Virgil?" Cass said.

"Victoria," I replied.

"We know someone named Victoria?" Cass asked.

"Close enough," I said, stuffing the sheet into my back pocket. "We know a Victor Rafael Quiñones."

CHAPTER SIX

FACE-TO-FACE

"TORQUIN, WHERE ARE the shards?" I called as I ran out the hospital entrance.

Torquin turned. In the heat of the late afternoon, his fire-blackened skin was covered with sweat. I could see a large, angry-looking, round lesion on his arm, where he must have caught a glob of vizzeet spit. He looked at me blankly. "Huh?"

"Are you okay, Big Guy?" Cass asked, gazing at him with concern. "You know, one of my foster parents had diabetes. When their blood sugar was too low, they acted like you—"

"There is much I need to tell you. . . ." Torquin said in a raspy voice.

The robe. I realized that was why it fit him so strangely. There was something underneath. "Torquin, did my mom give you anything before you left the beach?" I insisted.

Torquin's eyes sparked. He shook his head as if waking out of a dream, and I repeated my question. Nodding, he lifted off his robe. Underneath he was still wearing his tattered rags from Greece, but now the plain brown sack of shards hung by a thick cord around his neck. "Yes, this."

"You could have told us!" Cass said.

"Nice, Tork!" I said. "Those are the pieces of the Loculus of Healing."

As Torquin took off the sack and held it out to me, an arrow whizzed out of the woods. It speared the sack, ripping it out of Torquin's hand, and pinned it to the ground near the hospital wall.

Cass ran for it.

"If that boy goes another step," came a voice from the jungle, "he will be pinned next to it by the throat."

"Cass, stop!" I shouted.

He fell to the ground and then bounced back up with his hands in the air.

"Now come join the others," the voice said. "I would like a proper welcoming committee."

As Cass hurried to my side, Torquin instinctively pushed him and me behind his back. Out of the blackness stomped six guys who looked like the Massa Olympic weight-lifting team. They surrounded a wiry woman in a long toga-like garment. Her graying black hair was pulled straight back, giving her face a hawklike intensity.

"On your knees before Number One!" shouted one of the goons, unsheathing a dagger from his belt.

"Please, Manolo, the Hulk auditions are in Los Angeles." As Aliyah stepped toward me, her eyes never wavered from mine. "You see, these young people are our salvation. Jack and I, in particular, have a trusting relationship. Isn't that right, Jack?"

I was growing sticky with sweat. My eyes darted upward to Marco's hospital window. "Please, Aliyah, Marco is—"

"Dying?" she said. "Pity. I know death well, having lost several of my best soldiers just in the last few hours. In case you haven't noticed, the beach side of the island rose quite dangerously. But here is the odd thing. The other shore sank. The island is tilting. Curious, isn't it?"

"Not . . . just rising?" Torquin said.

Her stare was knifelike. "It may surprise you to know that deep under this island we have a thriving nerve center, left to us by the Karai. In it is our team of seismologists. They are, to say the least, spooked. Something happened to destabilize the island. Something big."

Cass shot me a nervous glance. But Aliyah was now face-to-face with Torquin.

"Perhaps you're familiar with this nerve center, having

served so well as Radamanthus Bhegad's lickspittle," Aliyah said. "Perhaps you know something of the precious sack that was stolen. A sack that looks remarkably like the one that hung from your ample neck."

Torquin yawned. He flicked a massive fly off his nose, caught it in midair, and popped it his mouth. "Lick my spittle."

Instantly Manolo and one other goon reached for their gun holsters.

With a loud grunt, Torquin threw his huge frame toward the men. His bare foot, which was roughly the size of an armadillo, connected with Manolo's jaw. Without missing a beat, he brought his thick arm down on the other guy's neck. Both guards thumped to the ground. But now I could hear rustling in the jungle, new voices. Other people were approaching. Torquin turned to face them.

"The rebels," I whispered to Cass.

Cass reached for the sack. He yanked out the arrow, freeing it from the soil.

"Drop it!" Aliyah's voice called out.

We turned. I took the sack and held it behind my back. Torquin was flat on the ground, surrounded by four new goons who must have emerged from the trees.

"Rebels, huh?" Cass murmured.

One of goons grinned at Aliyah. "Kill the fat guy?"

"Not fat," Torquin said calmly. "Muscle."

Aliyah circled Torquin, eyeing him appraisingly. Behind her, more Massa were emerging from the dark.

"I am not convinced this man is the culprit. Common sense would suggest someone rather smaller and quicker." Aliyah glanced back toward the trees. "Say, perhaps, the young terror behind me."

"Yeeeoowww!" cried a deep voice, as three more burly Massa guards came out of the jungle—or staggered, really. They were pushing Eloise, who was gagged and blindfolded. Her hands were tied together with rope, but she was landing some sharp kicks at the ankle level.

Cass lunged toward her, but I held him back. "You're hurting her!"

"She's hurting us," one of the goons grumbled.

"Gentlemen, remove the gag from the girl," Aliyah said. "Cass, you will be kind enough to drop that little bag of stolen goods right now, if you care about the well-being of your sister."

His face red with anger and worry, Cass let go of the sack. Behind Aliyah, one of the goons was untying the gag from behind Eloise's head. She spat at him, and he threw her roughly to the ground.

"Ow!" Eloise cried out.

"You leave her alone!" Cass said.

Eloise lunged forward and sank her teeth into the guard's ankle. With an agonized scream, he fell to the ground.

The guards hovering over Torquin raced over to help out. Torquin bounced to his feet and followed them. Aliyah turned in bewilderment.

I lunged for the sack, scooped it off the ground, and ran for the hospital door. "Go, Jack!" Cass cried out.

"Get him!" Aliyah shouted.

I heard a loud *craaack*. And another. I felt one bullet whiz past my right ear.

And then I was sprawled in the dirt.

CHAPTER SEVEN

CYRUS THE GREAT

I **WAKE UP** in the sand. I have—or someone has—built a protective wall of sand around me. The sun is still a bulge of pulsing orange on the horizon. But leading to that horizon is an orderly row of crops, fed by canals dug at regular intervals and flowing with water.

I shift my leg and feel that it is connected to a canvas sack. In that sack appears to be a Loculus. As I shake off the fog of sleep, I rub my eyes with both hands and slap the sides of my cheeks.

I nearly cry out in surprise. They are stubbled with hair.

I must be Massarym in my dream. Once again.

The sight of water makes me realize how thirsty I am.

But as I stand and prepare to climb over the wall, I hear distant voices.

"Hello!" someone is shouting. "It's all right, brother, come out and face me. We can work together!"

The wall is chest high, and I peer over the top to see a gaunt, dark-bearded man walking along the border between the crop and the desert. He is the last person I would expect to see.

Massarym!

I duck out of sight. I grab a hank of my scrubby beard and pull it forward from my chin. Looking down, I can see the tips of blond hair in my fingers.

Blond.

In this dream, I am Karai.

I have stolen this Loculus from my thieving brother.

I should know where I am, but I am half in this dream and half out. Something is not allowing me to fall completely asleep.

But I am also gaunt and hungry. My feet are swollen and blistered. I have been following Massarym great distances. And now he is hunting for me. "Working together" is the last thing he really wants.

I hear another voice, and I allow myself to peek out briefly. Following Massarym is a wizened old man in a plain white robe, with a blue sash around his waist and a simple cloth band encircling his head and tied together tightly in the back. "Young visitor," he calls out, "is it not more likely the bandit has escaped to the city?"

Bandit? They are calling ME a bandit? When it was Massarym who snatched away the Loculi and hastened the destruction of an entire civilization?

Massarym spins around to the man. "If he is in the city, we may consider him gone. My brother is nothing if not crafty. You may be a wise man, old Ardashir, but your Persian leaders are dolts. It will be a matter of weeks, maybe days, that the Egyptians will regain control of their land. The cities are already being looted and they are the last places Karai would risk taking the . . . Atlantean treasure."

Treasure, meaning Loculus, of course. He doesn't want to give its name to the old Persian man.

I hold tight to the sack. My journeys have been fruitless until recently. But now things are beginning to turn. I will start with this orb. I have heard reports of the hiding places of some of the others—in Rhodes and Halicarnassus. I will not stop until I find them.

Massarym and Ardashir are walking to the edge of the field. As they disappear behind a furrow of growing plants—flax, I think—I cautiously stand.

Slowly I look around. The sight directly behind me takes my breath away. Rising above the desert like sleeping giants, the three pyramids greet the sunrise. Their sides are mottled with a kind of creamy white material, as if a

54

smooth wall has been eroding away to reveal the stones underneath. To the right, its back to the sun, the vigilant but bored-looking Sphinx watches over them. Its features are sharp and lifelike, and I almost sense that if I step too close, it will bite me.

I will lose myself there and then figure out a way to get to the sea—perhaps a kind farmer or merchant will guide me.

Strapping the sack over my shoulder, I hop the wall and begin to run. I cannot believe how weak I feel, and my sandaled feet sink into the sand. I make the best speed I can manage, but after a few moments I realize I am not alone. A young girl is walking out of another field, a small goat hopping at her side.

I stop suddenly but remind myself it is only a child, younger than I, and I have nothing to fear. So I look forward and continue.

A babylike cry makes me turn my head, and I stumble on my crude sandals.

The girl is covering her mouth and laughing. "One does not insult Cyrus the Great by ignoring him," she calls out. Although she is speaking Egyptian, I understand every word. It is one of the abilities I was able to develop recently as a result of my experiments with the royal blood of my most magical homeland, Atlantis.

I know I should not talk to this girl. But I do. "Cyrus the Great?" I say.

She scoops up the goat and holds up one of its hoofs as if it's waving to me. The animal looks like it's smiling, and that makes me laugh. "The humble Karai bids good morning to Cyrus, King of Kings!" I say with a bow.

"And to me, Lydia, too?" she says.

"And to you, Lydia." As a quick afterthought, I add, "The Great."

She is so friendly and I am so lost and tired. I make the very quick decision that I can trust her (and Cyrus). So I speak up. "Dear one, I have traveled from a far land without friend or family, and I have a great need to get to the sea."

She looked over her shoulder. "My father tells me the Egyptians have blocked the port. There is much fighting now. He believes it is a matter of days before the land is conquered."

"Are you not in danger?" I ask.

She shakes her head. "We are Egyptians. We support the Egyptian rebels. And as we have been here for generations, we know of places to hide."

With an impish smile, she begins to run in the direction of the pyramids. "Come, Karai! Come, Cyrus!"

With a bleat, Cyrus turns and runs the other way, back toward the fields. But I follow Lydia across the sand, until she stops at a column of stone about chest high. A stele.

It is covered with faded hieroglyphs, but miraculously I

can read them. "'Here will be the greatest monument of all, constructed to honor Cambyses the Second, Conqueror of Egypt.'"

Lydia laughs. "They started to work on it. But they will never finish. Now watch this."

She runs her fingers down the side of the stele, tracing along some of the hieroglyphs but not others. After a few moments of this, she steps back.

I hear a deep groan from within the sands below, and the stele begins to fall backward slowly. Lydia is nearly jumping with excitement as the stele's base lifts out of the sand and a square hole opens underneath.

Cool air blasts upward from the blackness. In the rays of the rising sun, I can see a small ladder leading downward. Lydia gives me an eager smile. "Want to see?"

"No," I reply.

"I insist," she says. "Because I know that otherwise you will go to the sea. And you will be taken by the soldiers, drawn and quartered, and the next time I see your face it will be atop a sharp wooden pole."

I swallow. This is not my plan. I know I can turn the other direction from the turmoil and run. But the other direction is miles and miles of scorched desert. Here, at least, I can wait out the conquest. "You really think the battle will be quick?"

She nods. "Father has laid out stores of food. Also games

to occupy our time and very comfortable quarters. Follow me."

Turning around, she begins lowering herself into the hatch, stepping carefully on the ladder's rungs. I wait until she is just out of sight before following.

I am three steps in when I hear Cyrus's bleating again distantly. I look up to see him scampering toward us, with a group of men following.

"Karai!" one of them shouts.

It is Massarym!

As I hasten my descent, the sun glints off something in my brother's hand. It is a scythe.

"Who is that?" Lydia calls up.

"Never mind!" I say.

"Father?"

She is climbing back up the ladder. "How do you shut this?" I ask urgently. "Lydia, please, someone is after me!"

She leaps down the ladder. A moment later I hear a deep groan. A shadow is forming over my head and I step down the ladder to avoid being crushed by the stele's movement.

At the bottom rung, I see that Lydia is holding a torch at the end of a long corridor. I quickly remove my sack and throw it toward her. It lands with a thump at her feet. "What is this?" she asks.

"Go!" I shout. "Hide this where no one will find it. Just go! I will find you in a moment."

"But—" she says.

I hear a loud clank of metal directly above me. I look up.

At the top of the ladder, Massarym has wedged the scythe between the bottom of the stele and the edge of the hole. His face, shadowed but recognizable, leers downward. "Good morning, my brother," he says. "And thank you dearly. You have helped me more than you know."

He swings his legs around and begins to climb downward.

CHAPTER EIGHT

RESURRECTION

TORQUIN'S BREATH WOKE me up. On the negative side, it smelled like a freshly killed hedgehog. On the positive side, it was the first indication that I was not dead.

As I turned my head away from the stench, I realized five things:

1. I was out of my dream, where I was about to be attacked.

2. I was back in reality, where I had been attacked.

3. Old Until-Recently-Red-Beard-but-Now-Beardless was carrying me up the stairs. Fast.

4. The sack of shards was still wrapped around my right arm, and

5. As far as I could tell, my body was bullet-hole free.

"Landed very hard on you," Torquin said. "Sorry. Bullet was close."

Holding me like a loaf of bread, he crested the stairs and burst into the hospital room. Brother Asclepius was hunched over Marco, but he spun toward us, startled.

"Step aside," Torquin said. "We cure him now."

Behind us, footsteps clattered up the stairs. Asclepius blinked his eyes and stammered, "I—I'm sorry, but Marco is . . . he's . . ."

Torquin set me down on my feet at the side of Marco's bed. The guards were now at the door, but I didn't care. As I stood over my friend, I felt as if the air had been squeezed out of the room. Marco was faceup, staring straight into the harsh fluorescent lights overhead. His skin was a sickly alabaster white. A tangle of tubes, bandaged to his arms, led to a bank of monitors. All of them were beeping angrily. And showing flat lines.

Which meant no heartbeat. No vital signs. His chest was absolutely still.

I was only vaguely aware of Aliyah ordering her guards to put their weapons away. Eloise and Cass were walking toward me now. "Is he . . . ?" Eloise asked.

Brother Asclepius put a hand on my shoulder. "I did as much as I could. . . ."

I wasn't hearing them. Wasn't listening. Instead I

yanked open the backpack, dug my hands into the debris, and pulled out one of the shards. Its edges were sharp, and they cut my finger. But it was at least four inches across.

It was all we needed.

"Jack," Cass said, "it's not going to—"

I jammed the shard flat-side down, on Marco's chest. "It's bigger than the one we used on Aly," I said.

"But Aly was alive," Cass said, his voice muffled with falling tears. "The person has to be alive."

Closing my ears. Not hearing this . . . not hearing this . . .

I pressed harder against the still chest. "Come on, Marco . . . come on . . ."

The doctor was trying to pull me back, holding my arm firmly. "Jack, listen to me. It's too late."

I felt a buzz in my head, maybe from one of the alarms. Sweat ran down my forehead, stinging my eyes. The shard felt warm now. The cut on my finger bled onto Marco's shirt. Out of the corner of my eye I saw Aliyah approach. I must have barked at her to go away, because she stopped short.

"How long has Marco been dead?" Aliyah asked.

"Almost two minutes," Asclepius replied.

"Let go of the boy's arm, Doctor," she said. "Do not try to pull him away from his friend."

"But—" the doctor protested.

"I said *let go*, Asclepius!" she snapped.

The doctor's fingers loosened. Now Cass and Eloise were by my side. Cass put his hand on top of mine. My fingers were cramping. I felt like the shard was burning a hole in my palm. It was shrinking like the other shard.

"It's . . . almost gone, Cass," I whispered.

Cass tightened his fingers around my hand and lifted it upward. "We need it, Jack," he said.

It went against every ounce of my will, but I let him do it. The shard had embedded itself in my palm. It was now the size of a nickel.

"It's not going to work this time, Jack," Cass said softly. "Marco's gone."

I slumped back. I turned from the sight of Marco, still and unbreathing. I knew it was something I could never unsee. Cass was right. This was a Loculus of Healing, not a Loculus of Resurrection.

But my brain was pulling up another image of Marco, just as painful. I'd seen him like this before. Worse, really. Crushed and damaged almost beyond recognition.

"Resurrection . . ." I whirled on Cass. "We can do that, Cass."

"What?" Cass said.

"Think back!" I said. "Marco fell into the volcano. But we brought him back—and we can do it again."

"The waterfall!" Cass said, his frown vanishing. "Of

63

course. We have to get him there now!"

Brother Asclepius gave Aliyah a confused look.

"The healing waters," Aliyah explained. "They're in the center of Mount Onyx. They work for Select. Jack is correct. We must help them do this."

I couldn't believe my ears. "Did you say you'll *help*?"

Her eyes were moist as she looked down at Marco's body, and for a moment I could almost see that she was human. "To bring a boy back from the dead . . . this is an extraordinary thing. The problem is, it is quite dark outside. . . ."

"Don't need you," Torquin said, holding up the backpack that contained the two Loculi. "Have flight reservation. Invisibility class."

Torquin's broad frame was blocking Marco's bed now. Aliyah eyed the backpack with shock. "The Loculi?" she said. "I will take those."

"I thought you said you would help!" Cass protested.

"Do not make this difficult," Aliyah snapped. "You stole those and I will have them back before another step is taken. Torquin, I will count to three and you will hand that pack to Manolo."

Torquin raised a hairless eyebrow. "Or?"

"One . . ." Aliyah said.

Manolo signaled the goons. I could see them grabbing their weapons.

Torquin yawned. "Two. Three. Come and get me."

But before anyone could move, Brother Asclepius collapsed to the floor with a dull thump. Torquin spun around. He let out a choked gasp and nearly dropped the backpack.

As he backed away from the bed, the corpse of Marco Ramsay stood straight up. "Sorry," he said, staring down at the doctor. "Was it something I ate?"

CHAPTER NINE

KARASSARYM

"M-M-MARCO," CASS SPLUTTERED. "Y-y-you were—"

"Is he—?" Eloise squeaked.

"Are you—?" I said.

"Hungry?" Marco said. "Yes."

Eloise let out a screech of joy so loud that it brought Brother Asclepius back to his feet. She leaped on Marco's bed to hug him.

Cass jumped around the other side, shouting, *"Elbaveilebnu!"*

"I'm—I'm so sorry," Asclepius babbled, staring at Marco in astonishment. "This sort of thing has . . . never happened."

It *was* unbelievable. Marco had beaten death. Again.

"Welcome back," I said, "to the kid of a thousand lives."

Marco drew me close, nearly smothering me in the crook of his neck and shoulders. "Whatever you just did, Brother Jack," he said, "thanks."

I wasn't sure what I'd done.

As Cass sat on the side of Marco's bed, launching into a blow-by-blow description of what had just happened, I pulled back. Turning my hand upward, I stared at the nickel-sized Loculus in my palm. What *had* just happened?

"Extraordinary . . ." came Aliyah's voice. I felt her hand on my shoulder. She was by my side, smiling at Marco.

The backpack.

I eyed the pack with the two Loculi, which lay on the floor. With my foot I carefully slid it across the room toward the window.

But no one seemed interested in it at that moment.

"You knew, didn't you, Aliyah?" I said. "You asked how long he'd been dead. The length of time somehow made a difference."

Aliyah turned away. "There have been reports throughout history of people brought back after they were declared dead. The public goes wild over these phenomena, calling them miracles, divine intervention, blah, blah, blah. But this kind of thing only happens within a few minutes after breathing stops. The human body goes into a temporary sort of limbo state . . . a reversible coma. This is when people report seeing white lights, angels and cherubim, celestial music, and so forth. With someone as unusually strong as your friend, I imagine this state lasts longer than most. At least . . . I hoped it would. So I asked the doctor to leave you to your devices."

I smiled. "Thanks."

When she looked at me again, her eyes had changed. They were softer, unguarded. "I am moved by your dedication. And your brains. I wish I had known someone like you when I was younger."

I nodded, remembering the story she had told me in her office. "You lost your brother . . . Osman."

"You have an admirable memory," she replied.

"To Queen Artemisia, at the Mausoleum at Halicarnassus," I went on. "Osman was a Select."

"Yes," she said softly. "I did not inherit the gene myself."

"Were you searching for the Loculi back then?" I asked. "Have you known about these from the beginning? Because I thought only the Karai Institute knew—"

She nodded. "As I watched my brother descend into the underworld, I had the Loculus of Healing in my hand. But I didn't know what it was. I was so young. Later it was taken from me by a scheming colleague of my father's, and I never saw it again. It is very moving to see it now, even if it is in pieces."

I let the shard drop back into the sack. We had used two shards for healing, and they had both shrunk. How was I supposed to put together a Loculus now? It would be like a jigsaw puzzle with two shrunken pieces. When it was all done, there would be holes.

And a Loculus with holes is not a complete Loculus.

"Who-o-oa, who invited Medusa and her Gorgoons?" Marco's voice boomed.

"I guess he just noticed you," I murmured to Aliyah.

"Good to see you, Marco," Aliyah said uneasily. "I mean that."

Marco raised a skeptical eyebrow. "I'm waiting for the but," he said. "Like, good to see you, but you're under arrest for treason and sentenced to death by quicksand—"

"Considering your betrayal of me and my organization?" I could see Aliyah trying hard to hold on to her authority. "Appropriate measures will of course be taken, in the fullness of time."

"Aliyah, why let me bring Marco back to life just to punish him?" I said. "You need him. You need *us*. You are now on the road to defeat. The island is tilting, not rising. What's happening to the geological plates now? Did your experts tell you?"

Aliyah nodded. "They said the whole thing may slide into the ocean. . . ."

"So there's not much time," I said. "Leave Marco alone.

We need him to the find the Loculi. And let us work with the Karai rebels. They're scientists, doctors, tech geniuses, Loculus experts. People who could help you. People who know stuff you don't. People who want the same things you do—"

"The same things?" Aliyah shot back. "These are people who want to destroy the Loculi—just as Karai wanted."

"No, no," I shook my head. "They want to find the Loculi, to save the world . . ."

"P. Beg never said *that*," Marco remarked.

"There was a lot Professor Bhegad never told you," Aliyah said.

Marco and Cass were looking at me in bafflement.

My mind was total chaos. Was this true? Did the Karai want us to collect the Loculi just to blow them up? Were they lying about wanting to cure us?

Focus, I told myself. She can spout lies, too.

"What aren't *you* telling us, Aliyah?" I said. "Why do you want to make an entire continent rise and force a global seismic catastrophe? Is it to bring the rest of the world to its knees?"

"It does sound pretty selfish, when you put it that way," Eloise said.

"Oh, dear, dear Jack," Aliyah said with a chuckle. "Let me set your mind at ease. This catastrophe would never occur. The surface area of the island is not large enough.

Perhaps there would be a few unusual high tides and local flooding. But that will be a small price to pay for the benefits of Atlantis's restored magic. Most important for you, if we were to get the seven Loculi in place, you'd all be cured. And you, Jack, would stand to gain the most."

She leveled her gaze at me.

The destroyer shall rule.

That was the prophecy in the Seventh Codex of Massarym, hidden in an old painting. A prophecy I supposedly fulfilled when I threw the Loculus of Healing onto a New York City railroad track. When that Loculus was shattered to pieces under a speeding train, I became the Destroyer.

I was supposed to be the ruler of the new Atlantis.

Me, McKinley the Extremely Unmajestic.

I would have been cackling hysterically if everybody weren't staring at me so seriously. Waiting for me to figure out what to do.

"Work with us, Jack," Aliyah said. "You will not regret it. Neither will your children or grandchildren."

"Um . . ." I said, with great wisdom and force.

Who was lying?

Who was telling the truth?

Aliyah was the head of the Massa. Professor Bhegad was not the head of the Karai. He might have been lied to. He might not have known what the KI really wanted to do.

But would Aliyah really want to raise up Atlantis to

form a new world order—with *me* as the leader? It seemed ridiculous.

I missed Dad. He was all about lists—pros and cons. His motto was *A problem is an answer waiting to be opened.* Which sounded so dumb when I was a kid, but not now. I remember he always started with two questions: What do you want? and How do you plan to get it?

What I wanted:

1. Aly, alive and well.
2. The Loculus of Healing, healed.
3. The Loculus of Strength, back from the clutches of King Uhla'ar on the other side of the rift.
4. The curse of the G7W gene to be over, and a long life for my friends and me.

How I planned to get it:

1.

Arrrrrgh. This part I didn't know. The Massa had the power. The Karai had my trust.

"Jack . . . ?" Cass said. "You better say something. . . ."

All eyes were on me. No-longer-dead Marco. Almost-killed Torquin. The reluctant siblings, Cass and Eloise. The head of the Massa, Aliyah. About ten very large, very quiet Greek guys in tunics. All waiting for my answer to Aliyah.

Work with her? A day ago I would have laughed in her face. But now, for a nanosecond, I felt a charge of power. As if I actually were the king.

It was scary.

But I had my answer. To my own disbelief.

"I'll do it," I said to Aliyah. "I'll work with you."

"Jack!" Cass shouted in dismay.

"Really?" Eloise piped up.

"Dude . . ." Marco said.

Aliyah's eyes grew to about twice their size. "Well. Yes, then. I knew you would see reason."

"But I have some conditions," I added.

"Oh?" Aliyah said, holding back a smile.

"A child does not dictate to Number One," Manolo said, stepping toward me.

Aliyah put her arm out to stop him. "Go on."

"The Karai-Massarym feud is over," I went on. "As of now. You will call off the hunt for the rebels and declare a truce. And Cass, Marco, and I will deliver the rebels to you, willing to be your partners in a new union."

"What?" Aliyah barked in astonishment. As if I'd just reported that all hands were actually feet.

"I like it!" Cass said. "Team Karassarym."

"Massarai sounds nicer," Eloise said.

While I had my courage up, I quickly added something that had been stuck in the back of my mind all along. "Plus, you will give me access to a cell phone so I can tell my dad I'm alive."

"What makes you think we have any service?" Aliyah

73

asked with a bemused smile.

"Do you?" I said.

Aliyah stared back at me silently and tight-lipped, while Brother Asclepius was shaking his head. "This feud has lasted centuries," he said. "It's fundamental. Not so easy to—"

"Do not waste your breath, Asclepius," Aliyah said. "We must be patient with children. Your bluff will not sway me, Jack. You need us more than we need you. Especially with the tasks ahead. Drop this foolishness and not only will I let you call your father but I will put our best scientists to the task of repairing the Loculus of Healing immediately."

Out of the corner of my eye I saw Cass kneel, open the sack, and spill the Loculus of Healing shards onto the floor. They formed a mangled pile, hundreds of sizes and shapes. He spread them out and examined them carefully. Then, picking up two, he tossed one to me.

We held the shards close and moved them to align the edges, the way we had done it in my room weeks ago. At a certain angle, those first two shards had stuck together like magnets. But we'd had to get the positioning just right.

I could feel my shard warming, vibrating, until my fingertips felt numb. Still, the shards were staying put. Not moving at all. Cass was sweating. His fingers shook. Aliyah was staring at us as if we'd lost our minds.

"It's not working," Cass whispered. His shard slipped

from his fingers. But as it fell to the floor, it changed course in midair and began to rise toward me.

With a soft *sshhhink*, the two pieces collided, fusing together into one.

Eloise's jaw nearly hit the floor. "That was so cool."

Aliyah stepped forward and grabbed the fused shards from my hand. She walked to the window and held the piece upward to the sun. "How were you able to do that?" she demanded.

"The power of the Select," I said.

The seam that had formed between the two shards was sealing, bottom to top, until it was gone. Startled by this, Aliyah dropped the shard to the floor. It changed direction in midair and jammed itself right into place.

I fixed my eyes on Aliyah and pumped up all the courage I had. "My terms," I said, "or nothing."

Aliyah swallowed hard. And she nodded.

"Deal."

CHAPTER TEN

HAPPY BIRTHDAY

SOMEHOW THE MASSA had tapped an untraceable satellite signal through a proxy server. Communication would be possible. I had no idea what that meant, but my fingers were trembling as I sent a text to my dad. I was missing him a lot and I needed him to know I was okay.

Hey dad! ☺

JACK!!! Everyone in the hotel is staring at me. I just screamed with happiness. How are you????

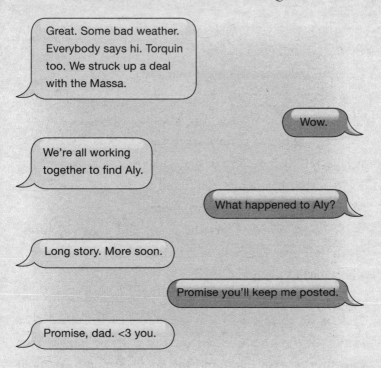

> Great. Some bad weather. Everybody says hi. Torquin too. We struck up a deal with the Massa.

> Wow.

> We're all working together to find Aly.

> What happened to Aly?

> Long story. More soon.

> Promise you'll keep me posted.

> Promise, dad. <3 you.

I couldn't do it. Couldn't tell him the whole truth. He would have wanted to fly here. And that's impossible, since no one knows where "here" is. I didn't want him to worry too much. But as I gave the phone back to Aliyah, I felt so guilty. What if I never saw him again?

She seemed to be reading my mind. "You're doing the right thing, Jack," she said.

"How do you know?" I replied. "You didn't see what I wrote."

"You're right," she said. "But I know you well. You and I aren't as different as you think."

Well, that was a cheering thought.

I turned away from her and watched Cass and Marco, who were hard at work on the Loculus of Healing.

"The leg bone's connected to the hip bone," Cass sang as he carefully moved two shards like tiny steering wheels.

"And the hip bone's connected to the neck bone . . ." Marco sang, maneuvering two more.

Sshhhink. Sshhhink. As the pieces slid together, Eloise nearly fell over laughing at Marco. "You're leaving out a whole part of the body!"

Marco shrugged. "Abs. They're so overrated."

I sat on the floor to join them. We each worked on a section of the Loculus, like areas of a jigsaw puzzle. Aliyah, Brother Asclepius, and the goons were all gaping at us. Asclepius had to hold on to at the edge of a table. For a doctor, I guess he fainted easily.

"Ramsay for the win—the biggest piece by far!" Marco said, holding up a section of Loculus that was curved perfectly, like the bottom of a wide bowl.

"Hey! He-e-eyy!" Cass's own large piece swept upward from underneath him and hurtled through the air like a mini UFO. With a loud snap, it attached to Marco's.

"Score!" Marco shouted. "How about you, Brother Jack?"

I was holding my section pretty far away. I figured I'd wait till I had more of it made, but hey, why not?

I held my piece out, and it instantly shot from my grip and clanked into Marco's big piece. Now the joined shape took on weirdly human form, a tiny head and huge torso that looked oddly like . . .

"Torquin!" Eloise cried out with a giggle.

"What do you think of that, Tork?" Marco looked around for Torquin, but he was nowhere to be seen. "Where is the Hulkinator, anyway?"

I caught a glimpse of the big guy out the window again. Just as before, he was perched at the edge of the jungle. Only this time, it looked like he was talking to himself. "Does he have a cell phone, too?" Cass asked.

I shook my head. "He's a little off his game ever since that explosion in Greece."

"A little?" Marco said.

"He is not normally like this?" Brother Asclepius asked.

"There's nothing normal about Torquin," Marco replied.

"That blast would have killed anyone else," I explained. "I'm amazed he survived. He's been acting strange since then. He didn't used to talk to himself."

Brother Asclepius nodded. "Let me go outside and see what I can do for him."

As the doctor headed out the door, we went back to

work. Piece by piece, section by section, the shards fused together and took shape. Aliyah and her guards watched us with a mixture of awe and wariness.

When we were done, it looked exactly the way it had when I'd held it in New York City. But with two big problems.

"Now what?" Aliyah asked.

I reached into my pocket and pulled out the original shard, the tiny one I'd been carrying since we tried using it on Fiddle.

"A baby tooth?" Eloise said.

"It's a shard," I said. "It shrank."

I held it up and said a silent prayer. It left my fingers and shot toward the Loculus. With a tiny click, it attached to the broken edge. The gaping hole was now a slightly less gaping hole.

Quickly I removed the shard we'd used on Marco. It, too, flew out of my fingers and attached to the other hole, filling it only partially.

"Uh-oh . . ." Eloise said.

"We could use it for Halloween," Marco said with a sigh. "A Loculus jack-o'-lantern."

Around me, everyone seemed to be deflating. "Is this all there is to the Loculus?" Aliyah said angrily.

"I—I guess so," I said. "Maybe if we wait?"

"Is that your plan, for it to magically repair itself?" Aliyah demanded.

"We have plaster," Manolo suggested.

Aliyah spun on him and he shrank back among the other guards.

"Correct me if I'm wrong," Aliyah said. "A Loculus full of holes is not a real Loculus. And without even one Loculus, there no chance of success. Now, *remind me of why we agreed to work together?*"

"He did the best he could!" Eloise protested.

As I walked closer to the Loculus, I heard sounds of a scuffle outside—muffled shouts and rustlings of leaves. I glanced out the window. Brother Asclepius, with a hypodermic needle in his hand, was scrabbling backward. Grunting like a caged animal, Torquin stomped toward him across the scrubby soil. "Torquin!" I shouted. "Stop that!"

"I—I'll be okay," Brother Asclepius shouted, not too convincingly.

"I'm getting a migraine," Aliyah said. "Guards, get that oaf!"

The room emptied. Marco was the first one out, then the guards, Eloise and Cass last. I turned to follow them, but something kept me in the room. It began as a soft buzz, like an insect had crawled inside me through the ear. The sound grew, slowly, droning and changing pitch.

I knew I had to help Torquin. But as irritating as the sound was, I couldn't stop listening. I glanced outside the window. The Massa guards had put themselves between Torquin and Brother Asclepius. But Torquin was on his knees now, head in hands, muttering.

I didn't know what he was doing, or what was going on in that head, but at least there was no fighting. And that was good.

The sound was drawing me to the broken Loculus. Like a distant orchestra of players bowing on damaged violins, on tin cans and barbed wire. I had heard this before—in the center of the volcano, near the remains of the Seven Wonders, and every time we got near a Loculus. It had a different tune every time, but it was always the Song of the Heptakiklos.

The Loculus began pulsating. The hole's ragged edges were smoothing out, growing inward, closing the gap.

Running to the window, I shouted: "Get up here—now. Something's happening!"

Aliyah immediately shouted to the guards, and they came running. So did Marco, Cass, Eloise, and Torquin.

I backed into the room. The Loculus began to rock back and forth. It lifted from the ground, spinning in place. The two holes, not much smaller than before, spat beacons of blue-white light around the room like lasers.

"Jack?" came Cass's voice from the door.

He was behind me. They were all behind me now.

"What the—?" Aliyah whispered.

Aliyah's goons closed ranks in front of her, forcing her to the door for protection. But they didn't get far before a thunderous boom threw us all backward.

My feet left the ground and my vision went white. For a moment I was aware of floating through the room, blinded by the light. Then my back smashed against the wall so hard that it knocked the wind out of me.

I collapsed to the floor, catching my breath. As my sight returned, I tried to sit upright but the pain in my lower back was intense. So I eased myself upward slowly, trying not to groan. Cass was helping his sister off the floor and Aliyah was cursing at her guards, who had fallen on top of her. Brother Asclepius was scrambling to his feet, and I could hear Torquin's heavy breathing somewhere.

But at the moment all I cared about was in the center of the room. The broken sphere was now a softly glowing orb, its dirt color now a sapphire blue. Waves of turquoise and indigo flowed like oceans inside, washing against the smooth, perfect surface. It was exactly as I remembered this Loculus of Healing, before I'd thrown it under the train.

"Welcome back," I whispered.

Aliyah's guards were now trying to help her to her feet. She stood, gawping like everyone else at the bright sphere. As I rose, I realized how hard I'd fallen. I felt like someone had clamped a vise to the base of my spine. I tried to walk normally to the Loculus but instead I hobbled like an old man.

"I don't remember it looking so cool," Marco said.

"Everything gets a little grimy in New York," Cass replied. "The question is, does it work?"

Reaching out, I placed my hand on the surface. Where my palm made contact, the swirls inside the Loculus began to gather. They formed a kind of cloudy image of my hand, neither gas nor liquid but somewhere in between. The blob swelled and darkened until it finally turned to black. Then, with a barely audible pop, it detached from the surface and shot into the center of the Loculus like a comet. I pulled my hand back and watched as the black blob was absorbed into the blue swirl, like a drop of ink into the ocean.

Whatever had been clenching my back released. I

straightened out slowly. No pain. I moved left and right. I did a couple of dance moves.

"Well, that's awkward," Eloise said.

"Did you see what just happened?" I said.

"The Loculus of Healing made you dance?" she replied.

They couldn't tell I was hurt. Or they'd been too busy looking at the Loculus to notice. But I could see a flash of recognition in Torquin's red, squinty eyes.

He was sweating badly. He had been looking worse and worse since he'd arrived back on the island. The burn marks on his arms looked like a botched tattoo job done by an angry orangutan, and his scalp was red from where his hair had been burned off.

I touched the Loculus again and reached out to Torquin with my other hand. "Torquin, let's get you back to normal—or as normal as a Torquin can be. . . ."

He shuffled toward me, raising his charred right arm. I placed my free hand on it and felt a kind of electric twang where my fingers touched. The feeling pulsed up my arm, across my chest, and clear through to my opposite palm, still placed against the Loculus. There, just inside the membrane, the dark patch began to form again—and again, it disappeared into the orb. Torquin shuddered briefly.

The black mark on Torquin's arm, nearest my fingers, was the first to vanish. Then the bruise directly above it. Like the movement of the sun, the healing spread up to his head and down the left side of his body. Angry, injured skin became thick and healthy. On his arms, legs, and head, the singed black clumps of hair fell to the floor. In their place came a growing crop of new hair, furry on the arms and legs and thick as ever on his head and cheeks—with one difference.

Although his hair was the old Torquinian red, his beard was now completely white.

Eloise smiled wanly. "Wow. You look almost not scary."

Torquin's face twisted into a strange grimace that I recognized as his smile. "Torquin feels fine."

"And that is why they call it a Loculus of Healing," I said.

"YEEAHHH!" Marco hooted, punching a fist in the air. "The Select, back in business! Once more with three Loculi! All hail King Jack!"

"No, don't call me that!" I exclaimed, but Marco scooped me up by the thighs and lifted me in the air.

"How about *Jack the gnizama*!" Cass shouted.

"Or maybe Spencer," Eloise said. "I always liked that name."

Marco set me down and I threw an arm around Eloise in a fake wrestling move until she giggled and pulled away—straight into the arms of a very stern-looking Aliyah.

"Well. That was a very impressive job. This is, as they say, a game changer." She nodded appreciatively, then turned, signaling for us to follow. "But we must move on. Manolo, will you please take the Loculus?"

As Manolo approached the glowing orb, Torquin stood in front. "No take."

Marco stepped between them. "Let me translate for old, um . . . White Beard. He means, 'Sorry, dude, but we're partners now, so let's all talk before you boss this crew around.'"

"Ah, of course, Manolo; they have legitimate concerns," Aliyah said. "So. We could have a little conference, with a celebratory cup of tea and some sensitivity training, and perhaps Manolo would play 'Kumbaya' on the lute. But this would take some time, and I am of the opinion that we move now, go back to the rift, and retrieve the Loculus your friend took with her."

"Now you're talking," Marco said.

"But before we rush willy-nilly into disaster, we must seal our bargain," Aliyah said. "Jack, you will follow your end of the deal and arrange to bring the rebel leaders to me. We have no time to waste. Can you do this in an hour?"

"An hour?" I said. "To broker a deal between the Karai and the Massa. That's crazy!"

Aliyah sighed with exasperation. "All right. Ninety minutes."

I turned to Cass, Eloise, and Torquin.

Then finally to Marco.

"Tell me, Marco," I said pleadingly, "that you know how to whistle."

"I can!" Eloise announced.

She stuck two fingers in her mouth and let out a blast that felt like an ice pick through my eardrum.

"Come with me," I said.

We raced downstairs and outside. Night had fallen, leaving only the light of the hospital windows to guide us across the scrubby patch of grass to the jungle.

"Okay, wait till I have my hands on my ears," I said, "and whistle 'Happy Birthday.'"

I pressed my hands as tight as I could. It didn't help. Eloise's whistle was like a police siren. It had the basic rhythm of 'Happy Birthday,' but the tune was pretty much unrecognizable.

Still, I was sure Nirvana would figure it out.

Our answer was a chorus of pained screeches from the birds and monkeys. After a minute or two Eloise tried again.

Behind us the hospital door creaked open. Aliyah was leading her guards toward us quietly, along with Cass and Marco. "What are they all doing here?" Eloise said. "They'll scare the rebels away."

"Aliyah, can you and the guards wait upstairs?" I called out.

Manolo had his hand on his gun. "Just want to protect

you," he said. "From monkeys."

"Wait a minute," Marco said. "If you guys think we're idiots, if you think we're going to call the rebels so you can ambush them, think again."

"Marco, keep in mind who you are speaking to," Aliyah said.

"When Number One gives her word," Manolo said, "it is as good as—"

His eyes went wide in midsentence and his mouth let out a choked little cry. As he fell to his knees, I could see a small, feathered dart in his neck.

CHAPTER ELEVEN

BLOOD OATH

"STOP!" I YELLED. "Don't—"

I felt the barrel of a gun against my neck. Another of Aliyah's guards pulled me to the ground, growling into my ear, "Move one strand of hair, and you are toe—"

I think he meant to say *toast*, but he choked on the word. His hand loosened and he fell away, gagging and convulsing, pawing at an arrow in his neck.

As I sprawled to the ground, Marco pulled Cass and Eloise down, too. Darts flew overhead like a cloud of insects in the growing darkness.

A bullet cracked loudly through the air, then another. Aliyah's goons were dropping to the ground, shooting blindly into the jungle. Each shot was followed by a volley of darts coming from the jungle's darkness. One by one the guards fell away, unconscious. I could hear voices in the trees now, distant footsteps.

Creeping slowly on the ground, Aliyah reached Manolo's side and grabbed his gun. Taking aim at a movement among the trees, she squeezed the trigger.

A shot rang out, followed by a loud shout of pain. A tall figure in a robe fell from the shadows, sprawling out onto the ground before us.

Aliyah dropped the gun. "Brother Dimitrios?"

As she raced toward him, more darts flew overhead. One of them lodged in her hair, barely missing her. "STOP SHOOTING!" I screamed. "WE'RE OKAY!"

From the blackness, Nirvana stepped into the dim light. She held up her right hand, in a signal to the rebels who must have been behind her. "Well, hooo-ee, this is a fine mess," she muttered, surveying Brother Dimitrios and the unconscious goons. Then, looking over her shoulder, she called out, "Enemy disarmed! Reclamation team, come forward! Bones, our special guest Dimitrios is down!"

Immediately three wiry-looking rebels ran out of the jungle. They went from one of Aliyah's unconscious guards to the next, scooping up weapons. Dr. Bones, the Karai physician, joined Aliyah and began gently examining Dimitrios. He'd been hit in the leg, and blood pooled below him. A moment later, Brother Asclepius raced out from the hospital with gauze, bandages, and some jars that looked like antiseptic.

"I'll get the Loculus of Healing," Marco said softly to Asclepius. "Ninety-nine percent more effective than ordinary Band-Aids. And no harmful side effects."

As Marco ran inside, the two doctors helped Dimitrios to a soft spot on the grass behind us.

"You used Dimitrios as a shield," Aliyah growled, glancing up at Nirvana. "A helpless old man."

"Actually, I'm not that . . . old," Brother Dimitrios said through a pained grimace.

"Not to put too fine a point on it," Nirvana said, "but your guys shot him."

"Self-defense, dear girl," Aliyah replied.

"Listen, you two," I said, "let's not argue—"

"That's how you guys operate, bullets for tranquilizer darts?" Nirvana blurted angrily. "We *rescued* this dude. He and his buddies were just asking to be vromaski snacks. They're all tromping through the jungle like the Seven Dwarfs, heigh-ho, heigh-ho, trying to bring you a present."

Now a whole team of rebels was emerging from the trees—along with a few robed Massa officials. The rebels were much skinnier and more raggedy, but the Massa looked like they'd just been to war—leaning on walking sticks, bleeding, and wearing bandages fashioned from tree bark. Two of them brought forward a massive wooden chest. Its hinges were rusted, its sides pimpled with barnacles. Seaweed hung wet and limp from every surface, and a huge padlock dangled from a broken hasp.

Aliyah rose, staring at the chest. "What on earth is this, Dimitrios?"

"It belonged to . . . *Enigma*," Brother Dimitrios called back. "As you ordered . . . before you left, Your Leadership. It was quite an operation, I must say. Believe it or not, one of our men nearly was bitten by a shark that had got stuck on board when the water receded."

"Shark?" Cass said, inching forward with his sister.

"Cool," Eloise added.

"I was not speaking to you, children," Dimitrios snapped.

Marco was racing out of the building with the Loculus of Healing. In a moment Dimitrios would be fine, but I can't lie. Part of me wanted him to suffer just a little bit longer.

"I ordered an *exploratory* committee," Aliyah said sharply. "I wanted a report, not a dangerous trip through the woods with an old chest." She glanced at a six-foot-tall woman with a chiseled face and short black hair. "Hannelore, you were supposed to head the committee. Have you no sense?"

"Begging your pardon, but this discovery was too urgent, Your Leadership," Hannelore replied. "Please, take a look."

As Aliyah reached for the chest, Nirvana stomped a black-booted foot down on the top of it. "Not so fast, Dora the Explorer. We have some business to take care of. You owe us."

Aliyah stood. "Yes, yes, Jack and I have been discussing this, and—"

"We could have taken this chest, no sweat, Numero Uno—and we could have let your minions be critter food," Nirvana barreled on, to a chorus of agreement from the rebels. "Now, our people are starving and dying. Which is bad for you, because we have survival skills in this jungle that you all could use. And in case you haven't taken a look down at your Sleeping Uglies, we have techniques that will disarm the worst of you. So listen closely because I have a proposition—"

"Oh dear, yes, accepted," Aliyah said with a weary sigh. "Now open the—"

I was trying to signal Nirvana to stop but she was getting all heated up. "Think hard before you say no to me, boss lady, because we can make your lives supermiserab— Wait. Did you say *accepted*? I didn't even tell you what we wanted."

"Whatever it is, yes," Aliyah said. "Food, shelter, medicine—and might I suggest from your general atmosphere, baths. We agree to work with you. With Jack and Marco and Cass and Torquin, too. We shall cease to waste energy fighting, and instead combine forces until we find the Loculi."

Nirvana's face was all twisted up into an expression that was part *duh*, part *I don't believe this*, and part *did I die and go to heaven?*

I nodded. "She means it."

"But they want . . ." Nirvana pointed to the goons. "And we want . . ." Nirvana pointed to the rebels.

"I know we have differences both operational and philosophical," Aliyah said, "but the seismic irregularities brought on by the abrogation of the time-space rift indicate the absolute necessity of our utilizing our mutual synergies to avoid cataclysm, and in my belief it is advisable to shelve the discussion of the ultimate fate of the Loculi until stability is achieved."

"In English, please," Torquin grumbled.

"I think she's saying that we're dead unless we work together," I whispered, "and we'll worry about what to do with the Loculi after we get them."

Behind Nirvana, the rebels were wide-eyed and confused, chatting and arguing. Nirvana slowly removed her boot from the chest and held up her hand. As the rebels shushed each other, she went face-to-face with Aliyah. "Blood oath?"

Nirvana whipped out a knife from the pocket of her ripped jeans. She slashed a small cut in the back of her hand, then held out the knife to Aliyah.

"I beg your pardon?" Aliyah said with utter disbelief, as

if Nirvana had just asked her to transform into a salamander.

But Nirvana stood firm. And now all the rebels were staring. As well as the Massa captives. And a couple of Aliyah's guards, who were just beginning to come to.

Aliyah's dismissive smile faded. With a weary sigh, she took the knife and pierced her own hand. The two women touched their wounds together.

"Ew," Eloise said. "Just ew."

Aliyah looked at her bleeding hand in disgust. "Antiseptic, please, Asclepius," she said.

With a big grin, Nirvana looked over her shoulder and let out a loud, clear whistle. "BOYS AND GIRLS, LOOKS LIKE WE ARE FINALLY FREE!"

More rebels poured out from behind trees, clutching their weapons. Fritz the mechanic and Brutus the chef both approached Aliyah warily. Fritz was the first to offer his hand.

While Asclepius tended to Aliyah's wound, she offered her other hand tentatively, as if she were about to stick it in dog turds.

I looked at Cass, and he gave me a nervous smile.

It was going to take a while for them all to become friends. The Massa had done a lot of horrible stuff. But it better not take too long. We had the three Loculi. We had Torquin. With the KI and the Massa on our side, we were back in business.

But we were without one crucial partner.

The island.

And we had to get Aly before it decided to slide into the ocean.

CHAPTER TWELVE

GREED OR NEED

I HATE WHEN grown-ups tousle my hair. But old Brutus was working my scalp so hard you'd think he was kneading bread. At least he was happy about the truce. "Big day," he kept saying. "Big day!"

"So," I replied, "can we get started—?"

Brutus turned to Torquin for a high five, but the big guy waved him away. "Waste of time."

There must have been two dozen KI rebels—way less than the original Karai Institute. The time in the jungle had taken its toll. Fritz the mechanic's once-bulging arms had grown thin, and his Harley-Davidson tattoo looked like a crushed tricycle. Some of the others were barely recognizable from weight loss and sickness.

The woman they called Hannelore was directing some of the rebels as they tried to pry open Wenders's chest. "Why are they doing this now?" Cass hissed.

"Because we need all the help we can get," Marco said. "We talked about this, Brother Cass. Wenders is the man. He covered every inch of this place. If anyone knew how to get in and out of the rift, it was him. So, what if his secrets are in that chest? Sometimes fast is the enemy of smart."

"Where'd you learn that?" Cass said.

"Fortune cookie," Marco said.

As the rebels pulled on the warped, waterlogged lid, Eloise clung to my side, openmouthed. I couldn't help looking either.

The hinges squeaked as the top swung open. A smell of rotting fish wafted upward. "Sweet," Marco said.

Eloise held her nose. "You are so strange."

Hannelore shone a flashlight, revealing a box inside:

"Greek to me," Torquin grumbled.

Marco peered closely. "I think it says 'This belongs to a Weird Bald Tot.'"

"Wenders was German, like me," Hannelore said, "as is this message. The translation is roughly, 'Whether you come with greed or with need, whoever opens this will soon be dead.'"

"Doesn't really rhyme," Eloise remarked.

As Hannelore reached for the box, Marco grabbed her hand. "Whoa. Don't do that."

"Why?" Hannelore asked.

"'Soon be dead'?" Marco said. "That's pretty strong."

"Ach, I am a scientist," Hannelore said with a little laugh. "This message was the scare tactic of a scared man. Besides, we've already opened this, and everyone survived."

Marco let go reluctantly, and Hannelore pulled up the box with both hands. It was sturdy and surprisingly heavy looking, like a giant car battery. She laid it on the ground and brushed off the seaweed. Pulling a small crowbar from a tool belt, she pried it open, releasing a soft sigh of air. "Remarkable for its time," she said, "this box is nearly waterproof. It must have been precision-crafted by the best German metallurgists of the day. But watch . . ."

Inside it was another box, wedged tightly. She pulled that out and opened it, to reveal yet another box. This one was dry and pristine, its oaken sides looking almost new.

"A perfect system of protection," she said. "The insides of this third box remained dry for more than a century underwater."

By now the entire crew—Aliyah, her guards, the Massa captives, the rebels, and the rest of us—were gawking silently. Hannelore jimmied open the final box and turned to us with a grin. "Voilà!"

Marco was the first to peer in. The box was packed solid with leather-bound notebooks, jammed side by side. Each spine was labeled with a number and date.

As Hannelore gently pulled one of them out, Eloise gasped. "These are sooo cool."

"Who's your daddy?" Marco crowed. "Are those Wenders's secret notebooks or are they not? So, what do they say, Brunhilda?"

"Hannelore," said Hannelore, leafing through the book. "The problem is that they are all written in Latin. Wenders was quite a scholar. He knew his classics, his Latin and Greek. I suppose he used Latin instead of his native German as a kind of code, to keep nosey people from understanding them. Which, unfortunately, would include us."

"Fiddle knew Latin," Nirvana added softly.

Great. All this effort and we were stuck with books we couldn't read.

"Wait," Marco said, reaching down into the chest. "Are you sure they're *all* in Latin?"

I felt Torquin's hand clamping on my forearm. He pulled me away from the chest with one hand and Marco with the other. "We go. To Mount Onyx. Now. She is waiting."

"But—" Marco began to protest.

"He's right," I said.

Aliyah was walking toward us, away from the chest. Marco, Cass, and Eloise were close behind.

"Have all three Loculi now," Torquin said. "Loculus of Flight to get there fast. Loculus of Invisibility to avoid creatures. Loculus of Healing if things go wrong."

"But even cases of extreme urgency cannot yield to recklessness," Aliyah said. "Night has fallen, and even if you are using your Loculi to travel, you must be able to see."

"Too bad we don't have a Loculus of Night Vision," Marco said.

Aliyah smiled. "You might."

Now all five of us looked at her blankly.

"If I'm not mistaken," Aliyah said, "you have visited five sites. But you retrieved Loculi from only four of them—the Colossus of Rhodes, the Hanging Gardens of Babylon, the Mausoleum at Halicarnassus, and the Statue of Zeus. You never found the Loculus of the Great Pyramid of Giza."

I flinched at the thought of our botched visit to Egypt. We'd been taken to the Massa's underground stronghold near the Great Pyramid. They'd tried to brainwash us the way they'd brainwashed Marco, but we'd managed to escape

102

and return to the island. It was a cell phone in my pocket that allowed them to track us—and eventually invade the island.

My fault. All my fault. For about the gazillionth time I fought back the voice that had been taunting me since the invasion. "We didn't have a chance to look," I said. "But after we get Aly, we'll go back. We have to."

"What makes you think you need to go back?" Aliyah said.

"Because, duh, we need seven Loculi," Marco said.

Cass held up a hand to shush him. "Wait a minute," he said. "What are you saying, Aliyah? Do you have it? *Do you have the pyramid Loculus?*"

Aliyah turned around. "Follow me."

"Why can't she ever give us a straight answer?" Eloise mumbled.

I turned back toward the jungle in frustration. In the distance, Mount Onyx was a deep black blot on the blue-black sky. "We don't have any time to waste."

"And I," Aliyah said over her shoulder, "am not in the habit of wasting time."

CHAPTER THIRTEEN

ORB MUSEUM

"SO, WERE YOU serious that there was a shark on board the *Enigma*?" Cass asked Brother Dimitrios.

"Hurry," I warned him.

We were racing into the ruined grand hallway of the building once known as the House of Wenders. The elegant tiled floor was covered with grime. A simple metal pole now lined the grand balcony, replacing the carved mahogany rail. And the destroyed skeleton of Herman Wenders's dinosaur had been piled up carelessly in one corner.

"It surprised us," Dimitrios said. "It was like something out of a horror movie. I thought we might be eaten."

"Doesn't happen that way," Eloise piped up. "Sharks use their stomachs for storage. Stuff can just stay in there, like, forever. They can choose which items to digest—and digestion happens in the shark's gizzard. That stuff in the stomach? If it starts irritating them or whatever, they just go . . . *bleeahhhh*! They throw it up, right out of their mouth. Their stomach is like this giant rubber slingshot. It's the coolest thing ever."

"How do you know all this stuff?" Cass asked.

Eloise smacked him. "They have school here."

"Will you stop chatting and step lively?" Aliyah called out.

She and Manolo were already at the elevator just beyond the hallway. It was the first we'd seen of the elevator since the Massa attack. The ornately carved metal door was pitted with shrapnel, but the up and down lights were working and the door slid open just fine.

I adjusted my backpack, which contained the Loculi of Invisibility and Flight. Cass was wearing the sack with the newly reconstructed Loculus of Healing. As we stepped inside, Brother Dimitrios settled against the elevator wall. "I don't believe I thanked you properly, Marco," he said. "For using the Loculus of Healing on me."

"No worries, Brother D," Marco said. "But you owe me one."

According to the buttons, the elevator descended seven levels underground, to the lowest level. But Aliyah pressed a swift combination of buttons, and it kept dropping.

"Where are we going? China?" Eloise asked.

Torquin, who had been grumbling and scowling the whole way, sighed. "Not hearing her anymore," he muttered.

"Not hearing who?" I asked.

"Voice," Torquin said. "Don't know who."

"Seriously?" Cass said. "Does Asclepius do psychiatry?"

"You look suspiciously healthy, Torquin," Brother Dimitrios said.

"We used the Loculus of Healing on him, too," Eloise explained.

Torquin glared at Brother Dimitrios. "You look suspiciously suspicious."

Dimitrios was the first one out the door when it opened. The air was at least twenty degrees cooler down here. It smelled like my basement in Belleville after a big flood two years ago. Like mildew and dead mouse.

"Phew, did you unwrap some mummies down here, too?" Cass asked.

Brother Dimitrios and Manolo shone flashlights into a cramped, dirt-walled cavern. The ceiling was not much higher than my head, and occasional stalactites dripped water onto the ground. Both Marco and Torquin had to stoop to walk.

Along the walls, four narrow tunnels had been dug. We followed Aliyah into one of them. Her flashlight outlined a long passageway with detours off to the sides. In the distance was a steady rhythmic banging.

"Th-th-this is scary," Cass whispered. "What if this is a dungeon?"

Aliyah turned. "Sorry about the noise. We are about to pass the auxiliary power room. We are forced to use it until the main power station is repaired. It was built by the Karai. I must give them credit."

Just next to the power room, Aliyah stopped before an unmarked door. Leaning low, she stared into a green-glowing metal plate. In a moment, the door swung open. "Iris recognition," she explained.

Manolo leaned inside and flicked on a light switch. I had to blink at the sudden harsh fluorescent light. As my eyes adjusted, I choked back a gasp.

The little room was actually a vast chamber at least fifteen feet high and stretching the length of a tennis court. Tables had been shoved against the walls, and shelves rose practically to the ceiling—every surface jammed with ancient artifacts. They were dull gray, jewel-encrusted, metallic, rocklike. The smallest was the size of a softball, and the largest approximately the circumference of Torquin's head. A couple had fallen to the dirt floor, and one lay smashed like a fallen Christmas tree ornament.

Every single one was in the shape of a sphere.

"Who-o-o-oa," Cass said, his head angled upward to take it all in, "this is an orb museum."

"Pah," Torquin said. "Looting. Illegal."

"We are all archaeologists and scholars," Aliyah said, "and we plan to return everything. Well, everything that is not a Loculus . . ."

I stepped inside, and it all became clear to me. When Aliyah said she and her people had found the Loculus, she'd been stretching the truth. They couldn't really *know*. They weren't Selects. "So . . . you found everything that *might* be a Loculus," I said. "And you brought it all here."

"We are reasonably certain *one* of these is the Loculus," Aliyah replied. "We took them from a hidden tomb that was not discovered by looters. Fragments of writing, presumably from Massarym, assure us that the Loculus was kept in the tomb, not in the Great Pyramid itself. Perhaps the pyramids, which had existed for millennia before Massarym arrived, were not deemed safe from looters. Whereas a hidden tomb . . ."

The Dream.

The memory came rushing back. The stone marker—the stele—had indicated the entrance to a hidden underground place. Lydia the farm girl had gone there to help Karai escape, only to be discovered by Massarym. "Karai and Massarym were both down there. . . ." I said.

"The writings do not mention Karai," Aliyah said. "But there have been rumors his body was buried under the tomb, with the Loculus beside it. Personally I think it's all bunk."

108

"Aliyah," I said, "the Loculi are all protected by creatures. If you did take the real one, you would have been attacked . . . by something."

"Perhaps," Brother Dimitrios said, "the Loculus must be activated in order for the creature to be summoned?"

I shrugged, looking around the room. The ancient jewels spat sharp beams of reflected light that danced against the walls. "Aliyah, there are hundreds of objects," I said.

"Can't you just wander around and listen for the Song of the Streptococcus?" Eloise asked.

"Heptakiklos," Cass said.

As I looked from orb to orb, the designs danced in the harsh light, distracting my concentration. I closed my eyes, but the fluorescents were giving off an annoying, high-pitched buzz, and the floor shook with the booms and thrums of the power station next door. How was I supposed to hear anything in this racket?

My foot jammed against something and I tripped, stumbling to the floor. "Nice move," Marco said.

"What do you hear, Jack?" Aliyah insisted.

"I can't do it," I said. "I need quiet. Less distraction."

"Manolo, can we move these to a more sealed location," Aliyah said.

"Will take days," Manolo said.

"Too long," Torquin grumbled.

"What if this is a wild-goose chase?" Marco said.

I looked desperately around the room, trying to ignore the sounds, the light, and now the bickering, which was starting to annoy me. *"STOP IT!"* I shouted at the top of my lungs.

The voices stopped. A moment later so did the other noises. And then a moment later, so did the lights.

Eight stories underground, we were plunged into total darkness.

CHAPTER FOURTEEN

LOUD AND CLEAR

"MANOLO!" ALIYAH CRIED out.

I couldn't see a thing, but I could hear the burly guard snapping on and off the light switch. "There is power failure," his voice shouted into the blackness.

"Oh, for the love of Massarym," Aliyah said. "We will have to do this another time. Let's go. We shall take the stairs. No power means no ventilation. And no elevator."

"Ooops," came Eloise's voice from the entrance. "Guess I should go back into that room and turn the lights on again?"

The room fell silent. "Did you say, go *back*?" I said. "Did *you* turn off the power?"

"I was just trying to help," Eloise pleaded.

"How is that helping?" Cass asked.

111

"Hello, Mr. Clueless, Jack wanted the noise and the lights to stop, right?" Eloise said. "So I went to the power room. And I saw this switch—"

Aliyah groaned. "This is why I never had children. Manolo, she tripped the master switch. Go back with her and . . . undo what she did."

I could hear Manolo muttering Greek curses under his breath. He must have bumped into a shelf because I also heard heavy objects thumping to the ground.

As the two passed into the hallway, silence fell over the room That was when I saw a glimmer of bright color on the opposite side.

And I heard a hum.

"What's that?" I whispered.

"What's what?" Cass said.

"The light," I said.

"Is no light," Torquin grunted.

"Okay then, what about the sound?" I said.

"There is no sound, Jack," Aliyah replied softly.

I walked toward the light, reaching forward with my hands. "Tell Manolo and Eloise not to pull the switch yet."

"Niko—go!" Aliyah commanded.

I could hear the burly guard thump out into the hallway.

The quiet was total now. I was aware that my eyes were not seeing the light, and my ears were not hearing the sound. The two things were like signals between the object and me—private signals that only we could detect.

You found me, Jack.

I laughed out loud, which I'm sure freaked out everyone else, but I didn't care. The object was totally visible to me, a swirl of blue and purple and green, like the earth itself. As I got closer the hum grew louder, until it seemed to be plucking the folds of my brain. I recognized the Song of the Heptakiklos loud and clear.

It was about chest high, on a shelf wedged between two volleyball-sized artifacts. "Gotcha," I whispered, lifting it off the shelf carefully with two hands. As I did, I could feel its energy coursing into my fingertips, through my arms, and up to my brain. "This is it. I got it!"

"Woo-HOO!" Cass yelled. *"Emosewa!"*

"Brother Jack . . . for the win!" Marco said.

I could hear Aliyah yelling into the hallway for Manolo to turn the power back on. With a thump and a whir, the lights bathed the room so brightly I had to close my eyes.

Cass and Marco were at my side now, thumping me on the back.

"FOUR! FOUR! FOUR! FOUR!" Cass said. "Well, five. But four in our possession."

I grinned as the Song of the Heptakiklos bounced off the walls. "Don't you guys hear it?"

"A little," Marco said. "I think. Like with the volume at one."

"How come it's so loud for Jack," Cass asked, "and we need hearing aids?"

"Because my man is da ruler!" Marco said. "So, what does the Loculus do, Brother Jack?"

"Huh?" I said.

"Are you going to, you know, spin spiderwebs? Climb the House of Wenders in a single bound? Wield a mighty hammer?" he asked. "See in the dark?"

"I can't tell yet," I said, "but I definitely don't think it's night vision."

Aliyah was staring intently at the Loculus. "You should know what the power is, am I correct? The other Loculi— did you know right away when you touched them?"

"Well, yeah," I said with a nod. "With the first one, we flew right away. We knew we were invisible with the second. The Loculi of Strength and Healing were pretty obvious, too. But this one . . . I don't know."

"We don't need to know that now!" Cass said, eyeing the door. "We have it. That's the important thing."

"Aly will be happy to know," I said.

Marco thrust his fist in the air and headed for the door. "To Aly!"

A loud thump echoed through the hallway. Eloise came racing in, then turned abruptly. "Ooops," she said. "Sorry."

Manolo limped in behind her, holding a hand to his forehead. "The foul, skinny little brat," he said. "She is the daughter of a jackal and a weasel, and she deserves to be spanked with broom!"

"Manolo, please," Aliyah snapped. "That is inappropriate."

I spun on him. "That's a little girl you're talking to, you jerk. Maybe you turned out that way because *you* got spanked with a broom! Tell him to apologize, Aliyah."

I glowered at her, but she stared at me as if I'd grown a third arm. So were the rest of them.

"Come on, guys," I said, turning to go. "Let's get out of here."

"Wait!" Aliyah called out. "How could you have said that to him, Jack?"

"Because he was being nasty to Eloise," I replied.

"But . . . I didn't understand a word he said," Cass said.

"Well, he mumbles," I replied.

Aliyah shook her head with a curious grin. "Jack, Manolo was speaking in Turkish."

CHAPTER FIFTEEN

A DIFFERENT SET OF EYES

HE TOLD ME I ate dirty socks for breakfast. Then he called me a fifteen-headed hydra and said I had the brains of a toaster. When he finally started making comments about my haircut, I stopped him. My test was over. I had understood everything Manolo had said in Turkish, I had repeated them correctly in English, and I didn't need to hear anymore.

"Bravo!" Manolo cried out, clapping his hands. It was the nicest thing he ever said to me, after the nastiest things he'd ever said to me.

"Well done," Aliyah said.

We knew the power of the fifth Loculus. It gave a Select the ability to understand languages instantly.

Of course, Marco had to jump in and give it a try, then Cass. This gave Manolo a chance to fire off a few more choice insults, which he enjoyed—a lot. But at Eloise's turn, when Manolo started yammering away, her face crumbled.

"Darling, he just said that you were a very smart girl," Aliyah said. "Manolo may be crude, but he does not insult small children."

Eloise shook her head. "It's not that. It's that I didn't understand him, even holding on to the Loculus."

"Hey, don't worry, the Massa recruited you because my m—er, Sister Nancy figured out how to determine G7W early. So the gene will kick in when you're thirteen." I tried to sound as reassuring as I could, but it felt weird. Because if I could, I would keep her from ever inheriting this ticking time bomb.

"That's four years from now!" Eloise replied.

"If I touch the Loculus, and then I touch you," Cass suggested, "the power will flow through. Right now."

Eloise made a sour face. "I'll wait."

There was barely enough space in my backpack for the Loculus of Language. Marco helped me zip it up, while the others headed into the hallway. "This is sick, Brother Jack," he said. "*They* brought the Loculus to us. And it's a good one. When we're back in Ancient Atlantis, we'll be understanding everybody, instead of listening to King Uhla'ar recite lines from *Everybody Loves Raymond*."

"Yeah, but we still have no clue how to get there," I said.

"We don't need a clue," Marco said proudly. "We had no clue for *any* of our adventures. We just went."

I looked at my watch—9:47. "Aliyah doesn't want us to travel to Mount Onyx in the dark. We can use this time to brainstorm."

Marco yawned. "Right. Or maybe sleep."

"How can you sleep at a time like this?" I said. But I was dragging, too.

"I know, I know," Marco said. "But what can we brainstorm with? There's no instruction book."

As I hooked the backpack to my shoulder, I thought about the group of Karai and Massa we'd just left. Right now they were poring over Wenders's notebooks, hoping to find something that someone could understand.

"Maybe," I said, "there is."

* * *

I could hear the sound of slasher metal when we were halfway to the hospital. Through the open door we could see the Massa gathered on one side, the Karai on the other, all of them on the floor poring over Wenders's notebooks. Well, almost everyone. Nirvana was jumping up and down to some pop punk tune, her hair whipping around wildly. Despite the sound, some people on both sides were fast asleep—which looked like a great idea.

Nobody looked too happy about Nirvana's music choice.

Nobody looked too happy at all. The truce was great, but it was going to take a long time for these two groups to become BFFs. As we walked inside, Fritz the mechanic touched an iPod dock and the music stopped. "Efferyone gets ten minutes! Zat vass eleffen minutes. But it felt like four days."

The sound of accordions and tubas filled the air. As Fritz began clicking his heels and yodeling, people threw food at him. At least both sides were united about that.

"I beg your pardon!" Aliyah bellowed.

Fritz spun around and turned off the music. "Zorry," he said, brushing a banana peel from his shoulder. "I got carried avay."

"It's lovely to see you all get along so well," Aliyah said drily. "Any progress?"

"A few interesting maps," Hannelore said, holding out a stack of papers toward her. "Some parts of the labyrinth that none of us recognize. Drawings, too—mystical, religious. Altars, priests, that sort of stuff. But Wenders was careful. Everything was either coded or in Latin."

As Aliyah took the papers, Cass, Marco, Eloise, and I knelt by the stack of notebooks. All three of them looked just as exhausted as I felt. I unhooked my backpack and took out the Loculus of Language.

I could hear a few gasps at the sight of the luminescent orb. Immediately Aliyah began explaining to the others what had just happened. Ignoring all that, I placed the Loculus on the floor and sat on it. Because I was wearing shorts, the backs of my calves made contact with the Loculus surface. With both hands free, I picked up the notebook marked Number 1 and began reading.

My eyes were heavy. It took all my concentration to focus. For a moment the Latin looked . . . well, Latin. Total gobbledygook.

The next moment, everything began moving. I blinked, thinking I was just too tired. But the ink was breaking up into blue-black filaments, spinning and colliding, scurrying around the page like cockroaches. A numbness rose from my feet and prickled up the sides of my body, until I felt like bees had been let loose in my brain.

"Jack, are you okay?" Cass asked.

"You look like you bit into a lemon," Eloise said.

I hung tight. Understanding what you heard and understanding what you read were different things, and I guess the reading part was more complicated. So I waited until the words came back into focus.

When they did, they were exactly the same.

But I wasn't.

It was as if I had grown a different set of eyes. As if instead of seeing a bunch of nonsense I was actually reading. Recognizing.

A daily journal of the woebegone crew of the ship

Enigma, including observations fantastical and dangerous . . .

"Wow," I muttered.

"What? Are you seeing the words in English?" Marco asked.

"No, it's more like an optical illusion," I said. "You know—you think you're looking at a tree but if you look at it a different way it's really an old woman's face?"

"You're seeing an old lady's face?" Eloise said, peering at the text.

"No!" I said, scanning the page. "I mean, the words are the same, but I can understand what they mean. Wenders began writing this after his son, Burt, died. 'It has been three weeks since we buried him, and only now have I the strength to write.'"

"'But write I must,'" Cass spoke up. He startled me, until I realized he'd dropped to his knees and was touching the Loculus with his hand. Around the room, both Massa and Karai were gathering around us, listening. "'Many of the crew have also perished, some have become feeble of brain or body. Others, I fear, are planning a mutiny and upon repair of my ship will attempt to return without me. If that is the case . . . '"

Now Marco was touching the Loculus. "'I shall be sure that this record travels with them,'" he read, "'hidden in a place unknown to any crew member but Burt, and in a language none of the crew will understand, hoping that someday, some kind scholar will record this for posterity. . . .'"

"'*In nomine Patri fili et spiritus sancti* blah, blah, blah,'" Eloise said, scowling with frustration.

"That's a sacred prayer, watch it," Cass said.

"Hmmph," Eloise replied. She flopped onto the floor with her hands under her face like a pillow. "Good night."

Aliyah found someone's jacket on the floor, rolled it up, and placed it under Eloise's head. "We have a few hours before sunrise," she said. "Rest will do us all good."

"Nema," Cass said with a yawn.

"That means 'amen,'" Marco said. "And I didn't even need the Loculus of Language."

A few more of the Massa and rebels had already curled up against the walls of the hospital lobby. Some of the sicker ones were in the rooms off the balcony, being treated by Brother Asclepius.

But as wiped as I felt, I couldn't stop. It was as if the words were leaping off the page to me, like prisoners sprung from jail. They kept me awake, beckoning me deeper and deeper into Wenders's story, into his observations and theories. "Just a few more minutes," I said.

The hospital clock behind us chimed eleven.

* * *

Bong . . .

Bong . . .

Bong . . .

No. It couldn't be.

Bong . . .

Four o'clock. What was I thinking?

I rubbed my eyes. I was the only one still awake in the lobby. Even Brother Asclepius was sprawled out on a gurney like a dead man.

I had just read about Herman Wenders's toenail fungus and his opinions about proper mustache grooming. The guy must have been totally bored all alone in this hot place.

But I also learned about secret passages in Mount Onyx and tunnels that ran through the jungle. I saw a list of all the creatures that Massarym had assigned to protect the Loculi. Supposedly the protector of the Pyramid Loculus was none other than the Sphinx, but maybe I'd read that one wrong. That old statue, as far as I knew, was still standing.

I'd copied some of the stuff down and ripped out pages of the journal to take with me in case we needed them. Still, as far as any clue about the rift, any hint about rescuing Aly, I had come up blank.

I would have been better off sleeping.

The room was spinning. Even if I slept now, the others were going to wake up in an hour or two. Me? I was going to be a basket case.

"*Arrrghh* . . ." I picked up one of the journals and threw it against the wall in frustration. It hit with a thud, and Cass woke up with a start.

"What are you doing?" he mumbled, rubbing his eyes.

"Go back to sleep," I said, plopping myself on the floor. "I'm fine."

Cass scrambled to pick up the journal. "Did you find anything useful?"

"No," I grumbled, shutting my eyes tightly. "Good night."

"Well, I'm awake now," Cass said, leafing through the pages. "If you give me the Loculus, I can pick up where you left— What the—?"

I let one eye pop open. Cass was staring at a page in the journal. "Did you see this?"

I crawled to his side. The journal was open to a page that showed all seven Loculi arranged in the Heptakiklos. Under it was a numbered list that included the words VOLATUS and INVISIBILIS. From the hours of reading, I remembered enough to know the first meant *flight*, and the second was obvious. *Invisibility.*

I grabbed the Loculus of Language and stuck it between us. Both Cass and I held onto it and waited for the words to become clear.

I read aloud an inscription at the top of the page. "'Although my memory fades, I must attempt to reconstruct the seven fantastical orbs and their powers, told to me by Burt, as told to him by a magical priest hidden in the mountain. Although I took these to be part of the delirious ramblings of a fevered mind, I now believe that he did indeed encounter some manner of being in that godforsaken catacomb. And so, should anyone ever desire to research further, I pray I accurately record the list of magical powers bestowed on these relics, whether real or imagined.'"

We fell silent, skimming over the list. He hadn't gotten them perfectly right. The Loculus of Flight "allowed the bearer great powers of leaping." The Loculus of Language "rendered the screeching of primates into the King's English." But the basics were there. Flight, invisibility, strength, healing, language—all five were on that first page.

"Turn it!" Cass said.

We stared, goggle-eyed, as I flipped to the next page and read the Latin translation in a whisper:

"'The sixth Loculus conveys upon the bearer the most unusual form of travel, whereupon the thought of a new location, combined with the desire to be located therein, results in the instantaneous achievement of this goal. . . .'"

"Beam me up, Scotty. . . ." Cass said.

"Huh?" I replied.

"*Star Trek*, the original," Cass replied. "Jack, this is teleportation! Your atoms vaporize and are reassembled in a different place!"

I nodded. But I wasn't really listening. Because my eyes were stuck at the description at the bottom of the page.

Forward is the thrust of growth
That makes us human, gives us breath
To travel back can now be done
Where death is life and life is death.

"Cass," I said, "I think we may have the answer to finding Aly."

"Whaaat?" Cass jumped to my side and I pointed to what I'd just read.

"The seventh Loculus—see?" I said. "It's time travel."

CHAPTER SIXTEEN

THROUGH THE
LOOKING-GLASS

THE ONLY THING more frightening than an angry leader of the world's most ruthless organization is an angry leader of the world's most ruthless organization who's been awakened from her sleep.

"Let me get this straight . . ." Aliyah paced the hospital lobby like a ghost in a country cemetery. Her voice was about an octave lower than usual, and if you weren't looking you might have thought Torquin was speaking. "You are proposing that instead of opening that rift, you just— whoosh—travel back in time to Ancient Atlantis and get Aly directly."

"Exactly," I said.

"Using the Loculus of Time Travel," Aliyah said.

"Right," I answered.

"Which you do not have," she said.

"But—" Cass, Marco, and I said together.

She cut us off with a red-eyed zombie stare.

"We're good at this," I squeaked. I meant it to sound brave, but it came out kind of lame.

"Even if so, even if you *did* have it, how do you know you can reach Aly?" Aliyah asked. "Will you be able to pinpoint the time travel so accurately?"

"The Loculi have a way of telling us how they work," Cass said.

"That's assuming a lot," Aliyah drawled.

"You're right," I said. "But I also assume this—if we just pull the sword from the rift, a humongous and not very friendly green blob will pop out to greet us and possibly have us all for dinner. Or if we're lucky, before he has the chance, the island will rise and sink and turn upside down, killing everyone on it. So . . . sword or Loculus? Pick one."

As Aliyah looked away, Marco elbowed me in the ribs. "Nice, Jack."

She walked slowly away, rubbing her forehead. Around her, sleepy guards, rebels, and monks were beginning to rouse. Although it was still dark outside, I could hear the first cawing of jungle birds. The sun would be up soon, and we would have to move. Fast.

Finally Aliyah spun around toward us again. She looked

128

about a hundred years old. "You have two sites left, if I'm not mistaken—one in Turkey and the other in Egypt."

I nodded. "The Temple of Artemis and the Lighthouse of Alexandria."

"Which would you go to?" she asked. "Did Wenders give any indication?"

I shook my head. "His information came from ancient records left before the destruction of Atlantis. Massarym had not taken and hidden the Loculi yet."

"That presents a problem, doesn't it?" Reaching into her tunic pocket, Aliyah pulled out a silver coin and flipped it high in the air. "Heads for Alexandria, tails for Ephesus."

"Heads!" Eloise screamed.

Aliyah caught the coin and slapped it down on the back of her wrist. "Tails."

Eloise plopped onto the floor, arms folded. "Figures."

"Now all of you try to sleep," Aliyah said. "Wheels up at seven."

* * *

The Dream begins again.

I try to force it away. There's not enough time. The sun is about to rise. Please.

But like a powerful magnet, sleep drags me down . . . down . . .

Until I am in a grassy field and the dark clouds are scudding overhead, while the Song of the Heptakiklos screeches like a siren on the hot wind. I hear the cackling of frightened animals. Townspeople are outside the gate, demanding to be seen. They are shouting the name Uhla'ar . . . Uhla'ar . . .

I keep my distance. I am . . .

Who?

I can usually tell if I'm Karai or Massarym in these dreams; it's always one or the other. But this time I don't know. I still feel like myself.

For a moment that gives me hope. Maybe I am still close enough to being conscious. Maybe I will jolt awake, adjust, and have a nice, pleasant dream about chocolate ice cream or Hoosier basketball or World of Warcraft.

Maybe if I smack myself in the face, hard . . . harder . . . HARDER . . .

"Jack, what are you doing?"

I turn. It's Aly, running across the field to me. She has the Loculus of Strength in her hand and King Uhla'ar is chasing her. Only somehow he's still a statue and so his steps are stiff and pieces of his marble skin are popping into the air. He's screaming, "I'll get you, Batman!" but it's not funny or weird, it's the scariest thing I ever heard, because he's gaining on Aly and she looks desperate.

"Jack, CATCH!" *she screams, and she tosses the Loculus high into the air.*

I jump, soaring into the air like a helicopter. But Uhla'ar leaves the ground, too. We are both reaching for the Loculus, and just as my fingers touch it, he transforms into a massive green beast with a mouth that's a gaping ring of fire.

As I feel myself being sucked into the flames, I scream as loud as I can. . . .

"She's not here," Cass muttered.

"Whaaaaa—?" I sat up so fast my back wrenched.

I was on the floor of the Massa hospital. Cass and Marco were sprawled out next to me, and beyond them were the rebels and the Massa.

"The Dream again?" Cass said.

"Yes," I said. "I mean, no. Not the Dream. It was different. I was in it. Me, Jack. And so was Aly . . ."

Cass wasn't really listening. He sat up, glancing out the window.

I looked at my watch—6:15. Outside I could hear the tromping of footsteps. Scores of Massa were now marching across the quadrangle toward the hospital. Nearly the whole compound had run to the beach the day before when the earthquake happened. Some of them had been killed by the Atlantean beasts. Others had brought Wenders's chest back last night. These were the rest. The survivors. They must have spent the night at the beach for safety.

They also must have gotten wind of the new alliance, because the brown-robed monks were talking with the raggedy Karai rebels. It wasn't exactly a yuk-fest, but no one was trying to kill anyone else. I had to blink my eyes a few

131

times to convince myself *this* wasn't a dream.

"Awwwww . . ." said Marco, shuffling over from his sleeping spot. "Maybe we can have a picnic around a campfire."

I jabbed him in the ribs. But my eyes were fixed on a tall woman emerging from the woods.

Mom.

I wanted so badly to scream out to her. I guess when you've been told at age six that your mom died, and the report was wrong, a part of you remains six forever. She spotted my face in the window immediately. I could detect the slightest nod, and then she looked away.

"Now that we're all friends," Cass whispered, "are you going to tell Aliyah about your mom?"

"Maybe," I said. Behind us, the lobby sleepers were awakening and running outside. "But not now. Come on. Let's join them. Act welcoming. Mingle."

"Mingle?" Cass whispered, as if I just asked him to dance naked on a tree stump.

I barged outside with the crowd. Most of the rebels looked relieved, but people on both sides seemed wary and guarded. A few stragglers by the edge of the jungle didn't seem to want to move any farther, as if preparing for some kind of ambush. But now Aliyah herself was striding toward them, flanked by her goons and smiling grandly. "My fellow Karai and Massa loyalists, come, come! Nothing to fear and everything to gain. The improbable news you have just heard is true. . . ."

As she continued, making her grand pronouncements, both camps gathered around her to listen. I hung out at the edge of the crowd, and in minutes, Mom was standing beside me. We both took a couple of steps backward, without looking at each other.

"Did I just step through the looking glass?" Mom whispered. "Or is all this true?"

I spoke soft and fast. I told her everything—about Marco's episode, the reconstruction of the Loculus of Healing, the truce between the Massa and the Karai, the new Loculus, and our discoveries from Wenders's journal. "We're going to find the Loculi of Teleportation and Time Travel, starting today."

Mom didn't reply at all.

"Did you get all that?" I said out of the side of my mouth.

"Yes. I—I'm just flabbergasted. About the truce. It's been so many years. . . ." She gave my hand a quick squeeze. It felt good. So good I wanted to jump up and down.

"Maybe we'll be able to go home," I said, "and be a family again."

Mom paused a few seconds, then said, "Yes."

"You—you don't sound happy," I said.

"I am deliriously happy, Jack," she replied. "I—I just fear it will all fall apart."

"We're going to find them, Mom—"

She shushed me. "Promise me, Jack, you will not call me that name, and you will keep our secret."

"Why?" I said.

"Because they will not be happy to know there has been an impostor in their midst all along," she replied. "And it isn't only the Massa we need to fear. Do not forget why I came to the Massa in the first place."

I could practically feel my heart thudding against my toes.

Mom had staged her own death in a crevasse in Antarctica. At the time she'd been working for the Karai, trying to find a cure for G7W. She figured the research would go much faster if the two rivals groups would join forces. But when she contacted the Massa to open talks, the head of the Karai assumed she was betraying secrets. He ordered a contract on her life. The only way she could keep from being killed was to fake her own death. When the coast was clear she went to work for the Massa under a false name, to continue research.

"This is exactly what you wanted—the uniting of the two groups," I said. "Maybe the Omphalos will forgive you. . . ."

"The Massa have starved, oppressed, and killed the rebels," Mom said. "I have no proof that the Omphalos approves of this union. But whether or not he does, if he finds that I have been living in disguise all these years . . . and if Aliyah discovers I've been lying . . ."

"What will happen to you?" I squeaked.

Mom sighed. Again she took a long time to answer, and when she did, her voice was barely audible. "I don't know. I'm not expecting kindness and understanding."

"You'll have to go into hiding again, won't you? I can't lose you and see you again—and then lose you forever. I can't!"

"No," Mom said. "Nor can I."

"I promise I will find those Loculi," I said, my voice quavering in my throat. "I promise we'll be cured and I will go home again. But I'll only do it if you promise me you'll be safe."

"If there's one thing I know how to do, it's take care of myself," Mom whispered. "On my life, I will be there to celebrate your fourteenth birthday, Jack."

I thought I felt a kiss on the back of my neck, but I couldn't have.

Mom's promise had left me strangely calm. And superdetermined. When I turned, she was gone, lost in the crowd.

I caught a glimpse of Brother Dimitrios's eyes, pinning me like lasers. Had he heard? He couldn't have. Frankly, though, at that moment I couldn't care less. I turned toward Aliyah and pretended to listen to her speech.

But I was hearing nothing.

CHAPTER SEVENTEEN

AMAZON CAFÉ

I DIDN'T REALIZE how much I missed Slippy the stealth jet until I saw her on the runway.

For a hunk of metal she was gorgeous, her gunmetal gray sides radiating swirls of heat in the morning sun. Unlike the rest of the compound, she had been completely cleaned, repaired, and shined over the last few weeks. She was shipshape and ready to take us to Turkey.

Unless Torquin and Brother Dimitrios killed each other first.

"My dear fellow," Dimitrios was saying as we walked toward the jet, "I served in the Greek military during my youth as a pilot, and have kept up my aviation license all my life."

"Pah," Torquin said.

"Oh, dear." Dimitrios threw up his arms in exasperation. "It is hard to argue with 'pah,' isn't it?"

"Good," Torquin said. "Then don't argue. Torquin fly."

Marco, Cass, Eloise, and I lagged a few steps behind the two squabblers. "Maybe we should take a referee with us," Marco murmured.

"Or just sneak away to Turkey on the Loculus of Flight," Cass said.

"I wish," I said.

"I call the copilot's seat!" Eloise blurted out.

"Your feet don't even reach the floor," Cass said. "Be glad you're even coming. You're *nine*."

"And you're asinine," Eloise shot back.

"Yes!" Marco bellowed. "Eloise for the win!"

I think we were all a little stressed from the lack of sleep. And worried. My head was spinning. We had hammered out our plan after Aliyah's coin flip, and she had made us repeat it aloud several times on the way to the airfield:

The expedition team would be Torquin, Brother Dimitrios, Marco, Cass, Eloise, and me.

We'd leave the Loculi here for safekeeping, except for the Loculus of Language. We'd need that. Torquin and Dimitrios both knew Greek, but neither of them spoke Turkish.

We would try to find *both* missing Loculi before returning.

Torquin and Dimitrios would each have smartphones.

At least it made sense when we planned it. But now, for the thousandth time, I wondered if we were doing the right thing.

"Hey, down there!" Nirvana was at the top of a ladder near Slippy's nose. She began climbing down, a paintbrush and bucket in hand. "I just finished my masterpiece—what do you think?"

Still drying on the side of the jet was a perfect image of Fiddle's face, smiling down at us.

I had to swallow back a lump in my throat. She had really captured him in his ponytailed glory, the way he was before the jungle sickness had made him so thin. "Pretty good likeness, huh?" she said. "Slippy was his baby. He was so proud of her, the old nerd. And he'd be very proud of you, too."

I smiled.

Fiddle was watching over us, Mom was thinking about my next birthday, and Nirvana was standing in front of me with her arms wide open.

Marco, Cass, Eloise, Nirvana, and I all shared a group hug. "Ready?" I said to my friends.

"No," Cass said. "But that never stopped us before."

"*Cowabunga, we are back in business!*" Marco shouted, taking the ladder two rungs at a time.

I raced up after him. We took the two seats directly

138

behind the pilot and copilot. Cass and Eloise climbed into the seats behind us. "No fair . . ." Eloise grumbled.

"Wait—are you nine, or five?" Cass asked.

As the two squabbled, Brother Dimitrios planted himself in the cockpit, donned his headset, and started to take taken control of the jet. Torquin was the last to climb in. With a yawn, he sat sideways on Dimitrios's lap. "Yeeooooww!" Dimitrios screamed, squirming to get free.

As the monk slid to the copilot seat, Torquin grabbed his headset. "No Loculus of Healing. Be careful."

He pulled on the door. It slammed shut so hard I thought the jet would topple over. And in a moment the jet was spinning down the runway. The only sound louder than the engine was Dimitrios howling in pain.

And Cass and Eloise arguing in the back.

"Fasten your seat belts," I said.

* * *

"Okay, so the first Temple of Artemis was destroyed— *floosh*—by a flood," Cass said. As Slippy soared over the Mediterranean, he read from a tablet screen built into the seat's armrest. "And the second one? They spend ten whole years building it—and everyone's like 'Wow, this is the etamitlu in emosewa!'"

"I beg your pardon?" Brother Dimitrios asked.

"Ultimate in awesome," Torquin grunted. "Duh."

"And then, *wham*, one day some crazy pyro burns it to

the ground," Cass continued. "But do the Greeks give up? No! They spent twenty years building the third temple, and this one is totally off the charts. Like, gnilggob-dnim!"

"Will somebody pull his plug?" Brother Dimitrios moaned, rubbing his forehead. "I am a bit of a scholar of antiquities myself, and if it's information you need, I'd be pleased to give it to you, regarding the site, the architecture, and the history, in coherent English, not from some fly-by-night Interweb site."

"Yeah, but Cass isn't boring," Marco said.

"I beg your—" Dimitrios said.

Torquin yanked the steering wheel of the plane downward, and Brother Dimitrios grabbed for a barf bag. I was tempted myself. Torquin was the worst pilot in the history of aviation, but I have to admit, it did feel good to see Dimitrios so uncomfortable.

"So, there's this guy named Antipater," Cass barreled on, reading from the screen. "He's like, hey, I've seen the Statue of Zeus, the Hanging Gardens of Babylon, the Colossus of Rhodes, the Pyramids, and the Mausoleum at Halicarnassus, but . . . okay, here it is. . . . 'But when I saw the house of Artemis that mounted to the clouds, those other marvels lost their brilliancy, and I said, "Lo, apart from Olympus, the Sun never looked on aught so grand."' Wouldn't it be cool if we found it?" Cass looked up, a huge smile on his face.

"I'm hungry," Eloise said.

"Blurg," barfed Dimitrios.

"What does *aught* mean?" Marco asked.

The plane dropped so fast I thought I would lose my lunch. "Coming in for a landing!" Torquin grunted.

I closed my eyes and prayed.

* * *

I think Torquin felt guilty about taking control of the flight from Dimitrios, because he let the monk drive our rented car. Which would have been okay idea if Dimitrios weren't ghost white and on the verge of falling asleep. The ride from Izmir Adnan Menderes Airport to the temple's site near a town called Selçuk took a little more than an hour, but it felt like two days.

Torquin sat in the front passenger seat. "There!" he said, pounding Dimitrios on the shoulder and gesturing to a road off to the right. A sign pointed to the Temple of Artemis site, but Dimitrios steered the car farther up the road, to a boxy-looking building with a sign that said AMAZON CAFÉ.

"Please," Dimitrios said. "I must use the restroom."

"Pah," Torquin said.

Eloise looked longingly out the window. People were eating from heaping plates of fried food in an outdoor scating area, while soft music was being piped in through speakers. "I'm hungry."

"Amen, sister," Marco said.

141

The monk pulled into a spot, and the rest of us bolted out of the car and took seats at a free table. I made sure to hook my backpack tightly over the back of a wooden chair. I knew we needed to visit the temple, but my mouth was watering, and first things first.

As a waiter began pouring water, Eloise asked, "What's calamari?"

"Squid," Torquin replied. "Very good fried appetizer. Waiter! We take eight orders calamari."

Cass looked up from his menu. "But there's only six of us."

"Five for me, the rest for you," Torquin said.

I felt something brush against my ankle, and I jumped so quickly that I nearly knocked over the water glasses. As I scraped my chair back, the people in the nearby tables all stared.

A scrawny black cat slunk away along the tiled floor. As it looked back at me, its eyes flashed bright orange and it hissed, baring its teeth.

"Out of here, devil cat!" the waiter said, giving the feline a swift kick. "I'm sorry. Would you like something to drink?"

"Did you see that cat's eyes?" I whispered said to Marco. "They were—"

"I'll have a chocolate shake with extra ice cream," Marco announced to the waiter.

As we went around the table ordering, I couldn't help but notice the cat had circled us and was now sitting just outside the café railing, staring at me. Its mouth seemed to be moving, as if it were speaking.

"Jack?" Marco said. "Earth to Jack?"

"Uh, juice," I said. "Orange juice. Marco, does that cat look strange to you?"

"Looks hungry," Marco said with a shrug. "If I find a mouse in my food, I'll share."

Brother Dimitrios was coming out of the restroom now, and I realized I had to use it, too. I excused myself and went to the back of the café. I felt light-headed inside the restroom and made sure to wash my face. Something was odd about this café. I couldn't wait to leave.

Maybe it was because we were so close to a Wonder. And that always meant some kind of danger.

As I finished up and pushed the door back open, it thumped against someone. I held tight against the frame and looked out, but there was no one on the other side. And I realized I hadn't hit someone at all, but some*thing*.

The black cat had backed up and was waiting for me. With a low, growly meow, it inched closer, its orange eyes brightening. "Heyyyy, I don't have any food, buddy," I whispered.

But as I tried to walk back to my table, it leaped in my way, placing its front paws on my pants. "Stop!" I blurted.

143

I could see the waiter running over. The cat glanced sideways at him and then cast a reproachful glance at me. That was when I saw the pupils of its eyes.

CHAPTER EIGHTEEN
DEVIL CAT

I DIDN'T NEED the Loculus of Language to know that the waiter was throwing some choice Turkish curses at the black cat.

"It's okay!" I said. "Don't—"

But the cat had disappeared out of the café, and the waiter was looking at me as if I had a screw loose.

Maybe I did.

I left the café and glanced over the outdoor tables. Torquin and Brother Dimitrios seemed to be in some kind of argument. Cass and Marco were laughing, and Eloise was stuffing fistfuls of calamari into her mouth.

For a moment I thought of going back and telling them what I'd experienced. But even I didn't trust what

I'd experienced. A cat with lambda-shaped pupils? It didn't make sense. How could it even see?

I had to find it and look at those eyes again. Just to be sure.

To my left, the white stucco walls of the building ended in an alleyway. I casually walked to the alley and looked in. On one side of it was a tightly closed Dumpster. The ground was covered with cobblestones stained brownish gray with food. At the end, the cat was sitting on its haunches.

When I made eye contact, it stood and cocked its head, then walked behind the building. I ran down the alley and followed it around the corner.

And I tripped over the leg of a grizzled old man slumped against the wall. "Whoa!" I shouted, just managing to stay upright. "Sorry!"

The man pulled his legs in and looked up. He was wearing black sunglasses, and his face was covered with a scraggly salt-and-pepper beard. "Australia?" he said, rising slowly to his feet.

"Uh . . . no!" I said. "America."

He was blocking my path back to the café. I looked over my shoulder, but the cat was gone.

"Ah, good. America," he said. "You take me to America?"

Oh, great. A total wacko. I knew this was a dumb idea. I backed away, figuring I could sneak around the other side of the building. "Yeah. Sure," I said. "Uh, well, great to meet you—"

"Herostratus," the guy said. "And you?"

"Jack. See you!"

I turned on my heel and bolted, but I didn't get far. The back alley ended in a chain-link fence.

Spinning around, I said, "Oops. Look, I have to get back to my—"

"Orange juice," he said. "I know." He was reaching into his pocket, and I felt the hair prickle at the back of my neck. "Take this. We go to America someday."

Out of his pocket, he pulled a dirty, ragged-edged business card and held it out to me. I grabbed it, mumbled thanks, and shoved it in my pocket. He stepped aside, gesturing for me to pass by.

I couldn't help brushing against him as I squeezed by, back the way I'd come.

I bolted for the café, where the waiter was already serving the main courses. Someone had ordered me a cheeseburger. Marco was slurping the last drops of a chocolate shake. "Did you fall in to the toilet, bro?" he said. "You were gone a long time."

"I—I went looking for that weird cat," I said lamely. "It had . . . strange eyes."

"Did you find it?" Eloise asked.

"No," I replied.

"Chef probably needed it . . . for cheeseburger!" Torquin laughed at his own joke, a hideous snorting, choking noise that made the people in the nearby table drop their silverware.

"Well, there are plenty more cats," Cass said, gesturing around the café floor, where at least three more were twining around the tables. No one seemed to be paying them much attention.

And neither should you, I told myself. As I took a deep breath and picked up my burger, I noticed something strange about my sleeve.

Hairs. Black cat hairs, up and down the length. Exactly where I had brushed against the homeless guy.

* * *

"Slow day," Torquin remarked as we walked up the path to the temple site.

He was right. The sky was overcast, the air had a chill, and we were among the few visitors to the Temple of Artemis. "How much of it is left?" I asked.

Cass gestured to a marble column about two stories high that looked like it had been put together out of mismatched blocks by a baby giant. "That much."

"That's it?" Eloise said.

"The temple was destroyed by the attacking Goths in the third century B.C.," Cass said. "Many of the stones were used in other buildings over the years. Others were looted."

148

As we walked closer, we seemed to be the only visitors speaking English. I heard what sounded like German, Greek, Turkish, maybe Swedish. Aside from the patched-together column, the site was basically a flat field strewn with relics—a piece of column here, a chunk of sculpture there. Mostly weeds and soil, and a wide, swampy puddle.

"Some Wonder of the World," Eloise sniffed. "Are the others just as spectacular?"

Brother Dimitrios was stepping cautiously. "I have seen how this works," he said. "These children can conjure life out of rocks. They can cause the formation of statues, Loculi, and all manner of creatures. It is a terrifying thing to behold."

"I'm waiting. . . ." Eloise said, tapping her foot impatiently.

I walked around the field, but I felt nothing. Not the slightest vibration, nothing close to the Song of the Heptakiklos. "Be patient," I said. "This happened at the Mausoleum in Bodrum, too. All we needed was the right stone. . . ."

Cass was kneeling by a piece of column that was charred black. "Hey, maybe this is from the time that goofball burned down the second temple, before they built the third and most awesome one."

"Ancient goofballs," Marco said. "Sounds like a book series."

As I picked up a stone, Torquin pulled out his phone and began thumbing away. "Wikipedia. Temple arsonist wanted to be famous. Burned it down so people would know his name." He scratched his head. "Didn't work. Herostratus. Never heard of him."

At the sound of that name, I dropped the rock on my foot. But I didn't feel a thing.

Fumbling in my pocket, I pulled out the business card the homeless guy had given me.

CHAPTER NINETEEN

THE BACK DOOR

BROTHER DIMITRIOS MUST have tipped well at lunch, because the Amazon Café waiter just smiled and nodded as we barged back into the outdoor restaurant. I led everybody around to the back alley, but it was totally empty save for an old newspaper blowing lazily in the wind.

"He was right here!" I said, inching my way down the narrow passageway toward the chain-link fence. "I followed the cat with the orange eyes, but when I got here it was gone. That's when I saw the old guy."

"Wait, *orange?*" Eloise said.

"Yes, and its pupils were shaped like lambdas," I said. "I tried to show you, but you guys were all over the menu."

I saw Cass give Marco a look. "Are you sure you're

feeling all right, Jack?" Cass asked.

"The calamari did taste a little funny to me," Marco said.

I stopped when I reached the end of the alley. Just before the fence, in the back wall of the restaurant, was a closed door. From a distance, it looked black and featureless, but up close I noticed words carved into the metal but blackened with age and paint.

"I don't remember seeing this," I said.

"Restaurant kitchens generally do have back doors," Brother Dimitrios said.

"I mean the words," I said.

"Stand still," Cass said, reaching into my backpack. "This is a job for the Loculus of Language."

I took out the old man's business card. "I'm taking a wild bet this says Amazon Legacy Solutions."

"Uh . . . yup," Cass replied.

"It's on the card that weird guy gave me," I said. "He must work here."

"I guess Amazon's just starting out in Turkey," Marco said. "Maybe we should order a book."

I knocked on the door and heard it echo on the inside. "Hello?" I called out.

After waiting for a few moments, I knocked again.

"No one there," Eloise said. "Can we go now? This places stinks, and it gives me the creeps."

I pressed down on the latch. With a deep click, the door swung open into complete blackness. A blast of cold, dry, musty air whooshed out.

"Anyone home?" I couldn't remember the name on the card, so I checked it in the light from outside and said, "Um . . . Herostratus? Hello?"

As we all stepped in, Brother Dimitrios said, "This is clearly some sort of meat locker. Unless you would like to have a run-in with a side of beef, I suggest we—"

"*Yeeeeeeiiiiii!*" A baby's scream pierced the darkness. I jumped back, knocking Eloise off her feet. As we tumbled to the floor, I heard a click.

I scrambled to stand up. Above us a single lightbulb flashed on, and from it hung a long string almost all the way to the floor. At the end of the string was a fuzzy, chewed-up plush mouse.

A black tail disappeared into a half-open doorway. "That's it!" I said. "That's the cat!"

My heart thudding, I took in the surroundings—an empty, square room with a vaulted ceiling that seemed higher than the building looked from outside.

"Close the door!" a voice with a thick accent called out from the next room.

"Herostratus?" I called out. "Is that—"

"Am I not being clear?" the voice boomed.

Torquin reached behind him and pulled the door shut.

The room fell silent. Everything we had been hearing— distant car horns and revving motors, planes, radios—was totally gone. Not the slightest hint of a sound.

"Echo!" Marco called out. "Echo! Echo!"

Eloise poked him in the side. *"Will you stop that!"*

For a moment, absolutely nothing happened. Slowly, the light from above seemed to soften, and I blinked, thinking my eyes were adjusting weirdly to the light. Near the half-open door, the harsh white wall seemed to be darkening. Its flatness grew wavy, as if it were suddenly melting. But one by one, the waves swelled and took on solid form. They became rounded like cups, bowing outward until each one took the shape of a sconce, each holding a flickering candle. Their surfaces took on the weight and shine of polished marble, carved with faces, shoulders, and arms of women. Each one looked as if she were holding up the light herself, the sconce fires dancing brightly.

"Jack, look!" Cass exclaimed, pointing upward.

I craned my neck to see the ceiling, which was now at least twice as high as it had been. Its squarish shape was now vaulted marble, its walls carved with the shapes of vines, leaves, and jumping deer. The bare lightbulb at the top was now a chandelier made of deer antlers, their tips blazing with candlelight.

Brother Dimitrios let out a gasp and began to dance weirdly. I felt a movement under my feet, and I realized he was just spooked over the fact that the bare cement floor was changing shape, transforming into a mosaic of colorful glazed tiles.

Eloise let out a scream. "I want to go home!"

She headed for the door and pressed down on the latch, but it wouldn't move. Brother Dimitrios joined her, but he wasn't having much success either.

Marco ignored them both, creeping toward the half-open door, where the cat had disappeared. "Here, kitty, kitty, kitty . . ."

I stepped closer to him. At the transom, we both leaned inward, pushing the door open. I reached in and felt around the inner wall. "There's got to be a light switch some-where. . . ." I said.

"Careful, Brother Jack," Marco said.

I stepped into the room. And I put my foot down on . . . nothing.

Losing my balance, I grabbed Marco. But his weight was pitched forward, too. "Whoa!" he said. "What are you—"

Marco reached for the doorjamb but I felt my weight pitching downward. I let go of Marco's shirt and wind-milled my arms.

"DOOOOIIINNNNG!" Marco's voice echoed against the walls as we both fell into blackness.

CHAPTER TWENTY

HEROSTRATUS AND VROMASKI *FLAMBÉ*

I'M NOT SURE how Marco hit the floor first. But I was really glad he did. He may be all muscle, but he's way softer than a hard marble surface.

"Yeow, Brother Jack, that was your butt and my kidney!" Marco said, jumping to his feet with a tight grimace.

"Sorry!" I rolled off onto a carpet that was woven with threads of deep reds, greens, and blues—hunting scenes, woodland games, meetings in meadows. The fact that I could see this rug, and Marco's grimace, meant that somewhere on our way down, someone turned a light on.

As I looked around, I realized it wasn't just one light, but about two dozen fiery sconces, fancier and bigger than the ones above. I sat there, winded, catching my breath.

The view into the room was blocked by a big marble desk balanced on thick columns, but a foot or two away from me was a wooden ladder leading up the wall to an arched doorway above. Cass, Marco, Eloise, Torquin, and Brother Dimitrios were gathered there, looking down.

"You could have used ladder," Torquin commented.

"Thanks for the suggestion," I said.

My gaze rose further upward toward the ceiling, which was capped by an enormous dome, painted with an image of a goddess surrounded by women with long, flowing hair. The height of the room was freaky enough. The Amazon Café was a one-story building. It also very much did not have a dome.

"How did they light all those candles so fast?" Marco turned, rapping his fingers on the marble desk. "Whoa, glad my kidney didn't land on this hard thing—"

He froze in the middle of the sentence, looking over the desk.

I jumped to my feet. On the other wall of the room, a cavernous fireplace crackled. The flames rose at least three feet high, licking the sides of what looked like a pig, slowing turning on a spit. A horrible smell, like burning rubber and puke, made me suspect it was actually a vromaski.

Off to the side, cranking that spit, was Herostratus.

I elbowed Marco. "That's him," I hissed. "That's the guy!"

The old man turned, and his face broke into a huge smile. "Ah, so good of you to . . . *drop in!*"

"Who are you?" I asked.

"Did you hear what I just said?" Herostratus exclaimed. "'*Drop* in?' Haaaar-ha-ha-ha!" He threw his head back in a high-pitched, barking laugh.

Marco narrowed his eyes as he moved closer to the old man. "My, Grandpa, what orange eyes you have."

He was right. The light flashing from the man's eyes were an unmistakable dull orange. "The color of fire," Herostratus said.

"You . . . *you* were the cat!" I said.

He nodded. "They love me in that restaurant. Such nice people. Especially the Greeks."

"Okay, Garfield," Marco said, "tell us who the heck you are and what you're doing."

The old guy stepped away from the fireplace, shambling a few steps toward us in his broken sandals, and bowed stiffly. "Humble Herostratus, at your service. And this"—he gestured with a grand flourish toward the roasting animal—"is Hog Warts."

"Now that," Marco said with a sneer, "is not funny."

Herostratus shrugged. "That joke killed at the last boar sacrifice." He glanced cautiously toward an arched doorway that led to a long hallway. "They cursed me—the Zons. Like them, I live for an eternity. But unlike them, I have the power to shift shape into animal form. But it is for their pleasure only. For their amusement."

"Who are the Zons?" I asked.

"They hunt me. They trap me all alone and slaughter me. You cannot imagine the pain of dying, only to be brought back to life—only to be killed again. And for what? Because of my personality. I am being punished for who I am, for what I enjoy—a little laughter, a little flash!" Herostratus moved closer. "Would you like to see me juggle three flaming willow branches?"

"You're the guy who set fire to the Temple of Artemis," I said.

He looked fearfully over his shoulder. "Please. That name is not to be mentioned here!"

"Whoa, hang on, Thermostatus," Marco said, "let's cut to the chase. We're here for a reason."

"Yes, yes, the Loculus, isn't it?" Herostratus replied.

"You know?" I said.

Herostratus clapped his hands. "Of course! I have been waiting ages—literally—for you, young man." He looked curiously at me. "Erm . . . your name?"

"Jack," I said. "But how—?"

Herostratus spread his index and middle finger and pointed them downward in a lambda shape. "The mark! You have it."

Instinctively I reached for the patch of white hair

160

shaped like an upside-down V at the back of my head. How did Herostratus know about the G7W mark? All of us had this. It was part of way the gene expressed itself. My hair had been shaved off when I first arrived on the island, but the mark had grown back. Professor Bhegad had called it a lambda, because it resembled the shape of the Greek *L*.

A belch erupted from behind us, echoing loudly in the room. Marco and I spun around to see Torquin leading the others down the ladder. "Sorry. Calamari," Torquin explained.

"By Adonis's curls!" Herostratus blurted out, pointing at Marco and then at Cass. "You have the mark also . . . and you! Oh, the Zons will be absolutely thrilliated. Oh, dear eyes, do not fall out of this head! I have been despairing to see even one of you—but now *three*! Oh!" He cast another nervous glance toward the hallway. "We have a few minutes. You must be hungry. Calamari are such miserably small things. Sit, sit. The only way to properly eat a vromaski is *en flambé*. Flames rising to the ceiling—"

"STRATO!" bellowed a deep voice from the hallway.

Herostratus jumped. "Strato is my . . . how do you say it—nickname Hm. Yes. Hrmmph. YES, MY ALL-POWERFUL, ALL-KNOWING, WISE, AND BEAUTIFUL HIPPO?"

Cass groaned. *"Hippo?"*

Clomping noises resounded from the hallway, and we all instinctively backed away. From the top of the arch, a face peeked down at us. Her eyes were a deep brown, her hair jet-black and pulled back with a tightly tied string. I figured it was a woman standing on stilts or on the bed of some kind of vehicle. But when she fully emerged, she was on her own two legs. Which were themselves almost as tall as I was.

She strode in, her thick hair bouncing against her back like an animal pelt. Her feet were the length of my forearms, shod in sandals whose crisscrossing straps wrapped upward to her knees. As she set down a shield against the wall, a saber clattered against her leather tunic. She wore a black leather belt threaded with deep pouches, out of which peeked blowpipes, bows, and darts. Across her shoulder was a quiver strung over a thick, embroidered silk sash.

"Awesome," Marco murmured.

"Can't be," Dimitrios rasped.

"Let's go," Eloise squeaked.

"Beautiful," Torquin grunted.

"I am *Maximo*!" the woman growled at Herostratus. "*Maximo*, not *Hippo*. When will you ever get that right? I sound nothing like that clumsy, lazy, bulbous-nosed lizard!"

Immediately after saying that, Maximo cocked her head to one side like a nervous tic. A spear came ripping out of the tunnel behind her, inches from her ear, its point slicing through the air and thudding into the center of Herostratus's chest.

We all jumped back. Eloise screamed. Marco rushed toward the old man as he fell to the carpet.

CHAPTER TWENTY-ONE

THE ZONS

"HOW COULD YOU do that?" Marco cried out, looking up at Maximo. "Just because he called you—"

"*Pkaaaaach!*" Herostratus let out a cough and lurched upward from the floor, yanking the spear from his chest.

I have never heard Marco shriek so loud. He scrambled away on all fours. The rest of us were pretty freaked, too.

Herostratus threw the spear into the fireplace, his tunic unstained by even a drop of blood. "Great gods, that hurts!" he said. "You see? They do this all the time. Kill, back to life. Kill, back to life. They love tormenting me!"

Maximo burst out laughing. Now more enormous people were emerging from behind her—all women, all dressed in warrior garb, all at least eight or nine feet tall. Their shoulders were the width of bookshelves, their voices deep, their legs as sturdy as tree trunks. One of them slapped Maximo on the back, scowling at her over a nose as big as a softball. "You may mock me, but you must admit I am a good shot," she growled.

"You are full of surprises, Hippo," Maximo said.

"A barrel of laughs," Herostratus murmured.

Detouring to the roasting vromaski, Hippo ripped off one of its legs and began gnawing on it like an ice-cream cone.

"Welcome to the set of *Seven Brides for Torquin*," Marco muttered.

Torquin was staring, mesmerized, and I realized it was the first time I ever saw him look *upward* at another person.

"*Pssst . . . psssst!*" Herostratus hissed from the floor, where he had fallen to his knees, bowing low to the ground. As he signaled for us to do the same, Hippo walked to within an inch of his face and let the steaming fat from the roasted vromaski leg drip onto her massive, dirt-encrusted toes. "Dinner, Strato," she said. "Come and get it."

"Lick the feet! Lick the feet! Lick the feet!" the others cried out rhythmically.

I turned away from the sight and waited till the cheering was over.

"That is so disgusting," Eloise mumbled.

"*I—I don't think we belong here!*" Brother Dimitrios said.

"Perhaps we can leave now, Ms. Maximo?"

"Strato, where are your manners?" bellowed Maximo. "Are you not going to get up and introduce us to your guests?"

"Jack and Marco," I said. "And Cass, Eloise, Torquin, and Brother Dimitrios."

Shaking in his robe, Brother Dimitrios was now saying prayers under his breath in Greek. "Well . . . a Hellene?" Maximo said. "Perhaps we should be speaking your language?"

"English is . . . f-f-fine," Dimitrios said, holding on to the ladder as if he were either going to keel over or try to run away.

Herostratus was standing now, a thin line of vromaski grease across his lips. "Jack and friends, it is my great pleasure to introduce the strongest, the largest, the longest lasting, the most beautiful and durable, exalted and all-powerful . . ." He cupped his hands to his mouth and let out a fake trumpet fanfare. "The Zons!"

Maximo bowed low from the waist. "Until we become better acquainted, Amazons will do."

"I am dreaming, tell me I am dreaming," Dimitrios said, pinching his own arm repeatedly.

Eloise smacked him. "That's real. And so are they."

"Do you not know who the Amazons were?" Dimitrios said. "They were not human. They were the woman warrior tribe of Ancient Greece—dedicated to Artemis, goddess of the hunt, known for their skills at killing. *They had the bravery and cunning to attack Hercules himself!*"

"Yes, well, we all make mistakes," Maximo said with a sigh.

Cass nodded. "The name of the café upstairs . . . the company on Herostratus's card. You've been here all along. Your name has stayed alive."

"We protect our brand." Maximo turned to the others. "Soldiers! What do we do with visitors?"

The women stepped forward, one by one, introducing themselves. After the first one shook my hand, I thought my fingers would come off with it. So I just waved hi to the rest of them. Myrto . . . Pitane . . . Priene . . . Anaea . . . Ephesos . . . Lysippe . . . Their skin color ranged from peach white to dark brown, and although they were thickly muscled, they moved like dancers, with smoothness and grace.

They seemed happy to see us. Weirdly happy.

"Um . . . guys?" I finally said. "Do you know why we're here?"

Maximo chuckled, which began a ripple effect of laughter around the room. "Do you assume that because we are physically powerful we do not possess adequate brain resources?"

"I get that all the time," Marco said.

"All of you, sit," Maximo commanded. A pair of

enormous hands pushed me downward to the carpet. "You would like to pursue the gift of the Atlantean. The Loculus. Yes?"

Marco, Cass, Eloise, and I exchanged a wary look. "Yes," I said.

"Massarym told us you would come someday, of course. We just didn't think it would take this long." Maximo gestured to the open door overhead. "Do you have others in the antechamber, perhaps? I see three of you carry the mark, but it will be to your advantage to have a female."

"I'm going to get the mark in four years, when I'm thirteen," Eloise announced. "But I might dye it."

"Ah, well, we shall see, but until then you are still just a child." Maximo turned, clapping her hands. "Sisters! Phase two begins! The feast!"

A couple of the Amazons bounded into the tunnel, laughing and chattering. A moment later they emerged with cloths, bronze bowls, and plates. Herostratus put on a pair of thick animal-hide gloves and removed the vromaski from the flames. Even roasted with savory spices, the beast smelled awful. As he began slicing it, his knife blade broke. "Hmm, this one may be a bit gamy," he said.

I hated the confusion. The noise. The chattering. The smell. I hated that we were about to eat the inedible with a bunch of loonies while Aly was lost and suffering.

This was enough.

"Stop!" I finally shouted. "We're not here to eat! Please, we do not have time. Our quest is urgent. If you have the Loculus, we need it—now!"

The Amazons fell silent. They all looked at Maximo.

"Very well, then," their leader said, snapping her fingers. "Clear the feast from the carpet and proceed to phase three."

With a murmur of voices, the Amazons tossed their bowls against the walls and kicked aside the supplies on the floor. Chewing messily on the remains of their dinners, they spread around out the edges of the thick carpet. When Maximo snapped her fingers again, they dug their hands under the borders and lifted upward.

Before we could do a thing, the carpet rose around us and closed at the top, and we were in total, smothering darkness.

CHAPTER TWENTY-TWO

THE TIP OF A KNIFE

TORQUIN YOWLED IN anger. I could feel him fighting against the confines of the carpet, trying to break through. We all were trying, but the material was tough and thick. We had nothing to cut it with, and no leverage. Our arms and legs were all jammed together as we rose up off the floor, being hoisted through the room we could no longer see.

I could feel Eloise's short, frightened breaths on my shoulder. I tried to put my arm around her but couldn't get the angle right. As thick as the carpet was, I could hear the murmur of Amazon voices chattering excitedly.

It wasn't long before we jolted downward onto something hard and vaguely lumpy. Above us, where the carpet was gathered, a rush of cool air entered—and daylight.

The carpet fell away, flattening on all sides. I had

to blink my eyes against the brightness. A field of grass stretched out before us. I squinted up into the bottom of a vast dome that arced high overhead, ringed with bright lights. It looked like some kind of stadium, only there were no seats. Surrounding the structure on all sides was a wall of solid rock.

I heard a deep, echoing thump-thump behind us.

"Jack . . ." Cass said.

I spun to see that we were at the base of three wide stairs of white quartz, leading up to a platform. On it was an empty golden throne, so studded with jewels that it seemed to be firing bullets of light. To the left, the team of Amazons stood at attention, each woman clutching a leather ammunition sash draped over her shoulder.

One of them lifted a polished white tusk to her lips. It must have been hollowed out, because when she blew into it, an enormous *blatt* echoed through the stadium.

A stone door opened at the base of the wall. Four more Amazons emerged, younger than the ones we'd met and dressed in finer tunics, with gold thread and inlaid stones. They marched in formation up to the throne platform, singing a strange anthem.

Nurturer of Persians, Grecians,
Spartans, Thebans, and Ephesians.
Bow thee to the temple goddess,
Wise and strong and fair and modest!

"I wrote that," Herostratus whispered proudly.

"Figures," Marco said.

"I told them to use the English version—and for once they listened to me," Herostratus said. "Now bow down!"

As we sank to our knees, an old woman stepped into the stadium through the archway. She wore a crown made of antlers that seemed too large for her head, and her tunic was made of fine, silken brown fur. A young Zon led her by the hand, but she didn't need the help. She seemed to float as she walked, as if she were made of air. Her eyes were moist, the color drained from her irises. She stared straight ahead, and for a moment I thought she couldn't see at all. Then her head turned, her eyes settled on me, and I felt as if someone were running the tip of a knife from my ankle to my neck.

The Zon led her up the stairs and settled her into the throne. Immediately Herostratus stood up and bowed. "Would your godliness like the usual half hour of comedy and song? In honor of our guests, I have some biting political satire about the American presidential election!"

The woman reached into an ornately carved marble urn at the foot of the throne and fished out an ugly dagger. Herostratus's face turned white. Closing his eyes, he threw his arms wide to give the queen a target. "Here we go again. . . ."

She held out her left hand, palm out. Pointing her

gnarled fingers upward, she began using the dagger to clean her nails. In a voice hollow and raspy, she hissed, "No satire."

Herostratus's eyes popped open. With a look of relief, he gestured frantically for us to stand. As we did, the woman stared silently. "Introduce yourself," Herostratus mouthed.

I stood on shaky legs. What was the protocol for meeting the Greek goddess Artemis? "Um, hi," I said, my voice a ridiculous squeak. "I'm Jack McKinley, and these are Torquin, Brother Dimitrios, Cass and Eloise Williams, and Marco Ramsay."

She stared off to the distance as if I hadn't said a thing. As if she couldn't make out my presence in front of her.

"Say thank you," Herostratus mouthed.

"So," I said, "we'd just like to thank you for hearing us, O Great Goddess Artemis—"

She pounded her fist on the throne's arm and sat forward. "Do not . . . ever . . . call me by that name."

I jolted back, ramming into Marco. "I'm sorry if I offended you, but isn't this . . . *wasn't* this . . . the Temple of Artemis? That's what we're looking for."

"There is no Artemis!" she thundered. "Tell me, do you mean that odoriferous javelin thrower Aeginaea of Sparta . . . or Alphaea of Letrini who hides her hideous face behind a mask, or that mousy twit Locheia . . . or Aphaea of Athens or Kourotrophos or Potnia Theron or Agrotera—or me?"

173

"I—I don't know!" I stammered.

"Of course not," she said, blinking rapidly. "Every god—every last minor male god—has an individual name, oh yes. But we hunter goddesses? We are all strong, we are all excellent shots, so we are lumped together . . . under the name *Artemis*."

She drew out that name with a nasal lisp.

"Wh-wh-what shall we call you, O Great Goddess?" Brother Dimitrios stammered.

She smiled. "I am from Mount Cynthos, on the island of Delos. So you may call me Cynthia."

The name hung in the air for a moment, until Marco burst out laughing. "*Cynthia?* The Temple of Cynthia? That's a joke, right?"

The woman snapped her fingers, and the six frontline Amazons instantly reached for their bows and pointed them at Marco.

"Not a joke," Marco said, hands in the air. "Not a joke at all. Oh, and BTW? That thing your pal Stratocaster does—popping back to life—that's not in my wheelhouse. At least not here. So, arrows, very dangerous. Just saying."

"Up! All of you!" she said.

We stood, and the Amazons surrounded us. Slowly Cynthia rose, and two of the Zons jumped up to help her. Squinting as if the light were too strong, she descended from the throne, circling us. "Do you think they built the most wondrous structure in the world—more than a hundred columns, a marble roof that scraped the clouds—for someone who could merely shoot a deer? Look around you. I was not merely a goddess of hunting but of something greater: womankind. I trained them in the hunt, tutored them in trade and in music, taught them to build and to read, helped nurse their babies. The Amazon race flocked from the mountains to worship at my feet. Then, upon the arrival of the Atlantean, it all ended."

Now the Amazons were grumbling again, spitting on the floor, and muttering Massarym's name.

"Massarym was a scholar and a gentleman!" Brother Dimitrios protested. "The Massarene monks have devoted centuries to his writings—"

"This gentleman lured us with the sad tale of his mother the queen, persecuted for her scientific genius," Cynthia said. "He financed the building of the third and grandest temple, after the idiot Herostratus burned the second—"

"For which I have been dutifully doing penance ever since," Herostratus broke in.

"By the time that temple was destroyed by the Goths, Massarym was long gone—but only then did his curse take effect," Cynthia continued. "We were banished to live deep in the earth, tricked into protecting his Atlantean treasure until the rightful heirs came to claim it. Our time here has been long, and we are ready to be freed from our task."

I couldn't believe my ears. "We can help you with that."

"The curse stated that we would be doomed to protect the Loculus against attackers, and that no man would ever succeed in removing it," Cynthia said. "These were Massarym's words—no *man*."

"We're boys," I said.

"Speak for yourself, Brother Jack," Marco grumbled.

She shook her head. "You have the mark. All three of you. Even with my eyesight, I can tell. It will be impossible for you. Have you no female among the marked?"

"Yes, but she's been kidnapped," Cass said. "We're trying to rescue her. We need your Loculus to do that. Actually, you would like her a lot—"

"Silence!" Cynthia said.

"Wait! I'm going to get the lambda in four years," Eloise said brightly.

The Amazons all began murmuring. Cynthia signaled Maximo over for a private talk. They mumbled in some odd language with their backs to us.

"Why did you say that, Eloise?" Cass whispered.

"Because it's true," Eloise said. "I'm trying to help."

"Hey, maybe they'll just give the Loculus to her, because she's a girl," Marco said. "This could be the easiest gig yet!"

"See?" Eloise said, sneering at Cass. "You so do need me."

Now Maximo and Cynthia were turning back toward

us, with grim looks on their faces.

Cynthia put a hand on Eloise's shoulder. "I suppose, dear girl, you'll have to do."

Eloise's face turned three shades paler. "Wait. Do *what*?"

"*Zons—prepare!*" Cynthia shouted.

Amazons were bounding over toward us with armfuls of battle equipment—shields, swords, quivers, torches, darts, tubes—and plopping them down around Eloise.

Maximo dropped a helmet over Eloise's head. "Acchh. Too big."

Eloise ripped it off. "What is going on here?"

"The only way you can get the Loculus," she said, "is to fight us for it."

CHAPTER TWENTY-THREE

ELOISE, MARCO, AND CHINGGIS

"YOU'RE MY BROTHER!" Eloise screamed. "You can't let them do this to me!"

She was pacing the small, stone-walled gladiator chamber attached to the stadium. Outside, Amazons were lining the walls, chattering and passing around baskets of food.

"Jack will figure a way out of this!" Cass said.

"I will?" I said.

Eloise glared at me. She looked like she was about to cry.

"I will," I said.

It was about the least convincing thing ever out of my mouth. Eloise's leather helmet drooped down to her ears, and the silk fabric Maximo had stuffed inside was flapping out the back like a tail. Every time she turned, her sandals slid off her feet, and her tunic kept falling down even though they'd clipped it to the strap of her quiver.

"Look at those freaks out there!" Eloise said. "Look what they're eating! They're gross!"

I peered outside. The Amazons were passing around buckets, reaching inside, and pulling out cooked animal heads and feathered bird wings. They were picking their teeth with armadillo tails and having contests over who could spit eyes the farthest.

"It's . . . a different diet from ours," I said.

"It's heads and butts and guts," Eloise replied. She took her helmet off and threw it to the ground. "I'm out of here. I am not doing this."

The helmet rolled to Marco, who scooped it up. "Hey, this would fit me," he said, putting it on his own head.

"Then *you* do it," Eloise said.

I looked out at the crowd. Their backs against the wall, they were far away from the center of the stadium. There, Amazons in helmets and thick armored gear were throwing spears, sparring with knives, leaping, racing each other. In their outfits, they all looked the same.

"You know, Eloise, that might not be a bad idea," I said.

"Ha-ha," Marco drawled.

"Seriously, look at them," I said. "They're all about ten feet tall. You walk out there, Marco, all covered from head to toe, and they won't know the difference. To them, we're all shrimps, even you."

"But Cynthia—" Cass said.

"Her eyesight is horrible," I said. "Did you see the way she was squinting at us? She's hundreds of years old. My dad's, like, forty and he needs glasses to see the fridge. Also, look how far away she's sitting."

We gathered at the door. Cynthia's throne had been moved to the far end of the oval stadium. She was at least fifty yards from where the action was going to be.

She stood, and the entire place went silent except for a few deep belches. Through one of the archways, a team of four Amazons carried in a platform on their shoulders, supported by wooden poles. On top of the platform was what looked like some kind of statue, shrouded in a thick, embroidered cloth. Behind the team, two more Amazons pounded a drumbeat on animal skins stretched over hollowed-out tree stumps.

They crossed the stadium and set the platform down before the throne. Cynthia slowly descended the stairs. With a flourish, she removed the cloth.

Sitting at the top of a golden base inlaid with red jewels was a pearl-colored orb. As it caught the glare of the overhead stadium lights, the Amazons oohed and aahed.

"Warriors, scholars, women of thought and courage!" Cynthia said, her voice robust and piercing. "It is with great happiness but a heavy heart that I inform you our Council of Elders has met and decided that we have reached, at long last, our day of reckoning!"

Torquin stared at the Loculus with greedy eyes. "So close . . ."

Marco took a deep breath. "Give me that Amazon uniform. Now. Before I change my mind."

* * *

"Ow! Ow! Ow!" Marco winced as Eloise plucked hairs from his leg. "What's up with the tweezers?"

"My foster mom used to do this," Eloise said.

"I'm not your foster mom!" Marco protested. "The boss lady's not going to see my peach fuzz. Besides, have you seen Maximo's legs?"

Brother Dimitrios hurried in, carrying a huge leather sack—which he nearly dropped on the floor when he saw Marco. "By Massarym's spear—what on earth?"

"Where've you been?" Marco asked.

"Our dear friend Herostratus gave me some extra weapons," Brother Dimitrios said. "But I was expecting—"

"Today, the role of Eloise will be played by Marco Ramsay," Marco said.

Outside, Herostratus had emerged from another tunnel and begun performing a kind of clown act, setting fire to a five-foot-high wooden replica of the Temple of Artemis. It was pretty amazing looking, even in a small version—with its rows and rows of white columns inside and out. As it went up in flames, Herostratus came out with a tiny bucket of water and tried to throw it on the fire, while Amazons rushed in from the entrances with massive hoses.

For a special crowd-pleasing finale, they quickly doused the fire and then turned the hoses on Herostratus—while he transformed into a pigeon, a cat, and a squealing monkey.

"I think they're almost done with the opening act," I said.

Cass was wrapping the sandals all the way up Marco's calves to the knee. "You still don't look dainty enough," he said.

"I could wear a tutu," Marco said, adjusting his helmet.

I tied a colorful silk scarf around Marco's thick neck. Torquin pulled tightly on the tunic, trying to get Marco's shoulders to look a little less broad.

"Don't stand with your legs so far apart," I suggested.

"Don't pound your feet when you walk," Brother Dimitrios said.

"Can you make your arms look less muscley?" Eloise asked.

"Don't speak like boy," Torquin said.

"Smile more," Brother Dimitrios said. "You look pretty when you smile."

Marco pressed his legs together, pulled his arms in,

tiptoed toward the door, made a pained smile, and said in a mousy voice, "How's this?"

"Terrible," Eloise said.

"Ladieeees and ladies!" Herostratus shouted, to a chorus of boos and hoots. "Sit back and relax, 'cause now it's time for the main event!"

A whinny sounded in the stadium, and a masked Amazon in full battle gear—helmet, armor, spear—came galloping out on a horse through one of the archways. The steed was brown, massive, and powerful looking, and it reared up on its hind legs to the roar of the crowd.

"Where'd they get a *horse*?" Cass asked.

"Where'd they get two?" I said.

Through the opposite archway, another Amazon yanked on the reins of a second horse. This one did not want to enter the stadium, snorting and rearing defiantly. Now another Amazon joined the first—two nine-foot-tall women pulling on a beast that didn't want to move.

Finally the horse charged forward, kicking left and right and sending both warriors flying. It ran into the stadium, bucking and snorting, until three warriors lassoed its neck.

The animal shook its head side to side, but it knew it was caught. With a final fling of the neck, it turned its eyes toward our little archway.

"I think it likes me," Marco said.

"Mounting the noble steed to my right will be your

favorite Zon and mine—Maximo!" Herostratus bellowed.

Maximo climbed on the calm, powerful horse and took a galloping lap around the stadium, to a roar of cheering.

"And to my left, battling for the Loculus of Massarym, upon the notorious wild horse of Mongolia known as Chinggis," Herostratus yelled, "let's give a Za-Za-Zon welcome to the . . . er, precociously powerful Eloise of the mortal world!"

"Za! Za! Zon!" the crowd chanted slowly and rhythmically, then faster and a faster.

"Wild horse?" Eloise said.

Cass tapped Marco on the shoulder. "Go get 'im, Tex."

Marco stepped out of the archway, taking tiny steps and keeping his arms tight to his sides. He lifted his right hand and waggled his fingers to the crowd, then began blowing kisses.

Cass was turned away, his eyes shut. "I can't look. How's he doing?"

"Very bad actor," Torquin said.

The three Amazons who were handling Chinggis could barely keep the horse from bolting. They weren't paying much attention to Marco as he walked closer. But Marco didn't try to jump on, at least not right away. Instead, he walked up to it closely, mumbling words I couldn't hear. The horse snorted a few times, pulling at the three lassos, but its eyes didn't move from him.

He touched the side of its head and began stroking its forelock gently. Then, one by one, he unlooped the lassos from Chinggis's head. Freed, the horse pawed the ground once and bowed.

Marco dug his foot into the stirrup and mounted, to an explosion of applause.

"And they're off!" Herostratus shouted.

Well, one of them, anyway. Maximo was whipping her horse into action. Her entire face was covered with a thick leather mask; and as she leaned forward, she pointed a blunt-tipped wooden lance directly at Marco.

"They never gave me one of those!" Eloise said.

As Maximo charged closer, Chinggis reared up on her hind legs in surprise. As she came down, Marco gave her sides a firm kick.

Now Chinggis began charging, too. But Maximo had much more speed. I could hear her bloodthirsty "HEEEE-AAAAGGGH!" echo into the dome—and the Amazons whooping with expectation.

Marco let go of Chinggis's reins and threw his arms out to the side as if to say, "Come get me."

And Maximo rammed her lance directly into his chest.

CHAPTER TWENTY-FOUR
THE WRATH OF CYNTHIA

MARCO'S SCREAM DEFINITELY did not sound Eloise-like.

With the blunt tip of the lance against his chest, Marco grabbed the shaft with both hands and yanked his arms upward. Still holding tight to the lance's hilt, Maximo went flying into the air.

Her horse charged by at full speed, riderless.

With a loud grunt, Marco swung the lance over his shoulder—with Maximo still on it. The lance snapped in two, and the Zon leader somersaulted head over foot, landing in the dirt with a loud thud.

The place went dead silent. Most of the Amazons were slack-jawed with disbelief.

"Such action! Such courage! Hoooo-hoo!" Herostratus shouted. "This sort of thing has never been seen before in our stadium! Is Maximo dead, ladies and ladies? Ha! Of course not! Amazons are immortal . . . *OR ARE THEY?* Now the question is . . . for the lives of all the Amazons . . . will Eloise get the grand prize?"

Marco spurred Chinggis toward the Loculus. Cynthia sat up in her throne, watching stonily. At the other end of the stadium, Maximo was struggling to her feet.

Swooping down with his hands, Marco snatched up the Loculus and held it high over his head.

"Yyyyes!" Eloise screamed, jumping onto Cass and nearly knocking him over.

I breathed a sigh of relief. I knew the Loculus had to have the power of teleportation or time travel, and either one would get him out of there, so I called out, "Use it, Mar—er, Eloise! Use it!"

But he was on the other side, making Chinggis promenade before the Amazons. He held the Loculus under his arm like a football and shouted while pumping his fist, "We got it. We got it. We—we—we got it!"

"What the heck is he doing?" Cass said.

"WATCH OUT, MARCO!" I yelled.

Across the stadium grass, Maximo was racing on her own two feet toward Marco. Her stride was huge, her calves as muscular as an Olympic runner's. With a scream, she jettisoned herself into the air, diving toward Marco.

Her hands closed around the Loculus and she snatched it away, knocking Marco clear off the horse. He tumbled to the ground and rolled, his helmet flying off and bouncing away on the grass.

Now Marco's face was visible to the crowd. Seeing who he really was, they began screaming angrily, storming the field. Cynthia rose to her feet, her jaw hanging open.

Marco scrambled to put the helmet back on, but it was too late.

"Forfeit!" Herostratus cried out. "The mortals are disqualified!"

Cass, Eloise, Torquin, Brother Dimitrios, and I all ran out onto the field. *"Grab the Loculus, Marco!"* I shouted.

Marco dove toward Maximo, but she jumped away, holding tight to the Loculus. From his left and right, Amazons ran from the sidelines into the fray. Out of nowhere, a half-eaten roasted vromaski's head flew through the air and landed on Chinggis with a dull splat.

The horse ran toward Marco, kicking at the attacking Amazons ferociously from both sides. I had to watch where I was running, because nine-foot women made deadly projectiles.

One of them landed next to me with a loud "oof." As she sat up, dazed, Eloise leaped over her. She snatched up the broken half of Maximo's lance and began swinging it wildly.

She clipped two of the Amazons at the ankle and tore through another's weapon belt, which fell to the ground. Then, weaving under the legs of the fighting nine-foot warriors, she began yanking on their sandal straps, untying them.

I scooped up the fallen weapon belt and ran to the sidelines. There, out of the chaos, I was able to take out a blowpipe and stuff a leather pouch full of darts into my pocket.

In the middle of the stadium's confusion, I saw the Loculus roll toward Brother Dimitrios. He picked it up, his face full of disbelief. "By the gods, I've got it. *I've got it!*"

Hearing this, one of the Amazons whirled away from the melee and ran toward him, brandishing a club.

I thought I heard Dimitrios muttering, "Oh dear."

"Toss it over here!" Torquin shouted.

Over the moving scrum of bodies, all I saw now was the Loculus flying high over the crowd, into Torquin's arms. I tried to see what happened to Brother Dimitrios, but the crowd was parting now to let someone through.

I froze.

Out of the madness, Cynthia was float-walking toward me, brandishing a bow. Before I could do a thing, she was on her knees and aiming an arrow at my head. "You do not cheat Cynthia," she said.

"No-o-o-o!" Torquin's voice boomed.

I heard the twang as the arrow left the bow. I saw the

point heading for my eye. I knew I had no time to duck.

The line drive blur from my left was a total shock. It connected with the arrow in midair, creating an explosion that knocked it off course. I dropped to my knees, as Cynthia let out a cry of anger in Greek.

To my left, Torquin was staring slack-jawed, the Loculus no longer in his hand. To my right, Cynthia's arrow lay on the ground.

All around it was a pile of shattered Loculus, being stepped on and kicked around by Chinggis.

CHAPTER TWENTY-FIVE

LOSS UPON LOSS

THE SCREAM BEGAN as a tiny wail and grew to be the loudest siren I had ever heard. It caromed off the round dome, magnifying and echoing against itself so that it sounded like a chorus of the dying.

Cynthia was on her knees, looking at the broken Loculus in horror.

I ran up beside her and fell to the dirt, sweeping up the pieces of the Loculus in my hands. "Marco, Cass!"

They dropped to my side and tried to help. We all had to be careful to avoid Chinggis, who was still in a frenzy from all the commotion. The shards were sticking into my palms, drawing pricks of blood. "It . . . looks like glass," I said. "Whoever heard of a Loculus made of glass?"

"Back!" Torquin ordered, pulling me by the shoulder

just in time to avoid Chinggis's flying hoof.

This Loculus was way more fragile than the one I'd thrown under the train in New York City. Instead of a few dozen thick, jagged pieces, there were millions. And whatever we could have collected was being kicked away and ground in the dirt by a wildly confused Chinggis. "What are we going to do now?" Cass asked.

I shook my head, speechless.

Now the Zons were gathering around their leader, falling to their knees, bowing their heads. Some were wailing in sympathy. No one had time for us anymore.

"Come," Torquin said. "Let's go."

"But—" I protested.

"Must get out of here," he said. "Now."

I stood, backing away. The whole thing was hopeless. Torquin was leading us through the jungle of Zons. They were trying to gather up the shards, rushing to comfort Cynthia, picking odd fights with one another for no particular reason. It was utter chaos. I knew Torquin was right. We had to leave now while we had the opportunity.

But as I turned to go, I caught a glimpse of Brother Dimitrios lying on the grass. Eloise was leaning over him, and she looked up in shock as we ran to her. "What happened?" Cass asked.

"He threw Loculus to me," Torquin said. "And Zons hit him."

Blood was pooling under Dimitrios's head. His face was losing color, and as he turned to me, I could see a gash down the side of his face. "J—J—"

"We have to get him some help!" I shouted.

"No!" Dimitrios said with a grimace. "Too late. You must . . . continue . . ."

"Come on, Jack, let's lift him," Marco said.

"No . . . ! No!" Dimitrios said. His eyes fluttered and his words were halting. "J-Jack. I did . . . I was . . . wrong . . ."

"What are you talking about?" I said. "You threw the Loculus to Torquin. That saved my life!"

He made a coughing sound, and blood spurted from his mouth. When he looked at me again, tears sprang from his eyes. "Jack . . . Hero . . ."

"*You're* the hero," I said.

". . . stratus . . ."

Dimitrios's eyes fluttered again, and then shut.

"Dimitrios—wake up!" Cass said, slapping his cheek. "What did you mean by— Jack, why did he say that?"

"I don't know," I said. "Brother Dimitrios, what about Herostratus?"

The old monk's lips quivered as if he wanted to speak, but instead his head rolled to one side. And his body went limp.

Torquin pressed his fingers to the side of Dimitrios's neck, feeling for a pulse. "Dead," he said.

Eloise began to cry softly. "No. Just no," she said between sniffles. "Dimitrios was kind of creepy, but he didn't deserve this. . . ."

Cass put his arm around her silently.

I sat back, numb. I knew we had to go. I knew that every second we spent here was one second closer to being captured by the Zons. But I couldn't move. I felt nothing.

Professor Bhegad . . . Daria of Babylon . . . and now Dimitrios. All of them gone in the quest for the Loculi. A quest that was now hopeless. "This was my fault . . ." I muttered. "It was my idea for Marco to impersonate Eloise. And because of that, Dimitrios is dead and the Loculus is destroyed."

"Brother Jack, did you see that bronco?" Marco said. "No offense, but Eloise wasn't ready for that."

"My fault," Torquin mumbled. "For throwing Loculus."

Now, over by Cynthia, one of the Zons was pointing toward us, shouting to the others.

"Uh-oh," Torquin said. "Have to go."

"We can't just leave him here!" Eloise said.

"*Go—now!*" Torquin bellowed, lifting Eloise off the ground with one hand and Cass with the other.

Marco had to pull me up by my shirt. "Dude, don't lose it. You don't want to end up like him."

I got up and ran. Together we headed back toward the entry archway. A spear whistled over my head. It barely missed Torquin but cut a straight row through the top of his hair. Arrows began raining on either side of us. "Yeeeow!" Marco yelled.

"Are you okay?" I shouted.

"Only . . . a flesh wound . . ." he said through gritted teeth. Turning in midstride, he scooped up the fallen arrow with his noninjured hand and hurled it back. "Bull's-eye!" he shouted.

"Hurry!" I called out.

We headed for the tunnel where Herostratus had emerged. As we plunged in, I could hear another spear clank against the rock wall, just above the opening. "Does anyone have a torch?" Marco called out.

"Oh, sure, Marco, I always keep a torch in my pocket," Eloise shouted.

"Ow!" Torquin grunted. "Hit wall. Go left."

We were running blindly now. From behind us came the thumping of size-gazillion feet. I could see the dull glow of light against the walls—*they* had torches! At least I could see walls, ceilings, and shadows now. We ran straight, past two side tunnels. But just ahead, Torquin was coming to a stop. He'd reached a fork and was sniffing left and right. "Smell air. One of these leads outside."

An arrow skittered under my legs, sliding on the floor and into the tunnel on the right. "They're close!" Eloise said.

That was when I saw a shadow moving in the right-hand tunnel, near the floor. Two eyes stared up at me in the darkness.

They were bright orange.

CHAPTER TWENTY-SIX

PLAYING WITH FIRE BOY

"GO RIGHT!" I said.

"Why?" Cass asked.

"That cat—it's Herostratus!" I replied.

Following Herostratus might have been the dumbest decision I could make, but I had to go with my gut. His name was the last thing Dimitrios had said.

We ran right, following the shadow of the cat into the tunnel.

I was expecting a hail of arrows or a flying lance. But I didn't expect the loud scraping noise behind us. It made me jump in midstride and turn around, as a wall of solid rock closed across the tunnel, sealing it off to us at the fork.

"What the—?" I muttered.

Marco had seen it, too. "It's a trap, Brother Jack. They're locking us in."

I whirled around. "Not much we can do. Come on!"

Torquin had waited for us at the next fork. He signaled us to go left.

Our path was uphill and I was sensing a change in the air. We were nearing some sort of exit. But as we bolted around a curve, Torquin came to a quick halt. "Whoa, apply air brakes!" Marco yelled.

We pulled up behind them. I peeked over Eloise's shoulder to see Herostratus standing in our way, trembling. He was reaching into his pants pocket, fumbling with a set of keys.

"You betray, you pay!" Torquin said, balling his fists.

Herostratus shook his head. "Not me, babies," he said. "I'm not the one who betrayed you."

His hands shaking, he inserted the key into a door in the wall. It took him a few tries, but he finally pushed it open and stepped inside. "Please," he said. "Hurry."

I heard a scrape and saw a spark. A torch came to life, and we could see Herostratus using it to light three sconces. They sent flames shooting up into a long, narrow shaft.

We crowded into a room that was a perfect cylinder, almost too small to fit us. Aside from the sconces, the only other feature I could make out was a huge wooden crank at about waist level. "Please, step back from the center,"

Herostratus said. "You'll just have to squeeze."

As we spread out, he began turning the crank. It squeaked loudly, echoing upward. Now I could hear frantic chittering above us as the shaft filled with the shadows of bats. "Ignore them," Herostratus said. "They're friendly. Except Fuzzy. He bites."

"I hate bats!" Eloise shrieked. "Which one is Fuz—"

A black streak darted downward. We all ducked, screaming. But with a quick flick of his arm, Herostratus swatted it against the wall, inches from Torquin's head. "That one."

"Yum," Torquin said. "May I take—?"

"No!" we all shouted at once.

Ignoring us all, Herostratus cranked and cranked. The floor began to shake, releasing a cloud of dust—and a perfect circular section of the floor popped out and began to rise.

A cylinder made of polished amber-colored marble thrust upward, inches from Torquin's belly. It moved painfully slowly and with an ear-splitting groan, as the marble rubbed against the stone opening. I had to close my eyes to the dust cloud, and everyone was coughing.

But through all that noise, I was feeling a sensation in my brain that was a lot like the Song of the Heptakiklos.

When the noise stopped, I squinted through the settling dust. Near the top of the shaft, I could make out a section of the shaft's wall that had been hollowed out. In the flickering light of the sconces I saw a perfect sphere, the size of a basketball. The Song was screaming now. "This is it," I said. "This is the Loculus! But that one . . . back in there . . ."

Herostratus sighed. "The Zons will realize it is a fake, if they have not already. They are crafty, but over the eons have grown a little soft in the cerebrum."

"The who?" Torquin said.

"The brain," Eloise explained.

"So Brother Dimitrios died for a *fake Loculus*?" I could barely spit the words out.

"Brother Dimitrios," Herostratus said, "was the one who made me swap it out. He met with me while the girl was preparing for battle. I told him I had made ceremonial replicas of the Loculus. We used them for pageants and such, so the real one would not be damaged. I was ordered by Cynthia, of course, to use the real one today. But I couldn't help bragging about the craftsmanship of the replicas. Even though it is not in my nature to boast—"

"Go on," Marco said.

"Well, I am the Custodial Storage Executive," Herostratus continued, "so a few centuries ago I fashioned this hiding place. Clever, no?"

I thought back. Dimitrios had been gone while we'd made the decision to substitute Marco for Eloise. "But . . .

why would Dimitrios want you to swap the real Loculus for a fake?" I said.

"Because he thought the girl would be torn to shreds," Herostratus said. "A not unreasonable assumption. Which would ensure that the Loculus would remain here forever. Well, he didn't like that. And neither did I."

"I find this line of thought very upsetting," Eloise said.

"So you switched the Loculus for a fake," I said. "And then what? We would leave Eloise's body in the stadium, run back here with you and Dimitrios, and then—whoosh—back to the island with the Loculus?"

Herostratus shook his head. "No," he said softly. "Brother Dimitrios would. Alone. That was his plan."

"You're lying!" Cass said. "It makes no sense. The Loculi don't work without the Select—which would be us. Dimitrios needed us to bring them back!"

"He had a different plan," Herostratus said. "He was upset over being forced to accept some kind of truce between enemy camps."

"The Karai and the Massa," I said.

Herostratus nodded. "Yes, that sounds right. Well, Dimitrios had a list of young people who also had the mark—a database, I believe you call it. He thought that if he returned with this Loculus, he would be a hero. He would persuade his superior to recruit new . . . Selects. He believed that with you children on the island, he would never achieve the power he deserved."

From the hallway outside, I heard a dull thump, and then another. Herostratus jumped. "They are breaking down the barrier. We must escape."

As I reached for the Loculus, Marco grabbed the latch on the door. But it wouldn't budge. "Let us out, dude," he said to Herostratus.

A third thump was followed by a huge crash. And the pounding of footsteps.

"On one condition," Herostratus said. "Take me with you."

"*Whaaaat?*" Cass said.

"They are gods, and by the curse of Massarym, they will disappear upon the taking of the Loculus," Herostratus said. "But my curse was not set by Massarym. It was set by *them*. When they are gone, I shall become human again."

"Heck no, Fire Boy!" Marco spat. "You were going to go through with Dimitrios's plan."

"You're as bad as he was," Eloise said.

Now the footsteps were settling outside the door. Something pounded on it with a force that shook the entire shaft.

"Please!" Herostratus said. "Have mercy on a fellow traveler."

The pounding was louder now. The center of the door was cracking, the latch beginning to warp. In one or two tries, they would be in.

Herostratus was looking at me desperately. His eyes were glowing an extrafierce orange now. I knew he'd suffered under the Zons. But he'd been punished for setting fire to one of the great structures of ancient history. And he'd been ready to sacrifice us for his own freedom. He couldn't be trusted.

"Sorry, Herostratus," I said.

I placed my hand on the Loculus.

Cass and Marco, on my left and my right, put a hand on my shoulder. Torquin and Eloise touched them.

At that moment the door crashed open, shattering the marble shaft that housed the Loculus.

And I heard the screaming of a cat.

CHAPTER TWENTY-SEVEN

THE DESTROYER DESTROYED

I NEVER THOUGHT I'd miss the Dream. The horrific, end-of-the-civilization Dream that puts me at the brink of death. But I do miss it now.

I want the world to be opening beneath my feet, the kingdom to be crumbling around me. I want to be frightened by griffins and vromaskis and running to save my own life.

Because these new dreams are worse.

In this one, I am floating in nothing. I don't know where to go or what to do. My body is as tiny as an atom and as large as the solar system. It is expanding and contracting in a blink of a nanosecond. I can see nothing. I can hear, smell, feel nothing, but I know I am not alone. First a blot of black whisks into my vision and disappears into a cloud. Then I see Cass, and Marco and Eloise and Torquin. What is going on? All of them are as scared as I am.

They are calling to me without sound, pulling on me without touch. JACK, GET US OUT. JACK, DO SOMETHING.

Why me?

WHY?

I don't know how we got here. I don't know where to go. But I am the one who must make the decisions.

Somehow, it's on me. But how can I? I am Jack the Nothing. Jack the Failure.

I am the Tailor unspooling.

I am the Destroyer destroyed.

I hurtle and bounce, grow and shrink. I hear screeching tires and hospital beeps, submarines and waterfalls, howling vizzeets and whispering zombies, death threats in sitcom dialog, the Song of the Heptakiklos.

And somewhere in the mix, as if to taunt me, are the old sounds from the Old Dream. They want to torture me, too. The explosions and screams. They know that I want out. They know that I will trade this for the destruction of a continent.

So I decide.

We are going there. Now.

But I fail there, too. Because now, as clear as my hand, Aly is pushing me away.

Aly is telling me there is work to be done.

Aly is pushing me back, back to this dream, to this place

that is ripping me apart.

Where do I go? I ask.

WHERE DO I GO?

But her face fades.

Home!

Yes. Home. All I want to do is go there. My yard and my bike and all the things I like. My bed, which I see now.

I reach out to my bed. From here it is a thousand light-years away.

From a thousand light-years away I see that something is under the covers—WHO'S BEEN SLEEPING IN MY BED! So I yank the cover off and I scream.

It is a skeleton, grinning at me, its teeth chattering, surrounded by a swarm of bugs that rises into the air in the shape of a globe. A Loculus of Flies.

I clutch the Loculus closer. It's still in my hands.

Number six.

NO, it COULD have been number six. But it's not.

Because one Loculus is lost to the Rift. Because Jack the Tailor is Jack the Failure.

I remember the moment we lost it—Aly screaming, clutching it as she sinks . . . sinks . . .

And now all I can think of is that. The rift and the sword. The rift and the Heptakiklos and the island that is tilting . . . tilting . . .

CHAPTER TWENTY-EIGHT

THE THINK SYSTEM

ON THE POSITIVE side, the sun was bright, and the air smelled like the sea.

On the negative side, I felt like someone had reached into my gut, squeezed hard, and pulled me inside out like a shirt.

All in all, I would rather have been in Disney World. Or even in a vat of vizzeet spit. Anything but in the pain that I was feeling right then. I think it took me fifteen minutes to stop screaming, and another fifteen to feel like my skin had finally found my body and attached itself again.

The first thing that came into actual focus was Marco's face. I'd never seen it so contorted with pain. *"Do not. Ever. Let that happen. Again,"* he said.

I nodded dumbly. That was a no-brainer.

Where were we? I blinked until the surroundings came into focus. I could see the columns of the House of Wenders-aka-Massa. Soldiers, monks, and rebels were pouring out of the surrounding buildings, shouting to one another. I could see Torquin stumbling about, rubbing his back and arms against a brick wall as if to test if he was really there.

"What the heck just happened, Brother Jack?" Marco said. "I feel like I was just taken apart and reassembled."

"Marco," I said in a choked whisper, "where are Cass and—?"

Before I could finish, Marco grabbed my arm. He pulled me up, and I stumbled after him across the compound.

Not far from the cafeteria, Cass and his sister were lying like rag dolls in the dirt. As Massa surrounded them, Brother Asclepius raced out of the hospital. He knelt by them, feeling for their pulses. "Alive," he said. "Bring them inside."

Already a team of technicians was exiting the hospital with two stretchers. They carefully loaded Cass and Eloise on them.

As the team went through the hospital doors, I could see Aliyah and her guards sweeping down the steps of the House of Massa. She was carrying a sturdy golden box. "The Loculus of Healing is inside," she explained, holding it toward me. "I think they need it. The blessings of

Massarym on them. I will wait. And then I have many questions for you. Go."

I took the Loculus from her and ran to the hospital.

I hadn't a clue what had just happened, but figuring that out would have to wait.

* * *

"So, back in that chamber, you just touched that Loculus—even though you didn't know which one it would be?" Cass said, lying on a hospital bed next to his sister's bed.

I nodded. It felt great to be talking to a totally normal Cass and Eloise. The Loculus of Healing had worked on them. Aliyah and Brother Asclepius were watching their vital signs in a state of awe. To be honest, Marco, Torquin, and I had put hands on that Loculus, too. All of our bodies had taken a beating.

"I knew it had to be either Time Travel or Teleportation," I said. "And either one would get us out of there."

"Well, everyone around here looks the same age as when we left," Eloise said. "So it wasn't Time Travel."

"Good choice," Marco said. "Better than being speared by Amazons."

"Teleportation hurts," Eloise said.

Torquin nodded. "Take body apart, put back together. Very painful."

"I don't think that's what happened," Brother Asclepius said. "That's the *Star Trek* version—you know, the molecules

209

dissolve and reappear like magic somewhere else. But think about it. When you talk on the phone, your voice doesn't travel. It's turned into *information*—little bits of data that are decoded at the other end."

"That can happen with bodies?" Marco said.

"Theoretically," Brother Asclepius said. "Atoms are atoms. They're all the same. So if the information on how to build a Marco is sent to a new set of atoms somewhere else, *they* assemble themselves. The thing is, that process would take an extraordinary amount of energy! It's a miracle you didn't die from the experience."

"When it comes to Atlantis, some things are best left unexplained," Cass said.

"What I don't understand is, how did you get the Loculus to place you back precisely here, on this island?" Asclepius asked. "As opposed to someplace random, like the middle of the Arctic or West Africa?"

I took a deep breath. "I'm not exactly sure. I wasn't really thinking. We went into some weird state, sort of like sleeping. I could feel my body growing and contracting. I thought we were all going to explode. Then I started thinking about Aly and Atlantis. I could see her yelling at me. It was crazy—like *she* was guiding me, telling me to go back to the island. When I concentrated on this place—boom, we were here."

"That's how all the Loculi work," Marco said. "It's the

210

think system. You think about what you need to do, and they do it."

Brother Asclepius scratched his head. "As a man of science hired by the Massa, I have had to accept many things. But I'm afraid there's no scientific basis for the think system."

"Can't wait to hear what you say about time travel," Marco said.

Aliyah, who had been quiet this whole time, finally leaned forward on her folding chair. "Jack, where is Brother Dimitrios?"

The room fell into a heavy silence. I tried to think of a way to word it, but Eloise beat me to it.

"He died," she said softly, "trying to get us the Loculus. Which was fake anyway."

As I explained what had happened—Dimitrios's death and the news of his betrayal, Aliyah's face grew ashen. "Dimitrios . . . had a strong will and could be devious," she said softly. "But this kind of treachery? I find this very hard to believe. Your source . . . was he, or she, trustworthy?"

I shrugged. "That wouldn't be the first word I'd use to describe Herostratus."

"Then I—I don't know what to believe," Aliyah said, standing up. "I will choose not to convict him without proof. And I will miss him. While you prepare for the final part of your journey tomorrow, I will arrange a service in his memory."

"Tomorrow?" I said. "Aliyah, I don't know if we have that kind of time."

"If I'm not mistaken," Aliyah said, "the last Wonder of the Ancient World is in Egypt—the site of the Lighthouse of Alexandria. How do you expect to go there?"

Her question lingered unanswered. I thought about Slippy, which we'd left at the airport in Turkey.

"Jack, if you're going to suggest the Loculus of Teleportation," Cass said, "I will personally throw you to the vromaskis."

"Well, you will be pleased to know I have given this some thought," Aliyah said. "I've made arrangements with our agents in Turkey to retrieve the stealth jet from Izmir. Upon its arrival here, shortly before sunrise, we will inspect it and prepare it for your departure."

"Sunrise?" Cass said. "But that's nearly a half day—"

"You will use that time to peruse the writings of your hero, Wenders," Aliyah said. "We have been examining them to the best of our ability during your absence. He appeared to have written extensively about the Lighthouse. I urge you, with your linguistic abilities, to be fully prepared this time. We cannot risk losing another of our respected comrades. Please wait here while we get the material."

She turned and walked toward the door, with her guards in tow.

"Respected . . ." Torquin said. "Pah!"

"She's right," Cass said. "We can't be sure Dimitrios said those things."

"Dimitrios lying, conniving slime," Torquin said.

I nodded. "But why would Herostratus lie to us?"

"Herostratus lying, conniving, obnoxious, delusional, pyromaniac slime," Torquin said. "Pick your poison."

"The dude begged us to take him with us," Marco said. "Maybe he was trying to win our trust."

"All he had to do was touch one of us," I said. "He would have teleported with us."

"Are you sure he didn't?" Cass asked.

"Would have swatted him away," Torquin grumbled. "Good riddance."

Now Aliyah's guards were bustling in, carrying Herman Wenders's chest. With a thump, they dropped the oaken box onto the floor.

Aliyah swept in behind them. "The Loculus of Language is inside this box," she said. "I advise that you use it. Knowledge is power, my children, and the lack of it can be fatal. I believe my brother's death years ago could have been prevented. I would never forgive myself if I allowed you to succumb to your youthful eagerness as he did. Am I understood?"

"Understood," I said.

"Come, gentlemen," she said, turning toward her guards. As they left the hospital room, Marco opened the chest and began taking Wenders's notebooks out. I lifted the Loculus of Language from the box and placed it on the floor.

"Where do we start?" Eloise asked.

I placed my hand on the Loculus and began reading the Latin titles on each cover. There were seven altogether. On the covers of six were dates. But the seventh book was different.

I read the title aloud: "'Notes on the Nature of Writings Left by Prince Karai of Atlantis and Retrieved from a Devastating Fire in a Chamber of the Labyrinth of Mount Onyx'—"

"That's got to be the bat guano cave!" Cass turned to his sister. "I almost died there."

On the first page, Wenders had written an introduction.

"'I write this in a state of hunger and despair. My sanity leaks away by the day. Praise God for the return of my Malay deckhand, Musa, having survived an abduction by monkeys. His company, and his doggedness, have kept me alive. And his retrieval of these scrolls, after a brave foray into the labyrinth of Onyx, has compelled me to believe that our work must be preserved and will be someday discovered—and that a cure for whatever befell Burt will be found.

"'The notes that follow were written in runes of the Atlantean Late Period by Prince Karai upon returning

214

to his devastated homeland after a search for his brother. They give insight into Massarym's aims and fears. I have attempted to translate as best as possible, but I leave the notes themselves to some future scholar with deeper knowledge. What follows are Karai's words. Humbly, Herman Wenders.'"

I put aside the leather book. Under it, carefully folded, was a stack of brittle-looking parchment, filled with ancient symbols.

Holding onto the Loculus, I lifted the first section and laid it flat. The symbols danced before my eyes, their meanings flying up from the page to me like voices. "I—I can understand this!" I said.

Now the others were looking over my shoulder, not bothering to touch the Loculus, as I began to read slowly:

"'I, Karai of Atlantis, do hereby record for history the diabolical plan of my brother, Massarym, who travels from city to city in search of structures in which to hide the seven Loculi containing the power to animate the most perfect civilization in the history of the world. I have learned of several locations and traveled to them myself. I believe I found one in a great city by the sea called Ephesus. A temple to the goddess Artemis, it was a work of exceeding majesty and beauty, and a fitting tribute to Massarym's pride. Upon inspection, though, I was nearly consumed by a fire set by the most wretched of human beings. Who

215

would destroy such a holy site? Only a criminal of basest intent, a subhuman lackey by the name Herostratus, whose loyalty was assured by Massarym with the smallest amount of money . . .'"

"PAH!" Torquin shouted, pounding the windowsill. "Now I wish he came. Want to pound him into the ground myself."

Cass sat back, his face darkening. "Jack, are we sure he didn't touch one of us when we jumped?"

Before I could answer, the cry of a griffin ripped the evening air. Startled, we all looked out the window.

The beast fell from the sky in a swoop of red, its talons outstretched. Below it, a small, dark creature that had been near the base of the hospital now ran for the jungle.

The little thing wasn't fast enough. The griffin plucked it from the ground, screaming with triumph. As it rose into the darkening sky, the griffin's prey dangled helplessly.

We caught a quick glimpse of it as it passed our window. It was a black cat, with unspeakable fear in its eyes.

Which were bright orange.

CHAPTER TWENTY-NINE
LI'ANU

THE REST OF the night, it was hard not to be bothered by Torquin's giggling, a rhythmic wheezing that sounded like a bulldog with allergies. We were trying to decipher Karai's notes and diagrams. Lots of them were ripped, stained, burned, or missing.

"You can be cruel, Tork," Cass said.

"Did not like Herostratus," Tork said. "Not as man. Not as kitty cat . . ."

As he went into another fit of giggles, I looked at my watch—3:07 A.M. I think we were all feeling a little giddy.

We hadn't really looked at Wenders's notebooks. We'd spent most of our time on Karai's scroll, which had been carefully cut and divided into four sections. Cass, Marco,

Eloise, and I had each taken one.

Mine was the last. The very bottom of it had been burned away. But I was determined to read all of it. "Okay, guys, this is our last Wonder and Loculus," I said. "We don't want to mess it up. Did we learn anything here to help us?"

Cass raised his hand. "I had the earliest part of the scroll. Okay, so, Massarym is like the big show-off of the two bros, right? He goes to the Mediterranean on a ship he steals from the royal Atlantean fleet, and what does he do? Shows off. He figures, 'Hey, I want everyone to think I'm some kind of god. Then I can park the Loculus in some kind of cool gnidliub—or get some architect to build one. Then—boom—I put some kind of spell on it and—moob—I make sure it's protected by a beastie.' He goes to Greece, or whatever they called it back then. They love him so much that this group becomes the Massarene monks. Generous old Massarym rewards them by leaving his seven beautiful codices, woo-hoo!"

"What's a codice?" Eloise asked.

"Singular is *codex*, plural is *codices*," Cass said. "A codex is an ancient text. So, the monks find an architect to make the Colossus, where Massarym hides the Loculus of Flight, guarded by a griffin. Trouble is, Tweety likes to eat monks, so Mass takes the bird back and puts this spell on the statue. It's totally stone until someone tries to steal the Loculus—then it comes to life and pounds the thief into human moussaka. The monks are like, 'Great, what a deal!' and he leaves. Problem is, Massarym's carrying around those Atlantean beasts on a ship. And the crew are freaking out. The big green blob is oozing out of its cage and managing to eat them."

"The one Marco the Magnificent stabbed in the rift?" Marco said proudly.

"Well, not *that* one, but maybe its little brother or sister," Cass replied. "Anyway, that's where my part ends."

"I got the part where Massarym's sailing up the Euphrates and he meets this shaman from a place called Sippar," Eloise said. "The guy takes him to Ancient Babylon. When Massarym goes to the palace, the queen is throwing shoes at the king. And her royal highness has *a lot* of shoes. The king is embarrassed and says she's really homesick. She's like a mountain girl, and Babylon is superflat. So Massarym goes, 'Build her a mountain! You know, like a big structure with Hanging Gardens and stuff, which *looks* like a mountain. And I'll leave you with these foul creatures that will protect it and, oh, yeah, can I keep this orb inside it?' That works out well. Then he gets back to his ship, and there's been this mutiny. He offloads a bunch of the monsters, which have been spitting acid on the crew and messing up the ship. But that still doesn't make the crew happy. They're so angry they nearly kill Massarym. Anyway, that's all I got."

Eloise put her part of the scroll down and looked at Marco. "You guys went to all these places? I am so jealous."

Marco shrugged. "Dude, it wasn't all fun times."

"I'm not a dude," Eloise said.

"And you're not fun times." Marco spun away to avoid being slapped. "JK! Anyway, so yeah. Massarym starts ramping up the magic spells. He gets rid of the crew and enchants a bunch of new sailors to obey his every wish. He makes sure extra guys are on board in case Greenie eats some. And he heads to Halicarnassus, where he knows this famous guy Mausolus has died. He gets the guy's wife, Artemisia, to build this awesome structure, the Mausoleum. Only now his dad, King Uhla'ar, is hot on the trail, and he shows up in Halicarnassus with his toga in a twist. So Massarym tries to throw him off the trail by pretending to throw the Loculus off a cliff—"

"And then they meet again near Olympus," I said, "where Massarym puts a spell on his dad, trapping him in the Statue of Zeus. That's in my part of the scroll. Afterward, Massarym is feeling guilty about what he did to Uhla'ar. But he got what he wanted. Dad is off his trail, the crew is a bunch of yes-men. The problem is, Greenie has escaped."

"That big thing?" Marco said.

"Yup," I said. "So most of my scroll is about Massarym's *li'anu*."

"Which means?" Eloise asked.

"Well, I couldn't figure that out, even with the Loculus of Language, but I think I got it from context—you know, get the meaning from the words around it," I said, reading aloud: "'Although Massarym was brilliantly skilled in the magic arts and persuasive among the people he met, although he was able to trap his own father and assemble a new crew, he lacked control over many of his fearsome Atlantean beasts. These often acted with wills of their own. Those who lived in or traveled by water proved to be the most difficult. Although Massarym brought them to the Great Lands by cage, the most fearsome of all, the great Atlantean Mu'ankh, broke free. Thus Massarym began his great *li'anu*, following the sea up through the vast north lands.'"

"So, *li'anu* is some kind of search," Eloise said.

"Exactly," I replied, continuing onward: "Anyway, he's in Greece now, so he sails over to Rhodes to borrow the Loculus of Flight . . . 'Under cover of night, Massarym traveled to lands covered by forests and swamps. The crude, warring tribes there took him to be a kind of god, which he enjoyed greatly, of course. He created detailed maps of his travels, some of which I was able to steal, some of which I copied. And it was in these cold, dank, horrid places where he heard of sightings of a great green sea beast. There were many names given to it by these people, the most common being *kraken*. After much searching, he finally found the Mu'ankh frolicking in a long and narrow waterway, frightening the local tribes.'"

Cass grabbed the map from me, staring at the circle that had been drawn on the map. "Guys, this is Europe," he said.

Eloise rolled her eyes. "Tell us something we don't know."

"This area . . ." Cass went on. "It's Scotland."

"Wait," I said, pointing to the circle drawn on the map. "So this waterway would be . . . ?"

Cass nodded. "Loch Ness."

"Wait," Marco said. "Nessie is Greenie? How cool is that?"

"Wait, don't people claim to see Nessie even now?" Eloise asked.

"Falsely," Cass said. "It's the power of suggestion. The legend sticks and then people see it for years and years . . . mostly because they want to."

"'It took Massarym a great deal of time to guide the Mu'ankh out of the lake and onto the land,'" I read. "'He proved too unwieldy to fly through the air, so Massarym by necessity used the most dangerous Loculus of all, that of . . . *de'alethea'* . . . ?'"

"That's got to be teleportation," Cass said. "He teleported Greenie—but where?"

I kept going: "'The beast was nearly dead upon arrival. Great was Massarym's woe, and he set to restoring the hideous monster to life. For while he was gone, the architect Sostratus had completed plans for the greatest of all . . .'"

"Greatest of all *what?*" Marco said, slapping his hand down on the Loculus.

"That's it," I said. "That's where the scroll ends."

"Wait. What's that guy's name?" Cass raced to the hospital desk and sat at the computer there. As I spelled out the name *Sostratus*, he did a quick search.

Torquin, Eloise, Marco, and I followed, looking over his shoulder.

"Bingo," Marco said.

Our answer was glowing on the screen:

SOSTRATUS: ARCHITECT OF THE LIGHTHOUSE OF ALEXANDRIA.

CHAPTER THIRTY

SEESAW

"IT'S DEAD," MARCO said as the Jeep bounced along the road toward the airfield. "Greenie, I mean."

Eloise glared at him. "How do you know it's d— Owww! Torquin, will you slow down?"

Much as we begged Aliyah not to let him, Torquin was our driver. Heading directly into potholes at top speed had always been one of his favorite things to do. But today his driving seemed more absentminded. Like he just just wasn't paying attention. "So . . . sorry," he said, jamming on the brake. "It is difficult . . . to maneuver a wheeled vessel . . . such as this."

"Not funny," Eloise said.

"Maneuver a wheeled vessel . . . ?" Marco narrowed his

eyes. "Torquin, you don't need to impress us. Just drive, dude."

Torquin immediately began speeding up again.

"To answer your question, E—think of what that Loculus did to us," Marco said, putting his hand over his head to cushion his banging against the roof. "Greenie has a gazillion times the number of atoms we have. Like Brother Asclepius said, it's all about atoms. The more you have, the more complicated it is assembling them all. There's no way that thing survived being teleported."

"What if Massarym had the Loculus of Healing?" Eloise said.

"What if he didn't?" Cass replied. "What if it was already hidden away in the Mausoleum at Halicarnassus?"

The Jeep jolted so suddenly I thought we might have hit a tree. "Yeeeow, I only have one head, Tork!" Marco shouted. "Dang, *we're* the ones who need the Loculus of Healing."

"Huh?" Torquin grunted as the Jeep fishtailed onto the tarmac. He slammed on the brakes and we did a complete three-sixty, just before plowing into a crowd that nearly covered the entire field.

The people nearest the Jeep jumped back. Manolo grabbed Aliyah and threw her to another guard who was farther back in the crowd. Torquin skidded to a stop, nearly colliding with Slippy's landing wheels. He jumped out of the driver's seat and held his hand up to the waiting crowd.

"My badness," he grunted.

The rest of us were staring, dumbfounded. It looked like every single Massa and every single rebel had shown up to see us off. Streamers hung from Slippy's wings, along with shining cutout letters spelling GOOD LUCK, SELECT!

On the fuselage, next to Nirvana's portrait of Fiddle, was another one of Brother Dimitrios. I wasn't sure how I felt about that, but I guess fair is fair.

As we staggered out of the Jeep, Torquin turned toward us, sheepish looking and even more red faced than usual. "They hate me. . . ."

"Turn around, please!" Aliyah barked, emerging from the crowd and walking directly for Torquin. "I would like a word with—"

But as Torquin slowly shuffled around to face her, his face beet red, his shoulders slumped, and his brow scrunched up like a field of just-planted corn, she spat out a laugh.

Her guard's shoulders began to vibrate up and down as they struggled to contain their merriment. A couple of rebels let out a giggle, and then Nirvana blatted out a "HAAAA!" that made every person completely lose it.

They were surrounding us now, and I realized that they were even more excited than we were. Finding the last Loculus would fulfill the dreams of both organizations.

Standing maybe ten feet away was Mom. I couldn't

jump into her arms, but she was mouthing "I love you," which felt just as good.

I knew we had a long way to go. I knew that even if we were successful in Alexandria, we still had our most impossible task ahead of us.

But, boy, could I feel the love. And I let out a whoop at the top of my lungs.

* * *

A few hours later, as we swooped, jerked, and spun over the Mediterranean, the love was pretty much out the window—along with my stomach.

"I've got my mouth pointed toward the back of your head, Tork," Marco said. "Keep flying like that and you get the shampoo of a lifetime."

"Doing best I can," Torquin said. "Promise."

As bad as Torquin's driving is, his piloting is like riding a roller coaster rejected by Six Flags. He jammed the throttle back, and the jet began a nosedive. Both Eloise and Cass started screaming. I don't need to tell you what happened to Marco. Suffice it to say Torquin managed to radio ahead for someone to meet us on the tarmac with a hose.

Our landing wasn't a pretty sight.

Afterward we freshened up in the restrooms and then waited at the terminal arrival gate for Torquin. Cass was staring at his tablet, madly doing research. "Okay, the island of Pharos, where the Lighthouse stood? It isn't an island anymore," he said. "In ancient times they carted out some rocks and dirt and connected the island to the mainland. The strip of land is called a mole. Do you know how long the mole was?"

"Is this necessary information?" Eloise said. "Because I could use some quiet right now. And maybe ice cream."

"Back then, instead of miles they measured land by the length of a stadium—which was six or seven hundred feet, give or take," Cass said, his eyes brightening. "The land connector to Pharos was a *heptastadion*—seven stadiums!"

"Massarym was all about those sevens!" Marco punched a fist into the air. "Proves we're on the right track. He must have been there."

"Turns out, the Lighthouse lasted a long time," Cass said. "Like, nearly two thousand years, until an earthquake nuked it. Some of the stones were used to build a fort on the site. It's still there, and it's called the Qaitbay Citadel."

Torquin came lumbering toward us from the restroom. "I rent car now."

"No!" Eloise shouted.

Cass immediately ran to the curb, where a cabdriver was standing idly by a beat-up old taxi. "You need cab?" the driver called out, yanking his door open. "Of course you do!"

We all climbed in before Torquin could say a word.

* * *

It was a tight taxi ride through Alexandria, with Torquin hogging the front passenger seat and Cass, Eloise, Marco, and me squeezed into the back. The driver led us down streets of squat, whitewashed buildings. Most of the women wore head coverings and long dresses, everyone walked in sandals, and the smell of the sea got stronger the farther we got from the airport.

The cabdriver spoke fluent English, and he wouldn't stop. "First time? Of course it is! You from New York? London? Ha!"

"Actually, we're not," Marco said.

"Of course you're not!" the driver said. "Those big American cities, European cities? Brand-new. Paint is not even dry on these cities!"

"But we don't live in any big American or European—" Cass began.

"Here, we are founded by Alexander the Great!" the cabdriver barreled on, ignoring Cass. "Of course we are! Because is why we are called *Alexandria*, you see? More than three hundred years B.C.! We had largest library in the world—five hundred thousand volumes! You think New York Public Library had that in ancient times? You think Library of Congress or Harvard?"

"Of course they didn't!" Eloise said.

"Smart girl!" the cabdriver said. "Alexandria greatest center of learning in history. I take you there now?"

"To a *library*?" Marco said. "Shoot me first."

"I like libraries," Eloise piped up.

"Of course you do!" the cabdriver said, swerving to the right across two lanes of traffic. "We go!"

"No!" Torquin, Marco, Eloise, Cass, and I all shouted at once.

"To the Lighthouse," I said. "I mean, the Qaitbay Citadel."

* * *

We got there at the height of the sun. The taxi's air-conditioning couldn't quite crank up high enough to make up for the heat-generating machine known as Torquin, so we were already sweaty by the time we got out.

The sea breeze helped. Seagulls cawed and swooped down toward food left by a group of kids on a railing. I could hear a buoy clanging out to sea. Qaitbay Citadel was a massive stone castle at the end of the long arcade lined with cannons. The castle's roof was crenellated along all four sides, with a great turret on each corner. Arched windows like two giant eyes gazed at us from above the entrance as we walked the length of the arcade, past tourist families posing for selfies. "You feeling the Song of the Heptakiklos yet?" Marco said. "Like Brother Cass said, some of the castle stones are from the Lighthouse."

I shook my head. Not even a hint.

Off to the left, a dark-haired woman in a head scarf

clapped her hands and then spoke into a megaphone: "Three minutes to the start of the English-speaking tour, ladies and gentlemen! We will be discussing the history of the Qaitbay Citadel from its days as the famous Wonder of the World, the Lighthouse of Alexandria!"

I was so busy listening for the Song that I barely noticed. "Come on," Cass said. "We might learn something."

"If I knew we were going to a lecture, I'd have brought my sleeping bag," Marco said.

"Can't we just go into the citadel now?" Eloise asked.

"So, I suppose you are the only customers this afternoon," the woman said, now walking toward us with a huge smile.

"Customers?" Marco said, his eyes widening in panic. "We're—"

"Eloise," Eloise said, extending her hand. "And this is my brother, Cass. And my friends Jack, Marco, and—where's Torquin?"

I looked around, but he was gone. "Restroom, I guess."

"Good idea!" Marco said.

"My name is Sima," the woman said. "Come. These tours are better when they're small. More intimate, no?"

As she began leading us toward the castle, Marco pantomimed a big, theatrical yawn.

"Too late for us to join?" a voice piped up from behind us.

232

I turned to see a group of tourists heading our way from a chartered van. There were about ten of them, about half men and half women, each wearing baseball caps and colorful T-shirts. All their arms were covered with tattoos, and most of the guys had beards.

The first guy to reach us must have been in his late twenties. His beard was thick and dark brown, and he wore narrow, black-rimmed glasses. "Americans?" he said.

"Yup," I answered.

But my eyes were fixed on his shirt, which showed a print of the Lighthouse of Alexandria. As his friends ran up next to him, I couldn't help staring at their shirts, too. And their tattoos. I saw a great statue astride a harbor . . . a tremendous structure flowing with plants and flowers . . . a magnificent lighthouse . . . "The Seven Wonders," I said.

"Can you recite them all?" he said.

"Yes," I replied. As I reeled them off, he looked surprised, but not as surprised as I felt right then.

His baseball cap—all their caps—were emblazoned with an unmistakable familiar symbol.

"Who the heck are you?" Marco asked.

"Actually, I'm Cooper, from Bushwick—that's Brooklyn," the guy said, spinning around to show the back of his T-shirt, which said SEESAW. "And that acronym, in case you were mad curious—which of course you are—stands for Society for the Earthly Edification of the Seven Ancient Wonders. You've heard of us?"

"No," Eloise said.

"The . . . upside-down *V*," Cass said, "on your hats. What does that mean?"

At once, all of them held their hands out, fingers pointed down in a lambda shape. Scissoring the fingers open and closed, they cried out in unison, "Ka-ku, ka-ku."

Then they cracked up, nodding toward one another with great satisfaction.

I felt like I was being flung to the outer reaches of the nerd universe.

"Please tell me I'm dreaming," Marco mumbled.

"That's our sign," Cooper said. "It went over really big at Comic Con. The inverted V was discovered by the Alexandrian archaeological diver who founded our group. We think we have a pretty good idea it relates to the actual origin of the Seven Wonders of the World!"

Now I was listening. "You do?"

One of the group members, a girl with purple hair and three nose studs, pointed straight upward. "There," she said with a grin.

We all looked up, into a clear sky with fluffy clouds. "Where?" Eloise replied.

The entire group burst out laughing again. "I know, I know, you think we're weird," Cooper said. "Okay, we're on a pilgrimage to all the sites. To show that the Seven Wonders are the proof of . . . wait for it . . ."

"We're waiting," Marco drawled.

". . . Extraterrestrial life!" Cooper said.

"Extraterrest— whoa, you guys think the Seven Wonders came from outer space?" Marco said.

"Ka-ku, ka-ku," Cooper said. "Just kidding. But, yes. Seven other planets . . . seven wonders. Coincidence?"

"I don't think so," said the girl, who shared a high five with Cooper.

"According to the carvings discovered by our founder, each Wonder contained a magical sphere," Cooper went on. "These, we're pretty sure, were made of cosmic matter . . . wait for it again . . . from each of the other planets of the solar system! Seven planets, am I right?"

"Did the Greeks even know there were seven planets?" Cass asked.

"Not according to history, smart guy," Cooper said, "but we're sure some of the mystics knew. We just haven't found the docs yet."

Now the guide was calling out to us, looking at her watch. "Erm, I believe we shall begin the tour!"

"Sooo psyched!" said Cooper. "Hey, we have open

membership. Our meetings are fun, and we have chapters all over the place. Here's our contact info. Farouk, our founder? Awesome. Lives in Alexandria, dives for shipwrecks. Coolest way to make a living, ever."

He reached into his pocket and pulled out a business card:

SEESAW
1-800-555-WONDERS
Brooklyn * Los Angeles * Toledo * The Cosmos
Founder: Farouk Assad

The Seesaw members were already following Sima toward the citadel entrance. "Think about it," Cooper said, turning to follow.

"Ka-ku, ka-ku," I said.

CHAPTER THIRTY-ONE

CRAZY FAROUK

"FAROUK NOT THERE," Torquin said, shoving his phone back in his pocket.

"Bummer," Marco said.

We had found a cab just outside the citadel and now were riding down the so-called mole, the land connector back to town.

"Two . . . three . . . four . . ." Cass was counting.

"What are you doing?" Eloise asked.

"Measuring out stadiums," Cass replied. "I'm curious how long a *heptastadion* is."

"About three-quarter mile," said the cabdriver.

"I still think we should have taken the tour," I said. "We would have learned something."

"We're not here to *learn*," Marco said, as if *learn* were a synonym for *have our fingernails pulled out*. "Well, we are. But not to learn about castles and museums. This guy Farouk dives for wreckage, right? He's probably found stuff we can use!"

"If we have to go to Mars, will Torquin have to drive the spaceship?" Eloise said.

"The Seven Wonders did not come from outer space!" Cass said. "Those guys were a couple of sandwiches short of a picnic. I mean, come on—'ka-ku, ka-ku'? Have you ever heard of anything so ridiculous?"

"Never," Marco drawled. "Because the Loculi of Flight and Invisibility and Strength and Healing and Language and Teleportation are so reality based."

"Hah!" Torquin rumbled. "Tushy."

"I think you mean *touché*," I said.

The taxi went left at the main harbor road, which led along the Mediterranean. I checked the card Cooper had given me. On the back he'd written Farouk's local address.

Soon we were winding through the streets in an industrial part of town, outside the tourist area. There, the road was pocked with holes and the buildings were huddled close together. Cats watched lazily from doorsteps, and every few feet a different spicy smell would waft into the cab windows. Seeing us, a group of kids gave chase, shouting in Arabic until the driver sped up. As he wound through ever-narrower alleyways, the smell of fish became overpowering.

Finally he pulled up to a small dock, where the crew of a sturdy boat was hauling in a net full of squirming, silvery fish. As we got out of the cab, they'd begun dumping their haul into big buckets. Some of the fish spilled over the bucket sides and slid along the decks, where a big, burly dockworker caught them and tossed the escapees in with the others.

"Farouk?" Torquin called out.

Three men looked up.

"Guess it's common name," Marco murmured. "Dudes! 'Sup! Anybody here speak English?"

"How can I help you?" the big dockworker said, turning our way. He had a massive chest that seemed to be in competition with his belly, and a beard so thick you could imagine small animals hiding inside. "I am Naseem."

He stuck out his right palm, which was enormous and covered with calluses. Fortunately Torquin stepped forward to shake it, and I escaped having my hand crushed. "Looking for Farouk Assad," Torquin said.

"Ohhh, *Crazy* Farouk you want!" With a big smile, Naseem shouted in Arabic to the fishermen, who all laughed and went back to their catch. "Crazy Farouk shows up sometimes . . . sometimes no. Are you people . . . ?" He twirled a finger in a circle around his ear, rolled his eyes, and made a "cuckoo" whistling noise.

None of this was giving me hope.

"No," Torquin said.

Naseem looked at his watch. "My son and daughter run the bakery, up the street. It is Wednesday. Right now they are taking the last loaves of rosemary bread out of the oven. You like rosemary bread?"

"I don't know her," Cass said.

"Well, Crazy Farouk does!" Naseem said. "Where is rosemary bread, there is Crazy Farouk."

We thanked him and walked the short distance to the Citadel Bakery, which sat next to a weed-strewn lot. As we neared the building, the stink of fish soon gave way to the warm, yeasty smell of bread. People were appearing from around dark corners, heading toward the shop. "Forget Farouk," Marco said. "I'm starving."

He began running. But as he got near, a thin young woman in a head scarf bustled out of the shop carrying a basket with a loaf of bread wrapped in paper. Wordlessly, she set the basket down on the dock, directly in front of Marco. Giving him a quick glance, she turned and went back in.

Marco's face exploded with a smile. "Whoa—thanks!" he said, kneeling down to take the basket. "When people see Marco the Magnificent, they can't help themselves."

"That's not yours!" Eloise said.

Marco took a deep sniff, then began unwrapping the paper. "So maybe this was an offering to the fishies? I don't think so. Dang, it smells good—"

A rock whistled toward Marco from the empty lot. "Whoa!" he said, stumbling backward onto the pavement.

We looked to our right. A woman, shrouded in gray scarves, stood next to a small structure made from branches and old patched sheets. "Hands off the bread," she said.

"Sorry!" Marco replied. "I was just smelling it. Awesome."

The woman had silvery hair pulled back tightly into a bun. Her skin was dark and leathery, as if she'd spent her entire life outdoors without sunscreen. As she strode across the junk-strewn lot, she fixed each of us with a sharp, green-eyed gaze. It wasn't until she was halfway across that I realized she was wearing flippers.

"Um, excuse me? Do you happen to know someone named Farouk Assad?" I asked.

Snatching up the basket with one hand, she ripped off a hunk of bread with the other. "I am Farouk Assad."

"Oh," Eloise said. "We thought Farouk was a man's name."

Farouk nodded. "That's one of the reasons they call me crazy. Also, the flippers. Eh. What do they know?"

With a shrug, she stuffed the bread into her mouth and held out the rest of the loaf toward us. "Rosemoof burr?"

she said, which I assumed was "rosemary bread?" with her mouth full.

Marco was the first to accept her offer, but Cass and Eloise gave me wary looks.

I was too hungry to resist. The bread was steamy, spicy, and warm. It tickled my nose as I ate it. We all sat on the edge of the thick wood rail that lined the harbor, dangling our feet over the water. "We met some of your group members at the citadel," I said.

"The Americans," she said. "They are strange."

"Ohhh yeah!" Cass said, laughing with relief. "They believe the Seven Wonders came from outer space! Haaa-ha-ha-ha—"

Farouk swallowed her bread. "They did."

Cass fell silent. My heart thumped. Torquin's face was turning pink and I could hear a few random squeaks coming from him, which meant that he was on the verge of laughter.

Ask a few questions, I told myself, *and if she's a total wacko, cut your losses and move on.* "We hear you are a diver, and we're searching for—"

"The Lighthouse of Alexandria, of course," she said. "And, like everyone else, you are looking in the wrong place."

"But . . . this *is* Alexandria," Cass said. "And we were just at the island of Pharos—or what *was* the island. That's where the Lighthouse used to be, right? So where else would we look?"

Farouk gave me a deep, appraising glance. Then she quickly stood. "I have work to do. Please feel free to finish the bread. It is my gift to you."

As she turned to go, I called out, "Wait! Does this mean anything to you?"

I was wearing a baseball cap, which I now took off, and then turned around, fluffing my hair to be sure she saw the Λ.

She cocked her head, then grabbed my hair with her fist and yanked hard. "Yeow!" I cried out.

"Hey!" Torquin said, reaching for her arm.

"It's real!" Cass said. "Not sprayed on or anything. We all have it!"

Farouk let go. "I left a very good job in banking to pursue my dream. To learn about the Seven Wonders of the World. I put all my money into diving and excavation and archaeological digs. I took a vow of simple living. It took years to find more believers, to form SEESAW. If you are here to mock me, to write about me in sarcastic terms—"

"We are descendants of the royal family of Atlantis!" I shouted. "We have been searching for the Seven Wonders ourselves. We think you may have some clues left by a prince named Massarym. Please. Work with us. We need to find the remains of the Lighthouse!"

"Massarym . . ." Farouk thought for a moment and then threw her head back. *"Atlantis?"* She burst out laughing, an obnoxious jackhammer-like sound that echoed up the alleyway.

"What's so funny?" Marco said.

"You're just as crazy as I am!" she retorted.

"Farouk, please," I said. "We're not here to mock SEE-SAW. But we've seen a lot. We've been in contact with some ancient scholars. And if we don't have your help, we'll die. All four of us were taken to a remote island. We are part of a mission to solve this ancient, deadly problem. We all have this gene called G7W—it causes the white lambda on the back of our heads. What it does is—"

Farouk abruptly held up her hand. "This gene . . . I would like you not to talk about it right now."

"But it means everything to us," I said. "It will—"

"Kill you. I know this." Farouk's face was darkening. From a tattered pocket she pulled a cell phone, tapped something out, and held it to us. The screen showed a faded image of a grinning, black-haired boy. "My son, also Farouk, had the mark."

Had. Past tense.

"I'm sorry," I said softly.

Farouk pocketed the phone. "We have different theories. But I know what is in store for you. And I would never forgive myself for denying you the chance to realize your quest."

She turned and began walking toward her ramshackle tent. "Are the relics . . . there?" Marco asked.

She laughed. "No, my boy. If you would like to see the remains of the Lighthouse, we must go by ship. I will get some equipment. It is a long journey. And I warn you, you may not like what you see."

"Wait. So the Lighthouse was taken from the island?" Eloise asked.

Farouk began crossing the street, her flippers slapping the pavement. "Not exactly," she said. "The island took the Lighthouse."

CHAPTER THIRTY-TWO

OUT OF THE OORT CLOUD

THE ALEXANDRIA HARBOR faded into the distance, then completely disappeared. As we motored farther into the Mediterranean, the water became a deep blue, almost purple. It was nice to see the crew on each fishing boat wave to Farouk as we approached.

It wasn't so nice to see them cracking up as soon as we passed.

"Massarym," she said, "was, I believe, a survivor from the Oort cloud."

"The *who*?" Marco said.

"The vast belt of shattered planets and space debris at the outer edges of the sun's gravitational reach," Farouk replied.

"Um . . ." Eloise said, looking at me nervously.

"Maybe you can tell us exactly what you discovered," I said carefully. "If Massarym left writings, wouldn't they be in a language you didn't understand?"

"I cannot decipher all of his writings," Farouk continued, "but there are similarities to Greek and Arabic and ancient Egyptian. After many years, I have figured out that he flew to these parts through the air—that much I'm sure of."

"You got that part right," Marco mumbled. *But he got there on a Loculus*, he didn't say.

"I also discerned that there was a large green vessel," Farouk continued. "From what I can make out, the vessel was called Mu'ankh."

"It . . . wasn't a vessel," Cass said.

"And it didn't come from outer space," Eloise added.

Farouk sighed. "I know, I know, most people cannot wrap their minds around something like this. *Crazy* is the word most often used. But I think it is crazy to assume that the Seven Wonders were built by coincidence—all around the same area, all with concepts in architecture far advanced for their time. Having studied other options, I can only conclude Massarym was from a civilization that simply does not exist on earth—"

"Atlantis does not exist now," I said. "But it did, trust me. Atlantis sank. Its language had elements of Greek,

Arabic, and ancient Egyptian. Massarym was an Atlantean prince. All of what you're describing can be explained by those things."

Farouk cut the throttle. She looked from Cass to Marco to Eloise to Torquin to me. "All right," she said. "I vowed I would be respectful. Do tell."

I took a deep breath. The fishing boats were far behind us. There was no sight of land, and she controlled the boat. I figured we were stuck together, like it or not.

"Well," I said, "it began with these two brothers. . . ."

*　*　*

By the time I finished telling the story, it felt like even my eyeballs were sunburned. Farouk had taken some fishy-smelling sheets out of her ship's hold, soaked them in water, and had us put them over our heads for coolness and protection. She hung on every word.

"Extraordinary," she said. "But I must say, it absolutely defies rational belief."

"Oort cloud is more rational?" Torquin said.

Farouk smiled and pulled out a cell phone from her pocket. "Have you been keeping up with the news?"

"Not really," I said.

"A giant found dashed on the rocks in a beach in Rhodes," she said. "Sightings of floating two-headed beings in the streets of New York City. A statue coming to life in a small Greek village. Eight-legged creatures flying through the air. The Sphinx of Egypt disappearing overnight."

"Wait," I said. "*The Sphinx?* Are you sure that wasn't just a rumor?"

"All corroborated on the internet!" Farouk said.

"Yeah, we know about some of those," Cass said. "But not the Sphinx. You can't believe everything you read on the web."

"Ah, you accept those bizarre occurrences, but you doubt my theories?" Farouk's eyes drifted out to the water, and she began to pull hard to the left on the tiller. The boat was puttering slowly now. "There," she said, pointing out to sea. "About seven kilometers out. *That* is where the island is— the one on which the Lighthouse was really built, that is."

Cass, Eloise, Marco, Torquin, and I bunched together at the railing. Or rather, Torquin grabbed the railing and the rest of us hung on and hoped the boat didn't tilt into the sea under his weight. "Which island?" Torquin asked. "See nothing but water, water, water."

"Exactly," Farouk replied. "It is submerged."

"So . . . you're saying the Lighthouse wasn't built on Pharos?" Cass asked. "And the ruins are out there some- where?"

Farouk nodded. "You see, long before the Lighthouse was built, the island you visited was a treacherous place. For centuries ships were pulled to its rocky shoals by the cur- rents and the trade winds. Leaders believed the land itself was accursed. Torches were set up on the island to warn the ships, but the great winds made a mockery of this. Alexandrian engineers wanted to build a structure, atop which would sit a mighty torch protected from the elements. But no one could conceive of a way to do this that would not be destroyed by nature. The technology to do this was too advanced for the time. Until one visitor arrived. A visitor who could not conceivably have come from this planet."

"I'm guessing you mean old Massarym-o," Marco said.

Farouk nodded. "Dressed unlike anyone in Egypt. Speaking a strange tongue. The technology he brought was so beyond the engineers' capability, so sophisticated, that they thought him a god. Massarym saw that the harbor would be safer if the Lighthouse were farther out—on *another* island. By placing it just a few meters farther out, the water would be deeper, safer. The ships would be diverted long before they even caught the strong current. 'Another island? But there is none!' the wise men noted. I am certain women noted this, too, but in these stories it is always men. . . ."

"I hear you, sister," Eloise said with a sigh.

"Massarym said he would conjure an island himself," Farouk went on. "A movable island."

"Seriously? Like a gigantic float?" Marco said.

Farouk smiled. "With enough mass to support a lighthouse the size of a forty-story building! Well, he said he needed time for this. He left plans for the architects to build the Lighthouse while he traveled to gather the necessary magic. Many doubted Massarym, but he assured them that he would leave a powerful protective talisman of great magic inside the Lighthouse. Well, the workers created a base massive enough to support such a structure. And as they were building up the walls of the Lighthouse, Massarym returned. Imagine the astonishment as the people woke up one day to see in the harbor exactly what he had promised—another island! Eventually the Lighthouse base was rolled on massive logs to its new home. This new island was given the Greek word for lighthouse—*Pharos*. Most of the time this new island stayed close, so it seemed like an extension of the bigger island. During storms it traveled. Before long both islands were known by this name."

"So why is this movable island all way out to sea now, stuck here at the bottom?" I asked.

Farouk shrugged. "There is much we do not know. We can only assume Massarym was trying to impress the people of Egypt. This would make sense. World domination by aliens is not an easy sell to humans. And clearly, he failed. I believe his people could not survive our atmosphere. The drifting of Massarym's island, its sinking—these happened long after he died. Perhaps they were the result of the powerful earthquakes."

I didn't want to argue about the alien stuff. But the rest of the story made a crazy kind of sense. I guess if Massarym could travel through Europe on Loculus Air Express, wrangle the Loch Ness monster, put a curse on his own dad, and create most of the Seven Wonders of the Ancient World, it stood to reason he could create a movable island. He wanted to create a home for the Loculus, and allow it to be protected by Mu'ankh. If anyone tried to steal the orb, the island itself would come to life.

"The thing is," Marco said, "creating a whole island? That's a huge deal. And Alexandria had this crazy library, right? So the place must have been crawling with writers. Wouldn't someone would have written this down? Why don't we know about it?"

"Maybe because the last part of Karai's scrolls was burned in bat guano?" Cass said.

Farouk nodded. "And, of course, the Library of Alexandria was burned three times. Countless records were lost. This is why the writings we found were so valuable."

"How do we get to the island?" I looked out to sea but still saw nothing but water.

"You don't," Farouk replied. "I will not allow it."

"We have to," Cass insisted. "That's why we're here."

"There are plenty of relics strewn about for miles around," Farouk said.

"Farouk, that magical talisman you spoke about—the thing that Massarym promised the people of Alexandria?" I said. "*That's* what we need."

"After what happened three years ago, I have restricted my explorations to a maximum of a half kilometer from the site—about a third of a mile," Farouk said. "And that is what I will permit you to do. I am used to crews of up to six people, so there is enough diving equipment. But I must insist—my boat, my rules."

"What happened three years ago?" Marco asked.

"Four divers went down to the site," Farouk said. "When they came back up, they were in pieces."

CHAPTER THIRTY-THREE

ROCK CYCLONE

I HAVE BEEN grateful for Torquin's size many times since arriving at the island. Unfortunately, this day was not one of them.

When we already out to sea, Farouk discovered that she didn't have scuba gear that was big enough for No-Longer-Red Beard. Which meant that during the dive, he would be the one staying on the boat. Which also meant Farouk would be going with us.

I was hoping it would just be us and Torquin on the dive. If there was any chance we could sneak away from Farouk's safety zone and actually explore the submerged island, those plans would be much easier with Torquin on our side. "Remember, all of you," Farouk said, helping

Eloise with her wet suit, "you descend very slowly, and you rise even more slowly."

"H-h-how slowly is slowly?" Cass asked. "Do we have a speedometer?"

I elbowed him, and he gave me a sharp look, mouthing the words "I'm a terrible swimmer, you know that!"

"Diving is easier than swimming," I whispered to him. "Besides, you took the KI training course, right?"

We all had. For me, it had been sandwiched between learning to be a chef and a mechanic. I was terrible at both. And I barely remembered the diving rules.

But Farouk's nagging brought it all back.

"If you need to, you can jettison your belt in an emergency," she continued. "It contains lead weights, and dropping it will help you rise. But you must be careful. At the high pressure deep underwater, your body collects excess nitrogen. If you rise too fast, that nitrogen will get into your blood system and your joints, which causes decompression sickness."

Marco nodded. "Otherwise known as the bends."

"Exactly," Farouk said. "You must check your depth and pressure gauges regularly. And don't forget, you have an alternate air source, and it's called the . . . ?"

"Octopus," I answered as I adjusted my mask, snorkel, air tank, fins, buoyancy vest, and the little emergency-air knob.

"Ready!" Eloise shouted, stepping up to the railing. "I call first!"

Farouk looked very reluctant. "You know, it is highly irregular to let a nine-year-old do this."

"I trained her," Marco said. "Long story. She's little, but she's a fish. If she does anything wrong, I'll reel her in."

Eloise kicked him with her flipper. "All right then," Farouk called out, looking at her watch. "Keep your eyes on me. I found Massarym's writings in an area safely far away from the sunken island, and I hope to find more with your help. Be careful not to go farther than that spot, for your own safety. And remember, the underwater currents can be strong, so stay close together. We will return in a half hour. You will not have enough oxygen for any more than that." She took off the watch and handed it to me. "This is waterproof. Rely on it."

"Roger," I said. As I slipped it on my wrist, I noticed the time—2:49. We would have to be back by 3:19.

"'Bye, Tork, don't be too jealous!" Marco said. *"Geron-imo!"*

He leaped over the side, sending up a wave of water that hit Torquin squarely in the face.

"Raaamphh," Torquin grumbled.

"That's not fair!" Eloise shouted, jumping in after Marco.

The tank and gear were weighing me down, and I was

already sweating. I rolled onto the railing of the boat and pitched myself over. In the water, I made sure to wet the inside of my mask, to prevent fogging up. Then I slipped it on. Cass finally let himself in last.

Farouk took the lead. We sank slowly, then began kicking out with our flippers, away from the boat. Marco pulled off a few somersaults and caught a fish in his bare hands, but that made Farouk stop cold, so he gave it up.

Show-off.

The sea was murky, but our masks contained headlamps. I had to hold my nose and breathe out, to equalize the pressure. I knew this could be dangerous. I looked over to Cass, Marco, and Eloise. I couldn't see their faces. Could we find signs of the Loculus far from the sunken island? If we didn't, how could we persuade Farouk to let us go there? I could hear my own breathing . . . *too fast* . . . a buzzing noise from inside my own ears . . .

Calm down, I told myself.

Before long I caught glimpse of the bottom of the sea. A couple of long, thick-bodied fish undulated lazily. A huge lump of sand came to life and swam away, which scared me until I realized it was just a squid.

Farouk had stopped moving and was pointing downward. I caught a flash of excitement in her eyes through her mask. Below us was a mound of oddly shaped debris. She was pointing to it excitedly. I guess she hadn't seen it before.

We all dived closer. In the center of the pile was a thick, broken, drumlike cylinder. Even covered with sea grunge, it was obviously part of an ancient column. Farouk began pulling away some of the seaweed, trying to get to the surface. Marco planted his feet and lifted another piece of wreckage clear off the sea bottom, releasing a stingray. As Marco jumped away, his legs made the sand churn, and I saw a knife-shaped sliver rise into the muck, turning end over end. It caught the light of my headlamp. Somehow it had escaped being covered with barnacles and seaweed. It glowed back a golden color.

I swam toward it. The buzzing noise in my ears seemed to get louder. I tried to ignore that and concentrate on my breath. *In . . . out. In . . . out. Slow . . .*

The sliver sank, and right away the muck began swallowing it up greedily. Just before it disappeared, I grabbed a corner of it and pulled.

It was about a foot long, an almost perfect crescent-moon shape. I turned toward the other three, but they were huddled around the wreckage, their backs to me. I could feel myself drifting away from them and kicked hard to get back. *Be very careful of the underwater currents*, Farouk had said. *They can be strong.*

Finally I grabbed onto Marco and pulled myself into their huddle. Spread out before them on the seabed were now four objects, including the section of column. But it was a simple, cracked building stone that made my breath quicken.

I reached down and lifted it out of the sand. A lobster-like creature scurried away. This stone had to be part of the Lighthouse. Maybe when the island moved, it dropped pieces on the way. I looked over my shoulder to the place where we'd seen the dark blotch.

When I looked back, the others were at least fifteen feet away. I had drifted in some kind of current, moving fast. I angled my body back toward them and kicked hard, making sure to hold on to the crescent-shaped relic with one hand and the lambda stone with the other.

But no matter how hard I tried, the others were growing smaller and smaller. Why weren't *they* caught in this current?

I turned to look over my shoulder. The water on the sea floor seemed to be darkening.

No. Only a section of it. It seemed to be growing larger, a thick oval shape that sat on the ocean floor. Somehow, Massarym had managed to create a floating mass about the size of a baseball diamond that was now stuck down here. And the current was pulling me directly toward it.

I was gaining speed, and I noticed that I'd flipped around. My hands were extended forward, toward the sunken island. It wasn't the current bearing me along. Those grungy pieces of rock, the two relics—*they* were pulling me. Like magnets.

Four divers went down to the site, Farouk had said. *When they came back up, they were in pieces.* As the shadow moved closer, I wondered if those divers were pulled into the island, like I was, by some weird underwater riptide. Did they smash into some deadly sharp coral?

I tried to let go. I opened my fingers. But my palms were

pressed against the relics, jammed tight. I was moving fast enough that I could feel the water pushing against my air tanks, hard. The straps were straining against my shoulder. If they broke, I was dead in the water. Literally.

With every ounce of strength, I yanked my hands downward. They slid off the two relics. I braced myself for them to hit me in the face.

But the relics continued to jettison forward, into the light. And I began to slow down.

Light? My brain finally registered the strength of the eerie glow. Where had that come from? My headlamp wasn't strong enough to create the pulsating yellow-white blob directly ahead of me. I thrust hard with my flippers to spin away. I took a quick look over my shoulders, but the others were nowhere in sight.

The buzzing sound was deafening now. It felt like it was in my bloodstream. I knew that if you didn't adjust to the pressure, bubbles could form in your blood. You could die from the bends. Maybe that was what this noise was. I couldn't survive down here. None of us could.

But the light was mesmerizing. From all sides, schools of fish began swarming into it, like moths circling a flame. As I floated closer, I realized they didn't look like fish. No fins, no sleek shapes. They were pieces of rock, chunks of marble, twisted shards of metal, all gathering.

Despite the muffling of the water, the sound of their

collision was deep and bone shaking. I could hear the thump-thump-thump-thump of stones shooting into place, forming a shape. It was thick and square, rising upward in a spiraling swirl of debris. Some of the chunks were enormous. If one of one of them hit me, even underwater, I'd be toast.

I felt something grab me from behind, and I nearly jumped out of my wet suit. Turning around, I saw Marco's grinning face through his mask. Cass and Eloise were behind him, looking scared out of their wits.

I held on to his arm and Eloise's. Marco towed us farther away from the rock cyclone. When I turned back around, the column of light had risen to a tapered shape, its top obscured by the dark, murky water. Fewer stones were shooting toward it now, and the light intensified.

Slowly the brightness rose up from the base. As it climbed, it illuminated what looked to me like a soaring skyscraper with a grid of windows and marble sides.

The light finally emerged at the top, sending a beacon that blazed through a wide opening. I've seen Empire State Building and it was awesome, but this staggered me. I had to force each intake of breath. Triumphant music blasted like some weird underwater orchestra of crabs and bottom feeders.

It took me a moment to realize it was the Song of the Heptakiklos.

Just below the beacon of light was the stone I had lifted up from the sand.

CHAPTER THIRTY-FOUR

TO THE LIGHTHOUSE

"WHERE IS FAROUK?" I mouthed to Cass.

He shrugged. "I don't know."

I looked back into the murk. Farouk had warned us about getting close to the sunken island. She was probably too afraid to follow us. Or too smart. Were we in danger? Had we gone too deep too quickly?

I wanted her to see this. Someday, I wanted the whole world to know about the Seven Wonders and why they existed. I looked at the watch Farouk gave me—3:01. We had eighteen minutes.

"We should go back," Eloise mouthed.

Cass didn't say a thing, but the look on his face was definitely *Are you nuts?*

I began swimming toward the Lighthouse. The light that we'd followed had floated to the top, and the base of the thing was a lot darker. Still, I could make out the shape. The base was a superwide structure about the size of a city block and maybe four stories tall. The tower's tall shaft rested on top of it.

I headed for an arched doorway in the base's center. If the Loculus was inside, we had to start somewhere. The others followed. I waited at the door, floating.

My watch read 3:03. Sixteen minutes.

Marco pressed down on the door's latch and pushed it open. A small school of fish swarmed upward around our masks as if we'd interrupted class. Cautiously we swam in.

The Song of the Heptakiklos was loud and clear. I expected to see a Loculus any moment, but the room was pitch-dark. The Lighthouse's beam was high overhead, at the top of the shaft—but down here in the base, the ceiling was thick, blocking all light. As we swung our headlamps around, we could see rows and rows of stout columns, once straight but now thickened and warped by crusts of barnacles and coral. They seemed to move and dance in the crisscrossing beams, like awkward old men, and I made sure to avoid them as I trained my lamp on the floor.

I saw a sharklike fish, lazily flapping its tail. A gigantic crab. A couple of gallon plastic jugs. A splayed-out creature that was either a drowned pig or a dropped kid's toy.

No Loculus.

We met at the other end. Eloise gave me a shrug. *See anything?*

I shook my head.

Cass pointed to his ear. Hearing the Song of the Heptakiklos?

I nodded. I was hearing it all right. And, believe me, when it's jangling and twanging away at your nerves and bloodstream, while you're in a wet suit, that's not a whole barrel of fun.

Marco pointed up. We would search this thing top to bottom.

Together we swam out of the base and back out into the sea. I still hoped to see Farouk, but she wasn't there. With a powerful thrust of his flippers, Marco quickly rose above the thick base and swam upward toward the tapering Lighthouse shaft.

Higher up, the glow of the beacon cast the building in a dull amber green. The sides just above the base were octagonal and pocked with windows like an office building. But as we squirmed through a door at the base of the section, I could see that there were no offices inside, no floors. Just a huge, spiral staircase flanked by stone buttresses connecting it to the wall.

As we got closer to the top, the sides slanted inward. The octagonal shape gave way to rounded walls tapering to maybe ten feet in diameter. At the top we could see a hatchway leading up into the chamber that contained the great light.

Marco and I both swam up carefully through the hatch, which was way over to one side of the circular floor. We peered inside the top chamber to see a steep pedestal supporting a giant rotating ball of light. The ball made a low moaning sound as it turned, and it was too bright to look at it directly.

Cass and Eloise were in now, too, and she was pointing upward. "Loculus?" she mouthed.

"Too big," I mouthed back.

Besides, the Song of the Heptakiklos was weaker up here, not stronger. With frustration, I realized we must have missed something at the base. I pointed downward through the hatch. *Let's go back.*

I looked at my watch—3:12. Seven minutes left. My air gauge was low, and I hoped Farouk had left us a little margin of safety in case we got stuck.

I led the way this time, spiraling down the stairwell. Sure enough, the Song was growing stronger now.

Obey the Song. Follow it.

I could feel it leading me down into the base, until I found myself nose to the floor. It was then I knew that the Song was pulling me lower.

The Loculus was not in the Lighthouse shaft or the

base. It was in the island itself. Had to be.

I turned and waited for Cass, Eloise, and Marco, then pointed downward. "Inside the island," I mouthed. They all looked at me as if I'd gone completely bonkers.

Which was pretty much how I felt.

I swam out the latched door. With a strong kick, I propelled myself along the surface of the island. The Song of the Heptakiklos was raging, but I couldn't tell if it was getting louder. Like the rest of the sea bottom, the island was covered with muck and shells and slimy waving tubes. But the surface itself was so much darker than the rest of the sea bottom. What was this island made of? And how had Massarym been able to move it?

I swam down to the surface of the small island, planted my feet, and started to clear away sea growth. As I pulled up some slimy grass fronds, sand sprayed upward. But under that sand was a rock-hard smoothness, way too hard for me to dig through without tools. Whatever material the island was made of, it seemed to be tinted green—maybe from algae, or maybe Massarym had figured out some space-age material, an industrial-grade structure that could support a Wonder of the World.

Whatever it was, the Loculus seemed to be inside it, and we needed to find a hatch, or a way to dig.

I reached down and rubbed my gloved hand along the island surface. I tried to pry away some of the barnacles, but they were stuck tight. Marco joined me. He took out his knife and began hacking away at the barnacles, trying to see what was underneath.

With a mighty, Marcoish thrust, he managed to bury the blade into the surface.

The ground below us heaved violently. Marco and I were flung upward into the sea. I could see him mouth "Earthquake!"

Bad timing. What were scuba divers supposed to do during an earthquake? No one had taught us that.

Eloise and Cass had swum away from Marco and me, investigating the sunken sides of the island. They must have noticed it, too, because I could see the whites of their eyes as we swam toward them.

But instead of coming to meet us, they veered away, as if we'd just farted.

I could tell Cass was trying to say something. He and Eloise were both pointing to something behind us.

Marco and I turned. The island's side, now rising through the water, showed two burning white spheres. For a moment I thought we'd somehow found two Loculi.

But Loculi didn't blink. And they didn't have beady black eyeballs. And they weren't set into a massive, dragon-like head.

I felt my legs kicking like crazy. But they weren't fast enough to get away from the giant, gaping mouth that thrust forward out of the green island and closed tight around me.

CHAPTER THIRTY-FIVE

IN THE BELLY OF THE BEAST

OF ALL THE ways a person could die, being digested by a prehistoric creature posing as an island had never crossed my mind.

I somersaulted helplessly into a massive gullet. My flippers hit the top of the creature's throat, making a gash that spurted yellow goop. Then they bounced off the sticky, toadstool-dotted tongue, which nearly sucked those flippers off my feet.

My poor fried brain was trying so hard to latch on to something normal. It was conjuring up images of the Walk on the Moon bouncy house in the Mortimer P. Reese Middle School Annual Kidz Frolic. But the rest of my nervous system was telling me I'd just made the transition from human being to fish food.

This could only be Nessie. The Kraken. Mu'ankh. Greenie. When Massarym went on his trip to "find a movable island," he brought back this escaped Atlantean beast to protect the Loculus.

And now we were inside it.

I raised my arms over my head to protect my headlamp. As I tumbled, I caught glimpses of Cass, Marco, and Eloise. Cass had lost one of his flippers to the Amazing Suck-o Tongue. I was veering downward now, toward the thing's throat, where it was getting narrower but no less gross. I finally stopped when I crashed into a wall.

Well, maybe not crashed. *Squelched* would be more like it. The wall was fleshy and gray, with a thick, lined seal running from top to bottom like a tightly shut curtain.

As the other three barreled into me, the curtain of flesh began to open, bowing outward from the center on both sides. Showtime.

I screamed inside my mask, even though I knew I was the only person who could hear me. We were passing through the opening, tumbling downward. If my knowledge of anatomy was correct, we had just entered the beast's esophagus.

We slid downward through a smooth, narrow tube that hugged us on both sides. I have never not wanted to be hugged so much in my life. The light from my headlamp was useless here; the creature's fluids made it nearly impossible to see out my mask.

Finally the tube ended, and I somersaulted downward into a cavernous chamber. I spun a couple of times and landed with a splat on a gelatinous floor—well, it would have been a splat if I could have heard it.

Marco and Eloise landed next to me, and a one-flippered Cass tumbled to a stop not too far away. Cass jumped up, holding his side. But even just standing up proved not to be too easy. The floor wasn't exactly flat—or steady. Cass teetered off-balance. As I wiped the slime off my mask, I could tell Cass was angry about something. He was also pointing downward, to where he'd landed.

An old television set, in pretty good condition, was sitting there, minding its own business, on the floor of . . .

The stomach.

That was where we were. It had to be.

I was feeling the Song of the Heptakiklos like crazy right now. I was afraid the beast had the Loculus in its clutches, maybe right underneath us. I was tempted to stab through with my knife, but I was pretty sure this thing would kill us if I tried. I shone my beam around. The chamber was about the size of my sixth-grade classroom, and not that much more attractively decorated. Not far from the TV was a hair dryer, a hardcover book, and a soggy Elmo doll—all just passing the time. I guess the beast just ate whatever it saw.

"What now?" Marco was mouthing.

I held my hands to my ears and mouthed back: "Song of the Heptakiklos." It wasn't an answer to his question, but at least he would know that we were close. For what it was worth.

Cass lifted the TV, a look of utter confusion on his face. The box was pretty well embedded. The stomach floor stretched up with it.

As Cass tried to tug the TV free, I heard a deep rumble. Without a chance to brace ourselves, we all pitched violently upward. My head bounced off the stomach ceiling, dislodging my headlamp. I dived for it, but the lamp changed course in midwater. Instead of falling downward it veered off, straight through the valve that went back up into Mu'ankh's throat.

Marco turned to me, and his lamp shone into my face. I pointed up to my own mask. *No light.*

This was getting worse by the minute.

Marco stayed by my side as we all floated back down to the stomach floor. Cass was pointing to the TV and shaking his head. "I will never do that again," he was mouthing. Which was wise. Irritating the beast that swallowed us wasn't exactly a good strategy.

But what was?

My watch said 3:18. In one minute we were going to run out of oxygen.

You are dead.

Dead. Dead. Dead. Dead.

No one will ever know what happened to you. Not Mom on the island. Not Dad in Greece. Not Aly in Atlantis. No good-byes. Nothing.

My brain had decided not to be an optimist at this time. I tried to shut down the thoughts, or at least switch them to the great dilemma of How to Get Out of a Stomach. This was not something they taught you in biology. Stomachs were where things got digested. Digestion was the breakdown of food into components for your bloodstream, your respiration, and your excretion—the last part of which I did not want to think about. All of this, I knew, was accomplished by stomach acid.

Acid!

I looked around. My friends' lights were bouncing off the stomach walls. I could see the outlines of all kinds of debris down here, not just the TV but some fishing nets, a wooden lobster pot, a baby carriage.

Baby carriage?

All this stuff must have fallen off ships. But if the stomach was supposed to digest, why wasn't all this stuff eaten up by acid?

Why weren't we?

Cass was pointing frantically toward an area of the stomach wall above us. It was round and darker than the rest of the wall, with another closed valve running top to bottom.

I could feel my own stomach churn as I imagined where that led. Because after the stomach came the . . . well, the nasty stuff that I'm not supposed to talk about in polite company.

I did not want to end my life as nasty stuff.

Eloise was swimming around in a weird way now, with her left arm twisted around to her back so that her palm was raised upward. Her fingers were tight together, and I realized she was trying to imitate a fish with a dorsal fin. Which, I figured, was a shark.

I did believe at that moment that Eloise had lost her mind. Until I looked at Cass, who was mouthing a word that I took to be *China*. Maybe they'd both lost their minds. It was Williams-Mind-Losing Day. I swam closer and realized he wasn't saying *China* at all.

He was saying *Jonah*.

As in Jonah and the whale. As in, the character who may or may not have been swallowed by a beast who may or may not have been a whale but possibly instead a shark. And sharks were cool because they are one of the few survivors of prehistoric beasts. Scientists love them for their weirdnesses.

I tried to remember what those weirdnesses were. Eloise had told us.

Sharks use their stomachs for storage. Stuff can just stay in there, like forever. They can choose which items to digest—and digestion happens in the shark's gizzard.

Storage.

That's where we were. Whatever happened to old Jonah, we were in the belly of some kind of prehistoric beast. And I had a strong feeling we had more nutritional value than a TV. Which meant a possible Journey to the Gizzard. Which was where we would find our acid bath.

Now Cass was balling up his fists by his chin and tossing his fingers outward. At the same time he opened his mouth and stuck out his tongue. It took me a moment to realize he was pantomiming the act of puking.

Great.

I shook my head with a vigorous *no*! A mask full of barf would not be a helpful thing right now. But he kept doing it, adding a new motion—pointing upward, too.

Barf. Beast.

As I tried to figure that one out, Eloise swam by him, still "sharking."

Barf. Shark.

Well, if we were about to fry to death in a gizzard, why not end it all with a friendly game of charades? I was sweating like crazy, teetering between laughing my head off and crying like a baby. But Marco was swimming over to the TV. In my state of mind, I wouldn't have been surprised if he'd manage to pick up a vintage broadcast of *Sesame Street*.

Barf. Shark. Sesame Street.

Oh.

The roiling mess that was my mind finally began to snap to attention again. There was a connection, and I knew it. I tried to remember what else Eloise had said in the House of Wenders.

That stuff in the stomach? If it starts irritating them or whatever, they just go . . . bleeahhhh! They throw it up, right out of their mouth. Their stomach is like this giant rubber slingshot. It's the coolest thing ever.

I looked at Eloise. She caught my glance and smiled.

We could do this. I knew it. I had an idea, but it was certifiably crazy. Which had never stood in our way before.

I took another look at my watch—3:19. We were done. I prayed that Farouk had given us some extra air.

I swam to Marco as fast as I could, and I grabbed his arm. Underwater he was much easier to maneuver than on land. I forced him to swim with me, training his light around the chamber. The TV was a thick old thing like one my grandparents had, from the pre–flat screen days. So it had been here awhile, undigested.

I wanted to know what else was down here. I wanted to know everything.

As we gazed downward at the folds of the stomach floor, I let the Song of the Heptakiklos burrow deeply into me. It was getting way stronger.

There.

It was, at first glance, a bulging fold of flesh where the stomach floor met the stomach wall, like a gigantic pimple. But it was glowing.

As we neared it, my suspicion proved true—something *underneath* it was glowing. Something round.

Cass and Eloise were right behind us. I didn't bother looking at their faces. I needed to focus, because I could feel myself getting sleepy. My oxygen was running out.

The octopus. That was the name of the little emergency hand-sized knob. I grabbed for it, turned it, and took a deep breath. And another. I signaled for the others to do the same.

Then I reached for my knife. I held it tight against the beast's pimple, which was trapping our last Loculus.

With a deep thrust, I pierced the skin and sliced the pimple open.

CHAPTER THIRTY-SIX

A LESSON FROM JONAH

I FELT LIKE someone had thrown a can of thick yellow paint in my face. Knowing it was Mu'ankh blood was pretty disgusting, but I guess if it had been red it would have really topped out the sick-o-meter. At least Marco had the presence of mind to wipe off my mask, so I could see the path of my knife. Despite the thickness and gooeyness of the skin, I managed to pull the knife downward through the pimple that encased our Loculus. I had to hold tight, because the creature was clearly feeling this and not liking it one bit. Its body was moving, tilting one way and then the other.

When I had cut about halfway around the trapped orb, I felt the stomach lurch. Hard. I let go, hurtling backward. My knife went flying. It embedded itself in the stomach

279

wall above me, dangling from a gash that spurted more yellow blood.

Marco had hung on. With one hand, he hung on to the sliced flap of skin around the Loculus. With the other, he was coaxing the orb free.

Spinning around, he held aloft a glowing Loculus of luminous deep green. The Song of the Heptakiklos was ringing through every molecule in my body.

It had never sounded better.

"Yeee-HAH!" I screamed. My own voice was muffled inside the mask and no one else could hear me, but I didn't care. Cass and Eloise were swimming up beside Marco, flailing their limbs in an underwater celebratory dance. But the big guy was holding out the Loculus toward me.

He knew that this Loculus had the power to get us out of here. Its power was time travel. It could take us to a farm at the break of the Civil War, the hospital on the day I was born, a gladiator match in Ancient Rome, or a dinner with King Arthur and his knights at the Round Table. But it could also send us back to the time and place that started it all. To Atlantis on the brink of its own destruction.

And it could give us what we wanted—Aly.

The stomach wall was undulating wildly now. It looked like a battalion of gremlins were flinging themselves at it from the other side. Mu'ankh was feeling the cuts, big-time, and the cuts were only deepening with the movement.

Yellow Mu'ankh blood was coating the TV and the baby carriage, gumming up the whole stomach. Our wet suits were flecked with it. I snatched the Loculus from Marco's hands. I knew I needed direct contact, so I ripped off my gloves and let them float away. The water was much colder than I expected, but it was offset by the warmth of the Loculus itself as I held tight.

The think system.

The others had pulled off their gloves, too, and they were holding my wrists. I closed my eyes and thought of Aly. Her hair, dyed some crazy purple not found in nature, was pulled back straight like a ballet dancer's. She was tossing her head back, laughing. Making her laugh was a hard thing to do, and it always made me smile. I could feel my own face relaxing and my heartbeat quicken . . .

A deep, ominous *gggggglluuurrrmmmm* shook the water. I felt something snap upward from below me, throwing me off balance.

I opened my eyes. We were nowhere near Atlantis in the ancient past. We were still in the belly of the beast, and the beast had only gotten angrier.

My oxygen levels were near zero. Even the octopus was spent. What had I done wrong? The Loculus was supposed to respond to my thoughts. My thoughts were commands.

Maybe the command was too vague. *Atlantis in the ancient past* wasn't exactly specific. Maybe Loculi were like toddlers. They needed to be told exactly what to do. For now, I would pick a year, any year. Just to get us out of here.

July 4, 1999. Noon. 121 Elm Street, Belleville, Indiana. My bedroom. I don't know where that came from, but you couldn't get more specific than that.

But I opened my eyes to the same murk, the same rumbling chamber, the same scared friends in wet suits.

Year 1776. Signing of the Declaration of Independence.

Ditto.

Marco was glaring at me, palms upward. *What's happening?*

It wasn't working. I could feel Cass's fingers let go of my wrist. His body went slack, his eyes fluttering. Eloise had grabbed the back of his mask with one hand and was knocking on it with the other. Her mouth was saying "Stay awake."

Marco wrapped his arm around Cass's arm and managed to grab both Eloise and me. He kicked hard, trying to lift us all, trying to get to the opening at the top of the stomach.

I knew I needed to help him. His hands were full, and the least I could do was try to pry open the valve, so we could climb out through the beast's throat.

As we neared the valve, I realized there was a better way. I thought about Jonah. About that weird digestive system of prehistoric fish.

Irritation.

Forcible ejection.

Stomach functions like a giant rubber slingshot.

I broke loose from Marco and swam right up to the stomach wall. Holding tight to the defective Loculus with one hand, I plunged the knife into the beast's stomach again and again. The yellow goop was all over the place now, but I didn't care.

Feel this . . .

FEEL THIS . . .

I heard a pop in my ears, like the change in air pressure on a plane. Something was sucking me away from the stomach wall. Fast. It was all I could do to hold tight to the Loculus, which I did with both arms.

Cass, Eloise, and Marco were nowhere to be seen. All around me was blackness. I felt my body lurching wildly. I glanced at my oxygen gauge, which was at dead zero.

A moment later I felt my strap snap, and the gauge was gone. Along with the octopus. Along with my oxygen tank.

I tried to look for the others. My mask must have still held some air, because I was breathing. I was also shooting through the water like a cannon ball, unable to do a thing about it, clueless about where I was going. My flippers were yanked off my feet by the pressure.

Then, whatever held the mask on couldn't take the strain. It ripped clear off my face, and the water rushed in.

CHAPTER THIRTY-SEVEN
I AM NOBODY

AT FIRST I *think Aly has been caught in the rain. Her face glistens with wetness.*

But the sky is clear, the earth parched, and her eyes are clouded and sad.

I realize she is crying.

She has heard. She was hoping we would come, and now she knows we can't. She clutches the Loculus of Strength against her body, but it does not give her what she needs.

Now there is a knock at the door. The walls are thick, the windows barred. It is time, *a voice says.* The tumult has been put down. For now. The fields are clear and safe.

It is time to visit the Heptakiklos. To return the missing Loculus to its rightful place.

284

King Uhla'ar stands behind his queen. Here in Atlantis, home after his centuries of exile, he is a different man. Intelligent, reasonable. Aly's eyes focus on him, with frustration and disappointment. She has talked to him at length. Almost convinced him that Qalani's plan is doomed. That the past is the past and nothing can change it. That he must send her back through the rift.

But he cannot, or will not, stand his own against Qalani.

Aly looks my way.

I panic. Am I Massarym in this dream? Am I Karai?

I realize I am nobody.

I do not exist.

Aly rises. She holds the Loculus to her face. Following the Atlantean guards, she walks out the door.

CHAPTER THIRTY-EIGHT

FISH MOB

ALL THESE CENTURIES underwater hadn't done much for the Mu'ankh's teeth. My bare, flipperless feet banged against a fang with three gaping cavities, and it cracked clear off at the base.

The tooth shot out into the sea through the open mouth, and so did I. Cass, Marco, and Eloise were tumbling along with me. The beast had ejected us. *Like a slingshot.* I could feel the water's frigid coldness against my cheeks. The Loculus was still tight in my hands, but I had no flippers, no tank. . . .

No mask.

I stiffened with panic, nearly dropping the Loculus. No mask meant no air. How long had I been holding my breath? How much longer could I?

Why on earth wasn't I dead?

Cass, Eloise, and Marco were floating lifelessly in front of me. Their oxygen, like mine, had run out. I swam toward them. This seemed impossible. *How could I be functioning and not Marco?*

I could feel the Loculus moving and I looked down.

In . . . out . . .

I was holding it tight to my chest. *That's* what was moving. I was . . .

No. Impossible. I couldn't be breathing underwater.

But my mouth was shut. My nostrils were sealed. What on earth had just happened to me?

The Loculus.

I let go of it briefly, letting it float in front of me. Immediately my lungs seized up. I grabbed it again and my chest began to move.

I was getting oxygen, somehow. Like a fish.

This was not a Loculus of Time Travel. But it was the Loculus we needed.

I quickly pulled back the sleeves of my wetsuit so I could grip it with my bare elbows. With one hand I grabbed onto Marco's wrist, with the other, Eloise's. I tried to maneuver myself so I could secure Cass's wrist with outstretched fingers, but he was floating away and I wasn't coordinated enough.

I felt Marco jolt back to life. It took him all of two seconds to size up what had just happened. I nodded my head frantically toward Cass, and Marco managed to grab his hand, too.

Marco still had his flippers. He began kicking as hard as he could.

The Mu'ankh was writhing in the sea bottom, sending up a dark cloud of mud that slowly plumed its way up the Lighthouse, enveloping it bottom to top.

I saw the lambda stone crack and break off. A chunk of wall crumbled. The great lamp teetered twice, and then rolled through the opening of its chamber. After rising from ruins, the Lighthouse was breaking apart.

We raced to avoid being hit by the fiery sphere or swallowed up in the debris. Cass and Eloise were breathing now, and the kicking of eight legs was gaining us more speed. Finally we emerged through the cloud of debris and into clearer water.

As I looked down, the Lighthouse of Alexandria collapsed completely, into a mushroom of yellowish-gray foam.

I knew we were getting close to the surface. For one thing, the water was beginning to grow lighter. For another, I was no longer crazed with fear. I was thinking about the awesomeness of what had just happened. We had the seventh Loculus. We had found every single one—woo-hoo! But if I thought about that too much, I wanted to cry. Partly because one of the found Loculi had been lost again. But mostly because that made me think about Aly and the fact that we had failed to get her back. Whoever had told Herman Wenders about the powers of the Loculi, they'd sure gotten this one wrong.

I couldn't stop thinking about the Lighthouse and the Mu'ankh. Even though the beast had eaten us, I wished we'd managed to escape without killing it and destroying the Lighthouse. How cool would it have been to have a team dredge it up? People from all over the world would come to be amazed. As a bonus, their kids could drag their parents to a massive aquarium where, behind a thick Plexiglas wall, the great green beast would eject TV sets from its mouth on cue. We could call it the Mu'ankhseum. Or not.

Marco was exhibiting his happiness in more Marcoish ways, like letting go every few moments and doing loop-the-loops and dolphin imitations. Which always made us nervous, because whenever he stopped holding on to us, he had to hold his breath.

During one of his stunts, I had my eye on him so intently that I was only vaguely aware of a shadow passing over us. I heard the distant rumbling sound of its motor but didn't pay it much mind. But I did notice that Marco had stopped in the middle of a somersault. He was just hanging upside down, waving to us.

I had half a mind to veer away. Forcing him to follow us

would teach him a lesson not to show off. But I didn't have a chance even to try. Because something swept up from below us, forcing us off our course.

I looked down. A massive flash mob of fish and crustaceans was pressed against our feet. A fish mob. They were packed together, squirming against one another, and we were swept upward with them. Cass and Eloise struggled to hold on to my wrists. In a moment we had been pushed up against Marco.

He wasn't floating in the water upside down. His foot was caught in a net. A net big enough to catch all of us and about a gazillion fish. Marco reached down and freed his foot, lunging out with his hands to grab the Loculus. The choked expression on his face softened as he start to underwater breathe like the rest of us.

"Where are we going?" Eloise mouthed.

The only answer I could give was "Up."

We finally broke the surface into the hot sun. I had to squeeze my eyes shut against the brightness. We were being hauled up the side of a fishing boat in a net. Dying fish slapped at my face and body frantically. Cass, Marco, and Eloise had finally fallen away from the Loculus and were fighting with the silvery swarm, laughing and screaming at the same time.

I opened my mouth to breathe in my first breath of air, amazing air!

But nothing came in. I began to choke. I felt my face turning red. I looked up to the ship, where the entire crew had gathered to gawk at the humans in their catch. I heard Cass shouting for help. I tried to shout, too. But I could feel myself passing out.

"Let go!" Marco said.

I was frozen in fear, barely hearing him, sinking helplessly into the mass of fish.

"The Loculus!" Marco said. "Get your hands off it, Brother Jack!"

He was making his way toward me through the fish, part swimming, part crawling. I saw his fingers close over the Loculus—and the next moment it was flying up over the railing of the fishing boat to the utter bafflement of everyone on board.

"*Kaaaachhhh!*" A cough exploded from my mouth. I began gasping uncontrollably, taking huge, deep, gulping breaths. I felt like my throat was going to rupture and my lungs explode.

Marco held tight, coaxing me back. "It's all right . . . just breathe. . . ."

"What . . . happened?" I finally managed to croak out.

"Dude, you have to think like a fish," Marco said. "The Loculus gives you something they have. You can dance around forever underwater and get your oxygen just fine. But look at them now, right? By next week they're going to be breaded and formed into tasty little fish sticks. Because they can't breathe in the air. And when you're holding that Loculus, neither can you."

I thought about it a minute. I felt my lungs expand and contract. I took a deep whiff of fish.

It was the most beautiful smell I'd ever experienced.

For some reason, I burst out laughing. Seeing the goggle-eyed expressions on the faces of the fishing crew only made it worse. I began to howl uncontrollably, and that made Cass and Eloise crack up, too.

As we collapsed into giggles on the deck of the ship, Marco stood up and held out his hand to one of the crew men. "Dude!"

The guy's face was tanned a deep brown. He had a thick black-gray mustache and narrow blue-green eyes. "Dude?" he said, shaking Marco's hand. "So you are American. Tell me, why are you with my fish?"

That did it.

Cass, Eloise, and I were rolling on the floor, paralyzed with laughter.

"Well," Marco said, putting a hand on the guy's shoulder, "it's kind of a long story."

CHAPTER THIRTY-NINE

SEE CHOICE ONE

I **GUESS IN** the Egyptian fishing community, Crazy Farouk was a pretty familiar name. Because when Marco mentioned it, the entire crew shouted a knowing "Ahh-hhh . . . ," rolling their eyes to the sky. As if the mere mention of the name was enough to explain four kids with a shiny orb showing up in their net full of mackerel.

Whatever floats your boat, I guess.

The fishing vessel sped toward the shore. The breeze felt great in my hair, and it kept the fishy stench behind us. I kept the Loculus underneath me, pressed between my legs, taking care not to touch it with my skin.

Muhammad, the guy with the mustache, radioed someone who radioed Crazy Farouk. It turned out she had returned to her boat. When they reached her, she was crying and hung up on them three times. Finally Muhammad called a fourth time and shouted: "DON'T HANG UP JACK IS HERE I WILL PUT JACK ON THE LINE!" and he shoved the phone to me. "She is crazy," he muttered.

"Hey, Farouk?" I said.

After a moment of silence, I heard a flurry of Arabic words in rhythmic chant like a prayer. And then, "Oh, Jack—oh, I am so relieved to hear your voice! I thought you'd died. You all flew away from me. It was as if you were being summoned. Your friend Twerking was so upset with me."

"It's Torquin," I said. "Where is he?"

"He grew very agitated and insisted we come back to shore," Farouk said. "I will radio him. He will meet you at the dock. I will return, too, but it'll take a little while. I am halfway back out to the site. I was going to see if I could salvage—er, rescue you. Now, please, tell me what happened?"

I told her the truth—or, a version of it. I said we had found nearly the entire Lighthouse, but it was being guarded by a fearsome creature that ate people. I didn't give many details, but that didn't matter, because she filled them in herself.

"Yes!" she said. "Oh my dear. Oh wait till I tell SEE-SAW. This confirms the existence of Xinastra!"

"Who?" I said.

"A lizard creature from the star system Alpha Centauri, brought here on a comet in the fourth century B.C.!" she replied, as if it were the most obvious thing in the world.

I didn't disagree. She wished us luck in the future. I just thanked her and said good-bye.

For a long time, no one said anything. I think we were all still a little shell-shocked. Finally Eloise piped up, "So . . . how'd we get from 'Loculus of Time Travel' to 'Loculus of Breathing Underwater'?"

"I think we'd need the 'Loculus of Explaining the Misunderstanding of Words on a Parchment Despite the Use of the Loculus of Language' to find that out," Cass said.

"That one is in the Eighth Wonder of the World," Marco replied.

"We'll have to check those scrolls again when we get back," I said. But I wasn't really thinking about that. I knew we were all avoiding the bigger question. And someone was going to have to bring it up.

"Guys," I said, "you know, we were counting on this Loculus to take us to Aly."

Cass's shoulders slumped. "There goes my fizzy mood. Down the niard."

"What do we do now, O King of Future Kings?" Marco said.

"As I see it," I said, "we have two choices. Choice One:

295

pull out the sword, go into the rift, and hope it magically takes us back to where and when we need to go."

"And Choice Two?" Marco said.

"See Choice One," I replied.

We all leaned on the railing. In the distance we could see the marina. The people on the dock were all sticklike figures from here, except for one that looked like an animated tree with red and white leaves.

Torquin was waving to us.

We waved back. As the boat cut its speed and drifted toward the dock, we all stared straight ahead in total silence.

* * *

I can't see her.

All I can see is water.

The Dream isn't supposed to be like this. Am I too late? Has Atlantis sunk? I look for Aly. I am airborne and I'm not sure where to go. I scream out her name.

Aly . . .

ALY!

"Jack, wake up!"

My eyes sprang open, and the Dream dissipated into droplets of black. I was slumped in the plush leather of Slippy's passenger seat, my head jammed against the window. Cass was shaking me by the shirt.

I sat up straight, forcing myself awake. "Sorry!"

"You were calling Aly's name," he said.

I nodded. "Yeah. Wow. I was back in Atlantis. Or flying over it, I guess. But I couldn't find her. I couldn't find where I was supposed to land. Because the island was submerged already."

Cass's face turned about three shades whiter. He glanced over his shoulder. Marco and Eloise didn't look much better. They were staring at me like refugees from the underworld at Bo'gloo. "What's up?" I said. "You guys look like you just took your zombie pills."

I could tell we were descending. But unlike Torquin's usual habits, our angle wasn't totally nose down. We seemed to be on a gentle decline. "Not sure what to do," he muttered.

That didn't sound good.

Right now the bag that contained our new Loculus was strapped into the copilot's seat. We had picked it up in Alexandria, a thick, touristy shoulder bag that said MY PARENTS WENT TO QUITBAY CITADEL AND ALL I GOT WAS THIS LOUSY TOAT BAG. Mainly so we could carry the Loculus without touching it. And also because of the bad spelling.

I set it gently on the floor, sat in the seat, and looked through the copilot window. We were in the middle of a tropical downpour. Through the windshield wipers, I saw what looked like a lake surrounded by trees. "That is . . . airport," Torquin said quietly.

"Where?" I asked.

He trained a set of spotlights so I could see more clearly. A helicopter was floating on the lake. "Underwater," he said.

He banked the jet to the right. We flew over a set of roofs, arranged in an oval shape, all peeking up above a sea of water.

"No . . ." I said.

Below one roof was a set of columns, topped by a familiar marble carving:

HOUSE OF MASSA

CHAPTER FORTY

WHERE DEATH IS LIFE AND LIFE IS DEATH

"HAAAAANG ON, SLIPPY, Slippy hang on!" the voice sang over Torquin's console.

I knew exactly who it was. "Nirvana!" I shouted. "We're over the airport! What happened?"

"Hey, that must be Jack!" Nirvana said. "The reception sucks, but I know it's you because of the full sentences."

"Not funny," Torquin said. "Can't land."

"Yeah, well, we had a little seismic event while you were gone," Nirvana replied. "When last we saw you, we'd determined the island was . . . shall we say, unstable? Kind of like a dreidel when it loses speed—you just don't know which way it's going to fall? Okay, maybe that's not the best analogy, but suffice it to say the island has . . . tilted. In the other direction. I'd never been in a flood before. It's pretty scary."

My stomach knotted up. All I could think about was Mom. "Did anyone get hurt?"

"Not a soul, thank goodness," Nirvana replied. "But the *Enigma* is back underwater playing with its old fishy friends. *Way* underwater. So far underwater that the opposite side of the island has risen up like the White Cliffs of Dover."

"Who?" Torquin said.

"The Palisades?" Nirvana tried.

"Huh?" Torquin asked.

"They rose really high, okay?" Nirvana said with exasperation. "Tork, are you pilot enough to pull off a water landing?"

I could see the hairs of Torquin's beard angle upward. "Whoa, what's happening to your face, Torquin?" Eloise asked.

"He's smiling," I murmured.

"That's what I was afraid of," Cass replied.

With a loud "PAH!" Torquin yanked back the throttle and left our stomachs somewhere over the flooded compound.

* * *

The only thing worse than being on a plane with Torquin is being on a plane with Torquin during an emergency.

Well, there is one conceivably worse thing. You could

crash and die. But this comes close.

He lowered the pontoons with such force I thought they'd drop into the ocean. He landed so hard on the water it felt like solid rock. Despite the airtight compartments, seawater came seeping up to our ankles.

Swimming to a muddy shore and then scaling a steep wall of slime was pleasant in comparison.

At the top of the hill was a long, flat, treeless field of mud. The Karai rebels and the Massa had slapped together a small compound of tents and makeshift buildings of driftwood and tarps. Although the sun had just set and a steady rain fell, I still could see the outline of Mount Onyx looming in the distance. Being in the center of the island, it hadn't submerged. But its familiar cone now canted to the south.

"Thank you for getting everyone back safely, Torquin," was Aliyah's greeting. "That was a monumental feat."

"Would do it again any time," he said.

"Not with us," Cass murmured.

Eloise leaned over to me. "Did she just say Torquin had monumental feet?"

As we gathered inside the largest of the tents, a team of rebels served us hard crackers along with lukewarm tea. "We managed to salvage some provisions, electronic materials—and, naturally, all of Wenders's records," Aliyah said. "The rebels have been an enormous help, having survived in the wilderness for so long. There were no casualties, I am happy to report."

My eyes kept darting out the flap, hoping to see signs of Mom. "So . . . people like, um, Dr. Bones . . . Sister Nancy . . . ?" I asked, trying not to be too obvious.

"All fine," Aliyah said. "Scattered about on various recovery projects. But as you can see, we are running out of time. There is no telling what this island will do next. It is as if it has a life of its own. Now . . . please, tell us some good news." She looked greedily at my shoulder bag from Alexandria.

I felt my shoulders shaking. I was cold, and I took a sip of tea. Eloise started telling our story, with the rest of us chipping in until we covered everything. Torquin was quiet—even for him. The whole time he stared at Mount Onyx as if he were afraid it would fly away.

As I finished, with the account of how the new Loculus saved our lives, Aliyah's eyes drew together with confusion. "You mean the power of the Loculus is not time travel?" she asked. "How could you have gotten that wrong?"

"Did you bring back wrong Loculus?" Manolo grunted.

We'd hardly been back on the island a half hour, and already they were yelling at us.

"Uh, yeah, I'm really glad we're alive, too!" Cass said.

Aliyah's voice softened. "I'm sorry. Of course I'm glad you're all safe. This information throws me, though. If we are to manage the Loculi, we must not make mistakes."

I shook my head. "Something about the description. I must have read it wrong."

Aliyah snapped her fingers. In a moment, one of her goons had laid out the boxes with Wenders's notes, and next to them the Loculus of Language. I had marked the part where Wenders described the powers of the Loculi, so it didn't take long to find it. Cass, Marco, Eloise, and I leaned over it, touching the Loculus of Language. We stared at it intently, the silence broken only by the tapping of rain on the tent canvas.

The words appeared to me in Latin first. Then they began to change before my eyes. Most of them transformed instantly into their English meaning, bold and clear. Others were slower, their print soft and murky. I waited until I had something definite, and then read slowly: "'Forward is the thrust of growth/That makes us human, gives us breath/To travel back can now be done/Where death is life and life is death.'"

Manolo scratched his head. "Sounds like the time travel to me!"

"How do you do that so fast, Brother Jack?" Marco said. "The words are still forming for me. Some are supereasy. Like, *the*. But the rest . . ."

"Me, too," Cass said.

"Which ones are you stuck on?" I asked.

"Well," Cass replied, staring hard, "most of them are

303

there by now, but the place where you see 'growth'—I've got nothing definite yet."

Marco was frowning. "Weird. Something is forming for me, but it doesn't begin with *g*. I've got an *e* . . . *v* . . . *o* . . . *t* . . . ? What the heck?"

I blinked at the text. Marco's suggestion was making stuff happen on the page for me, too. My brain was scrambling the letters again. "Could that *t* be an *l*?" I asked.

"Yeah, maybe," Marco said.

The word was transforming before my eyes. "*Evol* . . . *ution* . . ." I said. "Whoa, okay, that makes sense. My first reading was *growth*. That's one of the possible definitions. But what Wenders meant was *evolution*. Maybe that changes the meaning?"

Aliyah's eyes lit up. "Wenders lived in a world that was being rocked by the publications of Charles Darwin. Everyone was talking about evolution. About how humans began as so-called lower life forms—single-celled organisms to amoebas to fish to amphibians to reptiles to mammals—"

"'Forward is the thrust of *evolution*'?" Eloise said. "That's what he meant?"

Cass nodded. "He's saying it makes us human and gives us breath. And evolution can only go forward, not back."

"And now, with this Loculus, we can 'travel back'—not through time but down the evolutionary cycle!" I said. "To some kind of amphibious state. Which made us able to breathe."

"So while using the Loculus in water we can breathe, but if we keep holding it out of the water we can't—just like fish," Eloise said excitedly. "And that's what he meant by 'where death is life and life is death!'"

"Bingo, Sister Eloise!" Marco said, slapping her a high five.

I heard the crackling sound of a rock slide in the distance. Torquin stood up abruptly and peered out the tent flap, his eyes trained on the weirdly tilted silhouette of Mount Onyx.

I felt my body moving from side to side, as if some ghost had decided to wiggle me with invisible hands. Through the open flap I could see the tide at the bottom of the cliff sweep out with a swift sucking sound and then crash to the shore, throwing Slippy into the mud like a toy.

Aliyah held tight to my arm until the motion stopped. After a moment of eerie silence, monkeys began screeching bloody murder from the jungle.

I left the tent and looked down over the cliff. The shore had shifted about the length of a football field.

No one had to say a word. But our eyes were all speaking volumes.

We had to act.

Now.

Before we were underwater permanently.

CHAPTER FORTY-ONE

WWDD

"NO," ALIYAH SAID. "And that is final. You will not be taking the Loculi from this island."

"Technically, they'll still be on the island," Marco said. "Just, like, thousands of years in the past."

Aliyah shook her head. "You didn't take them on your last journeys, and you were quite successful—"

"If we'd had the Loculus of Strength, we would have defeated the Zons so much easier," Cass said.

"If we'd had the Loculus of Teleportation, we could have gotten out of the Mu'ankh's belly in a much less disgusting way," Marco said.

"If we'd had the Loculus of Healing," I added, "Brother Dimitrios might still be alive."

Aliyah turned away. Her face darkened.

The tent flap opened, and three Karai rebels stepped in. One of them bowed to Aliyah and reported, "We've rerouted the fresh water lines, but Nirvana is still having trouble getting the electronics to work again."

The rain had stopped, the full moon was peeking through, and people were busy reorganizing the camp, repairing damage from the latest quake. The noise and the level of activity were distracting. I needed Aliyah's full attention to convince her that going into the rift without the Loculi would be crazy. I needed to talk to her alone.

I stepped toward her and put a hand on her arm. "Let's go outside and, um, take a walk," I said.

She gave me a funny look, but then she nodded. Slinging a pair of binoculars around her neck, she ducked through the flap with me.

Aliyah took my arm, and we walked a path parallel to the shore. After the last tremor, the sea had receded again. Now Slippy rested on mud about fifty feet up the slope. In the full moon's light, the jet glowed an eerie amber white that made the eyes of Brother Dimitrios's portrait seem to follow us.

"I miss him," she said. "He could be so dull and even coarse at times, but he was dedicated and trustworthy. And surprisingly wise. To me, at least."

"WWDD," I said.

"Excuse me?"

"What Would Dimitrios Do?" I said. "Listen, Ali-yah. Cass, Marco, and I—we're only thirteen. We've been through a lot, but we're still kids. So far we've been lucky. But for what we have to do now, we need help. Your help—"

"Are you gaming me?" Aliyah spun on me. "Jack, let me be blunt. Your chances of succeeding are wildly bad. You are entering what has always been a physical impossibility—a breach of time. How can I justify your taking six Loculi? What if you don't come back?"

"Exactly. If we don't come back, then what will you be left with?" I said. "Six Loculi, Aliyah. Tell me what you can do with only six of them. Six Loculi won't raise Atlantis. You'll be stuck on this island and what happens to your plans? To the memory of your brother? Is that what you want?"

Her eyes fell. She didn't say a word.

"Without the Loculi we're just normal kids jumping into that rift," I went on. "With the Loculi, we have power. Superabilities. We stand a chance of succeeding. Of return-ing with all seven. Which is the only thing that matters to you. And to us."

Nothing. No comment at all. How could she be so dense? "Come on, this is a no-brainer, Aliyah!" I blurted out.

Ugh. Nice job, McKinley. Way to be disrespectful to the

leader of the Massa.

Her face hardened. She looked away from me, inward to the island.

"I—I don't mean to be disrespectful," I said. "We can quietly fly over the jungle and avoid the beasts, then drop into the caldera—"

Aliyah shook her head. "No," she said quietly. "If you're going to do this, I would like us all to go to Mount Onyx together."

"Wait. Did you say—?"

"But for all our safety, you will take the Loculi with us through the jungle," Aliyah continued. "I will have Manolo get them. And the rebels will help protect us."

I grinned. "Common sense wins out—woo-hoo!"

"Not so fast," Aliyah said. "When we reach the caldera, I will make a decision as to whether you'll take them further. Meanwhile, please get some sleep. We will leave at first light."

"Thank you, Aliyah," I said, as she turned away. "And, hey, let's win this one for your little brother. Full steam ahead for Osman."

As she walked back to the tent, the wind lifted her hair on the tendrils of a gray-white mist. I thought I saw the glint of moisture on her cheek. "As you wish, my liege," she said with a smile.

* * *

My liege. She had called me that before. She always said it like it was a joke, but I knew it wasn't. Not really. It was a reminder. They didn't want me to forget I was the Destroyer, and the Destroyer would be king. But king of what? Some kind of New Order, after Atlantis was raised?

This made me nervous. It also made me think about something we'd never really figured out: What the heck were we going to do if we did finally get all the Loculi? Raise Atlantis, the way the Massa wanted, and risk destroying the world? Or destroy the Loculi, Karai-style, and give up any hope of surviving past our fourteenth birthdays?

The worst part was, we didn't have time to talk about it.

I thought about this all night. I tossed and turned when I was supposed to be sleeping. Finally I just got up and had a breakfast of stale crackers, rainwater, and some kind of foul-tasting jerky that only Torquin seemed to enjoy.

Now we were racing the sunrise.

As soon as we got up, a rebel named Felix, who had been Karai's "Director of Design, Electronics and Wardrobe," began fitting us with special dual-pouch vest packs. Each vest had two compartments and each compartment was big enough to contain one Loculus. A pack for each Select meant we could comfortably carry all six Loculi. Along each side Felix had added a quick-release tab, a rawhide cord that pulled down a huge zipper.

"It's too tight." Marco hunched his shoulders forward to

show how badly his new backpack fit.

Felix, eyed him skeptically. "I think it's slimming."

"Marco the Magnificently Slim," Cass said.

Marco struck a heroic pose. "I kind of like that."

"How'd you make these so fast?" Cass asked.

"I made them lo-o-ong ago, baby," Felix said with a laugh. "For when you guys would make a heroic return and join us in the revolution. Which isn't going to happen now. Lucky us. Anyway, you guys practice releasing those side tabs. I salvaged the zippers from Karai storage. They're industrial grade. The leather should be nearly indestructible. Drying and tanning those vizzeet skins was no easy task."

"These things are made of *vizzeets*?" Cass said.

Felix put his hands on his hips. "Well, they're not *alive. . . .*"

"I'm not going to ask about the jerky I just ate," I said.

The tent flap opened, and Aliyah strode in. "Well, the ground has not shaken, vibrated, or heaved in five hours. And the sun rises in sixteen minutes. Are we ready?"

"To risk our lives doing something that every scientist in history says is impossible?" Cass said. "Oh, sure."

"Number One, ma'am?" Eloise piped up. "Are you sure I can't go?"

"You're so polite when you want to do something totally dumb," Cass said.

As she drew back her arm to smack him, Cass lurched away. With a growl, Eloise jumped at him, and he caught her in his arms.

I thought they were going to tear each other apart. But they wrapped their arms tightly around each other and rocked back and forth. "When you come back," Eloise said, "can we go home?"

Cass's eyes were red. "Mom and Dad—"

"Are in jail," Eloise said. "I know. But that doesn't matter, right? You and me—we can make a home and take care of each other until they get out, right?"

"Right," Cass said.

"And we can move next door to Jack," Eloise said.

Cass smiled. "And Aly and Marco will come to visit all the time."

"Emosewa," Eloise said. "And gnizama."

They stood there without moving while everyone else bustled around in preparation.

For sixteen minutes.

CHAPTER FORTY-TWO

ONCE MORE INTO THE RIFT

"EEEEEE!"

The monkeys were on a time release. It was like they were programmed to scream at the top of their lungs the moment the sun peeked over the horizon.

Which wasn't the most pleasant way to start what might be the last day of our lives.

As we walked through the jungle, we were flanked by rebels and Massa soldiers armed with blowpipes and guns. "Ignore them, they are merely making mischief," Torquin said. His voice seemed weirdly calm and un-Torquinlike, as if being with the Massa put him on his best behavior. But his face was dripping with sweat.

"You feeling off your game again, Torquin?" I asked.

"I suppose you could say that," he replied.

Marco barked a laugh. "Dude, you are the only person I know whose vocabulary gets better when he's sick."

"It's the white beard," Cass said. "It makes him feel distinguished."

"*EEEEEE!*" agreed a chimpanzee.

"Would be so easy to blast those obnoxious pests!" Manolo said.

Another monkey dropped down from a tree, grabbed Manolo's head, and planted a big fat kiss. As it swung away, screeching, the guard staggered backward. "Uccch! Did you see that? Request permission to—"

"Stay on task, please, Manolo," Aliyah said.

"Perhaps they recognize a kindred spirit," Torquin grumbled.

"Ha! Good one, Tork," Marco said.

"*Pah!*" Torquin's response was so loud, so explosive, that we all jumped a little.

"Torquin? You're scaring us," Eloise said.

"Sorry," Torquin grumbled. "Passed out . . ."

"Uh, no, you didn't," I said. "You were right here with us. Hiking."

Torquin nodded. "Huh. Okay. Follow me."

He took the lead, bushwhacking through the jungle with a machete. Marco rolled his eyes and circled his index finger around his ear. "Cuckoo," he mouthed.

314

We walked carefully. Every rustle in the trees made my hair stand on end. Cass was shivering, despite the fact that the temperature must have been close to ninety already. A rustle in the brush made him jump so hard he hit his head on a tree. *"Hyyeaaaahh!"* shouted one of the Massa guards, slicing a machete through the undergrowth.

A small bush went tumbling away, and an iguana skittered for its life.

"That was close!" Cass shouted.

"It was a lizard," Eloise said. "How did you ever survive a griffin attack?"

"Barely," Cass said.

Eloise sighed. "Brothers . . ."

A couple of hours in, the sun began to pound. Last night's moisture was rising in thick, fetid-smelling waves from the ground. All we could hear was the crackling of branches and leaves beneath our feet.

But I was starting to get a little creeped out. Not by the fear of attack but by the lack of any. No vromaski growls, no griffin calls, no vizzeet screeches. And as we neared the volcano, even the monkey cries receded into the distance. The last time we hiked through the woods, we'd left a trail of poison-darted beasts by this time.

Nirvana hiked back toward us, her face drenched in sweat. "Sorry, guys," she said. "No fun today. The beasts are pretty quiet. Maybe they don't like the heat."

"Quiet is good," Cass shot back.

"I'm suspicious," Marco said.

"I think they're waiting to give a surprise party at Mount Onyx," Eloise suggested.

"Don't say that!" Cass barked. "Even as a joke."

"Well, what do *you* think it is?" Eloise asked.

"The island flooded, right?" Cass said. "When that happens, things drown. That means lots of easy meals. So if I were a griffin or a vromaski or a vizzeet, I'd be filling up on some of that roadkill and not bothering to hunt things that can still run away and fight back."

No one had the energy to argue. We were all grateful for the peace. As we reached a clearing near the base of the volcano, we could see a team of Massa scientists waited by the cave entrance, near a carved number 7 in the rock wall.

One of them was Mom. As usual, I had to restrain myself from running to her. "Hello, Sister Nancy!" I cried out, maybe a little too energetically.

"Hi there," she said. Her eyes were appropriately friendly, but as corny as it sounds, I swear I could see *I love you* in them. Which made my face heat up embarrassingly. I turned around and started coughing, causing Marco to pound me on the back. I forced myself to stop before I lost my breakfast jerky.

"We'll be joining you," Mom said. "We have a map of the route. This will help us avoid wrong turns."

316

Torquin waddled up next to her. "Bravo. Excellent idea."

"Well . . . thank you, Torquin," Mom said brightly.

"He's got a rare germ that makes him sound like a real person," Marco explained.

Aliyah looked over her shoulder. "We've been lucky so far this morning. Are we ready to continue?"

"I guess," Eloise said.

"Um . . ." Cass said.

"You bet," Marco said.

Felix circled around behind us and began helping Cass unhook his Loculus vest.

"No, we're not ready," I said, staring at Aliyah.

She gave me a weary look. "Jack, please . . ."

I put my hand on Felix's arm before he could go any further. "We go nowhere unless we can take the Loculi with us."

Aliyah's guards stepped forward menacingly.

"You told me you would think about it," I reminded her.

"I did," Aliyah said. She pulled a small silver chain from around her neck. At the bottom hung a simple, orb-shaped locket.

Quietly she hung it around my neck, and I held the locket in my hand. "What is this?"

"Open it," she said.

As I popped it open, we all gathered around to look at a yellowed school photo of a dark-skinned, grinning gap-toothed kid about nine years old. Across the bottom was a white-on-black placard that spelled out OSMAN BARTEVYAN.

Aliyah gave a signal to Felix, and he backed away from Cass.

She glanced to the sky, sighed, and in a soft but clear voice said, "Once more into the rift."

* * *

It was the fastest we had ever reached the waterfall. It was also the loudest I'd ever heard it. The water raged from its opening high above, crashing over the rocky wall and thundering into the pool below. It didn't quite block out the Song of the Heptakiklos, but it sure gave it a good run for its money.

Marco knelt by the waterfall's pool and splashed water on his face. "Feels great," he said. "Even if you're not dead."

He was right. All of us were tired, and we took a moment to refresh ourselves in the rejuvenating water. It had been a real slog through the labyrinth. Even though Mount Onyx was on the highest part of the island, rainwater had seeped into the paths, maybe two inches deep in some places. Our legs ached and our feet were wet and blistered.

"Okay, before we do this, do you all know which Loculi you're carrying?" Aliyah asked.

I adjusted my pack and stood. "I have Language and Flight."

"Invisibility and Healing," Cass said.

"Bert and Ernie," Marco said.

Aliyah glared at him.

"Okay. Underwater Breathing and Teleportation," Marco said.

"Then let's roll," I said.

Aliyah nodded. I touched the silver locket, and we all turned toward the caldera.

We weren't expecting to hear the loud, steady sound of breathing from inside, like the hum of a jet engine.

"Whoa," Marco said. "Is that Torquin?"

"I—I don't think so," Cass squeaked.

I looked over my shoulder. I couldn't see Torquin, but there were maybe twelve people crowded into a narrow space. So I walked up next to Marco, and we both crept toward the center of the volcano.

"Jack and I will do some recognizance," Marco called out.

"Reconnaissance," I whispered.

"That, too," Marco said.

The sun was just about directly overhead, so we had to shield our eyes. White light scorched the rocky walls and highlighted each stain and scuffle left from our last battle.

Only the corner that contained the Heptakiklos was in darkness. Because of the wall's angle, that area was dark, day and night.

With the Loculi on our backs and the Heptakiklos about fifty feet away, the Song of the Heptakiklos twanged in my head. It obliterated just about every other noise—except the deep, scratchy breathing, which I heard loud and clear.

"Sounds like a hose-beaked vromaski with a bad cold." Marco took my arm and we both stepped forward. "Go slowly, Brother Jack. Remember, they're more afraid of you than you are of them."

"Famous last words," I said.

"Dude, we have the Loculi," Marco reminded me. "Piglet doesn't stand a chance. You hold on to Flight, I'll hold on to Teleportation, and we'll kick his butt from here to Halicarnassus. Deal?"

"Deal," I said.

We both yanked down the quick-release side zippers, pulled out the Loculi, and stepped into the darkness. Instantly the temperature dropped about ten degrees. I could feel the mists of the Heptakiklos swirling around me.

As our eyes adjusted to the darkness, we both froze.

Sitting on its haunches in the middle of the Heptakiklos was a silhouette of a beast whose folded wings touched two of the caldera walls. In the darkness I couldn't see its color, but it had the body of a giant lion.

"Check it out, Tweety's back!" Marco said.

The creature shook its head slowly. It had no beak, and its face was smooth and round. "I-it's not a griffin, Marco,"

I said. "This thing must have flown here while we were away. Or escaped through the rift . . ."

The creature's wings unfolded with a whoosh that nearly knocked us over. I could hear Eloise shrieking behind us.

"I would thank you," came a deep voice that sent vibrations directly up my spine, "not to call me a thing."

CHAPTER FORTY-THREE

THE RIDDLE AND THE SWORD

FOR A MOMENT I was convinced someone was playing toy drums, until I realized it was just my knees knocking together.

Marco dropped a Loculus on the ground, then quickly recovered it. "Dude. Sorry. I take it back. I didn't know you could talk."

The creature was striding toward us on four stout legs, spiked with stiff fur. Its shoulders, at least ten feet high, drove up and down like pistons. But I still could not get a good sense of its face.

"Oh, I can talk," it said. "And in many languages. If your friends know what is good for them, they will put down their weapons. I believe they have something of mine."

Guns began clicking behind me. A dart came flying over my head, embedding itself into the creature's right leg to no effect. *"Stop!"* I called out.

I heard a flurry of shouting and commotion. Aliyah was yelling at Manolo. I was too afraid to turn away, too intent on seeing what this creature looked like.

Marco and I backed away. The creature's wings were leathery and thick, resting on either side of a deeply furred body. It wasn't a griffin. Griffins were sleek, fast moving, and nervous. This thing was broad and hulking and deliberate.

"We come in peace!" Cass shouted.

"I'll be the judge of that," the creature replied. "Besides, I'm the one who's supposed to ask questions. I'm famous for that."

As the beast stepped forward, light began to soften the shadow. I could see the outlines of its face now—a square jaw and chiseled cheeks, its fur combed straight on either side of its head. If I had any lingering thought this might be a griffin, that was totally gone now. Griffins did not have broad, humanlike noses and piercing round eyes, like this creature did.

"Don't you know my face?" the beast bellowed, its breath hot and musty. "Don't you know my name?"

"Let's see. The hair . . . um, you're George Washington?" Marco said.

"NOOOO!"

Aliyah was on her knees. "Get down, you fools," she whispered. "I don't know how this thing got here! It was protecting the Loculus. I thought we'd managed to sneak away from it in Egypt."

"THING? THERE'S THAT WORD AGAIN!" the beast roared.

It lunged toward Aliyah, reaching to swat her with its paw, but she rolled aside with the quick reflexes of an extremely scared ninja warrior.

The creature retracted onto its haunches, sitting tall.

Wings. Body of a lion. From Egypt. Looks weirdly like George Washington. I had an idea what this was. "The Sphinx of Egypt, disappearing overnight . . ." I murmured. "That was what Crazy Farouk said. She'd heard it on the news. And Wenders's notes . . . also mentioned something about a sphinx. . . ."

"What?" Eloise blurted. "But that's impossible! The Sphinx is a statue. Statues don't just come to life!"

Cass pressed his eyes shut. "Hasn't she learned *any-thing*?"

"As you know, I am here to collect something," the Sphinx said, its eyes moving to focus on me. "And I believe *you* have it."

"M-m-me?" I said.

"The Loculus of Language," Cass whispered.

I stood, backing away. I needed to make it to the tunnel. The entrance would be too small for the Sphinx, and it would get stuck. It was my only hope. Manolo stood beside me, eyeing the Sphinx defiantly. I could sense the others gathering, too.

With a sudden roar, the beast reared its head back and belched a plume of fire. It scorched a stray tree root that jutted from the caldera wall. "I do not fear your bullets, nor will your meager brains outwit me. You will return what is mine or you will die."

The Sphinx leaped into the air and landed inches from me. I felt the burn of its breath like the sun. "I was inanimate until the prince of Atlantis gave me inner life. Though caught in stone, I could see the world, the beauty of the pyramids. What glory! But this magician knew the nature of Sphinxes. We are creatures of logic. We feed on choices. Riddles. So he presented me with one: What in peace sees all but moves not, in distress sees death and moves swiftly, in success is released to eternal life, in failure is turned to dust?"

"I—I give up," I said.

"The answer was me," the Sphinx said. "You see, I was given a choice if I wanted life. Would I remain in stone and watch over the magical orb he had placed in the Great Pyramid, coming to life only to retrieve it in the event of its theft? My reward for success upon Massarym's return would be freedom, like the birds and lizards! But if the Loculus were stolen and not found, I would turn to dust. To this I agreed. And to this I remain faithful."

"But Massarym can't return," I said. "He's dead."

The Sphinx glared at me with colossal eyes. "I have no reason to believe this. But I am who I am, and as Massarym did for me, I will give you a choice. Answer me this question correctly, and I will take back the Loculus and let you live. Answer it wrong, and I will kill you for it."

"What kind of choice is that?" Cass blurted. "It's not fair!"

The Sphinx turned to Cass. "Then you shall be the one I ask."

Cass gulped. "On second thought, it is fair. Very fair. But there are people here a lot smarter than I am—"

"What is it," the Sphinx said, "that has four feet in the morning, two at noon, and three at night?"

"Ooh! Ooh! I know!" Eloise said.

Cass spun around. "You do?"

"Of course!" Eloise replied. "Everyone does. It's famous!"

"I asked the boy!" The Sphinx reached out with its paw and placed it on Cass's head. "He must answer or he must die."

"Um . . . um . . . wait," Cass said. "So . . . four feet, you said? Hmmm, let me narrow the possibilities. Actually, can you repeat the question?"

The Sphinx let go of Cass and sat back on its haunches. As it glanced at me, it began to drool.

"Wait!" Cass said. "I'll get it! I will. Just let me think. Do I have a time limit?"

Shaking, I unzipped the Loculus of Language from my pack and held it out, ready to hand it over. I wouldn't let Cass die, not like this. If the Sphinx took back the Loculus, we would just have to return to Egypt and get it—after we got Aly.

"Jack . . . ?" Aliyah said.

"It's a dude!" came Marco's voice from the caldera. "He crawls on all fours as a baby, walks on two legs as a grown-up, and has to use a cane in old age! Ding, ding, ding! And Marco wins the daily double!"

The Sphinx spun around. "I did not ask you!" the beast roared.

But Marco wasn't worried about the rules. He raced out of the darkness, holding aloft the golden, bejeweled sword that had been keeping the rift shut. The magic sword King Uhla'ar had called *Ischis*.

It had been stuck in the rift for centuries. It regulated the flow of energy and kept the rift from blowing open. Removing it had let loose all the beasts and destabilized the island.

If Marco could have picked the one colossally idiotic thing to do, this was it.

"What are you doing?" I shouted. "You can't remove the sword!"

With a roar, Marco leaped at the Sphinx. The beast unfurled its wings and lunged toward him. Spinning away, Marco swung Ischis and sliced off the tip of a wing.

The creature's screech filled the caldera. Blood spurted from its wound. It planted its feet, bared its teeth at Marco, and went into a crouch.

As it pounced, the ground lurched. A low moan echoed in the caldera. The Sphinx tilted and fell to the earth on its side.

Leaping to his feet, Marco plunged the sword directly into the Sphinx's chest.

CHAPTER FORTY-FOUR

NO MERCY

"RUN!" MARCO SAID.

"What do you mean, run?" Aliyah said. "Where?"

The Sphinx was writhing on the ground. Nirvana raced to a pile of supplies and tools that the rebels had collected in the caldera. "We can subdue it!" she said. "We have shackles!"

"We don't have time for that!" I shouted. "Marco, put the sword back. Close up the rift—now!"

Marco turned back toward the Heptakiklos. But the rift was widening, a mass of green flesh emerging from underneath. I could make out one jewel-like eye, rolling slowly to take in the surroundings. As the creature rose higher, two more eyes emerged. And then two more. Its body began spilling out of the rift, billowing like the ooze from my science fair volcano. It had the rolling flesh of an octopus and the wet sheen of an impossibly massive slug. And it was ripping open the gash farther and farther.

Eloise screamed. "What is that?"

"An ocean of blob?" Marco said, moving closer. "If it keeps this up, it's going to take over this whole space."

"Marco, th-th-this is the thing you stabbed after Aly was pulled into the rift," Cass said.

"Dude, excuse me—are you related to Greenie the Hungry Mu'ankh?" Marco called out. "Like his ugly uncle?"

My hands were shaking. I couldn't even grip the zipper of my pack, let alone return the Loculus of Language to its pouch. The orb slipped out of my grasp and rolled onto the ground, toward the creature.

As I stepped toward it, Cass grabbed my shoulder. "Leave it alone!" he said. "Or that thing will turn you into Jack McSlimely."

As the creature rose, its many eyes moved independently, sizing up the space. It spilled out over the empty dug-out bowls of the Heptakiklos, the places where the Loculi were once kept.

The Sphinx let out a screech, causing the enormous creature to turn its eyes in her direction. "Do not let this monster free, not under any conditions."

"We—we weren't planning to," Cass stammered.

"Send it back!" the Sphinx pleaded. "Send it back NOW! This is the Great Atlantean Behemoth. It is a killing machine, built of the earth itself, with no capacity of intelligence or mercy."

"Yeah, unlike *you*?" Nirvana yelled out.

"Does it speak?" Cass asked.

Marco circled it, holding tight to his sword. "How could it, Brother Cass? It has no mou—"

Spinning to face Marco, the beast lifted its slimy body upward like a cobra. As the rolls of flesh unfolded under its eyes, a gaping hole opened. It was a perfect black circle ringed with saberlike teeth. The Behemoth let out a hiss, spitting a thick, clear liquid.

"Never mind," Marco said. "Anybody have some Altoids?"

"Marco, this is not a joke!" Eloise screamed.

The Behemoth's eyes rolled toward Eloise—and Marco pounced. With a loud cry, he swung Ischis like a home-run hitter. Bases loaded, bottom of the ninth. He made contact just below the creature's mouth.

The sword sliced through cleanly and emerged through the other side of the creature's body, sending up a gusher of yellowish fluid. The Behemoth's head tumbled off and splatted heavily on the ground, a network of severed veins dangling like wires. The rest of its body drooped, then fell limply in a pool of slime.

Marco jumped back, his eyes wide. "Whoa. That is some sword . . ."

The Sphinx was moving now in the shadows. Limping. Its eyes were on the Loculus of Language, which had rolled to the opposite caldera wall. "Heads up!" Nirvana yelled.

I sprinted toward the wall, beating the Sphinx to the Loculus. As I snatched it off the ground, she screeched and shot me a furious glance. "This was not wise," she hissed, as she flapped her wings and crouched into attack position.

I bolted. Despite her injury, she managed to pounce fast. One of her claws ripped through my shirt as I jumped away. She hit the wall with a thud and a shred of shirt fabric, howling in anger and frustration.

I got up fast, clutching the Loculus of Language, and I raced toward the Heptakiklos. Toward Marco. But behind him, the Behemoth's beheaded body had begun moving again, undulating slowly. It was still stuck in the rift, plugging it up like putty. Its severed veins and arteries were moving, melding back together. Their pale yellowish-white color was turning green. Before my eyes the beast was growing again, forming into a smooth lump.

Marco swept his arm back, keeping me from getting too close. "This doesn't look good, Brother Jack," he said, staring in awe at the Behemoth's transformation.

"Watch your back!" Eloise cried out.

We both whirled around to see the Sphinx hobbling toward us. Marco kept it at bay with a threatening swipe of his sword. "En garde! Take that!"

"En garde?" the Sphinx hissed.

"I heard that in a movie once," Marco replied. "Loosely translated it means come any closer, you're Sphinx patties!"

A gurgling noise bubbled up from behind us. I looked over my shoulder to see the Behemoth's body repairing itself, sprouting eyes, growing a new mouth. "I don't believe this . . ." I moaned.

Marco's head whipped around. "Oh, great. It's regenerating. Just what we wanted."

"Jack!" Nirvana screamed.

The Sphinx took advantage of the distraction. But instead of attacking us, it catapulted on its good leg, managing to leap over our heads. Marco swung at it with Ischis, but the creature cleared him easily and landed just beyond me.

It stood between us and Behemoth now. With the glob growing behind it, the Sphinx seemed smaller but no less fierce. "This fetid hole has become quite unpleasant," she said. "So I will have that Loculus right now, please, and leave for Egypt."

"Or . . . ?" Marco said.

"Or the ground will slicken with the blood of children!" the Sphinx snapped.

"Lame dialog, drama queen," Marco said. "You need a new writer."

The Sphinx jumped toward us. Marco swung but

managed only to chop off a few feathers. Off balance, the beast landed on my foot, nearly wrenching it off. I saw red. All I could do was scream.

The ground lurched. A chunk of stone, soil, and roots smashed to the floor from high on the caldera wall.

The sword. Up till now I figured that with the Behemoth stuck in the rift, the energy was still trapped underground. But the crack was spidering outward in lightning jags. The rift was becoming a network of cracks. Clenching my jaw against the pain in my crushed foot, I looked for Ischis but couldn't see it in the chaos.

Marco leaped into the air and landed a kick directly in the Sphinx's face. As the beast fell back, I could see someone rushing toward me. I had to blink away the pain a few times to see it was Cass. He knelt over my legs, touching the Loculus of Healing to my ankle. "One Mississ-ss-ssippi, two Miss-ss-issippi . . ." he stammered, while the orb did its work.

The pain quickly disappeared. I thanked Cass and stood, surveying the mess around us. Marco was emerging from behind the Heptakiklos, Ischis aloft. He had found it in the shadows.

The Sphinx fixed a cold glare at him, but she wasn't going to go near Marco as long as he had the sword. The Behemoth was moaning, resuming its rise from the rift. Its new head was darkening, solidifying. Cass ran back to the pack of Massa and rebels. Many of them were firing at the green blob, but that was having no effect. Their bullets disappeared harmlessly into its gelatinous skin.

"Anybody got salt?" Marco said.

"What?" Eloise shot back.

"Ever see what happens when you put salt on a slug?" Marco said. "The thing shrivels up and dies."

"You need a salt mine for that thing!" Cass said.

The Heptakiklos was a mess now. The seven stone bowls, where the Loculi were supposed to be placed, were being split by the network of cracks. "What do I do now, King Jack?" Marco said. "As long as that blob is stuck, we're protected. If it escapes, or if I chop it to bits . . . what happens to the rift? It'll just grow, right?"

"I don't know . . ." I said.

Nirvana was shouting at me now, waving her arms, gesturing toward the tunnel. Something about Eloise. "What's she saying?" Marco asked.

His sword drooped. That was all the Sphinx needed. She leaped again, out of the shadows. Marco swung wildly. I jumped away, landing closer to the Behemoth. It was rising, changing by the second, nearly fully formed now. Its mouth gaped like the opening to a furnace.

The Sphinx rolled on the ground, her legs twitching. Obviously Marco had done some damage.

In that moment, I knew what to do. But I would have to

channel some of Marco's ability.

I stood, holding the Loculus high. "Sphinxy!" I shouted. "You want it? You really, really want it?"

The Sphinx righted herself, shaking off the pain.

"Jack, what the heck are you doing?" Marco shouted.

"Yes . . ." the Sphinx rasped. "Of course I want it, accursed child."

"Well, go get it!" I said, rearing my arm back and holding tight to the Loculus.

Turning to face the Behemoth, I threw it with all the strength I had.

I watched the Loculus leave my hand. It arced high into the air. The great green beast roared, turning its mouth upward.

And the Loculus disappeared into the wet, gaping blackness.

CHAPTER FORTY-FIVE
KARST POOL

I KNEW THE Sphinx would go nuts, and I wanted to be out of its way.

Everyone else in the caldera thought I was nuts, too. And maybe I was. I ran toward Cass for safety. I felt the whoosh of the Egyptian beast's injured wings as it flew, shrieking, toward the Behemoth.

"Jack, why the heck did you do that?" Cass shouted, stiff with shock.

"'In failure . . . is turned to dust . . .'" I said, catching my breath. "Remember? The Sphinx's job is to protect the Loculus. Or it turns to—"

"*Eeeeaaaahhhhh!*" With her front paws extended, the winged beast dove after the Loculus.

The Behemoth bit down tightly. I could hear a muffled screech. The Sphinx was stuck, trapped below her front haunches. Her head, shoulders, and wings were deep inside the blob. The two beasts shook violently—but the mighty Sphinx was like a toothpick in some extremely ugly Jell-O.

The Behemoth slid slowly back into the rift, pulling the Sphinx in, with a sick, slurping sound. It scooped up soil as it swept over the caldera floor, squeezing its mass back through the crack. As the last slimy piece of it disappeared inside, the rift contracted. The spidery cracks filled with rocks and dirt.

All that remained was the rear end of the Sphinx, jammed into what remained of the crack. Her rear legs were stuck in our world, kicking furiously.

"Follow me," I said to Marco.

"Dude, that," Marco said, staring in awe. "Really. *That.*"

"I said follow me!" I think I sounded way more confident than I felt. The guards and rebels were staring, dumbfounded. I headed straight past them, farther from the Heptakiklos, into the light. We needed to act fast. With one plan.

I could see Cass, but not his sister. "Where's Eloise?" I demanded.

Nirvana was standing by the tunnel, looking helpless and agitated. "Gone, Jack," she said. "With Torquin."

From inside the tunnel Aliyah came running, her

footsteps sloshing in the puddles left by the waterfall. "I followed them, but that big oaf is faster than . . ." Her eyes drifted toward the Heptakiklos, where the Sphinx's butt was gyrating helplessly.

"I needed to immobilize them both," I explained quickly. "The Sphinx wasn't going to give up until it got that Loculus. So I threw it into the Behemoth's mouth."

"You gave up a Loculus?" Aliyah said.

"We'll get it back," Marco said.

"If I hadn't given it up, that Loculus would be heading back to Egypt in the Sphinx's paws," I said. "And the Behemoth would be all over us. The rift is blocked now, so there shouldn't be more disturbances on the island. At least for now."

"It's brilliant," Nirvana said.

"Until it's not," I replied. "Which might be soon. What happened to Eloise?"

Nirvana's face was lined with worry. "Okay, we're standing there being all ineffectual while you and Marco are whaling on the beasts, and I see Torquin taking Eloise's hand and walking her back, farther from the action. This seems totally okay to me, Mr. Protector and all, but I'm noticing he's saying stuff like, 'My dear, I'm afraid this is too perilous a venue right now.' Which would be borderline normal for anyone else to say—"

"But not Torquin," Aliyah added. "Next thing we know,

Eloise is pulling at him, telling him to leave her alone. Also not an unreasonable thing to do, but under the circumstances no one paid much attention. The screaming came a few seconds later."

"I told you he was acting weird!" Cass said.

"I've sent Brutus and a couple of others to follow them," Nirvana replied, looking back into the dark passageway. "They were on Torquin's tail. Come."

She handed Cass and me flashlights. Marco followed. We raced past the waterfall and into the tunnel. At the first fork in the path, where we would turn left to get through the maze, Brutus stood pointing to the right. "Hurry."

Going as fast as we could, we raced to the next intersection, where Fritz pointed us to the left. "I asked them to do this," Nirvana said. "Sort of like the crumbs Hansel left to get out of the woods."

"Huh?" said Marco.

"The string Theseus left in the labyrinth to escape the Minotaur?" Nirvana called over her shoulder.

"What?" Marco said.

"Forget it," Nirvana replied.

"Left!" shouted a rebel who was just ahead of us.

"This is starting to look familiar," Cass said.

The tunnel was wider here. On the walls were paintings of griffins and hose-beaked vromaskis. Just ahead, on a corner that led off in another direction, I shone my flashlight on a mark carved into the wall. "I made that," I said. "And if I remember right, we should be pretty close to—"

My foot hit something that slid against the wall in a brittle-sounding crash. I quickly shone my flashlight downward to see a pile of human bones. "That is so gross," Nirvana said.

"Cass, we saw this skeleton—remember?" I said. "When we were first exploring the maze?"

"Right," Cass said. "It was after we fell—well, *you* fell— into that pool, in that weird karst environment."

"I don't want to sound like an idiot," Marco said, "but . . ."

"Karst," Cass said. "It's a geology thing. A place that has sinkholes, underground pools, cenotes. That's where Jack fell—a cenote, which is like a round pool. In Ancient Mexico they were considered holy and used for sacrifices and stuff. The weird thing is, you see this kind of stuff in areas that have lots of limestone—but not usually in a jungle."

"Sacrifices?" Aliyah's voice echoed in the hallway. Without another word, she barreled past us. We followed her in a hurry.

The tunnel narrowed. Nirvana was directly ahead of me, and she smacked her head on a long stalactite, which cracked off and crashed to the ground. *"Yeow!"* she cried out. "Watch your head."

"EEEEEEEE!" came a cry from directly ahead of us.

Monkeys?

What were they doing here?

Aliyah was standing at the entrance to the cave. As we gathered around her, we all stopped cold.

I remembered the layout of the place: Rock walls, dripping with water and rising up into darkness. A stone slab with a hole in the middle, about twenty feet in diameter, which dropped into a pool of icy-cold water. A room carved into the rock of the opposite wall, with a stone table and a set of steps.

At this point I could actually see little more than the walls. A few monkeys were climbing them, leaping from rock perch to rock perch. The last time we'd been here, the place was empty, but not now.

Old priesty-looking guys in gilded robes and sandals stood around the hole, chanting in a language I didn't recognize. They were more walking skeletons than men, all small and hunched and fine boned like birds. Their skin was papery and white, their movements excruciatingly slow. From thick candles on the floor, soft light shone upward, making the moisture on the walls seem to flicker with the rhythm of the chanting.

"What the—?" Marco said. *"Hello?"*

At the opposite end, one of the old priests began slowly climbing the steps into the room. He didn't react to Marco's call for a second or two. I think it took these guys time to do anything.

At last the priests turned toward us. They began to shuffle quietly backward, away from the hole, back toward the cave wall. In a few moments we could see the room from end to end. Back when we'd first explored the underground paths, this place had been bare and dusty. Now it had become a kind of shrine, decorated with leafy branches and flowers. The walls were painted with scenes of battle, a portrait of a royal couple with two sons, an armada of ships. Dozens of candles had been elaborately arranged, along with some kind of chalice with incense that smelled like pine trees.

A priest unlike the others stood in the center, with his back to us. He wore a jewel-encrusted hood and his shoulders were immense, completely blocking from sight the table that I knew was there.

"Who are you?" Cass called out. "You. The big guy. In the center."

But the man said nothing. Standing to his right, one of the older priests announced in a whispery voice, "I am R'amphos."

Now the giant priest turned. I could see, under the hood, a thatch of bright red hair and a thick white beard.

"Torquin?" I fought the urge to laugh. I wanted this to be a joke. Was there any other possibility? Why else would he be there?

"He's playing," Marco murmured.

"He's crazy," Cass said.

"He scares me," Nirvana said.

What scared me was Aliyah's reaction. I could see her trembling.

As Torquin descended the steps, the table behind him became visible. On it, lying unconscious, was Eloise.

"All bow," said R'amphos, "to the Omphalos."

CHAPTER FORTY-SIX

THE MOTHER OF INVENTION

IMPOSSIBLE.

Of all the crazy things we'd seen, all the unpredictable behavior, all the betrayals—this was the one I just. Could. Not.

Marco tensed up, clenching tight to Ischis. "Ohhhh, no, Big Guy," he growled. "You don't get away with this."

Springing upward, he leaped past the priests. He pinned Torquin against the wall, the sword to his neck. "Tell me this is some kind of joke, Torquin. *Tell me*. And then, guess what? Even if it is, I am going to kill you."

"What did you do to my sister?" Cass raced up to the altar.

"She is sleeping," Torquin said. "Don't worry, Cassius."

His voice was soft, not rough. His words were perfectly

formed. Had this been an act, all along? How could he have fooled us? How could we not know we were sharing all our adventures with . . . giving all our trust to . . .

The Omphalos.

Torquin was not Torquin. He was the head of the Karai Institute. The man who had accused Mom of betraying the group's ideals. This was the monster who had put a contract on her life, causing her to fake her own death. Because of the Omphalos, I spent years of my life thinking I did not have a mother.

As someone touched my hand gently from behind, I jumped. Turning quickly, I looked upward into a very familiar face. "M—" I started to blurt out but kept myself from completing *Mom*. "Sister Nancy! How—?"

"I was commandeering rowboats," she explained, "on a salvage mission. I came as soon as I heard."

"Did you hear . . . ?" I gestured toward Torquin. Tears began to flow down my cheeks.

"Yes," she said in a measured voice that didn't disguise her disgust. "I am as surprised as everyone else."

Marco hadn't budged, but Torquin didn't seem to care much about the blade to his throat. "How . . . how could you do this?" I blurted. "You won our trust. You took us to find the Loculi. You . . . you—"

"You nearly died for us in Greece," Cass said. "It makes no sense."

346

Aliyah walked forward, her face calm and quizzical. "Well, well. All these years I suspected the Omphalos was a figure of imagination. A lie. Perhaps a modern-day Oz, a figment dreamed up by a committee to frighten people. At other times I thought he was Radamanthus Bhegad. I'm not often wrong, dear Torquin. But this time you blindsided me. Free him, Marco. I will not give him the satisfaction of a swift death without an explanation."

Marco cautiously lowered his sword and let Torquin free. "Omphalos," Torquin said in his weirdly normal voice, "is a word the Atlanteans gave to the Greeks. Surely you know this."

"It means the center of all things," said Aliyah softly.

"It was the word used in Atlantis to describe the office of royal rule. You could call the king Omphalos, or the queen. This is called, in your tongue, an honorific?" Torquin smiled. "I believe you have already met my charming husband, Uhla'ar."

I didn't know whether to laugh or slap myself in the face just to see if I was dreaming.

"Dude, I don't know what these old geezers gave you to smoke," Marco said, raising the sword again, "but you are Torquin. Victor Rafael Quiñones. You are not and could not be married to King Uhla'ar of Atlantis of a gazillion years ago. And no offense, Tork, you're not Omphalos material. Now take off the costume, wake up Eloise, and let's book.

We got a Sphinx and green blob to deal with."

Torquin raised a finger and Ischis tore out of Marco's grip. It flipped over and flew toward Torquin, who grabbed it by the hilt and pointed it downward, the tip resting on the stone floor.

"Dude, okay, whatever," Marco said.

"Your beloved Torquin will be returned to you in the fullness of time," said Torquin. "You look upon his countenance. You hear his voice. This is because I, Qalani, no longer exist in my own form. My own consciousness is, shall we say, homeless? For the moment I am borrowing your large friend's body. Which has its great advantages, to be sure. But it is not easy speaking these words through lips untrained to move with such dexterity."

"I'll say," Nirvana squeaked.

Okay. Okay. Time out.

My head spun. I needed to sort this out. So the Omphalos was Qalani—had been Qalani all along. Only now Qalani was living inside Torquin—which would explain why he'd been acting so weird lately. The idea was crazy. It flitted around my brain like a lost bat, frantic and impossible to pin down.

"You don't believe me, my golden boy," said Torquin, aka Qalani, walking closer. "Yet you have seen evidence of Massarym's curse upon my husband, cruelly confined in the form of a stone statue."

"H-he cursed you, too?" I asked.

"Oh, yes," Qalani said. "After I created the Loculi, Massarym was the one who appreciated them most. I so loved watching his joy as he flew and disappeared and performed all the feats the Loculi allowed. Karai was wary of my achievement, but I shut him out, so proud was I. In this regard I, Qalani, had put myself above nature, taming and containing it! But as the attacks on Atlantis began from other armies, as the earthquakes and disastrous weather descended, Karai won my ear. He blamed my tampering for the disturbance of the Telion."

"Whoa," I said. *"Telion?"*

"It was the name we gave to the energy that seeped through the great rift," Qalani said. "And that energy, as you know, was the source of all that was good and perfect in Atlantis. Now, through Karai's wisdom, I saw that the Loculi *should* be destroyed. But when I urged Massarym to return the Loculi, he grew angry and vindictive. And, as I discovered, he had secretly learned magics I never even knew existed.

"He punished me, though I was his mother and the queen. I was to spend eternity as a fallen monarch, the lowest of the low. After my physical death, even my consciousness was cursed to remain fully sentient on whatever was left of Atlantis. Over time I learned to inhabit the consciousness of the basest of earth's creatures, the rats and vultures and crabs and bugs. It took centuries to grow strong enough to implant myself in more complex beings. And when I finally was able to inhabit the various monkeys of the island, my fortunes began to change."

"So the ones who guided us in the jungle to safety, back when we first tried to escape the Karai Institute . . ." I said. "They seemed so human . . ."

"Ah, you're welcome." Qalani chuckled. "I was heartened by the arrival of Herman Wenders, even more so at the development of the Karai Institute. I learned much in my animal disguises, spying on their procedures. As you can imagine, my capabilities as a scientist had been seriously impaired in my primitive physical state. But over the last century I was able to commandeer, then build, communication equipment—all in secret, all while in the form of a highly dexterous chimpanzee. Imagine! Without the capability of speech, I could make my presence known to Radamanthus and the others, in messages. Upon your arrival on the island, Jack, I was on the verge of cracking my most vexing problem—the ability to transfer my consciousness from monkey to human being. My breakthrough was Torquin."

"Figures," Marco said.

"So back when we were in New York City, running from Artemisia's Shadows," I said. "You summoned Torquin away from us . . ."

"The island had been invaded," Qalani said. "Necessity is the mother of invention. I needed a human surrogate. It took some time for me to figure out the details."

I swallowed, standing in front of my mother. The explanation cleared up a few things, but this was the person who had ordered Mom's death. He, or she, would have to get to me first before coming near her.

"Anne McKinley!" Qalani shouted. "Stand before the Omphalos!"

Aliyah's brow scrunched. "Who?"

"No!" I shouted. "You can't!"

Qalani focused directly on Mom. "Your son has proved worthy, Anne. And he bares an uncanny resemblance to my own fair Karai, you know."

"Wait," Aliyah said. "Sister Nancy is . . . *Jack's mother*?"

"Among everything else I learned today," Nirvana said, "that's actually pretty far down on the strangeness ladder."

I have no words to describe the utter weirdness of Torquin smiling at me like a proud grandmother. Qalani stepped down and began lumbering toward us. The sword sent up sparks as it scraped the stone floor.

Mom stood tall. Tears ran down her cheeks, but she wasn't shaking a bit. "What I did, Omphalos, was to prevent your taking me from my son. It is what any mother would do. I had to find a cure before he turned fourteen, if I was going to save his life. I gave up everything. I worked for people whose ideals I loathed. But I would do it again—in a heartbeat."

"You will not need to," Qalani said. "The time when your death might have served my purpose is long past. You have paid your price, as have I."

Mom's shoulders dropped. "Wait—the contract on my life is off?"

"Of course," Qalani said. "Things have changed. Our quest has come a long way. And I realize now that you acted not to stop us but to save the mission. Now, because of the brave actions of your son and his friends, Karai's dreams may finally be realized. You have a right to be proud, as do I."

I couldn't believe my ears. I didn't care that everyone knew the truth. I threw my arms around my mom for the first time since I was a little boy, and it felt amazing.

"So . . . you're going to help us?" Cass asked.

"Your cause and mine are inextricably linked," Qalani replied. Then she snapped her—Torquin's—fingers. "But we are Atlanteans, and this must be done the Atlantean way."

Four of the priests rose to the altar. They seemed to be floating above the ground as they walked, and together they lifted Eloise. Chanting in a weird, high-pitched gibberish, they carried her over to a hole in the stone floor. Her eyes fluttered, and then focused on her brother. "Cass?" Eloise said.

It was the only word out of her mouth before the priests dropped her through the hole.

CHAPTER FORTY-SEVEN

SOLDIER YIELDS TO TAILOR

THE LOUD SPLASH made me flinch. It echoed up into the chamber as Eloise hit the pool at the bottom of the pit. The other priests dropped to their knees, caterwauling at the top of their wizened lungs. Marco lunged for Qalani. Screaming his sister's name, Cass ran to the edge of the hole and leaped.

Qalani flicked the sword in Marco's direction. R'amphos pointed a bony finger at Cass. Both Marco and Cass were suspended in midair for a long moment. As if plucked by invisible strings, they both changed direction and landed harmlessly on the stone floor.

"You're a monster!" Mom said to Qalani. She, Aliyah, and I all tried to vault over the side to get to Eloise, but we bounced back, too.

"If you want to sacrifice someone, sacrifice me!" Cass yelled, scrambling to the edge of the hole. "ELOISE!"

His voice echoed in the darkness below. We were all on our knees now, shining our flashlights.

I heard a cough and a splash from below.

"ELOISE, CAN YOU HEAR ME?" Cass shouted. "ARE YOU OKAY?"

Eloise's voice floated up. "Well, the water's cold. But actually kinda refreshing."

Qalani knelt near us by the cenote and peered down. "How does your head feel, my child?"

"Fine, I guess—" Her voice dropped off, and then she screamed: *Yeeow! Ow, ow, ow, ow, ow!*

We all stiffened. What was happening?

Qalani smiled calmly and held out her hand. From an urn at the altar, R'amphos extracted a rope and gave it to her.

Kneeling at the edge, Qalani lowered the rope into the pool. When she felt the tug at the other end, she pulled up Eloise as if she were a rag doll.

She stood up and rubbed the water from her eyes and then hauled off and slapped Torquin's beefy face as hard as she could. *Why'd you dump me down a well? That really hurt.*

Before Qalani could react, Cass threw his arms around his sister and lifted her in the air. Standing behind them, Aliyah let out a gasp.

As Eloise and Cass spun around, I saw why. On the back of Eloise's head, as clear as can be, were two bright white streaks of hair in the shape of a lambda.

* * *

Qalani was still rubbing Torquin's jaw as we walked back through the tunnel. "You pack quite a punch," she said to Eloise.

"Sorry about that," Eloise said. But her face was alive with excitement, and she could not keep her hands from the back of her head. For about the tenth time, she asked, "So, I'm a Select? Really? I can go into the rift?"

"Yes, dear," Qalani said with a smile. "We need you. I have been admiring your progress for a long time . . . in my various forms. You're ready."

Marco, who was in the lead, turned and began walking backward. "So, if we're friends now, can I have KissKiss back?"

Qalani had to think a moment, then smiled. "Ah, you mean Ischis, the sword. I suppose so."

She handed the sword to Marco and he tucked it into his belt. As he kept walking backward, it clattered awkwardly against his leg. "So, Torquin—er, Clownie—"

"Qalani," the queen said patiently.

"So all that time I was working with those brats at the Massa training center?" Marco went on. "You were there . . . hanging around as, like, a bee or mouse or cockroach?"

"I hope I didn't step on you," Eloise said.

"Qalani," Cass said, "Why Eloise? Why did you do that to her in the cenote?"

"I have long been filled with impatience over the length of time necessary for G7W to express itself—and naturally for its, er, limitations," Qalani said. "I thought about these things as the time approached to go back to Atlantis. This must be done right, with maximal strength and effectiveness. The rift can only be transited by Atlanteans—and naturally, Selects. As Queen, I will be able to do this in Torquin's body, which will be a great boon, as we can certainly use his strength. As for Eloise—R'amphos is a wise and innovative scientist, and he can do remarkable things with a few spells and some holy waters. So in short, yes, Eloise has been accelerated to a Select. And we shall be that much stronger for her presence."

Eloise squealed happily and threw her arms around Qalani, then Cass and me. I smiled back at her. I didn't want to mention the fact that if we failed, her time clock ran out at age fourteen, too.

This was not the time to be a downer.

The rebels and Massa guards bustled around us as we strode past the waterfall and entered the caldera. Manolo gestured toward the Heptakiklos. Which, at the moment, was basically a Sphinx's butt embedded in a green blob.

"I think," Manolo said, "the two beasts are dead."

"A fortuitous circumstance indeed," said Qalani.

Manolo shrieked. *"Torquin?"*

"I know," I said. "Shocker, huh? But it's not him. It's a queen that took over his body."

Manolo shrieked again.

"Is it really dead?" Aliyah asked, walking toward the motionless Sphinx.

"Not chitchatting about the weather," Manolo replied.

"How do we proceed now?" Aliyah asked.

"Carefully," Nirvana said.

Qalani put her hand on the beast's furry, motionless flank. "Poor, dear creature. The Sphinx was the most cultivated of animals. What did Massarym do to this one?"

Marco crept forward, pulling the sword from his belt. "Turned it into one great big pain in the . . ."

He tapped the flat side of Ischis's blade on the Sphinx's hip.

With a muffled howl, the beast began kicking violently. A cloud of soil, dust, and rocks rose from the rift. A small crack began to grow and spread on either side.

Shards of bright white light shot upward like knives. The ground began rumbling beneath us. I fell, but Marco remained upright. He was staring directly at me. "Soldier yields to Tailor," he said.

"What?" I didn't know what to do. If the Sphinx shook loose, we were back to Beasts Unlimited. Only this time, maybe we wouldn't survive. "I hate that nickname, Marco."

"It fits, Brother Jack," Marco insisted. "Hurry."

"It was just Bhegad trying to make me feel better, trying to turn me into someone I'm not!" I shot back. "I can't hurry!"

My brain was a mess, thinking and overthinking. In my mind I remembered the day Professor Bhegad died. How he'd clung to my ankle as I flew through the underworld on the back of a griffin. How I watched him fall to his death. How I then lost a piece of my heart and soul when he disappeared forever from my life. And now a slideshow of other people flashed through my brain—Dad and Mom and the Ramsay family I'd met in Ohio and Mrs. Black in Los Angeles and Brother Dimitrios and my bike and the pathway through the woods to school. Everything a fragment of me. And all of it exploding into chaos.

You put things together, Bhegad said.

If things weren't together, they fell apart. Lives vanished. Worlds ended.

I leaped to my feet. My mind was jammed with thoughts. I had no plan. I wasn't ready to do anything. But plans, I knew, were overrated. We might not succeed. We might not make it back. But sometimes you just had to act even when you didn't know how. And that *made* you ready.

What I did know was this: possible success trumped certain death. My instincts were shouting at me loud and clear.

Sometimes, instinct was everything.

I grabbed Qalani's hand and pulled her toward Marco. "Remember, you're Torquin!" I said. "So act like him for a minute and do as I say." I turned, shouting over my shoulder, "Manolo, take the sword. Eventually you will have to jam it back into the rift, when it is finally clear. You'll know exactly when—and if you don't, ask Aliyah!"

Manolo stood rigid, his lips curled in disgust. "What does he think he's doing?"

"I'm not sure," Aliyah said, "but just do it!"

Marco handed the sword to Manolo. Grumbling, he took it. I took Marco's hand and Qalani's, held tight, and positioned us all close to the Sphinx but out of its kicking range.

I told myself I was crazy.

And then I shut myself up.

"Okay, on three!" I shouted. "Eloise, Cass, you come with us!"

"Come with you where?" Cass shouted.

"One . . ." I bent my knees. Qalani did the same, and then Marco. "Two . . ."

At the count of three, Marco, Cass, Eloise, the body of Torquin, and I leaped high. Our ten feet thudded hard on the Sphinx's flank.

Our weight caused the crack to widen again. The animal sank inside in a reverse shower of light.

We fell back onto the ground. Thunder cracked overhead and the ground jolted. From the rift came the howling screech of a griffin that flew straight upward—into the path of a falling boulder.

"Watch out!" Marco cried out, pushing me out of the way.

I felt myself rumbling side to side. Then upward. "What's going on?" Eloise screamed.

Behind us, Aliyah was holding the phone to her ears. "We're getting reports of an approaching tsunami!" she shouted. "East Coast!"

"*Go!*" Mom screamed.

"But what about you?" I screamed back. "What will happen to—?"

With a deafening boom, the walls of the caldera began to crack down the middle.

"*Just go!*" Mom ran toward me and squeezed my hand tightly.

"I love you," I said.

She nodded and then pushed me toward the rift. I took Eloise's hand. She took Cass's, and he took Marco's. Marco grabbed on to Qalani.

I did not look back.

On the count of three, we all plunged into the rift.

CHAPTER FORTY-EIGHT
THE END OF THE WORLD

UNTIL I GOT to the island, my most painful experiences were at the hands of Barry Reese, the Blowhard of Belleville.

Those were nothing compared to being squeezed by a Colossus. Or spat at by a vizzeet. Or attacked by a zombie army. Or swallowed by a Mu'ankh. Or having every atom of my body teleported.

But compared to the rift, the worst of these were 3 on a scale of 10.

I felt that the skin had been flayed from my body and then sliced thin and flayed again. I felt as if a thin electric prod had been inserted into the spaces between every molecule in my body.

My first thought was that I wanted to die. My second thought was that I should have died a nanosecond ago. After that my brain stopped thinking, and my senses shut down, one by one.

Sight.

Smell.

Sound.

Touch.

Nothing.

The Dream.

A ring of fire, screaming animals, the end of the world.

I am back to where it started, motionless, senseless, without thought. It begins again and I must endure all of it. I must fall to my death and wake up to the Ugliosaurus and wish that my dad were not in Singapore and bike to school and leap away from Barry into the street and be kidnapped to the island, where I will meet the nervous kid and the genius girl with the dyed-pink hair and the jock who can sink fifty-yard jump shots and the tweed-jacketed professor. It is the cycle of life and death stood on its head, past and present colliding, death and death everlasting, amen.

And this repeat cycle, more than the senselessness, more than the pain of all I have endured, more than death itself, is the one thing I cannot stand. The worst I can imagine.

"No-o-o-o!"

I shout at the top of my lungs, drawing my hands across the scene in front of me as if I can rip it apart and cause everything to vanish.

But it's . . .

"TOO LATE!"

I would say Eloise's scream woke me up. But that would imply that I'd been sleeping. I'm not sure I was. I'm not sure what state my body was in—dream or seeing, past or present.

Splayed out before us was a lake of green goo with three eyes and a Sphinx jutting from its mouth—both motionless. But gone were the walls of the caldera. We were in the center of what looked like a bowl, a vast circular field that rose all around to a steep, curved ridge. A waterfall cascaded from part of the ridge, and thick woods surrounded us on all sides. Below us the soil was parched, and I could smell the fires that smoked upward from the woods. I could also hear the distant scream of a creature that I recognized as a hose-beaked vromaski.

"Are we . . . in Atlantis?" Eloise said.

As Qalani struggled to her feet, she glanced at the countryside. I had never seen Torquin's features show so much emotion. They stretched and strained into an expression of both sadness and joy. "By Uhla'ar's staff, I never thought I would see this again . . ."

"I guess that's a yes," I said to Eloise.

"Because I—I just dreamed this, Jack," Eloise said. "And then I woke up, and there it was . . ."

I couldn't help laughing. "You're having the Dream, too, huh? Welcome to the world of the Select."

"Where's Cass?" Eloise said.

I looked around but saw no sign of him. He had to be here. We'd made it, so he must have, too.

Didn't he?

"Cass?" Eloise called out, heading for a thicket at the edge of the forest.

My eyes darted left and right, hoping to spot Cass. Rain was beginning to fall, and the drops felt prickly and sharp on my skin. I knew beyond any shadow of a doubt that I was wide awake, because I hurt from head to toe.

Marco was hunched over the Heptakiklos. The seven bowls were empty, but the carvings inside were sharp and new. Both his hands clutched the hilt of Ischis, which was stuck directly into the rift. I stood and walked toward him, adjusting my Loculus vest. "I thought you left the sword with Manolo," I said.

"I did," Marco replied. "This one was lying on the ground here when we came through. I think it must have been stuck in the rift, but we knocked it out. So I replaced it. Meaning the rift here, back in Atlantis. As opposed to the rift back in Team Karassarym Land. Because, let me see if I have this right . . . they are the same place, only we just went through Bhegad's mole hole in time, right?"

"Worm hole," I said. "Yeah."

"So why does the Heptakiklos look the same, but everything all around it is different?" Marco asked.

Qalani turned to face us, and I saw tears streaming down the face of Torquin. "Because Mount Onyx has not formed yet," she said. "The land has not buckled and sunk. It will before long. You see, you in the twenty-first century assume that the land changes slowly, over millennia. But in Atlantis, mountains rose and fell, shorelines changed swiftly—all for the benefit and protection of the people. This was the extraordinary work of the Telion, the unseen energy that nourished our land."

"Whoa," Marco said, "so if your people were like, dang, this place needs a good surfing spot, then the energy whips up a beach the next day?"

"Not quite as fast, or as frivolous—but that is the general idea." Qalani looked around. "Right now, we have arrived at a glorious time in my kingdom's history. You are seeing Atlantis is as it was and always should have been, vast and verdant and peaceful. I spent years constructing the Loculi. But it was only toward the end that Mount Onyx arose. I thought the Telion was causing this glorious mountain to form in order to protect the Heptakiklos. I should have known it was a volcano, not a mountain . . . a sign of the end . . ."

"*Cass!*" Eloise's shocked scream, from the direction of the forest, sent us running.

Cass lay motionless behind a bush, his head twisted to one side against the trunk of a tree. "He's breathing," Eloise said. "But look at his head! I—I'm afraid."

"Cass has the Loculus of Healing," Marco said, reaching for the straps of Cass's backpack.

As Marco began yanking on the zipper, Cass let out a shuddering moan, his face twisting into a grimace. "Let me do it," I said.

Gently I eased the zipper down and reached in. Cass also had the Loculus of Invisibility, but I could see this one, so it had to be Healing. As I slipped it out from under him, Eloise, Marco, and Qalani held his body still.

The rain was falling harder now, and I had to wipe it out of my eyes. I touched the Loculus to Cass's forehead, and he flinched. His head began to move, forcing itself away from the twisted position it was in, slowly straightening. Qalani pulled him away from the tree gently, gradually, to give his head more room to move. His eyelids began to flutter. "Hey, Brother Cass," Marco said. "Welcome to a rainy afternoon in Paradise."

"M-m-m-m" Cass said, his eyes wide and kind of wild looking.

"Marco," Marco said. "Or maybe you're reaching for the word *magnificent*? Or, *my hero*?"

"*Massarym!*" Cass shouted, pointing his finger.

We all spun around. Riding on a giant black horse across the field was a tall, thin figure wearing a hood against the rain. His eyes were hawklike, and the outline of a mustache and beard poked out from his smooth face. He looked younger than the guy in my Dream, maybe in his midteens. Behind him rode two burly men with tight-fitting hoods and belted swords.

I realized they would be asking questions and I would need to understand them. My hands reached instinctively toward my backpack pouch for the Loculus of Language, but I realized it was inside the dead green monster. Which still lay about thirty yards away, choked on a Sphinx.

Massarym shouted something to us in Atlantean.

"That didn't sound friendly," Marco said.

"He said, 'That was a fine use of the royal Loculi . . . for the benefit of petty foreign thieves' . . ." Qalani said, her voice distant and dreamlike. She was walking toward her son, holding out her hands. "My boy. My young, handsome son . . ."

Seeing the lumbering form of Torquin, Massarym's horse shied away, rearing back on its hind legs. The prince shouted to her angrily in Atlantean.

"Do you not recognize your mother, Massarym?" Qalani said.

"No, he doesn't!" Cass called out. "And by the way, you're speaking English! Which is a good thing, because you are a big, ugly, bearded guy and if you keep saying you're his mother, he may kill you!"

From behind Massarym came the clopping of another set of hooves. A powerful horse emerged from the woods, with bejeweled reins and a saddle studded with gold. It took me a moment to recognize the rider, a broad-shouldered man in a woven tunic and brocaded felt hat, staring at us with cruel steady eyes.

"Heyy, 'sup, King Uhla'ar!" Marco said. "Remember us?"

Qalani stared at her husband but said nothing. From behind the king trotted another horse, tethered to Uhla'ar's with a long rope. On it was a thin person with arms tied, a prisoner wearing a loose-fitting sack with a hood.

A clap of thunder resounded, and a bolt of lightning hit a tree not far behind them, cracking off a branch that fell in a loud thump. Massarym's horse shied again, and the prince beat its side with a whip. Rain began falling in sheets, as if bowl the size of the entire sky had just overturned.

But my eyes did not move from the small, serious face that peered out at me from inside the prisoner's hood. A face that broke into a slightly freckled smile, turned up more on the left than on the right.

"Jack?" said Aly Black. "What took you so long?"

CHAPTER FORTY-NINE

BACK TO BLACK

NOTHING CAME OUT of my mouth. Not "Aly!" or "I can't believe we did it!" or "I am about to cry," because my tongue had dried up and my feet were taking me at about a million miles an hour to Aly's side.

I could feel my own smile cracking my cheeks. For the first time in my life, I was moving faster than Marco. Behind me, he and Cass were whooping at the top of their lungs.

But Aly was staring at me with an expression of utter dismay. "Jack, no!" she cried.

I felt something thud against my chest and found myself flying backward through the air. Marco leaped out of my way but I collided with Cass, and we both tumbled to the wet ground.

"You morons!" Aly shouted. "Jack! Cass! Are you okay?"

Massarym barked a laugh. His pals howled. Uhla'ar's stony expression softened into a scornful grin. I sat up. My chest was killing me, but I didn't care. "It's so amazing to see you, Aly," I said.

She was crying. "You, too, Jack. And Marco. And Cass. And Torquin." She wiped a tear away. "Wait . . . *Torquin?*"

"It's actually Qalani," Marco said. "She's borrowing Torquin's body. Turns out, he's a step up from a monkey. Who knew?"

Hearing the flurry of English, the guards looked at each other in confusion. They were beginning to clutch the hilts of their daggers.

Aly sighed. "Guys, keep your distance from these goons. They can be brutal. Things are starting to get bad here. Qalani has just perfected the Loculi and Massarym has already begun stealing—"

"Silence!" Uhla'ar bellowed. "Do not make me attempt to speak English!"

"Aw, please," Marco said. "Just one time through the *Scooby-Doo* song."

"Watch it, Marco!" Aly shrieked.

With a blindingly fast flick of the wrist, Massarym's guard flung a dagger at Marco. But he contorted his body to one side in a kind of ninja hip-hop move. The knife whizzed past his chest so fast that it sent up a spray from the heavy rain.

"Dang, now how are you going to cut me a sandwich?" Marco said. "Qalani, don't translate that."

A distant thunderclap boomed. Massarym silently dismounted from his horse. One of his men jumped off with an umbrella that looked like it was made from animal skin. He held it over the prince's head as they walked together toward the tremendous green blob. With the Sphinx in its mouth, it stared upward into the rain through lidless eyes. The motionless hindquarters of the Egyptian beast were already matted and wet. I couldn't tell if either creature was alive or dead.

Massarym drew his sword and plunged it into the Behemoth's gut. The creature jolted. Its mouth stretched open, and the ragged Sphinx flopped lifelessly onto the wet grass. The Behemoth writhed and roared, shocked back to life after its trip through the rift. It tried to bite Massarym, who stepped nimbly out of its way but kept his sword firmly in place, yanking it left and then right.

The green beast howled as its body sliced in two. In the gusher of yellow fluid and entrails, the Loculus of Language rolled onto the wet grass.

With a triumphant smile, Massarym lifted the orb. Behind him the Behemoth was regenerating a new body before our eyes, quivering and slithering toward the jungle. The Sphinx lay motionless, just barely breathing.

Massarym held out the orb to me and nodded. Pretty

clearly, he wanted me to take it. It was covered with yellow goo, but Massarym didn't seem like the kind of guy you said no to.

As he dropped it in my hands, I fought back the urge to hurl.

"No doubt you are wondering two things," he said. "How did I know where the Loculus was? And how did I know that it was the Loculus of Language, which you could use to comprehend me?"

His Atlantean was perfectly understandable to me now. "Right now I'm wondering how I can keep down my lunch," I said. "But, yeah. Those, too."

I didn't know for sure what language I was speaking. But Massarym got the meaning and Cass, Marco, Eloise, and Aly were looking at me blankly, so it must have been Atlantean.

Massarym drew his face close to mine. His guard wasn't quick enough with the umbrella; I could feel the rain glancing off the prince's nose and into my own face. "I am connected to the Loculi in a deep way," Massarym said. "I know where each one is at all times. What I *don't* know is how you petty thieves could have gotten them. But I don't really care. Because when thieves are eliminated, so is theft."

"I didn't—we didn't—we just got here!" I stammered. "Sir. Your highness. See, we're from—"

"Enough." He held his sword high, nearly slicing through the umbrella, and another guard raced toward him with an animal-skin cloth, quickly wiping the sword of all the yellow blobby stuff the rain had not yet washed away.

"No—no, don't! I haven't even been born yet!" I cringed at my own words. "It's hard to explain. We're from the future. I live in Belleville, Indiana."

He cocked his head.

"Am I speaking Atlantean?" I said.

"Yes, but your words make no sense," Massarym said. "It is only the suspicion that you are crazy that makes me take pity."

"Good," I said. "Pity is good. But I'm not crazy. And I'm also innocent—"

"Oh?" Massarym said, bringing his sword to his side. "All right, then, I'm not an unreasonable guy. Tell me, how did my six Loculi disappear—only to show up in your possession?"

"Um . . . disappear?" I said.

"They were locked up in a chest, guarded by my most loyal men day and night," Massarym went on. "Not more than a few minutes ago, when I saw they were gone, I nearly executed my own best men on the spot. But I knew not one of them had the cunning or stupidity to do such a thing." He pointed to the Loculus in my hand. "And here are two Loculi, before my eyes. One in your hand, and the other, if I'm not mistaken, is the Loculus of Flight in a pack on your back."

I could feel my body shaking. There were rules about time travel. Bhegad had talked about this, in one of the many lectures he'd given us when we first got to the island. I'd forgotten so much of our training, but this stayed in my brain. *According to logic it is impossible*, he said. *But science has strange ways. If time travel were to occur, certain things could simply not happen. They would violate the laws of nature.* Like killing an ancestor, or preventing your parents from meeting—because you wouldn't exist. Like meeting yourself at a younger age, because you couldn't exist in two places at once.

Two of the same thing, you see, cannot exist in the same time, Bhegad had said.

I swallowed hard. Why hadn't I thought of this before? We were bringing Loculi into a time and place where they already existed. Something had to give.

Somehow, our Loculi had made it through the space-time rift. Which meant, by the crazy rules of time travel, Massarym's Loculi had to vanish.

They weren't stolen at all. The laws of nature had made them disappear.

From the woods came a fast clopping of hooves. I could hear Aly shrieking. But I didn't want to take my eyes from Massarym, who was stepping toward me with an angry glare. Once again he was raising his sword.

"Jacko . . ." Marco said from behind me.

"Seize the two other boys," Massarym grumbled to his guards. "I'll take care of this one."

"You can't kill me!" I blurted out, slowly backing away. "Or wait. Maybe you can. Give me a chance to explain, okay? It's kind of a long story. . . ."

"Sorry, I listened and I wasn't convinced," said Massarym. "Time's up."

He lunged toward me, bringing the sword down toward my head.

CHAPTER FIFTY

KARAI AND THE DEATH PART

I JUMPED ASIDE. But I was no Marco. I braced myself for a lost arm or at least a very lopsided haircut.

As I fell to the sopping wet ground, Marco jumped in to defend me. But he didn't have to. Massarym was frozen, arms in the air and sword still raised high overhead. He was struggling mightily to swing it but his arms were stuck. The umbrella was gone, and a taut rope was wrapped around the tip of the sword, pulling it back. As I crabbed away backward on all fours in the mud, I followed the line of the rope with my eyes. It led to a horseman at the edge of the woods.

"Dude, I had your back," Marco whispered, staring at the newcomer in awe. "But this other guy had your front."

My rescuer shouted something that was completely unintelligible to me. I realized that was because I'd dropped the Loculus of Language. Quickly I scooped it up.

Massarym was grunting, fighting against the pull on his sword. But the rope yanked the weapon out of his hand, and it thudded to the ground.

"Brother, have you lost your senses?" the attacker said, pulling on the rope like he was reeling in a trout.

Cass and Eloise were behind me now, too. "That's Karai," Cass said.

"Obvi," Eloise replied.

"Oh, my heart," Qalani murmured.

I turned to see Torquin's body go weak in the knees. She held on to Marco's shoulder with a thick, stubby hand.

"You have no idea how weird this looks," Marco whispered.

He, Cass, and Eloise all stood by me now, putting their hands on the Loculus of Language so they could understand.

"Bravo," Massarym said. "So, you've come to save the lives of your little robbers, who hide Loculi in the very monsters I have raised myself."

Karai came forward on his horse, ignoring his father. "If you strange children be robbers, I commend you. In Massarym, you have found your match in maturity. And in taking the Loculi, you have helped the royal cause." He turned toward the guards. "Men of the royal court, I command you gather these six orbs."

The guards looked at Massarym warily. "They do not move for you, Karai," Massarym said. "Surprise, surprise."

"Gather the Loculi or you will be held for treason!" Karai commanded.

King Uhla'ar, silent so far, put up a hand. "Hold!" he said. "Speak your piece, young Massarym. Circumstances do not augur well for a kingdom in which brother fights brother."

"Whoa, is that how he talks in real life?" Marco said.

"Shh!" I warned.

"Father, you know the evil plan of my brother, the prince Karai," Massarym said. "He seeks to destroy the Loculi created by our mother, Queen Qalani."

Uhla'ar turned his horse to face Karai. "Still on this quest, are you, my son? Do you not see our island paradise is sinking already?"

"Precisely, Father!" Karai protested. "With all respect, the queen has tampered with the sacred Telion. And only by destroying her creation will the balance be restored—"

"Son, we take your point," Uhla'ar interrupted him, "but do you not see it is too late? Our land will not survive."

Both Karai and Massarym began to protest, but Uhla'ar silenced them with a hand. "There is no point now to destroying the Loculi, Karai, other than soothing your mother's guilt. To this, I must agree with Massarym. We must take these orbs away and preserve them. Someday, when the time is right, we—or our descendants—will collect them elsewhere in the world. With the magic divided into seven components, held safely in the seven Loculi, the Atlantean energy will be unleashed again. In this manner, our way of life will last eternally."

Karai dismounted and approached Massarym, fixing him with a hard stare. "I do not scorn you for this statement, Father. Massarym has turned you against me. But if the Loculi are taken away, there will be no descendants of Atlantean royalty to lead this fool's paradise you envision. I have seen to this, by the use of my own science on samples of my own blood. I have unlocked the key to characteristics passed from parent to child and onward. Steal the Loculi, and our descendants will not survive past the age of manhood or womanhood."

"Karai was the one who planted the death part of G7W?" Cass murmured.

"He is gifted . . ." Qalani said softly. "A greater genius than I."

Massarym laughed. "You toy with human beings, do you? Perhaps you experimented with that witless, white-bearded fool?" He brandished his sword, gesturing with it toward Qalani.

"Where is your breeding?" Karai snapped. "A prince of

Atlantis treats every subject with equal respect. I apologize for my brother, kind sir."

"Thank you, my son," Qalani said quietly in Atlantean.

Massarym pointed his sword at Karai. "Such kindness to a half-wit lost in delusions, who dares call you son. Yet you would kill your own descendants!"

"No, *you* would, my brother," Karai replied. "For this marker will only become active if you carry out your quest. If the Loculi remain here and are destroyed, in the Heptakiklos where they first drew force, our descendants will be safe for all eternity. The magic they hold will be returned to the land from which they came."

"The land is doomed, Karai, no matter what we do," Uhla'ar said.

"Perhaps you are right, Father," Karai replied. "But the Telion has been disturbed, and the Telion must be appeased. By destroying the Loculi, we will show that we do not presume to control the energy of the earth. We will buy some time at the very least, of this I am certain. If necessary, our subjects will have the chance to escape on galleons to the four winds. They will establish their own wondrous lands, spreading what they have learned here. Like a flock of birds, they will travel close together yet each seeing a clear path ahead."

"How poetic," Massarym drawled. "And what if they do not travel together as a flock? How do you suppose they will know each other in these barbaric lands?"

Karai drew his own sword. "By my careful work, the descendants of Uhla'ar and Qalani will always recognize one another. From this generation forward, each of our descendants will exhibit a telltale mark of the Atlantean flock."

A flying flock. Birds flew in reverse V formations, with the leader in front and the others spread out so they could see. I felt my fingers touching the back of my head. "The lambda . . ." I said.

"*That's* what it means?" Cass said. "A flying formation of birds?"

"I thought it stood for lucky," Eloise said.

Qalani strode forward. She was owning Torquin's body now, not swaying so much in the hips. "Bravo, Karai," she said in Atlantean. "By order of the queen, I command my guards to deliver the Loculi to the Heptakiklos at once, where they will be destroyed in accordance to the proper ritual!"

"'By order of the queen'? From what pitiful land of hideousness are you, man ape?" Massarym said with a sneer.

Qalani's eyes widened, which was pretty scary in Torquin's body. She lunged forward and smacked her son's face. The impact of that meaty hand made Massarym spin around and tumble to the ground.

"Seize him!" Massarym shouted.

"Seize the Loculi!" Karai countered.

The guards raced forward. Qalani whirled, kicking one in the jaw, then the other. As the guards fell to the ground, King Uhla'ar jumped from his horse, brandishing a gold-handled sword exactly like Ischis. He took a swing at Qalani, who jumped aside with all the agility possible in Torquin's bulk.

Massarym and Karai had drawn their own swords and were facing off in a duel, as the remaining two guards began unhooking our vests.

"Ohhhh, no, Lancelot, you're not taking mine," Marco said.

Two guards pointed daggers at his eyes.

"On second thought," Marco said, "you are."

"Return the Loculi to the court, men!" King Uhla'ar commanded. As his men held us at the points of their blades, the king mounted his horse and brought it toward us. "I will agree to consider sparing your life on one condition. That you reveal the location of the one Loculus that is still missing."

"Wait—the Loculus of Strength?" I said.

"You took that one, King Ooh!" Marco said.

Uhla'ar's face twisted into a barely concealed rage. "They are lucky I do not slaughter them now. Guards, blindfold the visitors and take them to the dungeon."

With a roar, Qalani ran for the woods. One of the guards

threw an ivory-handled dagger, which landed directly in her thigh.

The advantage of having Torquin's beefy body was that she kept on running until she disappeared into the forest.

We had no such luck.

CHAPTER FIFTY-ONE

A BONE TO PICK

UNTIL BEING TOSSED into an Atlantean dungeon, I hadn't realized what an awesome invention deodorant was. The room was about the size of a basketball court with a ten-foot ceiling and an open window letting in the rain. The only two other prisoners in the place were two tiny, shriveled people hidden in corners, but their body odor had the power of a conquering army.

At least we were dry. Sort of.

Aly didn't seem to notice anything. She was pacing at the dungeon's gate. She seemed frustrated. "The weird thing is, I was getting through to Uhla'ar," she muttered. "Back in the woods. I was all tied up with a sack over my head. I figured they were going to kill me. So I pleaded with him. I knew I'd never get through to Massarym, but Uhla'ar's different."

"He's worse, the way I remember," Marco said.

Aly shook her head. "That was then. He's been different since we went through the rift. He stops by here and talks to me sometimes. Way more than he needs to. At first he's always all formal and mean, but then he softens up. Asks questions about history. He wants to know why people act the way they do in the twenty-first century. Also the twentieth and nineteenth and eighteenth, but I can't help with that. Think about it. I'm the only one who knows what he went through—being a statue all those years stuck in front of sitcoms, being covered with pigeon poop and dog pee."

"So why did he tie you up and put that sack on you?" I said.

"Massarym did that," Aly said with the sigh. "That guy—everyone thinks he's charming and cool, but he's one big sack of nasty."

"Well, Ooh La La seemed pretty nasty to me," Marco said.

Aly threw Marco a smile. "I missed you."

"I know." Marco turned away, his face turning red.

"And you . . . *you!*" Aly threw her arms around Cass until he squirmed away.

I wasn't jealous. Well, not totally. It was hard to be jealous when you're surrounded by stink and sweat and the threat of execution. Okay, maybe a little.

And then Aly decided to turn to me.

"You, too, Jack," she said. "You especially."

It wasn't exactly like gardenias dropped from heaven, but when she put her arms around me, I didn't squirm away at all. I closed my eyes and wished it would last until the twenty-first century.

We all jumped back when a broad-shouldered woman in a thick, official-looking tunic thundered down the prison corridor, banging on the metal bars with a stick. She grunted something in Atlantean and shoved a wooden plate under the gap at the bottom of the gate.

On it was a half-eaten cooked fish, charred beyond recognition, with its head, tail, and fins intact. Flies swarmed around it, buzzing angrily at our interruption of their dinner.

"Now that is totally . . ." Marco glanced at Cass.

"Gnitsugsid?" Cass said.

"Exactly," Marco replied.

I caught a new whiff of stink, as if it had been freshly sprayed into the room. From the corners, the two other prisoners were approaching us. The sight of their emaciated bodies was so sad, I felt like crying. Having G7W would have been mercy for them.

I knelt to pick up the fish, but stopped when I spotted some sharp, strong-looking bones that jutted from its midsection.

Lifting the putrid thing, I plucked the bones with my fingers. They were as hard as plastic. And that gave me an idea.

"Can you filet this, Marco?" I said.

"Say *what*?" Marco replied.

Aly and Cass looked at me as if I'd just grown another nose.

"We need these bones, separated and intact," I said. "I'm good at contraptions, but if I tried to extract these from the fish body, I'd leave a mess."

"Me, too!" Cass piped up, his lips curled in disgust.

"Yup," Aly said.

"But—" Marco sputtered.

"Hey, G7W gives you the ability to do awesome stuff with your body. Your fingers are part of that body, right, Brother Marco? Use them to extract the skeleton from that fish. You can give the meat to those two prisoners." I turned to Aly. "You can hack anything, Aly—fix anything, figure out anything. Can you pick locks?"

Aly cocked her head. "Well, *yeah* . . ."

"Do it," I said. "With fish bones."

"*What?*" Aly shot back.

"I forgot my bobby pins back home," I replied. "If you can't do it, that's fine. We'll stick around here until this building sinks into the earth."

Marco went to work, his thick, powerful fingers

somehow freeing the flesh from the fish skeleton with ease. "And . . . presto change-o, fish-o . . . Got it!"

He held up a perfect fish skeleton with nice, long spindly bones. One by one, he began carefully snapping off the thick, plastic-like ribs. As he gave the rest to our fellow prisoners, Aly collected the bones in her palm. "Here goes nothing," she said.

I turned to Cass. "You," I said, "are the one who's going to find a way out of here."

"Uh, dude, we came in blindfolded," Marco reminded me.

Cass shot him a look. "Dude, I'm Cass."

Eloise was leaning against the prison bars, arms crossed. "I guess I'll . . . you know, look out for videocams. Or play with the rats. Because that's all I'm good for."

I knelt next to her. "Eloise, I saw the way you handled a vromaski when Marco was training you. I've heard you speak Backwardish faster and better than your brother. I've seen you stand up to a Mu'ankh and survive a trip through the rift. You're just starting to be a Select. Sometimes even when you've been one, you don't know what you have. But my gut feeling is, yours is the most awesome ability of any of ours. Look at me."

She looked away.

"In the eyes, Eloise." I waited for her until she finally caught my glance again. "I didn't know what I had either.

I have watched your brother and Aly and Marco do all the things I wished I could do. It took me a long time to know that I had anything special—anything at all."

Eloise shook her head. "Come on, Jack . . . it's so obvious," she said. "You're the one who decides. You make all the other abilities mean something. That's the best thing of all."

I smiled. I felt a little lump in my throat, and it wasn't the nausea.

"Wait . . ." Aly said, working a complicated arrangement of bones into the keyhole. "I got it. I think I . . ."

With a teeny *snap*, the whole bone pick fell apart. *"Arrrrrgh!"* Aly groaned.

Eloise sighed. "Okay, Jack, maybe I take that back."

* * *

By the time Aly picked the lock, all that was left of the fish was a head and a tail. She also had to use the prong in Marco's belt buckle, which wasn't real easy to pull apart. It also meant Marco now had to tie the belt around his waist to keep his pants from falling down.

But we were out.

We stuck to the walls, tiptoeing down the dank stone hallways. From other prison cells, I saw pairs of bloodshot eyes peering from shadows, but no one seemed to care enough to make a noise.

"Okay, we make a left at the end of the next corridor,"

Cass whispered. "Eloise?"

On cue, Eloise raced to the corner, her step so light she didn't make a sound. She peered around, then signaled us a thumbs-up. "Maybe she's not so gniyonna after all," Cass whispered.

Left . . . right . . . right . . . up. We made it through a maze of cells, then up a musty flight of steps. The steps were just inside a castle wall. Our landing opened to a hallway that led to a huge wooden door. "That's where we came in," Cass whispered. "If no one's there, we're free."

Eloise raced ahead. She didn't even make it all the way before running back. "How do you do that so quietly?" Marco asked.

"I weigh negative five pounds," Eloise drawled, rolling her eyes. "Anyway, I heard voices. Like, ho-ho-ho-I'm-a-big-bad-prison-guard-with-muscles-and-a-sword kinds of voices. We can't do it."

Cass exhaled. On the other side of the landing, a door led into the castle chambers. "We're going to have to go through the palace," he said. "Let's just hope they're all busy running around worrying about the attacks and the weather."

Eloise pushed the door open a fraction of an inch and peered inside. "Looks empty to—"

The door swung open all the way, pulling the handle from Eloise's small fist. She screamed and jumped away.

From the other side of the door stepped the tall, powerful figure of King Uhla'ar of Atlantis. His bronzed, craggy features twisted into a smile.

"Scooby-Dooby-Doo, where are you?" he said.

CHAPTER FIFTY-TWO

UHLA'AR'S REVENGE

THE SURPRISE BLEW us all backward. I don't know how I kept myself from falling down the stone stairs and dying before I was born.

Aly's face was bone white. "Uhla'ar, please . . ."

The king looked back into the chamber. I thought he was going to order us inside and set up a nice, impromptu bow-and-arrow firing squad. But instead he forced us back into the stairwell landing.

As Uhla'ar shut the door behind us, he turned his back. I could see Marco quickly unwrapping his belt. I could tell he had some crazy plan. Did strangling a king count as changing the past?

As the king turned, Marco lunged forward, the belt

stretched between his hands. But his pants fell straight down, bunching around his ankles, and he fell to the floor.

The king gave him a baffled look. From behind his back, he produced the Loculus of Language and handed it to me.

"I refuse," he said, "to speak any more English than I just did. Rise, young man, and adjust your garment."

I nearly dropped the Loculus from shock. "H-h-hands on, everyone," I squeaked.

"Great idea," said Marco, his face three shades of red darker.

King Uhla'ar waited, staring at us with stony features as Cass, Aly, and Eloise all touched the Loculus. And Marco, after his belt was tied.

Finally the king continued, nearly spitting his words: "You all fought me, on the other side of the rift. You nearly destroyed me."

"Um . . . sorry," Cass said.

Uhla'ar whirled toward him. *"Are you?"* he snapped. "Because I would have expected no less of a warrior than to fight. You are small and slight, yet you stand your ground."

He was looking at Marco now. "I know what will happen in this world. I have lived a great long time. I have stood centuries in one place and observed much. I have watched arguments and killings, and I have seen families grow and die."

Marco swallowed. "Yup . . . well, there's a lot of good stuff on TV these days. . . ."

"You mock me," Uhla'ar shot back, but his voice seemed more hurt than angry. "As did Massarym, forcing me to live in that wretched town in Greece. But here is the conundrum—you also freed me."

"We did!" Cass quickly agreed.

Uhla'ar looked at him quizzically. "When I fought you on the other side of the rift, I wanted one thing: to return to my kingdom and preserve it. But I have learned so much since returning. Because I look at everything through the eyes of a different Uhla'ar. Having seen the future, I know now that it is too late to reverse what Qalani has done. The time for Telion has passed. The energy gave, and now it takes away."

"We could try to come back earlier in time. . . ." Cass said.

"There are reasons we are here, now," Uhla'ar said. "This I believe. For centuries I scorned the inferior life that I saw when I was stuck in Greece, the pettiness and greed. In the wild intensity of joy, in the moaning depth of tragedy, I saw only weakness. Before my eyes civilizations surged and fell, none as pure and perfect as Atlantis. *Weakness!*"

He took a deep breath. "But now, coming back here, I see more clearly. I was a fool. In that ragged humanity, progress was blindingly swift. It was not concentrated in one spot, one kingdom. It did not turn its back to the rest of the world. I see now that the passing of Atlantis was far from the end of civilization. That perhaps Telion was no longer our private domain, but that it was being spread across the world in smaller doses, for all people."

"Hate to break it to you," I said, "but that Telion is not as well distributed as you think."

"Ah, but it *can be*," Uhla'ar said. "And that is why my son Massarym's quest is a fool's errand. He would hasten to destroy his own land—in a quest to build it elsewhere artificially. Nonsense. Your world may be full of strife, my friends. It may seem hopeless to you. But the world of Atlantis was not equal. Yours at least has the potential to be that way. If we can stop Massarym now, there is no telling how much better it will be."

"So wait," Cass said. "You're . . . on our side?"

I nodded, remembering the visions I had of Massarym and Uhla'ar's massive battles. "In the Dream . . . you were fighting Massarym. You did try to stop him."

"Whoa, whoa, so if you're on our side, what was all about in the caldera?" Marco said.

"Confusion . . . frustration." Uhla'ar smiled at Aly. "My mind was—how you say, fried?—when I arrived through the rift. I didn't know what to think anymore. But this dear girl helped me. By listening. By forcing me to become a leader again. By leading me away from force and toward wisdom."

Marco shook his head. "Okay, we're getting there, Ooh. Little by little. But today, back in the woods, you were so on Massarym's side. . . ."

"A little trickery I share with Karai," Uhla'ar replied. "Massarym had hidden six Loculi. I have been trying to gain his trust, as he suspects my loyalties. Now, of course, because of your arrival, the Loculi are ours—except for one."

I smiled. "The Loculus of Strength. The one you brought through the rift."

"When you brought it through, did Massarym's disappear?" Cass asked.

Uhla'ar put his finger to his lips, then ducked back into the chamber. When he came out, he was holding a heavy box made of iron. Setting it on the floor, he yanked it open.

The Loculus of Strength nearly blinded me with its forceful glow.

"That's it, all right," Marco said, turning away.

"Karai and I have a plan of our own, a simple one," Uhla'ar said. "It is to happen at nightfall, in about two hours. You have proven your resourcefulness to me thrice— in Greece, in the volcano, and in your escape from the dungeon. I would be a fool not to think it would be useful to have you with us."

"What's the plan?" I asked.

"To smash the Loculi to bits, and with great joy," King Uhla'ar said. "As quickly as possible, right here in the dungeon."

I shook my head. "No."

"What do you mean, no?" Eloise said in disbelief. "We have a chance to save the continent!"

"If the Loculi are destroyed here, in the past, before they leave the island," Aly piped up, "G7W will not mutate into a killer."

"Dude, all those Selects, those unexplained deaths of thirteen-year-olds through history?" Marco said. "I mean, nobody heard about most of them, but there was that big one in the news—the kid who dropped dead in the bowling alley? Randall Cromarty! He lives. *We* live."

"Think about it," Cass added. "No big fight between the KI and the Massa. Herman Wenders will never discover the island because his son will be fine. He'll spend his life as a happy shoe salesman in Düsseldorf. And a couple of centuries later—*we'll all have our fourteenth birthdays*!"

I put up my hands. They weren't understanding me.

"Guys—I'm down with all of that!" I said. "What I mean is, we can't do it here in the dungeon. Karai was specific. He said the Loculi had to be destroyed *in the Heptakiklos where they first drew force.*"

I looked at Cass, who looked at Eloise, who looked at Aly, who looked at Marco. We all looked at King Uhla'ar.

"I shall call my carriage and notify Karai," he said. "I defer to his wishes."

* * *

For a king, it was a pretty modest carriage. But that was because Uhla'ar did not want to be noticed. One lazy horse pulled us through the woods in a creaky old dray with a stretched animal skin covering over the top. We jounced on every hole in the road.

"Feels like we're back home and Torquin's driving," Aly murmured.

"The island," I reminded her, "is not home."

Uhla'ar and Karai were disguised in dirty, loose-fitted smocks. Karai had managed to find rags for us all, and we covered our heads with thick kerchiefs. We'd draped an enormous blanket over the chest with the Loculi—except for the Loculus of Language, which I held swaddled in a blanket as if it were a baby.

"Guys," Cass said excitedly, "do you realize this is the first time all seven Loculi have been together?"

I nodded. "We thought this big moment would happen in Mount Onyx."

Aly leaned her head against me. I couldn't help it, but I sprouted goose bumps all over. "What's going to happen?" she said.

"Wh-what do you mean?" I asked.

"When it's all over," she said. "How do we get back? What if we can't?"

We all wanted the answer to those questions, but no

one knew enough to give them.

So no one did.

* * *

As we arrived at the clearing, I thought the cart had hit the biggest pothole in the world. It took me a moment to realize it was not a hole at all, but a sharp ground tremor. About fifty yards to our right, a tree let out a groan like a dying beast as it split down the middle and fell. The lightning was coming from all sides now, like an out-of-control electricity class in some sky-based school for the gods.

It was happening, and we all knew it. Atlantis was starting to destruct.

We had to shout to be heard. "Let's do this fast!" I said.

The cart's axle was broken, the horse shying and neighing in fear. We jumped out. Karai and Uhla'ar hurried the chest from the cart to the Heptakiklos.

Around the sword Ischis, smoke billowed out. The crack bubbled open a half inch as we watched. "It's going to blow," Marco said. "I can feel it."

Aly and Eloise pried open the chest. The Loculi of Flight, Healing, Underwater Breathing, Strength, and Teleportation all glowed up at us. I put the Loculus of Language inside, and I could hear it bumping up against the Loculus of Invisibility, which was, as always, invisible. "Let's get them into the Heptakiklos!" I shouted, turning to

Eloise. "Youngest Select goes first!"

She reached in and took the Loculus of Language. She looked for the bowl that had been dug for it in stone—the one with the carving of the Great Pyramid. Carefully she placed it inside.

Aly grabbed Invisibility and vanished from sight, only to reappear as she set it into its bowl.

One by one the Loculi took their positions in the Heptakiklos, where Qalani had built them.

"So, how do we nuke these guys?" Marco shouted over the rain.

I kept one hand on the Loculus of Language so I could understand Karai and Uhla'ar.

"Jack, Marco, Cass, Aly, Eloise, Father, and me—seven royals!" Karai shouted back, squinting his eyes as the water pelted them. "A perfect number! Okay, this must be done with precision. According to my calculations, the Loculi must be destroyed all at *exactly the same time*—otherwise they simply repair each other! As one goes down, another comes up!"

"Sort of like Whac-a-Loc!" Marco said.

"What?" Karai shouted.

"Never mind!" Marco replied.

"We will use these." Karai produced from inside his garment seven gleaming metal-forged wedges and spilled them onto the wet soil.

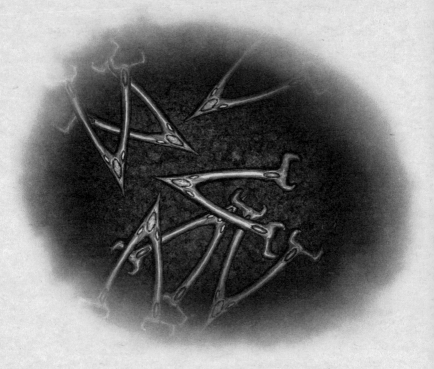

"Cool!" Eloise said.

"They represent the *kopadi*, the Atlantean word for a flock!" Karai announced. "Designed to pierce the Loculi with the appropriate force. But remember—it is crucial that this be done in one blow! By all seven of us."

As I translated for my friends, a maniacal shout came from the woods. We all looked up toward the ridge, shielding our eyes from the storm. Massarym emerged from the trees, his dagger pointed at the head of a captive.

Qalani.

Her hands—Torquin's hands—were bound at the wrists, and a bandanna covered her mouth. Her thigh was bandaged with a blood-stained tourniquet where she had been stabbed by the thrown dagger.

Trapped in Torquin's body, Qalani stared forward with the eyes of a mother who could not bring herself to fight back against her own son.

Massarym pushed her toward the edge of the ridge. Then, lashing out swiftly and mercilessly with his foot, he kicked her over.

"And one more," he called out, "makes eight!"

CHAPTER FIFTY-THREE

THE CIRCUIT OF POWER

QALANI FELL, ROLLING to the bottom of the ridge. I had to turn away. Seeing Torquin's body so out of control was painful. Knowing who was inside was unbearable.

She landed few feet from us, her face twisted into a grimace. Blood oozed from the tourniquet. Eloise calmly grabbed the Loculus of Healing and ran to her. As she pressed the Loculus to Qalani's leg, she untied her bonds.

I grabbed the Loculus of Language and held tight.

"Thank you . . ." the queen rasped.

"By Qalani's crown, Massarym, how could you be this cruel to a commoner?" Uhla'ar said. "Has this man attacked you?"

Massarym bounded down the rain-slickened ridge. "Ah,

well, maybe I will not kill this traitorous peasant after all! You do put me into a merciful mood, Father. For I see you have collected the Loculi for me!"

King Uhla'ar stood. "I have collected the Loculi indeed, Massarym. But not to serve your plans."

The prince strode toward us, placing his foot on the Loculus of Healing, jamming it down into Qalani's wound. Wincing, she cried, "Massarym, my son, please . . ."

"Do you not hear this blasphemy?" Massarym said. "This oaf claims to be the queen. And the queen is missing. Is that not an odd coincidence?"

"Missing?" Karai said. "Is that true, Father?"

Uhla'ar looked confused. "I—I don't know."

Eloise, Cass, and Marco were all touching the Loculus of Language, which was in my arms now. They knew exactly what was being said. And I felt the blood draining from my face.

Two of the same things cannot exist in the same time.

When Uhla'ar had come through the rift from the twenty-first century, he had simply replaced the Uhla'ar that was here. No one seemed to have noticed this, but that wasn't surprising.

But Qalani-as-Torquin had replaced regular Qalani. And that was a big difference, to put it mildly.

"What is your plan, Father?" Massarym said. "Why has no one seen the queen? Perhaps she has been fed to this animal of a man, who speaks in her voice?"

"Why would I do such a thing?" Uhla'ar retorted.

Massarym shrugged. "I do not understand your actions. One minute you are my helpmeet, the next you conspire with Karai to destroy the Loculi. What deeds, what foul magic, are behind the actions of Uhla'ar? Has my brother twisted your mind in his delusion to save Atlantis for himself?"

"That's preposterous!" Uhla'ar said.

"Stop this, my son!" Qalani said.

Karai stared at Uhla'ar in confusion. "Who is that man, Father? Why is he calling Massarym his son?"

The sky cracked with lightning. There was no time to explain Torquin to Karai. Massarym was delaying us. "Ignore him!" I shouted.

Karai shook his head. "But . . . there is something about that fellow . . ."

Qalani looked at me and I stared back, trying to drill my thoughts into her head. *Play along. Do not call him "son." They will not understand, and you will ruin everything.*

Another jolt shook the earth. Eloise grabbed the Loculus of Language from my hand and ran to the Heptakiklos. In her other arm was the Loculus of Healing, which she had taken to heal Qalani.

As she put them both back into their places, she shouted, "Let's do this—now!"

We all raced to the Heptakiklos. The Loculi were together now, all seven.

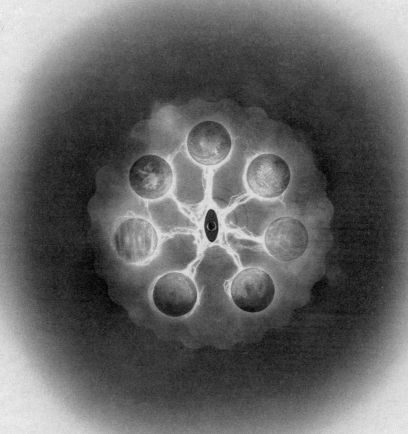

The Song of the Heptakiklos rang from ridge to ridge. I could feel the energy flowing from the rift, coursing through the seven orbs to create an unending circuit of power and mystery, healing and goodness. As we stood with our backs

407

to them, the light seeped in through my feet and filled me up to my knees, up through my spine, up to the white shape on the back of my head.

The rain poured down, but I felt bone dry. Marco staggered back, shielding his eyes from the glare.

Like a flock of birds, they will travel close together yet each seeing a clear path ahead.

"Take the kopadi—the weapons!" I shouted. "Now."

All seven of us turned and grabbed a lambda-shape knife.

"Give me those!" Massarym shouted.

He ran toward us, holding his sword aloft. I heard a loud, guttural yell.

Turning my head quickly, I saw Qalani's thick Torquin arms close around her son's legs. She wrestled him easily to the ground and stood, dragging him backward, his face in the mud, until he was unconscious. Then, turning him faceup at the base of the ridge, she gently daubed his mud-spattered, unconscious face with the edge of Torquin's shirt.

As Qalani knelt and kissed the cheek of her son, Uhla'ar held up one hand. "Wait."

Striding toward the wet, hulking figure of Torquin, the king held out his kopadi. "You are Qalani, my beloved wife," he said, his voice cracking, his brow dripping with rain and tears. "I cannot deny this. Nor can I bear returning to the time and place from which I traveled. I have lived

408

many lifetimes there, and I desire no more."

Qalani stepped forward. "My husband, my kind king," she said, "I shall remain here with my people. It is I who caused this, and I who must bear responsibility."

"If you remain, then you also deprive this man Torquin, whose person you fill, of his own life," Uhla'ar said, walking toward her. "He did not ask for this fate. Come."

He placed the kopadi into the thick, callused hand of Victor Rafael Quiñones, and then planted a tender kiss on the stubbled cheek. "We will meet again."

Qalani bowed her head. Weeping, she hugged Uhla'ar for a good solid minute.

At the crack of thunder that sparked an instant fire in the western woods, Qalani let go and stepped toward the circle. She lifted the kopadi high over her head, aiming the point at the Loculus of Flight.

"Lift!" I said.

All seven of us took our positions. The ground shook again, hard. With a jarring rumble, the rift split open, nearly to the edge of the Heptakiklos.

"And . . . strike!"

CHAPTER FIFTY-FOUR

IT BEGINS

ON THE MORNING I was scheduled to die, a large bare-foot man with a bushy red beard waddled past my house. The thirty-degree temperature didn't seem to bother him, but he must have had a lousy breakfast, because he let out a burp as loud as a tuba.

Belching barefoot giants who look like Vikings are not normal in Belleville, Indiana. But I didn't really get a chance to see the guy closely.

At that moment, I, Jack McKinley, was under attack in my own bedroom. By a flying reptile.

I could have used an alarm clock. But last night I'd been up late studying for my first-period math test and I'm a deep sleeper. Dad couldn't wake me because he was in Singapore on business. And Vanessa, the beloved au pair I call my don't-care-giver, always slept till noon.

I had known I'd need a big sound. Something I couldn't possibly sleep through. That's when I saw my papier-mâché volcano from last month's science fair, still on my desk. It was full of baking soda. So I got my dad's coffeemaker, filled it with vinegar, and rigged it to the volcano with a plastic tube. I set the timer for 6:30 A.M., when the coffeemaker would release the vinegar into the volcano, causing a goop explosion. I put a chute at the base of the volcano to capture that goop. In the chute was a billiard ball, which would roll down toward a spring-loaded catapult on my chair. The catapult would release a big old plastic Ugliosaurus™—a fanged eagle crossed with a lion, bright-red.

Bang—when that baby hit the wall I'd have to be dead not to wake up.

It worked like a charm. I jumped out of bed, washed my face, and ran downstairs. I wolfed down a bagel with butter, swigged from a carton of milk, and leafed through the travel brochure on the kitchen table.

I knew that when the week was out, I would be flying overseas for the coolest vacation of my life. Dad would be flying up from Singapore and Mom from Antarctica. We would meet at the airport and take a hydroplane to get to our resort.

I could not wait.

* * *

411

No!

I woke up so fast I got a humongous charley horse in my left calf. Groaning, I rubbed my leg and sank back onto the pillow, my eyes still closed.

The dream was all wrong.

It didn't happen like that.

Dad called from Singapore and I got a late start, so I rushed to school and nearly ran over Barry Reese, who picked a fight and caused me to dash out into the street, where I passed out and then woke up hours later in the hospital, where I saw a chaplain who was really Torquin in disguise. . . .

"Jack?" Mom's voice made my eyes pop open.

My room was icy cold. An air conditioner pumped like crazy from a duct overhead. My suitcase was wide open on a wooden stand by a flat-screen TV, and clothes were strewn all about.

By my bedside, a clock flashed 7:30 A.M.

It wasn't my clock. It wasn't my bedroom. And the Ugliosaurus was nowhere in sight.

What the heck was going on?

"Jackie! Time to wake up!" Mom's fingers rapped on the door three times. "Sleep well?"

"Mom!" I screamed.

She was alive. Smiling. Here.

"Awwww . . ." she said, cocking her head to the side. "Nightmares, sweetie?"

I jumped up and kissed her. I couldn't help it.

With a giddy laugh, she squeezed me and then ducked back through the door. "Somebody's still in dreamy land. Okay, get dressed. We have a big day ahead of us."

Dreamy land?

Nightmares?

I counted to three, then ran to the bathroom. I'd unpacked my toothbrush and toothpaste and a brush and . . .

There.

The hand mirror. It was the one Dad and I had bought at CVS when I was in second grade. I turned it and saw the laminated photo of four-year-old me sledding with Mom and Dad. Still there.

Quickly I turned my back to the bathroom mirror and held up the hand mirror so I could see the back of my head.

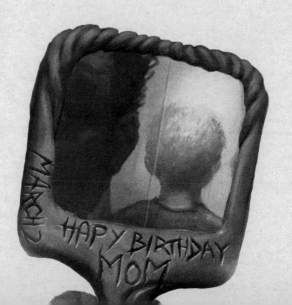

"Nice hotel, huh?"

Dad's voice made me jump. I nearly dropped the mirror onto the marble countertop. "Really nice," I said.

"Is something wrong?" he asked.

"No!" I snapped back.

"Come. Your mom and I are ready for breakfast," he said. "They have custom omelets. And your favorite—chocolate chocolate-chip muffins!"

"Yum," I said, pretending I had not completely lost my appetite.

After he left, I quickly got dressed. But my mind was racing.

What had happened? Where was the lambda? Where were my friends? Had this whole thing been a dream?

Where on earth were we?

CHAPTER FIFTY-FIVE

THE FLOCK

NISSI, THE LOST WORLD, WELCOMES YOU!

THE BANNER STARED down at us as we finished up breakfast. It was like some cruel reminder of everything I'd just experienced—or thought I had.

I half expected to blink and see the black tower of Mount Onyx, the odd brick buildings of the Karai Institute. But we were in some big old tourist resort, vast, manicured, and flat, with towering palm trees set against blue skies. All around us were dads wearing Hawaiian shirts and moms loading up strollers with stolen supplies from the buffet table. And vice versa. Just outside the door was a gigantic pool with a waterslide shaped vaguely like a green dinosaur. Mom and Dad spent the whole meal jabbering on about animals and exhibits. They both knew this scientist and that, and I was sure we'd spend many hours chuckling over tea and talking about genetics.

It all felt familiar. It all felt like I just woke up on Mars. So the two sensations canceled each other out, leaving me just plain numb.

Part of me wanted to run into the middle of the breakfast area and dance my butt off—because Mom was alive and Dad wasn't running away from home and we were together and nothing had ever been wrong.

But another part of me felt like my life was a great big PowerPoint presentation and a virus had just swept in and replaced all the slides.

Torquin . . . Marco, Cass, and Aly . . . the Seven Wonders . . . Professor Bhegad and Brother Dimitrios and Daria and Canavar and Crazy Farouk . . . they couldn't have just been thoughts and dreams.

Could they?

"Onward!" Dad trumpeted as he swigged his last bit of black coffee.

"Aren't you hungry, Jackie?" Mom asked, frowning at the untouched omelet on my plate.

"Tummy ache," I said.

She handed me a banana from her tray. "Well, take this,"

she said. "Just in case you do get hungry. It'll be gentle on your stomach."

I tucked the banana into my shirt pocket, which looked ridiculous, but in this crowd of tourists, no one would care. As we walked outside, the weather slammed me like a fist. Compared to the frigid AC of the hotel, the air was heavy and hot—and it was still morning.

We took a tram ride that raced along a lush tropical preserve. Our first stop was called Simian Surprises.

A canned voice spoke to us through the tram PA: "As on the island of Komodo, where the famed Komodo dragon survived to modern times, so, too, here in Nissi were found extraordinary examples of evolutionary anomalies not seen anywhere else in the world. At Lost World we preserve natural habitats, which necessitate sometimes dense tree covers, so walking visitors are urged to be patient. Do not under any circumstances attempt to feed the animals or even pretend to, and stay behind the Plexiglas barriers. . . ."

And blah, blah, blah.

I was tired and cranky before we even climbed down the stairs.

Our tour guide led us down a path between two extremely high Plexiglas walls. Kids had scraped words into the plastic, and by reading them I knew that Nick loved Jennie, and Taki "wuz hear," and someone felt the need to write FIXX about a zillion times.

All I could see behind the scratched plastic was thick clumps of palm trees and an occasional bird. I slowed down so the grown-ups would go on ahead and let my eyes wander upward. I heard a monkeylike screech and imagined Qalani becoming the Omphalos while trapped inside jungle animals. "Hello, my queen," I murmured.

The screech sounded again, this time a bit closer.

I looked left and right, and took the banana from my pocket. "Here, monkey, monkey, monkey!" I said. "Want some breakfast?"

"EEEEEEEEEE!"

A black figure dropped from the trees and slammed itself against the Plexiglas. I dropped the banana and fell to the ground as the creature spat a yellow glob that slimed the wall and dripped down.

The guide came running around the bend. He was trying to act all friendly, but I could see the anger in his face. "Oh dear, the black maimou must have smelled that banana, ha-ha!" he said with forced cheer. "This is exactly why we posted all the Do Not Feed the Animals signs!"

I bolted to my feet, staring into the yellow eyes of my assailant.

I knew that glare. I knew it very well. "It's not a maimou. . . ." I said.

"Excuse me?" the guide said.

The creature bared its teeth at me through the plastic and spat again.

"I'm not crazy. . . ." I turned to the guide and laughed. "I didn't dream it!"

"No, no, no, no," the guide said, "these animals are nightmarish indeed but very real—"

"It's a vizzeet," I said. "It's called a vizzeet and it spits poison."

"Uh, ladies and gentlemen, the maimou's venom sac has been surgically neutralized so that any contact with its saliva is perfectly harmless"—he chuckled—"if a bit unsightly."

As he walked onward with the group, Mom and Dad stayed behind. "Jack, are you all right?"

"I'm fine," I said. "I'm fine and I'm not crazy. I'm not. *Where is this place?*"

They gave each other a look. "We've been talking about this for weeks, Jack," Dad said.

"It's Nissi, the lost island in the tropics?" Mom added. "The place that somehow escaped being discovered until it was picked up by satellite a few years ago? *Ding, ding, ding* . . . ring any bells?"

"Right," I said. "That's right. The island didn't sink. This is it. We went through the rift and the rift closed. Forever. The Loculi are gone! They're gone and there was never a Karai Institute or any Massa. I'm not the Tailor anymore. Or the Destroyer. I don't have to rule! *Do you know what this means?* Woo-HOO!"

A maniac. A raving lunatic. I knew I sounded like that, but I couldn't help it.

Mom and Dad gave each other a look and burst out

laughing. "Another short story, yes!" Dad shouted. "I love the way your mind works, Jack. Everything a springboard for an idea. You will do this for a living someday. I know it. An author of a children's adventure series!"

"Make sure you include a little romance," Mom said with a wink. "Now come on. Let's do some more exploring."

As we walked on, all I could think about was Aly. And that made my collar feel about three hundred degrees hotter.

I had to find out about her. About Marco and Cass and Eloise. I had to know if they existed. But to do this, I would need some time alone.

We nearly ran into another family, a couple and three kids, heading into an enormous, high-roofed building that echoed with screeches. The eldest brother was maybe a year or so older than me, taking a zillion photos with his phone. Just inside the door, I could see a bright red dot in the middle of his image. I followed his line of sight to a branch on a tree way up by the opposite wall. The entire wall was constructed of caves, and at the very top one I saw a flurry of red.

To a hushed chorus of oohs and ahhs, a griffin flew out and perched on a branch. As it glowered down, it seemed to fix its icy yellow gaze on me.

CAAAAAAAAAWWWWW!

At the sound of its screech I gasped and instinctively dropped to the ground.

"What on earth is going on?" the guide said. "Shall I call nine one one?"

I jumped to my feet, staring warily up at the griffin. "Sorry," I said. "Sorry . . ."

The big red bird turned lazily on its perch and flew back into the cave.

Mom put a protective arm around me and smiled at the guide. "He hasn't seen one of those before, that's all."

The older kid was still clutching his phone. With his free hand he dusted the dirt off the side of my shirt. "It's okay," he said. "I was scared my first time, too."

"Thanks . . ." I said.

"Randy," he said with a smile. "You?"

"Jack."

As he turned to walk with his family, I caught a look at his backpack:

IF FOUND,
PLEASE RETURN TO
RANDALL CROMARTY
1167 LINKER ALLEY
SKOKIE, IL

I let out a laugh so loud, even the griffin looked.

"He didn't die. . . ." I murmured. "This kid. Randall. He didn't die in the bowling alley—he's alive. He's over fourteen and he's alive. And he's here!"

"Hmm?" Dad said absentmindedly, tapping away at his phone. "Just a sec, Jack."

I watched Randall Cromarty walk away. His hair was cut short, and as he walked around the bend to the cafeteria, the sunlight reflected against the back of his head.

I could make out the vague outline of a lambda.

Mom saw me staring. She smiled. "I noticed that. He's got it, too. Your birthmark."

"My birthmark?" I said. "But . . ."

"I saw you looking at your head this morning," she said. "It's not unattractive, you know. Just white hair. Some kids think it's cool. And hair dye does have chemicals . . ."

"Don't dye it!" I said. "I mean, please. Let's stop dyeing it, okay? I don't mind anymore."

She shrugged. "Sure, Jackie. No problem either way."

"Honey," Dad said. "We're late for that lecture."

Mom rolled her eyes. "The numerologist? Tamasi?"

"Archaeologist," Dad said. "He just loves analyzing finds based on numerical theories. Anyway, I like him. Hurry."

We raced out of the exhibit and back onto the tram. I could barely think straight. As the tram passed over the preserve, I heard screeches and snorts. I think I caught a glimpse of a hose-beaked vromaski, but I wasn't sure. It was a vast place, and I could not see far enough to any beach, but still . . .

This was the island. It had to be.

We had destroyed the Loculi with the kopadi. Which meant the Heptakiklos imploded, burying the great Atlantean power, the Telion. We had made it through the rift in time. Somehow.

If I was right, Karai's genetic engineering—the G7W death curse—never happened. And no Loculi were ever taken away to be hidden and protected.

"Penny for your thoughts, Jack," Mom said, as the tram stopped at the exhibition hall.

"Can we visit the Seven Wonders of the Ancient World someday?" I asked.

"The Lighthouse of Alexandria, the Great Pyramid of Giza, the Mausoleum at Halicarnassus, the Colossus of Rhodes, the Temple of Artemis, the Statue of Zeus at Olympia, and . . ." Dad squinched his eyes shut. "I always forget one. . . ."

"The Great Wall?" Mom guessed.

"The Hanging Gardens of Babylon," I said.

"Good one, Jack!" Dad said.

"So . . . they existed?" I said. "They were all built anyway?"

Dad snuck a look at Mom, as the tram came to a stop. "He's really in his own world today, isn't he? Come on."

We climbed down and ran up the stairs to an old building, past a sign that said, *Today! 9:00 A.M. Hear Professor Radamanthus Tamasi Discuss the Numerological Basis of Nissi's Archaeological Past!*

This was crazy. But . . .

"Tamasi?" I looked closely at the image—a craggy-faced guy with thick glasses, wispy gray hair, and a distracted look. "Isn't this guy named—?"

"Tamasi is his real name," Dad said. "But you're right, he never goes by it. Has this thing about the number seven. It repeats itself in nature and archaeology in all kinds of odd ways."

"One, four, two, eight, five, seven . . ." I said. "Every seventh is a combination of those digits in that order."

"Good for you, Jack!" Dad said. "So this guy decides to create a kind of stage name for himself—"

"Bhegad?" I blurted out.

"How did you know that?" Mom asked.

BHEGAD. Of course. It wasn't a real name. I couldn't believe I hadn't seen this before.

"Check this out." I grabbed a brochure from my pocket and scribbled on it:

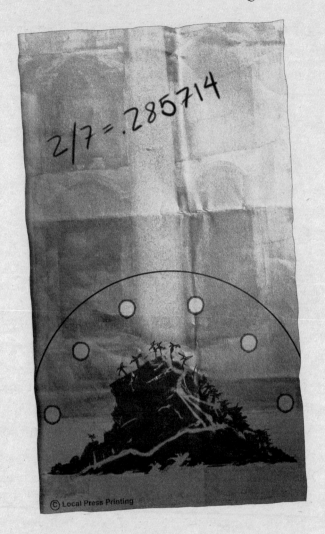

"Uh, okay . . ." Mom said.

"Right," Dad piped up. "Those digits that repeat themselves. The cycle of sevenths."

425

"*B* is the second letter of the alphabet," I said. "So here—watch. I take those numbers I just wrote down and find the letter of the alphabet that belongs to each number!"

Mom let out a hoot of laughter. "Hoo boy. What an old nerd!"

As Dad hurried us through the front door, a gruff voice called out: "Tickets five dollars!"

Behind a desk sat a very broad man with slicked-back red hair and black glasses, pointing to a price list. "Under fourteen free," he grunted.

"Torquin?"

I was nearly screaming, and he dropped his pen. "Excuse me?" he said.

"Your name is Torquin!" I blabbered.

He chuckled. "Sorry, dude. Victor. Vic Quiñones. I'm the professor's graduate assistant. Better hurry if you want to get a seat."

I was laughing so hard I can't believe they didn't throw me out.

Professor Bhegad was pacing the stage, muttering to two assistants. I didn't know what they were talking about—he'd probably forgotten his papers or something, but it made me so happy to see him alive.

As we waited for the lecture to begin, I thought about my friends again. Did Cass and Eloise know each other? Were their parents out of jail? Was Aly in California and Marco in Ohio? Or were they here on the island of Nissi somewhere?

Did they even exist? Had they made it through the rift, or was I the only one?

Bhegad . . . Torquin . . . Randall Cromarty . . . these were too strange to be coincidences. Weren't they?

I thought about the lambda. *No, not a lambda. A flock.* It was still there. Still on my head. Still on Randy's. But Cromarty had lived past fourteen. Karai had said the death curse would be lifted if the Loculi were destroyed, and that was great.

That was amazing. I was going to live!

Still . . . what about the powers? What about *that* part of

G7W—the part that opened up your ceresacrum and made your best talents a superpower. Did we still have that?

Tinker, Tailor, Soldier, Sailor.

I looked around. The auditorium was filling up, but Bhegad still didn't seem ready. I took out my phone and flipped through my contacts.

A. Black

M the M. Ramsay

C. Williams

E. Williams

I nearly screamed.

Yes.

All there.

I felt myself grinning at Bhegad. Sending him thoughts. *You told me about time travel. You weren't sure it could be done. You hinted the world would be changed in impossible ways.*

But he was still here. And so was I. Mom. Dad. My friends.

Someday, I vowed, I would tell him everything. About the life he never led.

I looked back down at my phone. First I had important business to take care of. If I could remember what had just happened—if I was aware of both worlds, both realities— then I hoped they would, too.

And we would share those memories at four birthdays in the coming year. Four of the happiest birthdays ever in history.

Clicking on Aly's name, I began typing out a text.

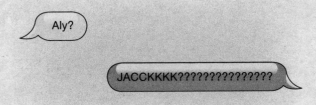

I smiled.

I couldn't wait.

SEVEN·WONDERS
of the Ancient World

BLACK·SEA

THE·TEMPLE·OF·ARTEMIS
AT·EPHESUS

ATHENS

THE·MAUSOLEUM
AT·HALICARNASSUS

THE·STATUE·OF·ZEUS
AT·OLYMPIA

THE·COLOSSUS
OF·RHODES

MEDITERRANEAN·SEA

THE·LIGHTHOUSE·OF·ALEXANDRIA

THE·GREAT·PYRAMID·OF·GIZA

NILE

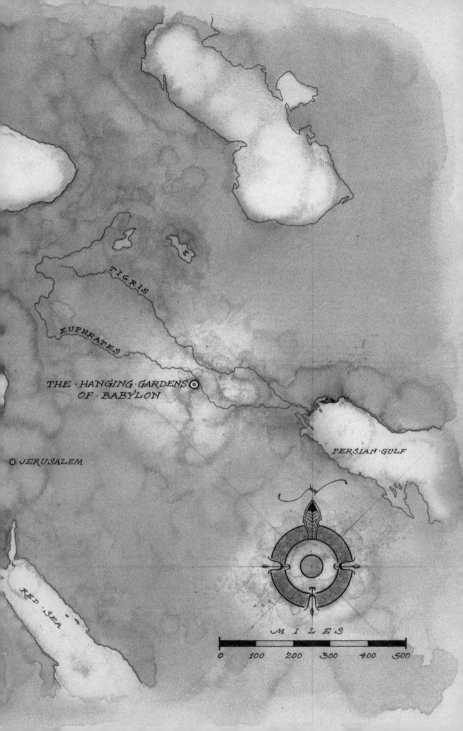

TIGRIS

EUPHRATES

THE · HANGING · GARDENS
OF · BABYLON

O JERUSALEM

PERSIAN · GULF

RED SEA

M I L E S

0   100   200   300   400   500

DROW LANIF A

WAIT. IT'S OVER?

Already?

Seven Wonders, five books, three years, one very sad writer. I'm going to miss this world. A lot. If you've come this far on the journey with me, I feel you deserve a final word. Because, let's face it, you're my hero.

Yup, you.

Authors don't say this enough: readers are the reason we exist. Well, other things are important too—oxygen and chocolate come to mind—but the truth is, without you the Seven Wonders would stay just the way it started. As an idea. A seed of a story.

You need to know that this seed was picked up, turned over, and grown by some very, very good farmers.

Like the megastar Dave Linker at HarperCollins. As head of the Seven Wonders team, he reads every word of every draft, finds mistakes, makes amazing suggestions, cracks the whip, coordinates with the art and publicity departments, and makes you feel like you're traveling with a brother. He's superarticulate, too, except when he calls to tell you that your book has made the *New York Times* bestseller list. Then he gets so excited he can barely form a coherent sentence.

The deep-down, roll-up-the-sleeves editing was done by a true legend in the publishing business, Eloise Flood. I first worked with her three decades ago and I'm still trying to get it right. Her input has made the characters rich and the plots knotty. Or the other way around. And she has a wicked sense of humor.

All of them answer to Emily Brenner, the world's most supportive and good-natured overlord. And she loves theater, so I love her.

Three mighty eagle-eyed people saved me from eternal embarrassment by poring over every word of every book, picking up all the mistakes the rest of us missed. Because you will never see those bloopers, I raise my talons in gratitude to Jessica Berg, Gweneth Morton, and Martha Schwartz.

I'm pretty bad at art but I know genius when I see it. Torstein Norstrand's cover artwork has knocked me off my seat so many times I believe I've sustained permanent hip damage. Joe Merkel has translated my impossible requests into interior art that's simply magical, and he's been helped by the supreme talents of Barb Fitzsimmons and Rick Farley.

But the words-and-images people are only a part of it.

If you have a publisher and managing editor like Susan Katz and Kate Jackson, you thank your lucky stars. Their enthusiasm has energized everyone since Day One. Two brilliant publicists, Cindy Hamilton and Lindsey Karl, have sent me to schools, bookstores, festivals, libraries, conferences, and TV studios in nearly forty states and three foreign countries. Marketing mavens Alana Whitman, Matt Schweitzer, Patty Rosati, Molly Motch and Julie Eckstein convinced me to dress up in a toga for my epic Comic Con video, and they continued to develop contests, teaching guides, and crazy Seven Wonders schemes. Alex Garber has manned the website with style and sometimes painful humor, with the subversive help of Colleen O'Connell. And Jeffrey "Scooter" Kaplan and Marissa Benedetto have managed to make great video footage despite a very shiny-faced author.

The task of getting books into your hands is a bit like wizardry. Boots-on-the-ground sales reps go door to door, to libraries and booksellers, while a team of back-office whizzes makes sure there are always copies to go around. Hats off to Andrea Pappenheimer, the Grand Master of this merry band, which includes Kerry Moynagh, Kathy Faber, Susan Yeager, and Heather Doss. A special holler to my brother from the South, Eric Svenson, who could sell sand to a camel.

An entire department exists to boot authors out of the country, and I kowtow to Austin Tripp, Sarah Woodruff, David Wolfson, Molly Humphrey, Christine Swedowsky, and Samantha Hagerbaumer for sending this wide-eyed boy to the Far East—and to Jean McGinley, Alpha Wong, and Sarah Oughton for spreading the Seven Wonders to other countries' publishers (and book clubs and movie companies).

Once the books leave the house, they take up residence on shelves all over the world. Readers, cherish your bookstores and book sellers. Love your librarians. They are smart, funny, wise, caring. Take advantage. I mean that. They will help you enjoy life and unleash the best inside you. (I wanted to list all the ones I've enjoyed meeting, but the book has a thousand-page limit.)

In the end, the book stops at you. All these people above do their work for that one purpose. So if you're reading this, if you're as sad to see the series end as I am, you're in good company.

Keep it up. Keep reading. Keep thinking. Keep feeling. You will never be sorry.

Okay, I said that you deserved a final word. Here it is. It's very short, but I mean it from the heart.

Thanks.

Peter Lerangis
New York City

SEVEN WONDERS

FOLLOW THE ADVENTURES OF

Jack McKinley in the mysterious, action-packed series that takes place throughout the Seven Wonders of the Ancient World.

For teaching guides, an interactive map, and videos,
visit **www.sevenwondersbooks.com**

READ THE FURTHER ADVENTURES IN THE SEVEN WONDERS JOURNALS